A Cast of
FALCONS

ABOUT THE AUTHOR

Steve Burrows has pursued his birdwatching hobby on six continents. He is a former editor of the *Hong Kong Bird Watching Society* magazine and a contributing field editor for *Asian Geographic*. Steve now lives with his wife, Resa, in Oshawa, Ontario. He has spent many hours birding in Norfolk, where the Birder Murder series is based.

A Cast of
FALCONS

STEVE BURROWS

**POINT
BLANK**

A Point Blank Book

First published in Great Britain and the Commonwealth by Point Blank, an
imprint of Oneworld Publications, 2016
This edition published in Great Britain, the United States and Australia in 2018

First published in English by Dundurn Press Limited, Canada. This edition
published by Oneworld Publications in arrangement with Dundurn Press Limited

ISBN 978-1-78607-428-7
ISBN 978-1-78074-948-8 (ebook)

Printed and bound in Great Britain by Clays Ltd, St Ives plc

This book is a work of fiction. Names, characters, businesses, organizations,
places, and events are either the product of the author's imagination or are used
fictitiously. Any resemblance to actual persons, living or dead, events, or locales
is entirely coincidental.

Visit our website for a reading guide
and exclusive content on THE BIRDER MURDER SERIES
www.oneworld-publications.com

Oneworld Publications
10 Bloomsbury Street
London WC1B 3SR
England

Stay up to date with the latest books,
special offers, and exclusive content from
Oneworld with our newsletter

Sign up on our website
oneworld-publications.com

To Hilary and Michael,
for all the stories we have shared.

ACKNOWLEDGEMENTS

I am grateful to my editor, Allison Hirst, my publicist, James *Jim Pub* Hatch, and the rest of the team at Dundurn for all their work in support of the Birder Murder series. I am fortunate, too, to now be in the capable hands of Jenny Parrott at Oneworld Publications in the U.K. Bruce Westwood, Lien de Nil, and Meg Tobin-O'Drowsky at Westwood Creative Artists have been creative indeed in finding solutions to the challenges I have brought them. On the very rare occasions I haven't been chained to a computer writing, ahem, I have enjoyed the company of many birding companions. Thanks to them for adding new species to my list over the past year.

And as always, love and thanks to my beautiful wife, Resa. In your predictions about the success of the Birder Murder series, you have proven, as usual, to be the opposite of left.

1

The noise. The deafening, terrible noise. The sound of air, rushing through his clothing, tearing at his hair, clawing his lips back into a grotesque grin. Ten seconds? Perhaps. Thirty-two feet per second, per second. A memory. School? Shadows. Sadness. Anger.

Lightheaded now, lungs unable to snatch the air rushing by. Panic. The rock face a grey curtain hurtling past at one hundred and twenty miles per hour. Terminal velocity. Another memory. School? Or college? Good times. Laughter. Women. Bars. Five seconds? Terminal! *I'm dying.*

He had seen the angel, a brief glimpse as he released his grip on the rock face. On life. Pure, white, beautiful. An angel that had brought him death. Angels. Heaven. Too late? Never too late, his mother said.

His mother. Regrets. Words not spoken. Actions not taken. Taken. Birds. Fear, now. Plunging down through open space. *I'm going to die.* Repentance. The key. *God, forgive me. For the birds. For—*

The man watching through binoculars fixed the body's landing place against the scarred granite backdrop, and then swept the horizon in either direction. Nothing else stirred. He focused again on the rock face and relocated the crumpled form, remembering the sickening flat bounce as life had left it. He lowered his binoculars and sat, deep in thought, seeming not to notice the fierce buffeting of the winds that scoured the bleak landscape. After a moment, he tucked his bins into a canvas bag resting against his hip, careful not to damage the other item inside. Things had changed now, but perhaps there was still a way; and perhaps this other item, now nestling gently against the bins, held the key. He rose from his crouched position and began to make his way toward the towering presence of Sgurr Fiona.

He moved with haste over the uneven terrain, beneath a sky that was grey and leaden. Swollen rain clouds were riding inland on the onshore winds. A fierce Atlantic squall was on its way and the exposed heath would offer no shelter once the storm arrived. The man wore only a heavy fisherman's sweater, denim jeans, and walking shoes. He had no coat or waterproofs to ward off the horizontal rains that would soon drive across the landscape.

He had estimated the distance to the rock face at a quarter of a mile, and he could tell now, as he crossed the ground with his steady, purposeful gait, that he'd been about right. Even experienced walkers underestimated distances in these parts. The stark, featureless landscape seemed to draw in the mountains on the horizon, making them appear closer. But the man had spent enough time in the natural world to be alert for its deceptions. It was those of the human world he found harder to detect.

He moved over the tussocks easily, barely noticing the sprigs of gorse and brambles that snatched like harpies at his trouser cuffs. Once or twice he stumbled over the craggy, moss-covered mounds, but for the most part his progress was sure-footed, even in the flimsy, well-worn soles of his walking shoes. On the horizon, the grey mass of a low cloudbank had begun its inexorable time-lapse march across the landscape. He would need to work quickly if he was to find shelter before the storm came. He had a window, a tiny chink of opportunity: the coming storm would discourage others from venturing out here. But squalls passed over these coastal areas quickly, chased into the inland valleys and hill passes by the relentless coastal winds. Behind the storm would come the clear white-blue skies of the North Atlantic. And then the walkers would return to the trails. It wouldn't be long before the body was found and reported. He must do what had to be done long before that happened. He needed to be far away by then.

The last of the vegetation died away and he emerged onto a slight slope of scree that led up to the base of the rock face. Sgurr Fiona towered above him, its peaks already lost in the greyness of the clouds. He stopped for a second to take in its grandeur, and as he looked up, he paused. Until now, only the images of the death, the violent impact of the man's body hitting the ground, had occupied his thoughts. But the initial shock was starting to wear off, and he began to recognize a meaning behind what he had seen; an explanation, perhaps. Had the other man recognized it, also, in those last, long terrifying seconds? Had he, too, acknowledged what it might mean? Either way, it was just him, now, standing alone on this desolate, windswept heath, who possessed this wisdom, this secret, entrusted to him by another man's death. He looked up at Sgurr Fiona once again, but the sky below the clouds was empty.

He approached the body and forced himself to look down at the broken, rag-doll form. It was clear the man had died on impact. The damage seemed to be mostly to the head and face. It was difficult to even make out the features now. He shook his head. It was as if the fates themselves had determined to cloak the death in a double layer of mystery: not only of who the dead man was, but of what he had looked like in life.

The man felt a momentary wave of sadness for the empty shape at his feet. All that was left of Jack de Laet, with whom he had drunk, and laughed, and swapped lies — and unknowingly, a few truths too — over the previous weeks. He was a bad man, Jack, one of the worst. But he had been a person, a living, breathing human being. And now he was … what? The man didn't have time to consider the question. Musing about the afterlife, the great beyond, was for a warm pub, where he would head after this, for a hot meal and a glass of single malt whisky and the comfort of a gently burning fire. Out here, at the base of a granite rock face, under a low, roiling, gunmetal sky, he had work to do.

He knelt beside the body and slowly began to withdraw the day pack from beneath Jack de Laet's stiffening form. He worked with great care. He couldn't see any blood coming from under the body, but if there was any, he knew the small pack could disturb it, smear it, perhaps in a way that a good forensic examiner might be able to detect. He breathed a sigh of relief when the pack finally slithered free showing no traces of blood. He lifted it to one side and peered in. "Ah Jack, you lied to me," he said quietly, without malice. Using a handkerchief, he withdrew a book from his canvas shoulder bag. It was battered and dog-eared, with a long-faded cover from which the images of a couple of birds, well-drawn and easily identifiable, stared back at him. He took a pen from his pocket and wrote two words on the flyleaf, holding the cover open with the handkerchief. Then he leaned forward to delicately lift the flap on one of De Laet's jacket pockets. He slid the book in.

He patted the pocket slightly as he closed the flap and rose from his kneeling position clutching the small day pack.

"See you soon," he said. But he wasn't talking to Jack de Laet.

2

Death had won again. As it always did in the end. Another man had challenged it, tried to face it down and defeat it with his frail human courage. And he had lost. In this case, Death had stalked its victim, pursued him silently through this leafy forest glade, treading the path parallel to this one that ran farther down in the ravine. At some point, it had moved ahead of the man so it could scramble silently up to this footpath, and lurk, hidden from view, until the man rounded the bend. To find Death waiting for him. A short struggle, perhaps, and then Death had claimed another victim, and dragged his soul off to its lair. And now it was up to Danny Maik to find out who had been Death's foot soldier this time, and to bring that person in to face the justice that Death itself never would.

They knew the choreography, and little bits more, from the trail of clues, footprints whispered into the woodchips of the two trails. But it was not enough to tell them who had been following the man, so they were still no closer to knowing who had decapitated him and left his body lying here in the centre of the path, and the head a few yards off, in the bracken to the right.

In this strange twilight aftermath of the event, not now fresh enough to be shrouded in shock, but recent enough that the horror had not yet faded completely, it was the jogger that

Danny Maik felt for most. The emotional trauma of those Philip Wayland had left behind would be understandable; their grief and despair justified. No one would consider it unusual if any of the family or friends fell apart for a few days. Or longer. But the jogger who had found the body was not in their circle, not really entitled to any of the emotions his death engendered in them. And so, this unremarkable woman, who had done nothing worse than decide on this path for her morning jog, must now deal with her own feelings only in the shadows. Maik could hardly imagine the shock she had endured. One minute enjoying the woods, hearing the rhythmic pounding of her running shoes on the trail, treating her lungs to the fresh, clean woodland air, and the next, happening upon the worst, most horrifying sight she would ever see in her life.

She seemed so shaken, so utterly traumatized by her discovery, as she was led away, trembling and sobbing into Constable Lauren Salter's sympathetic embrace. When the police arrived, they had found her standing beside the body, over it almost, as if unable to draw herself away. Or perhaps it was just that she was unwilling to leave the victim, feeling that someone should stay to watch over him, even in his brutalized, incomplete state, until the medics could come and treat him with the care and dignity the last moments of his life had denied him. If so, the woman's compassion would cost her dearly. Days and nights of images, things seen when her eyes had been inexorably drawn to the horror at her feet on the path; images that may never leave her. How could you confront such a sight — the headless body of a person — out here in the silence and the solitude of the woods, and not be damaged by your discovery? Domenic Jejeune, too, had seemed to recognize the toll the woman's discovery would take, had already taken, on her. The DCI made sure he organized her care and treatment before turning his attention to the body on the path. In truth, there had been no need to rush on that score. Both Detective Chief Inspector Jejeune and Sergeant Danny Maik had already long acknowledged the truth of the situation. Death had won again.

Maik looked along the trail again now and then turned his gaze to the right, peering through the undergrowth as if trying to judge exactly how far he was from the compound. Though this path was a public right of way, the battered sign on the fence made it clear to anyone veering from it that they were entering onto PRIVATE PROPERTY.

Public access through private land. Maik could hardly count the times as a beat constable he had found it necessary to go over the concept with tourists: *Yes, the path does go through private property. Yes, you are allowed onto it. No, you don't need the owners' permission. No, I don't understand it either.* And when the new foreign owners had acquired this particular property, the "Old Dairy" as they now called it, Maik had been present at the earliest briefings, when the questions about public access to private property had become even more pointed. *What exactly does the concept of land ownership mean in this country, when the public is granted rights of way into perpetuity?* But if the legal representative of Old Dairy Holdings had expected Detective Chief Superintendent Colleen Shepherd to quail under his withering glance, he was disappointed. Shepherd had told him politely that it meant whatever the Highways Passage Act meant it to mean. The discussion had ended there.

The world being the way it was, Maik had probably always known if any major crime was ever going to be committed around here, it would happen on this path, where jurisdiction and rights were at their most nebulous. Now, it would require all of DCS Shepherd's considerable diplomatic skills to get them the access and co-operation the investigating officers were going to need from Old Dairy Holdings to pursue their enquiries into this case.

Maik looked around at the glade again, drinking in its tranquility, the tangy hint of bark on its breezes. It had happened at dusk, the medical examiner had determined, at the far end of daylight's arc, when any protesters had long since gone home and the woods had returned to silence. *What brought you here, Mr. Wayland, to this path beside the place you had not worked at in more than a year? What, if anything, did it have to do with you being killed in such a disturbingly brutal way?* Maik smiled wryly. He was pretty sure his absent DCI would approve of these questions about Philip Wayland's final moments, even if he might not be too impressed by the high-minded affectation with which Danny's subconscious was composing them.

Absent, thought Maik. His *absent* DCI. Even for the famously disengaged Inspector Domenic Jejeune, the absence was puzzling. The call had come in from the Highland Constabulary just as the first analysis of the physical evidence in this case was starting to materialize. Not the ideal time, one would have thought, for the inspector to go haring off up to Scotland. Not at all the actions of a DCI fully engaged in the business of solving Philip Wayland's murder. Jejeune had certainly been invested enough in the case during the early days, even if his detached approach might have suggested otherwise. So when did a trip up to the Scottish Highlands suddenly take precedence over an active murder inquiry? When did investigating a book, a bird guide no less, found on the body of a fallen climber, become more important than pursuing a killer? Perhaps today was the day Danny would get some answers. Perhaps there would be a message waiting for him at the office, or an email, telling him the DCI was on his way back to north Norfolk.

Maik looked around the glade now, seeing the last remnants of the police incident tape flapping from one or two trees and the fresh bark chips on the trail that replaced the blood-stained ones gathered as evidence. It seemed inconceivable that this spot could have been the scene of such violence and brutality a scant few days ago. Shafts of light were beginning to filter through the leafy canopy, dappling the forest path into tawny patterns. Beneath the giant beeches on both sides of the path, patches of bluebells awaited the warmth of the early morning sun. This was a place of tranquility again now, a place that seemed to have gathered up the horrors of the past and laid a blanket of quiet over them. Nature providing a balm for the crimes of humans, forgiving them once again, as it always did.

Maik turned and headed back to his car, but not before pausing for one quick look back. The corner of an office was barely visible through the vegetation, the only evidence one could see of the research compound on the other side of the wire fence. DCI Jejeune had spent a long time staring at that office the last time he was here. *Just what was it you were looking at?* wondered Danny. *And why does it make you distrust the only witness statement we have in this case?*

3

The drive up had gone some way to helping Jejeune understand Lindy's look of disappointment when he had told her where he was going. Significantly, he had not told her why.

"The Western Highlands?" she said, shrugging off her work bag and slumping into one of the armchairs in their living room. "Oh Dom, I wish I could go with you, but it's this award thing. There are interviews and appearances and ..."

He smiled his understanding. In truth, he had gambled on the arrangements for the forthcoming awards ceremony preventing Lindy from being able to accompany him. If she'd tried to make it work, he would have thrown other obstacles in the way — extended the dates, invented some excuse that meant he had to travel alone. It was deception by intent, rather than by action, but it made him no less uneasy. They always said they told each other everything. They both knew that wasn't strictly true, but all pretense of openness between them had changed with the call from Scotland. Jejeune hoped these deceptions would be small, and short-lived. But now they had started, he knew they would feed upon each other, and soon, perhaps, it would be too late to rein them in. He had managed to mask all these thoughts behind an attentive smile while Lindy rhapsodized about the scenic wonders that awaited him on the wild western coast of Scotland.

"Each bend in the road, you think it can't possibly get any better, and then, next turn, there's another vista, even more breathtaking. The beauty is almost indescribable," she'd said, tucking her feet beneath her in the chair. The word *almost* told Jejeune she was going to try anyway. From an award-nominated journalist, he would have expected no less. He smiled again and squeezed into the chair beside her. Even if he had not wanted to listen just then, he would have done so, as his penance. But he always enjoyed listening to Lindy when she was passionate about a subject. She fell in love with her topics, and her enthusiasm coursed through her accounts.

"There's a rawness about the landscape, a stark, rugged bleakness. The mountains, *hills* they call them up there, they look like old prize-fighters, all battered and craggy and purple-grey. Even the lowlands have a kind of formidable harshness to them, gorse and brambles and ankle-breaking rocks. And the winds, God, sometimes they hammer across the land with such force you'd swear they are going to pull what little bit of vegetation there is out by the roots."

"If you're auditioning for the Scottish tourism board," said Jejeune playfully. "I wouldn't be expecting a recruitment call anytime soon."

"No, Dom, it's wonderful," she said earnestly. "It's all those things, but I can truly say it is some of the most beautiful scenery I've ever seen. And considering what we have right outside our front door here in north Norfolk, that must tell you something."

It did. And Lindy had been right. Jejeune had seen it all and drunk it all in, every crag, every heath-clad valley bathed in the milky Highland light. As he was doing now, sitting in the passenger seat of the van on his journey up to Sgurr Fiona, driven up the sinuous coast road from Ullapool by an officer from the Highland Constabulary named Ian McLeod. "Though most call me *Iron*," he had told Jejeune with a smile as he greeted him at the door of the local police station. It had been McLeod who had taken the report of the dead man at the base of Sgurr Fiona, going out to the scene himself to secure it and conduct the preliminary investigation. It had been McLeod, too, who had placed the call to the Saltmarsh Division's main switchboard on his return and left the message for Domenic Jejeune, informing him that a bird guide bearing his name had been found in the pocket of the dead man's jacket.

That had been yesterday. And now, less than twenty-four hours since McLeod's scanned image of the book's flyleaf had appeared on Jejeune's screen, here was the man himself, looking, he had surmised from McLeod's somewhat startled expression, a good deal younger and less distinguished than the Scottish detective had been expecting. It was not an uncommon reaction from those who were meeting Jejeune for the first time. Even to himself, to have achieved so much and risen so high, so quickly, seemed at odds with the youthful face he saw staring back at him from the shaving mirror every morning. But McLeod had inquired only whether Jejeune was tired after his long drive, and whether he might prefer to wait until tomorrow to make the trip out to the scene. But Jejeune wouldn't prefer to wait, thanks, and he would really appreciate it if they could go out to the scene right away. So they had.

The going became more jarring as they turned off the main coast road and took a narrow roadway leading up toward the base of Sgurr Fiona. The track twisted between steep-sided valleys that opened onto heath land every bit as rugged and uncompromising as Lindy had described it. McLeod pointed straight ahead, where a dark cloud lurked low over the sea, already draping a grey curtain of rain across its surface. "Another storm coming in from the Atlantic. Don't worry, though, she's a way off yet. We've plenty of time to have a poke about when we get there. Mebbe even have a wee scramble up the Fiona."

"I imagine this area sees a lot of bad weather," said Jejeune, looking out at the landscape rolling by. "It doesn't look like the kind of place you'd want to sleep rough."

"She can get a bit damp up here at times, right enough," agreed McLeod, breezing on by without ever stopping to consider if there might be more to Jejeune's observation than mere chit-chat. "Wettest place in Britain, in fact, and most of the rain comes in on the horizontal. The winds are so strong they can make the waterfalls flow upward." McLeod had his eyes on the twisting road and so he couldn't see whether there was any skepticism in Jejeune's look, but he was taking no chances. He took a weather-beaten hand from the steering wheel and laid it over his heart. "On my life."

"But the weather had nothing to do with the man's death, you said."

McLeod gave his head an economical shake. "Even though he was wearing a top-quality waterproof jacket, the body was still soaked through by the time I got to it, but our medical examiner reckons he was well dead long before the rains came. Everything was consistent with a fall." McLeod paused significantly. "He's seen enough to know."

Jejeune nodded. "But you can't say for sure how long he'd been there when he was found?"

McLeod shook his head. "Can't have been long, though. There were no signs of scavengers. Out in these parts, a deer can die and the Ravens and Hooded Crows will be on it before it hits the ground. This is us." McLeod pulled the car off the road onto a flat patch of grass that showed the wear of life as an impromptu car park for hikers setting out on the local trails. Above them towered the granite mass of Sgurr Fiona, the thousand-metre "Fair Peak" that drew climbers from all corners of Britain and far beyond.

They got out of the car and McLeod drew a generous helping of the clear mountain air into his lungs. "Just over there. Now,

remember, I did tell you there was nothing much to see anymore."
He nodded toward a small cairn that looked as if it had been constructed very recently. Perhaps even to mark the spot, thought Jejeune; passing hikers paying their respects to one of their own?

"Any idea what the man was doing out here?"

"Climbing, we think."

"With no equipment?"

McLeod shot him a look, one that told Jejeune he now suspected there might be something else behind his guest's inquiries, a faint shadow of accusation, perhaps, that the Scottish police should have done more to find out about the man who had died at the foot of this formidable mountain. Jejeune didn't mind. Anything that took McLeod's attention away from the real reason for his questions was welcome.

McLeod, though, had decided to let things slide, for now. "Your man wouldn't have been the first to try his hand at a spot of free climbing up the Fiona." He paused and looked up the sheer granite face towering above them. He shook his head. "He'll not be the last, either. These peaks attract some world-class climbers and hikers. Most of them have the good sense to give the hills a bit of respect. But like all wild places, An Teallach attracts its fair share of nutters. The local search and rescue boys are forever plucking some idiot off a ledge dressed in shorts and a T-shirt. Any squall comes in, and the poor fool would perish if they didn't. We think this one is probably just some cowboy who thought he'd come here to tame the Fiona, and she got the better of him."

No, thought Jejeune, *that wasn't what had happened.* He didn't know what had yet, but he suspected he would soon. And in the meantime, it was better to let Iron McLeod keep on believing this was all just some tragic accident.

McLeod pulled on a nylon jacket and handed a spare one to Jejeune. "If you're ready for a bit of a hike, I can show you something that will make it worth your while coming all the way up here."

Jejeune gestured for McLeod to lead on. Scrambling up the steep path in his faded jeans and heavy boots, McLeod didn't look much like an on-duty policeman, but he did look like a man who fitted these parts perfectly. Iron McLeod had the same uncompromising honesty as this landscape he clearly loved so much. It was a quality, perhaps, that Jejeune might have associated with himself, until the telephone call had come in. But the savage beauty of the wild Highland coastline was no place to be contemplating such things, and Jejeune instead concentrated on scrambling along behind his guide.

After fifteen minutes of strenuous, relentless ascent, they paused on a small ledge. Jejeune bent over, hands on his knees. McLeod stood barrel-chested against the elements, gratefully drawing in lungfuls of the still mountain air. Recovered, he was ready to press on. "C'mon," he urged, "we're nearly there. Just up around the next bend. It's worth the effort, believe me."

Jejeune followed the other man up the steep slope, his soft-soled shoes slipping occasionally on the scree scattered across the path. As they rounded a bend, he stopped suddenly. They were on a small promontory jutting out over a vast nothingness. In front of them, a spectacular vista of undulating purples and greens stretched off to a range of distant mountains, their peaks wreathed in mist. Broad shafts of sunlight broke through the cloud cover in one or two places, sending beams of light down onto the heathland. The fierce wind tugged at Jejeune's hair and scoured his face, making his eyes water slightly. He looked across to McLeod, who was gazing out over the scene in silence. He was wearing an expression born of pure joy.

"It's magnificent," said Jejeune.

"Aye, you'll no see a view like this without earning it, right enough," said McLeod, raising his voice above the winds. "But

I've climbed the Fiona in all seasons, in all kinds of weather. She never disappoints."

She, noted Jejeune. Another in McLeod's harem of females out here: the hills, the elements, the landscape. But Jejeune had an antenna for misogyny, and he detected none in Iron McLeod. If his use of the feminine pronoun revealed anything about the man, it was the deep affection he held for these wild places. The two men stood on the edge of the rocky outcrop and looked out over the landscape in silence, watching the light play over grasses and shrubs as they were tossed around by the keening winds below. McLeod pointed to a thin ribbon of silver light on the horizon. "Can you see that over there, Inspector, away in the distance?"

Jejeune leaned forward and squinted out over the ocean, but he could see nothing. He turned to McLeod and held out his hands, palms up.

"Canada," said McLeod with a smile. "C'mon, let's sit a while and you can tell me what it is about this old bird guide of yours that's special enough for you to drive all the way up here to get it."

Jejeune smiled back. *No, I won't tell you that,* he thought. *But I'll tell you a plausible enough story that it won't insult your intelligence.*

4

DCI Jejeune would not be returning for another couple of days. The desk sergeant had not exactly averted his eyes when he delivered the news to Danny Maik, but he hadn't been keen to let them linger too long under the sergeant's flinty stare, either. He consequently greeted DCS Colleen Shepherd's appearance in the doorway with more enthusiasm than she, or Maik, would normally have expected.

Shepherd had already received the news, and was looking for someone to tell how she felt about it. She fixed Maik with a look. "Anything I should know about, Sergeant? I understand that he needs to sort out why this unknown man had a book with his name in it; but really, how long can it take to convince the local police that he knows nothing about it? The death up there is not suspicious in any way, is it?"

Maik had received a call from a Sergeant McLeod just as Jejeune was making his way up to Scotland, and he had asked that very question, sergeant to sergeant. Which was the reason he was now able to confirm to Shepherd with such confidence that it was not.

"And why on earth drive? He is aware we have air service to the wilds of Scotland, I take it? Even down here in the tiny backwater of north Norfolk."

Maik said nothing. Loyalty was about not saying anything that might get your superiors in trouble. It had nothing to do with inventing explanations for their irrational behaviour.

"Walk with me," she said, leading him along the hallway. It could have been one of those Americanisms she was so fond of, but it could have been a literal request. Shepherd was looking trim these days, fitter and better toned, the results of an exercise regimen she had pitched herself into, in the throes of yet another failed relationship. Maik wouldn't have cared to speculate whether this newfound interest in her body shape was designed to improve Shepherd's self-esteem, or her chances on the dating circuit, but it didn't really matter much to him. His concern lay in the possibility of having to accompany his DCS on her rigorous daily walking circuit around the village streets. Maik regularly bemoaned the amount of paperwork that piled up on his desk during the course of a day, but he realized it might come in handy today if he needed an excuse to beg off from joining her.

"I take it there's still nothing to suggest anyone at the Old Dairy compound was involved in the Wayland murder?" she asked as they made their way along the corridor. Though she took a broad spectrum approach, both of them knew she was really only asking about one person.

"Prince Yousef's alibi remains firm, ma'am. A researcher who works up there is certain she saw Philip Wayland entering the woods at seven p.m."

Shepherd nodded. "And the prince was already in his helicopter by that time, in radio contact with ground control. So why does the Inspector want me to arrange an interview with him?"

She stopped walking and turned to look at Maik intently. It was impossible to tell from her expression whether Jejeune had mentioned his doubts to her, those same misgivings he had carelessly tossed in amongst his last-minute instructions to Danny Maik as he rushed out the door: "This statement that puts the

Prince in the clear, Sergeant," Jejeune had said, shaking his head doubtfully. "I'd like a word with him, the moment I get back."

Maik responded frankly. "Perhaps it's because Yousef's the head of the operation up there."

"The *de facto* head," said Shepherd, "in his older brother's absence. I don't think there's any doubt that Prince Ibrahim is the real power behind the Old Dairy project. He's coming over, by the way."

"The Crown Prince? Now there's a coincidence."

Shepherd eyed Maik warily. "Not at all. From what I understand, Prince Ibrahim is about due for his biannual visit anyway, though no doubt he'll want to assess what impact this murder investigation is going to have on the project. I've already told his representatives I don't see any reason it should interfere with their day-to-day operations."

Her stare seemed to be challenging Maik to disagree, but he just gave a noncommittal tilt of his head. Shepherd waited, but when it became clear the sergeant wasn't going to offer anything, she pressed.

"Agreed?"

"The investigative team are aware that neither the prince nor any other member of the Old Dairy Holdings board of directors are the focus of our inquiries at this time," said Maik, reverting to the formal language that was his safety net when he was in danger of losing patience with his superiors.

"So we're still looking at the protesters, then. Somebody who didn't like what Philip Wayland's research was going to mean for the north Norfolk coastline."

He saw the uncertainty in her face. Was it a strong enough motive, she was asking, to kill someone, especially in such a disturbing, violent way? Neither missed the irony; had it been Domenic Jejeune positing such a theory, they would have had no qualms about pointing out how flimsy it was.

"We didn't find anything the first time we looked," said Maik, trying hard to keep the note of exasperation from his voice. Shepherd's interest in keeping the investigation away from a research facility in which an Emirati royal family held a controlling interest was understandable, but throwing up improbable leads in its place wasn't making the sergeant's temporary leadership role any easier.

"Nevertheless, it's our best avenue of approach at the moment. Plenty of angry people, feelings running high. Get in amongst them, Sergeant, shake them up. If you still can't find anything, I might, just might, be willing to consider the DCI's request. But not until we have fully explored every other possible line of enquiry. *Fully explored*, Sergeant. Do I make myself clear?"

Maik nodded, but it wasn't the phrase she had emphasized that had caught his ear. It was another one. *At the moment*, thought Maik. Meaning until DCI Domenic Jejeune returned to take up the reins of the investigation. Before his absence, Maik had not really realized just what a sense of reassurance Jejeune brought to proceedings. Yes, he would likely haul them off in all kinds of improbable directions. Yes, there would be frustration and impatience at his unconventional, protocol-defying approach. But, beneath it all, there would be the same, single underlying refrain as always. I'll get you there. Follow me, keep your faith, and I'll deliver your killer. I will do it in my usual disinterested way. And it won't mean a thing to me when I have. But I will do it.

"Well, best be getting on with things," said Maik brightly. It seemed unlikely now that Shepherd was going to insist he accompany her on her power-walk around Saltmarsh. He was fairly sure she had covered all her agenda items. All the same, it was better not to leave things to chance. "Full in-tray, as usual," he added.

She regarded him dubiously. "If you're speaking to DCI Jejeune, you might want to mention to him that any royal interview wouldn't be a package deal. Prince Ibrahim, when he arrives, couldn't be more firmly off-limits if he was on the moon."

Maik nodded. But as he watched the retreating form of the slimmed-down Colleen Shepherd disappearing along the corridor, it crossed his mind that if Jejeune's niggling doubts turned out to have any substance, one prince might be all he would need.

5

Detective Constable Tony Holland peered out of the window of the incident room at two young community service workers stealing a smoke break.

"Mug's game," he announced, shaking his head sadly. "You've only got one set of lungs. You need to look after them."

Maik, who was bent over the desk at the front of the room, setting up for the morning briefing, looked up, puzzled.

"You'll have to excuse him, Sarge," said Lauren Salter, "He's just quit. Apparently, his new girlfriend disapproves." There was more than a touch of amusement in the detective constable's confiding tone.

Maik did not look best pleased. The last thing he needed today was one of his detectives going through the anguish of nicotine withdrawal. At his best, Tony Holland could be a good investigator. Maik would have liked him to be able to contribute a bit more than observations on the number of respiratory systems human beings had.

The stragglers took their seats and everyone turned their attention to the front of the room. Truth be told, it was more attention than Maik was comfortable with, especially with the progress report he was about to deliver. "Nil" would about cover it. Maik drew himself up to his full height and looked at them squarely. "Right," he announced, "let's get started."

"I see the organ grinder's still away then," said Holland, to the general amusement of the room.

Maik glowered at him from beneath a furrowed brow, as if to suggest that this particular monkey would be more than happy to grind any organ Constable Holland might be willing to proffer. He moved quickly onto his topic. "Okay, new development. The ME has found minute traces of leather in the neck wound," he said. "I suspect we all know where this leather came from?"

Holland raised an eyebrow. "A cow?"

Maik gave him a look. As entertaining as Holland's newfound joie de vivre was, in Maik's present mood, it wasn't doing anything for his long-term career prospects.

"Correct, Constable. From the shoulder strap of Philip Wayland's satchel. It matches the scuff marks we found, suggesting the weapon glanced off the strap on its way into the wound site."

There was a general stirring of unease in the room. This was it? The sum total of their new developments? Most in the room had put this much together from the evidence at the site. Danny Maik might have felt it necessary in his role as acting lead to pretend this was a significant step forward in the case, but they all knew he was fooling no-one, least of all himself. His next statement, however, went some way to explaining why such an insignificant detail would be given so much attention.

"I want us to have another look at this group of protesters," he said. He held up a hand. "I know we've been over it once, but let's dig a bit deeper this time, have a look at their backgrounds. Let's see if any of them make a habit of showing up at other protests, or have any affiliations with groups that do. And while we're about it, let's have another run through the victim's background. I want to see if anything pops out at us, something we might have missed first time around."

A few eyes dropped in the front rows, and others found different things on which to rest their gaze. This was Danny Maik telling them they had nowhere else to go, that he had run out of options. Inspector Jejeune's leads might not always follow the straightest pathways of police procedure, or seem even vaguely related to the case at times, but at least they were leads. Maik's entire approach seemed to consist of looking at a few disgruntled locals who gathered daily at the gates of the Old Dairy compound, protesting against who-knew-what, or sifting through the ashes of the late Philip Wayland's life. They had done all this already. The protesters were mostly well-known in Saltmarsh, and preliminary checks had thrown up no surprises. Similarly, Philip Wayland's life, while distinguished enough, had provided no footholds for further inquiries.

That Constable Salter was first in to try to help protect Maik from the awkward silence was no surprise. If the sergeant himself was oblivious to her interest in him, few others in the room were.

"I'm not sure there's much logic to some of these protesters' objections," she said. "This business about the environmental-ists believing if you provide a way to deal with the problems created by fossil fuels, people will stop looking for alterna-tives…" she shook her head. "As far as I can see, their arguments are based on flawed premises."

Maik steeled himself. Salter had recently been on a depart-mental Modes of Reasoning course, and as a result, they had all been hearing more lately about fallacies, validity and empir-ical reasoning than they ever wanted to. They hadn't bothered much about courses like this when Danny was making his way through the ranks. They had worked on the assumption that police officers would be able to come to logical conclusions without any training. Even if their faith was not always entirely justified, Maik was still of the opinion that if you needed a course to teach you how to think, you were probably better suited for a life of crime than one on the other side of the fence.

Nevertheless, opposition of any kind to the research going on at the Old Dairy project went to motive. "It probably wouldn't hurt to have a bit more of a look into this whole carbon capture business, Constable. Who's opposed to what, and on what grounds?"

"If you like," said Salter with an easy shrug. "But I still say inductive reasoning with no proven underlying principle lacks validity."

Maik closed his eyes and pinched the bridge of his nose between his thumb and forefinger. If this was an example of the sort of approach detectives would be bringing to cases in the future, about the only investigative tool you would have left would be to beat a confession out of a suspect. As far as he could see, the environmentalists' objections were based on a fairly astute understanding of human nature. Once something ceased to be a problem, people turned their attentions to things that still were. But he suspected a straightforward assessment like his wouldn't last long in the rarified atmosphere of Salter's logic, so he let the matter drop.

"There's not much in his background of note, Sarge," offered Holland. "An ex-wife, quite a looker by all accounts — tall, pretty. Bright, too, a doctor at the local clinic."

"Sounds like just your type, Tony," said Salter. "Before you became besotted, I mean."

Maik's look urged Holland to get on with it.

"They were both young, though, and it didn't last long. A lot of fighting, reportedly, though nobody seems to know why."

"And she's not in the picture now, at all?" Maik asked.

"Lives in South Africa. But she did post a tribute on Wayland's Facebook page soon after his death. So she must have been keeping tabs on him." He shook his head and snuck a sly look at Salter.

"Can you imagine not being able to let go of somebody like that? After all this time, even though he was engaged again."

"And we're sure there's nothing in the fact that Wayland was found so close to his old stomping ground?" asked Maik. "He worked at the Old Dairy compound for quite a while."

There was uncomfortable shuffling in the room at the sergeant's attempts to revisit yet more ground they had already covered.

"He hadn't worked there for more than a year," countered Holland. "And, strictly speaking, he was found on a public footpath, not on the Old Dairy property itself. The actual compound is all restricted access, electronic gates and pass cards. Wayland couldn't get in there unless somebody signed him in. Nobody did. We checked." A thought seemed to come to him. "Still, I suppose it wouldn't hurt to ask around, see if anyone ever saw him hanging about outside," he said. "I could look after that myself, if you like."

"Your new non-smoking girlfriend works up at the Old Dairy, doesn't she, Tony?" asked Salter with wide open eyes. "Planning on treating her to a bit of your in-depth probing while you were up there?"

"She works on the property, not in the compound itself," he said evasively. "She doesn't have any more access to the research facility than the general public." Holland paused, and switched to a tone that made everyone sit up and take notice. "But I'll tell you something. Whether they work in the compound or just on the property, the people up at the Old Dairy are all terrified. A murder like this one, it shakes people up. Not just that it happened so close to them, but the way he was killed."

With a metal blade, rusted on the cutting edge, thin, but wide. Much wider than your normal knife. Maik had deliberately avoided the word *machete* when he gave them the medical examiner's report at an earlier briefing, but he could tell from the expressions at the time that the assembled ranks were already there, long before he had finished speaking.

And that was what was at the heart of this palpable sense of unease that permeated the room, that had permeated the entire case, in fact, right from the very beginning. They all knew that most times murder was a heinous act committed by a normal person. It was a momentary action, a quicksilver escape from the shackles that held the human impulses in check. But this type of murder, the deliberate stalking followed by the mutilation, this was a different kind of crime. This was evil itself — deliberate, meticulous, cold. A person who could commit such an act represented a very different type of challenge for the detectives, and a far more dangerous one.

"Point taken, Constable," said Maik with a confidence he didn't feel, "but let's not lose sight of the fact that there is at least one very plausible motive in this case. You should feel free to remind your young lady, and anybody else up there, for that matter, that Philip Wayland was involved in a body of research that is highly controversial, and has already attracted a fair amount of criticism. It makes sense that he would be singled out as a target by people who were opposed to the work he was doing. That's the theory we're working on. We have no reason to believe anyone else is in danger."

One or two nodded, as if Maik had managed to take them along with him on his train of thought. But they knew, too, they all knew, that it wasn't the research itself that was controversial; it was the environmental impact it might lead to, months, perhaps years into the future. And the protests were not happening at the university, where Wayland had been working at the time of his death. They were aimed squarely at the Old Dairy compound, a place he had not set foot in, to the best of anybody's knowledge, for more than a year. That Danny Maik was willing to reach so far beyond the boundaries of credibility to reassure them spoke volumes about how important it was to him that everybody remain calm. And also, about how little real reassurance he could offer.

6

Jejeune was beyond weary when McLeod dropped him off at the station car park to pick up his Range Rover. The hike had been exhilarating and had given him a second wind for a while, but on the way back to Ullapool, the cosy warmth of McLeod's gently rocking van had drifted him once more towards sleep. At the inn, he decided to forgo dinner and head straight to his room. As he opened the door, he noticed the white slip of paper on the floor. It was a flyer from a local pub that had been pushed under his door. Jejeune splashed his face with cold water and turned to head out again. He would ask the receptionist. If the pub wasn't too far away, he would walk there. The brisk evening air might sharpen his senses. He had a feeling he was going to need them.

The interior of the pub was bathed in amber light. In the corner, a waning fire was burning, the firelight flickering orange on the whitewashed walls of the room. Small knots of drinkers, mostly men, were gathered at the bar and a few scattered tables. Only one table had a single occupant. Jejeune headed for it.

"Well, I came," he said, sitting down uninvited.

"That's it, after all this time? Not even a 'How the hell are you?'"

"How the hell are you? Now, I came, so what's this about?"

The man held up a glass. "Glenmorangie," he said. "Want one? They probably have Crown Royal, but just be sure to call it rye. They get very testy here in the Highlands about what's whisky and what isn't."

Despite his agitation, Jejeune recognized he was not controlling this agenda. They would get around to business only when the other man decided they would. He went to the bar and ordered a whisky. He didn't need to specify that he wanted it neat. Up here, anything else was a special request. When he returned, he leaned back in his chair, taking in the room, and then the man in front of him. The lines were more deeply etched around the eyes and mouth than he remembered, and the black hair was longer, parted in the middle now and hanging down shaggily, almost collar length. The beard was new, full and dark, but it looked right. The eyes, though, they hadn't changed. They were the same grey-green, wary and watchful as ever.

Jejeune picked up his drink and took a sip. Over in the corner, a light-hearted commotion flared up and abated again just as quickly.

"I needed to see you," said the man conversationally. "I thought the book would get you up here."

Jejeune said nothing. He simply continued to stare at the man.

"Relax, Inspector," the man said, reading the uncertainty in Jejeune's eyes. "It was just what it looks like, a fall."

"You saw it happen?"

The man nodded. "It wasn't great to watch, but if I'd have looked away, I might not have been able to get on him again. You know how it is through bins at a distance. So I tracked him all the way down." He was silent again for a moment. "It was a long fall."

"How far away were you?"

"Far enough not to have been involved, or to have been able to save him." There was no warmth in the man's smile. "I knew he was dead, but I went over anyway, you know, just to be sure. And then I realized, as I saw him lying there, that this was my chance. So I left the book. His name's Jack de Laet, by the way."

"You knew him?"

The man shrugged. "More than I wanted to. He arrived here by boat two days ago." He sighed and lifted his drink, taking a moment to look around the room before raising the glass to his lips. He set it back down in front of him again with care. "I'm not going to shed any tears for Jack de Laet, but I swear to you, I had nothing to do with his death."

Another explosion of laughter erupted from the table in the corner, and Jejeune saw a man at the bar cast a glowering look at the group. Perhaps in this environment, the DCI's senses were even more heightened than normal. It was as if he was not only on the alert for danger, but half-expecting it.

"You look good," said the man, bringing Jejeune's attention back to the table. "A little tired, maybe, but almost-married life obviously agrees with you."

There might be a time to tell this man how happy he was with Lindy, how much he loved the wild, open coastlines of his new home in Norfolk. But now wasn't it. Not when there were questions about Jack de Laet that could be cleared up.

"The local police think this was just some thrill-seeker looking to free climb that rock face," said Jejeune, letting his eyes play over the fire. It would need a new log soon. Would that be the job of the bartender, leaning casually over the bar swapping stories with the locals? he wondered. Or did the pub have a resident fire-jockey on staff? The warmth. The whisky. He realized his fatigue was returning, despite the new stimulus of this meeting, and this information. He realized, too, that his companion had gone silent. He was looking towards the bar, staring at someone.

Jejeune flashed another glance towards the man leaning against the bar, a hulking individual who seemed to be merely hanging on to the periphery of his companions' conversation, looking around constantly for something to upset him. A bad day at work? Trouble at home? Backstories, thought Jejeune, everybody had them, those hidden motivations for how we feel, how we think, how we act. Whatever it was, the man had turned his unfriendly eyes on Jejeune's companion and returned his stare.

"Tell me about this boat," said Jejeune suddenly.

"Newfoundland to Scotland almost via Iceland," said the man. "That's all you need to know. De Laet knew how to climb, Domenic. He was good at it. But he didn't come all the way here just to test himself against Sgurr Fiona. Ask your friend the police sergeant if there is something else up there that a free spirit like Jack de Laet might be interested in, a man who I'm going to bet isn't going to show up on any searches they do to try to identify the body."

Jejeune raised an eyebrow.

"They won't even find an address for him. He headed straight for the mountain as soon as the boat docked in Ullapool."

And you did the same, thought Jejeune. Both you and Jack de Laet managed to get ashore undetected, and you both headed straight for that mountain. Only you didn't go together. You tracked him, and made sure he didn't know you were there. Telling without saying; it was a skill that came in handy, but it depended on telling somebody who was going to understand the unspoken messages. This man seemed confident that Jejeune would.

At the bar, the man turned away from the TV in disgust as the football results flashed onto the screen. Could the source of his anger be as simple as that? wondered Jejeune idly. He drained his glass. It would take him ten minutes to walk back to his hotel through the rain-slicked Ullapool streets, and he felt he had no more than about fifteen left in his tank.

"So what happens now?" he asked.

"I'm guessing some of that will depend on what your friend in the local constabulary tells you when you see him next. Tomorrow?"

Jejeune nodded. "He's meeting me at breakfast at my hotel."

Neither man suggested it should be a party of three.

"And then back home, to the joys of Norfolk? You come by train, or do they fly celebrity detectives around the country these days?"

Jejeune shook his head. "I brought my Range Rover."

The man's face, a mask of guarded emotions to this point, melted into something softer. *Relief? Gratitude?* He gave Jejeune a smile, genuine and warm. "Is that a fact?"

"I'm thinking of going up to Dunnet Head tomorrow afternoon."

"And then?" Despite his earlier elation, the man still seemed uncertain, as if almost afraid to hope for Jejeune's answer.

"And then we can head on down to Norfolk together."

"You sure it will be okay? With your girlfriend, I mean."

"I'll work it out," Jejeune assured him.

The man relaxed finally and leaned back in his chair. "Man, it's been a while. *Road trip, road trip, road trip,*" he chanted, banging on the table. He was loud enough to cause everyone else in the bar to look around.

The hard-looking man detached himself from his group leaning against the bar and wandered over menacingly, his glass slung low against one hip.

"How ya doin'?" asked Jejeune's acquaintance pleasantly. "Just a few high spirits."

"Yeah, well mebbe you and your friend here would like to take your high spirits elsewhere, so the rest of us can enjoy a quiet drink." He set himself more squarely, ready to attack as soon as he saw the other man begin to rise. Although he was spoiling for a fight, it didn't necessarily need to be a fair one.

Domenic tensed as if he had witnessed such exchanges evolve into bigger things in the past. But his companion merely looked up to meet the other man's gaze. "No thanks, we're fine here," he said pleasantly. He left a long pause, into which any number of dangers could have trespassed. "But you're right," he said finally, "you should be able to enjoy a quiet drink in here. Please pass on my apologies to your friends at the bar, too."

The man shifted uneasily, thrown by the contrast between a stare that betrayed no contrition at all and the words that seemed to carry such sincerity in both tone and meaning.

"Aye, well," he said, backing away uncertainly. He returned to his friends at the bar, but while the other men continued to cast furtive glances at Jejeune's table, the original messenger chose not to make eye contact again.

Jejeune looked at the man sitting across from him, as if distrusting what he had just witnessed. The man leaned over and placed a reassuring hand on his arm. "It's fine. There won't be any trouble," he said, with the certainty of someone who knew it was within his power to ensure it. "Let's have one more for the road, and then you can get back to your hotel."

"And you? Where are you staying?"

The man smiled enigmatically. "I'll see you back here tomorrow when you've finished with the sergeant."

Jejeune eyed the man carefully. Was his evasion distrust, or merely an involuntary caution long bred of necessity?

The man raised his glass in a toast. He caught the eyes of the men still staring at him from the bar and smiled. But none of them heard his whispered words.

"To little Domino. The best baby brother a man could have."

7

Even to Maik's normally uncritical eye, the university complex's prosaically named New Building was a structure of soul-destroying ugliness. The sparse steel and concrete addition had been appended onto the glorious ivy-clad red brick of the earlier nineteenth-century building almost as if it was the architect's intention to provide as sharp a counterpoint as possible between the sensibilities of the two eras.

It was the usual way of things, thought Maik. Unable to match the achievements of a previous generation, the pendulum had swung violently, deliberately, to the other end of the arc. Music was a perfect example. The exquisitely crafted Motown songs of the sixties, with their seamless harmonies and impeccable musicianship, had left no room for improvement. So what had the world ended up with? Punk, the antithesis of all that Motown stood for. No proper singing, no pride of musicianship. In short, no discernible talent of any sort, at least in Maik's view. And here it was again, as he approached the entrance to the building, a confrontation with the same sort of reactionary disaster: architecture's punk rock, in steel and concrete.

Maik stood for a moment in the stark, unwelcoming foyer, orientating himself. Following the direction pointed by a sign on one of the walls, he headed down the corridor, his mood a mirror of the unrelenting cheerlessness around him. He reached his destination and paused in the hall, drawing a breath before he knocked on the door and entered. Xandria Grey was at a desk, poring over some charts when he entered. She stood and came towards him. She tried for a smile of greeting, but seemed to lack sufficient will to pull it off.

"Thank you for coming." Her gratitude was genuine enough, even though Maik could see the sadness in her eyes. Despite the advice Smokey Robinson had given him on his drive over, the sergeant didn't have to look very much closer to see the tracks of her tears. They had been there, he knew, since she had first been informed about her fiancé's death. She seemed too frail and childlike to be taking this on. Her pale, round face, her soft brown eyes, robbed of their light by sorrow. Even her hair, a neat, face-framing pageboy style, seemed too young, too innocent, to be on a woman who had suffered such an adult loss. Despite his resolve on his walk along the corridor, Maik couldn't bring himself to broach the subject of his visit just yet.

"I never did ask," said Maik. "Your name, Xandria …?"

She gave her head a small shake. "Dad said he never knew where Mom came up with it," she said, almost apologetically, "and we lost her when I was still too young to ask." Her sadness seemed to deepen a little. "She travelled to Egypt just before she had me, so perhaps it's a name she heard over there." She tried a careless shrug, but like her smile, it lacked conviction. "It does tend to be a bit of a distraction at times. Look at us, discussing it now, when there are other things we need to be talking about." Her brisk, businesslike tone suffered the same fate as her other efforts at artificial sentiment.

"It's a nice name, all the same," said Maik awkwardly. To his ear, he could not have told Xandria Grey any more eloquently that he wanted to avoid the other subject, that it was precisely the nature of those other things that kept him lingering out here among the light, before descending into the darkness that he knew awaited them both. He hesitated.

"Ms. Grey," he began uncertainly, "these questions you have, about the details of Mr. Wayland's death; it's not always best to know. Sometimes it's better with unanswered questions than —"

"Than the truth?" The guarded look suggested he had already given her the answers she was seeking, but she persisted anyway, as if something inside was urging her on, compelling her to come face-to-face with her own horrors. Maik knew he was not in a position to deny this fragile, broken woman the details of her fiancé's death any longer, and with a look, he gave her permission to finally ask her question.

"These rumours about Philip, about … about the way he was found. The ones everybody is whispering about when they think I can't hear. They're not true, are they?"

Maik was silent for a moment as he searched for a soft couching of hard truths, though he knew there would be none. With an expression of genuine regret, Maik told Xandria Grey, as quickly and concisely as he could: Philip Wayland had been decapitated.

The look on her face was not one that Maik had ever seen before. But then he had never delivered this kind of news before, even from the theatre of war, with the horrific injuries so many of his colleagues had suffered. Denial, shock, revulsion; they were all there in Xandria Grey's face as she listened to Maik's deliberately sketchy account of the condition in which Philip Wayland's body had been discovered.

"I'm very sorry," he said. He took her arm gently and guided her back to the desk. "Why don't you have a seat?"

She nodded vacantly. She would not have resisted, it seemed, anything Maik might have suggested. He sat opposite her. He would have preferred to remain standing, but he sensed she needed the comfort of an equal now, a confidant, rather than an interrogator hovering over her. She stared blankly out the window, her brown eyes moist with repressed emotion. Perhaps she intended to save her response for later, for the privacy of her own home, rather than this unfeeling concrete bunker of a university research facility. But perhaps, too, this was the only face she ever intended to show to the world now. Perhaps she would try to deny her emotions from this point on, in the hope that, if only she could push them down deep enough inside her, they would cease to exist. Maik hoped not. It was an approach he knew was doomed to failure.

"Philip was such a decent man," she said, without turning her gaze from the window. "Really, always thinking about the bigger picture, the greater good." She seemed unable to look at him, this messenger who had brought her such horror. Instead, she stared with a strange detachment at a world outside this room, a world that held promise, and life, and joy. One that perhaps held no place for Xandria Grey anymore.

Maik reached for his usual balm in these stilted situations. "This work you're doing here," he said, "its importance goes beyond the normal realms of academic curiosity, I understand."

Grey nodded vacantly, and then seemed to rally slightly, as if recognizing Maik's intent to coax her from her sadness, and willing herself to respond to it. "Carbon capture and storage is going to be our primary defence against climate change in the future, but while there are many methods to recover industrially produced carbon, we were … we *are* looking at a new approach to storing the carbon once it's been captured."

"Was Mr. Wayland close to a solution?"

Grey bit her bottom lip, fighting to hold on to her composure. "Philip was leading a project to explore the viability of sequestering it through the use of carbon-fixing algae. He was convinced it would change the way we approach carbon storage." Maik watched as she drifted off, gazing at a place beyond the papers on the desk, seemingly lost in her thoughts.

"Perhaps we should wait until my DCI gets back," he said softly, standing up. "I'm sure he'll be interested in hearing about all this. I should probably be going, anyway. If you're sure you're going to be okay?"

Grey stood up abruptly, as if to fight off the sorrow that was threatening to overwhelm her once again. "I'll walk you back to the car park."

Maik began to protest that it wasn't necessary, but she insisted. "It can be a bit of a rabbit warren out there," she said, trying another of her pathetic smiles. "Besides, it will do me good to get out of this place for a while."

She grabbed a sheaf of paper from her desk and fell into step beside Maik. They walked in silence for a few moments, their footsteps echoing hollowly off the walls of the corridor.

"Mr. Wayland was well respected in his field, I understand," said Maik tentatively, as if wary of highlighting the importance of his loss.

Grey looked at him. "It's all right, Sergeant. It upsets me to talk about Philip, but I can't help that. You must ask whatever questions you need to. Philip was an acknowledged expert on the subject of carbon sequestration. It's fair to say it was something of a coup for the university to land him, especially considering his long-standing relationship with Abrar el-Taleb."

"And nobody here resented his star status, anything like that?"

Grey shook her head. "Perhaps some might have, if he had been thrust upon us as the new Messiah, or presented himself as the man on whom all our futures depended. But it wasn't like that at all. For Philip, the problem of removing carbon from Earth's atmosphere came first, last, and every position in between. He saw no room for egos or personal glory. Philip's only interest was finding a viable industrial-scale solution to carbon storage. How that breakthrough came about, or by whom, he didn't really care. He was happy to be one part of the team here. He was the leader, undoubtedly, but he saw himself as a member of the research group all the same."

Maik nodded thoughtfully. "And this research he was working on, it's all still here? You're certain none of it has gone missing?"

Grey nodded certainly. "It was the first thing the University Oversight Committee asked us to check when they heard about Philip. There are backups on various drives, but a lot of this material is also in hard copy, stored in the vaults. Philip was very old school. Three-ring binders and manila file folders." Grey stopped for a moment. In the washed-out light, everything looked sallow: her lab coat, her papers, her skin. She shook her head slightly, and a wistful smile softened the corners of her mouth. "I used to tease him that going down to the vaults was like taking a trip back into the seventies."

Maik didn't necessarily think that that was such a bad place to be, but Grey misinterpreted his silence. "I can show you. I haven't been down there myself since Philip…" She took a shallow, steadying breath. "*Redolent*, that's the word, isn't it? A reminder of death?"

It wasn't the definition as far as Maik knew, but perhaps death brought its own interpretation to everything.

"However, if you think it's necessary."

Maik considered the idea, but the grinding oppressiveness of the building was already beginning to weigh on him, and more of the same, or worse, held no particular appeal. "Perhaps later," he said. "I see we're almost at the car park anyway."

They emerged into the daylight and Grey held out her hand. "I'll be all right, Sergeant. Eventually."

Was it a woman making a statement, or someone looking for reassurance? If it was the latter, then Maik wasn't sure he could oblige. Not based on the broken shell of a person he had seen staring vacantly through the window a few moments earlier; the one trying so hard now to project feelings she seemed unable to locate within her, even as she watched him every step of the way back towards his car.

8

The hulking form of the man in the olive green jacket was turned away from Lindy as she approached. He had binoculars up to his eyes, scanning a wide, reed-fringed body of water with care. Lindy halted on the dirt path, far enough away to avoid disturbing him. The man following close behind her did the same.

For a long moment, the two watched the man, noting the intensity with which he studied one area, before moving on to the next. Lindy knew such careful scrutiny was one of the reasons few birds in these parts escaped the notice of Quentin Senior.

"Still stalking poor defenceless birds to within an inch of their lives, I see, Mr. Senior," she said when he had finally lowered his bins.

He spun around and his ruddy face broke into a broad grin. "Ms. Hey, how delightful. I hear your better half is in Scotland at the moment. I do hope he finds the time to get in some birding. There are some particularly wonderful spots up there." He cast a curious glance at the tall, older gent standing behind her. "That is to say, if he still is your better half. Do forgive me. I shouldn't have assumed."

He looked at the other man again uncertainly, as if coming to terms with the fact that Lindy could very well be in a relationship with a man twice her age, especially one as distinguished-looking as this. Lindy seemed to read his thoughts, and, to his relief, found the notion hilarious, letting out a genuine, unrestrained laugh.

"Quentin Senior, this is Eric Chappell," she said, recovering herself finally. "Eric's my boss at the magazine."

"Ah, indeed. Pleased to meet you." A mixture of embarrassment and relief spread across Senior's features as he extended a huge hand. "I hear Ms. Hey has brought some welcome publicity the way of your magazine, Mr. Chappell."

Eric smiled. "Any time a journalist gets nominated for a national award, it reflects well on the publication," he said, "even if we so manifestly fail to meet her own high standards most of the time." He turned to raise his eyebrows toward Lindy before brushing away the joke with a sweep of his hand. "We're all delighted, naturally, and very proud of her."

"Something about King Lear?" Senior snapped his bins up at a shape on the water and lowered them again, so quickly it was like one fluid movement, over almost before Eric had realized what was happening.

"'Distaff and Sceptre: Lear and the Prospect of a Female Royal Line,'" said Eric, still recovering from Senior's sudden action. "Lindy here tied in the recent changes to the Succession to the Crown Act to aspects of Shakespeare's play. It was quite brilliant," he assured Senior in response to the older man's dubious look. "The nomination is well-merited."

Lindy reddened slightly. "It was just a bit of noodling around," she said modestly. "Besides, we're a long way from anywhere yet."

Senior looked at Eric for clarification.

"The announcement's not for a couple of weeks," he said. "No one knows quite when exactly. The committee adheres to the charmingly old-fashioned practice of notifying the candidates by post. The conventional wisdom was always *big envelope: good news, small envelope: disappointment*. Though, of course, our magazine has never had a winner, so we've never actually been able to confirm it."

Lindy had been doing her best to ignore the conversation, looking out over the landscape, drinking in the subtle shades of the swaying grasses as the light played over them. The surface of the water was still, an undisturbed mirror for the cloud-dotted sky. "Anyway, we're not here to talk about me," she said briskly. "I'm afraid Eric appears to be suffering from some sort of mental breakdown," she said, dropping her voice gravely.

"Oh, I'm sorry," said Senior, as if he didn't know quite why Lindy would want to share such personal information with him.

She nodded. "I'm afraid he's decided he wants to become a birder."

Senior barked a delighted laugh. "Well, then, welcome to the most wonderful form of insanity you'll ever come across, Mr. Chappell."

"It's been one of those areas that has fascinated me for years, to tell you the truth," said Eric. "You know, what do you people see in it? Am I missing out on something? So I decided to throw myself in at the deep end. Lindy says she can't think of anyone better to show me the ropes."

"I'm not sure about that, but certainly there could be no-one more willing."

"I thought I might like to turn it into a feature for the magazine, too, chronicling my experiences as I try to become a bona fide birder. That means we'd want to include some bits of your wisdom, a few tips, insights about bird behaviour, that sort of thing, if that would be okay."

"Of course," said Senior heartily. "If you're sure you want to expose your poor readers to my piffle, I'd have no objections at all."

"I believe Eric had me pencilled in for the feature part of it," said Lindy, smiling confidingly at Senior, "but I think we both know *that* was never going to happen."

"You'll have to forgive Ms. Hey," Senior said, turning to Eric with mock seriousness. "She's still fighting the call herself, you see. You strike me as a man of certain experience, Mr. Chappell. Is anything quite as tragic, I wonder, as watching a young heart deny its true destiny?"

Eric smiled, aware he had entered in the second act of an ongoing drama. But though he may not know Quentin Senior yet, he clearly knew Lindy well enough to decide that a middle ground was the safest. He marked his position on the matter with a measured silence.

"Right … birding," said Senior brightly. "Let's get started. Rule one, I suppose, is always try to give a bird a decent look. I was out here one day and I saw a female Reed Bunting. Didn't even give it a second glance. And then I heard that distinctive *tic*. — Little Bunting, can you believe it? I'd have passed right by if it hadn't given that call, and I'd have missed one of the rarest visitors to these parts. Since then, I've seen plenty of birds I couldn't identify, and failed to get on plenty more, but it's never been for want of trying."

As if to demonstrate the point, he snapped his bins up swiftly now, lowering them after a brief glance over the fields. Lindy couldn't help smiling. "Better buckle up, Eric," she said. But she could tell he was already captivated by Senior's enthusiasm, as she always was.

"Why don't we take a walk down toward the beach, see if there are any gulls to work on? Might as well throw you in at the deep end," said Senior breezily. "Would you care to join us, Ms. Hey?"

He undoubtedly already knew her answer, but she recognized it was courtesy, rather than mischief, that required him to ask. She had seen Quentin Senior stand as a woman left a dining table. Such old school manners would never have permitted him to take his leave today without first making his offer.

Lindy shook her head. "Other plans, sadly," she said with mock regret. "Besides, I'm expecting Dom home any time, possibly this evening."

From somewhere off to their left, a mixed flock of waders flushed suddenly, startling them. Senior raised his bins and tracked them as they flew off low across the exposed mudflat, peeping their alarm calls. Both Lindy and Eric saw the look of quiet contentment that spread across his features as he watched them go.

"And you could identify all those, I assume?" said Eric.

"Dunlin," said Senior, "Green Sandpiper, a Sanderling or two. Though I was once told that it is novices who identify birds. Apparently, experienced birders *recognize* them." He gave them a soft smile. "Or am I trying too hard to provide you with suitable copy? Curlew, Eric, behind you, flying to the left!"

Senior's sudden announcement caused the man to spin in time to see a large bird disappearing over the reed beds on low, lazy wing beats. As it rose over a distant berm, Lindy saw two other birders, in silhouette, standing to watch the Curlew's progress. It would have spoiled the scene a little for Dom, she thought, the presence of people. He liked his vistas pristine, empty of any evidence of humans. The non-natural things, he called them, as if human beings shouldn't be a part of this landscape, didn't belong. He was a man of such absolutes sometimes; it was difficult to see how life could ever satisfy such an exacting view of the world. But Domenic loved birding at Cley, and she knew he would come here as soon as he returned. Perhaps he would meet Senior, and Eric. Slowly, it seemed as if all the men she cared about were disappearing into birding. The thought made her strangely sad as she left the two men to their newfound friendship and made her way alone back along the trail to the car park.

9

"Now there's a man who looks like he didn't get much sleep last night," announced Iron McLeod boldly as he strode into the hotel's breakfast room. The other diners turned in surprise and suppressed grins at Jejeune's sheepish reaction to the good-natured ribbing.

The inspector was sitting at a small table nestled neatly into the bay window of the room. Weak sunshine was filtering in through the net curtains, spilling pools of light onto the white linen tablecloth.

"Strong night, was it, sampling the fleshpots of Ullapool?" McLeod nodded down at Jejeune's half-finished breakfast. "Never mind pushing it off to one side of your plate, man, you need to get some of that haggis and black pudding down you. That'll set you up for the day, right enough."

McLeod leaned back easily on the rear legs of the chair and gave a lavish wink to the waitress who had delivered a second silver pot of coffee to Jejeune. She smiled shyly in return, enjoying his attentions. With his short, sandy hair and his neatly trimmed beard, McLeod looked well suited to play the lead in a young girl's dreams, thought Jejeune idly, even if his florid features and rugged, powerful hands suggested he might be more the type for solitary outdoor pursuits.

"I was wondering," said Jejeune casually, "is there any thought that this business is any more than it looks?"

McLeod tipped forward and eyed him warily. "If you're not going to eat that toast, would you mind? My daughter was running late for school today, and I had no time to grab any breakfast for myself."

Jejeune pushed the untouched toast toward him.

"More than it looks?" said McLeod, taking an inordinate amount of care to spread marmalade onto the toast, a task which left him no attention to return Jejeune's gaze. "Now, why would you ask a question like that, I wonder?"

"Because you said the man was wearing a high-end waterproof jacket," Jejeune said. "And a person who invests that much in outdoor wear probably knows enough not to go out hiking without the proper equipment. But you said he had nothing with him, this man, no pack, no water bottle. It just seems strange, that's all."

McLeod nodded. "Plenty enough that's strange about this case, though, isn't there, Inspector Jejeune? Now that you've had some time to sleep on it, did you think of anything more that you could tell us about that book. Or about the man who had it?"

It hadn't been necessary for McLeod to take Jejeune down to the mortuary before setting out for Sgurr Fiona yesterday. He had texted a picture to the detective from the south and had a better-quality printed copy waiting to show him when he arrived. Jejeune confirmed that he'd never seen the man before, and had no idea who he was. The DCI suspected that, like himself, McLeod was not a policeman who made a habit of asking the same question twice. He would know, as Jejeune did, that people rarely changed their answers the second time of asking. If they had answered truthfully in the first place, there was no need to. If they had lied, they had no option but to stay with their first response.

Jejeune shook his head slowly. "Nothing comes to mind." *Other than his name*, he thought, *and how he came to this country*. The deceptions continued to mount. They were like ants on his skin. He couldn't wait to shake them off, get away from this place, get home, to shower off the lies and feel the freshness again of unguarded … what? Honesty? Hardly, with Lindy unaware of exactly who she would be harbouring under her roof. But if not honesty then, what? Truth, of a sort. No more lies, at least.

McLeod bit into the toast and chewed it slowly. He looked at Jejeune carefully.

"No, I didn't expect anything would," he said.

Jejeune seemed to find something interesting about the walls of the breakfast room, and it was a moment before he turned to face McLeod again. When he did, he found the other man's gaze waiting to meet him.

"Do you know when your department might be able to release the book?"

"Ah, now then, that would be down to me," said McLeod. "Would there be any more coffee in that pot, d'ye think?" He reached over to a neighbouring table and snared a cup from the place setting.

Jejeune drew the cup toward him and began pouring. "The book?" he said, in a tone which suggested that he, too, had all the time in the world.

"I'd be willing to release it to you right now. Just the one puzzle to be answered."

On the far side of the breakfast table, Jejeune finished pouring with an immaculately steady hand. He slid the cup across the table. McLeod stirred in cream lavishly and took a long drink. "Now that's a fine cup of coffee."

Jejeune said nothing.

"Fingerprints," announced McLeod. "The dead man's aren't on it."

Jejeune turned for a moment to take in life on the far side of the bay window. Whatever was out there, it didn't hold his interest for very long. "I can see how that would be a problem," he said at his most reasonable again. He turned his gaze to McLeod. "Although ..."

"Although, there could be any number of explanations for that." McLeod gave the table a resounding slap with his broad, weathered hand, making the cutlery bounce. "That's exactly what I said. He could have been wearing gloves when he put it in his pocket, for example, and then taken them off and left them in his room before he set out to climb the Fiona. All we need to do is find out where he was staying, locate the gloves, and Bob's your uncle. Mystery solved." He looked at Jejeune carefully, gauging the other man's face for a reaction.

"Did I mention I had a nice chat with that Sergeant Maik of yours down in Norfolk? He couldnae say enough about you. You can tell a lot about a person by the kind of loyalty they inspire in the people who work for them, I always find." He searched Jejeune's face with his eyes for a moment. "Can I ask you something, Inspector?" he asked, his tone more conversational now, more relaxed.

"Of course," said Jejeune guardedly, raising his coffee cup to his lips.

"You're obviously a birder, or else why would you have had that book in the first place. Have you ever seen a white eagle?"

Jejeune stopped drinking.

"I'm sure I saw one up on the Fiona about two months ago. Does such a bird exist?"

"Not as far as I know," said Jejeune. *No as in yes,* he thought. *More truth. More deception.* "Could it have been an Osprey? They're extremely rare up here, but they're all white below."

McLeod shook his head. "No, I've seen an Osprey. A gillie called me up to his salmon river one time, where he was losing

fish to one. Wanted to know if he could kill the bird as a pest."
He held up a hand to still the slow progress of alarm spreading across Jejeune's features. "Even I know enough about the Nature Conservation Act to know the answer to that one. No, the Osprey has a dark back, doesn't it? This bird I saw was pure white, I'm sure of it."

Ask your friend the police sergeant if there is something else up there that a free spirit like Jack de Laet might be interested in.

"There's no species like that which you could reasonably expect to see in Scotland," said Jejeune, adding the qualifier that helped him to hang on to a fragment of the truth. Deception was such an easy game to play, if you allowed yourself these moveable boundaries.

"I suppose it must have been a sea eagle, then. You've seen that light up on the Fiona. It's magical. It could transform almost anything into something else, I suppose, make you believe you've seen something you haven't."

McLeod paused and looked at Jejeune, who found something interesting enough in his coffee cup to avoid having his eyes meet the sergeant's.

"Pity," said McLeod finally. "This mystery man who had your book. Seems he must've been a birder, too. I was thinking if it was a white eagle, and he had heard about it, mebbe he went out for a wee look."

If McLeod was laying a snare to see if anyone was eager enough to jump into it, Jejeune wasn't going to be first. "You said you didn't find any binoculars on him."

"No, that's right. And anyway, if you're telling me there's no such thing, then I guess I'm on the wrong track." McLeod stood up abruptly, the chair making a loud scraping noise as he pushed it back. "Well, that's me away to the station. It's been a real pleasure to meet you, Inspector Jejeune." He leaned forward across the table, oblivious to the scattershot of crumbs lying on the tablecloth between them. Jejeune thought he was offering his hand, and had stretched out his own before he realized McLeod was handing him something. It was the bird book, wrapped in plastic. He passed it to Jejeune with a significant look. "You won't forget now, if anything comes to mind about this man, or what he might have been doing in possession of your book, you will let me know. Anything that could help us write this off as an accident once and for all."

Jejeune felt the tension flow from his body as he watched McLeod leave. He felt slightly queasy from the effort of stonewalling such a decent person; from the effort of … let's face it, deceiving him at every turn, even if he wasn't entirely sure at this point about what. He had just taken a steadying mouthful of coffee when a heavy hand on his shoulder made him start.

"Almost forgot," said McLeod. "Thanks for breakfast."

10

Danny Maik eased himself out of the small car, rounding to the passenger side to open the door. Constable Salter could have opened it, but why would she? Why spoil the fantasy she had been building for herself on the drive out here. Opening a door was something a man might do for his lady, especially a gentleman like Danny Maik. So if she wanted to pretend that she and Danny were just out for a drive on this beautiful summer afternoon, that they had come down here, with the dreamy sounds of Motown playing in the background, to this sun-kissed field to take in the beauty for a few moments, where was the harm in that?

They were on a gentle slope of land, mid-point between a rocky shoreline and a dense stand of trees that ran across the ridgeline. It was the glade where Philip Wayland had been killed. From here, there was no sign of the fenced-off compound just beyond the rise. Salter couldn't imagine owning such an immense piece of land, one on which you were unable to see a one-hectare compound from another point on your property. She turned to take in the swath of ground around them. It looked like it would have been able to yield valuable crops, with the proper care and attention. But Salter knew Prince Ibrahim al-Haladin had no interest in frivolities like agricultural practices. For him, these fields were reserved for another purpose.

Maik had parked the Mini next to Tony Holland's brand new Audi TT, in front of a large dome-shaped hangar. It was the only building in sight. Holland emerged from the hangar and approached them with what looked like a genuine smile of appreciation.

"You two didn't have to come all the way out here."

"No trouble, Constable," said Maik easily.

Holland nodded, showing that he recognized Salter's presence as necessary, too. Despite the fact that Tony was Darla Doherty's boyfriend, Maik would have insisted there be a female officer on scene, just in case.

Salter looked past Holland to the hangar. "Your girlfriend works here, Tony? At the prince's falconry?" Salter couldn't keep the amusement from her voice. "Blimey, no wonder you kept it quiet."

The connection to an interest for which Holland had so often derided DCI Jejeune forced him into an explanation. "These are birds of prey," he said defensively. "We're not talking about those useless bundles of fluff the DCI wastes his time with. I mean, these are proper birds — hunters."

"Shall we?" asked Maik. "The DCI would never forgive me if I had the chance to investigate a break-in at a falcon enclosure and I wasn't able to give him chapter and verse when he got back."

"Just so you know, it's called a *mews*, a falcon's pen," said Holland, causing Maik and Salter to exchange a significant glance. "I've already had a look around. As far as Darla can tell, nothing has been taken, but it does look like somebody's had a bit of a riffle around in one of the filing cabinets."

Salter knew Holland would be relieved that he had found justification for rushing out here after receiving the panicked call from his girlfriend. When he had left the station, his expression had told them he was uncertain whether it was just the overreaction of somebody still unnerved by the violent murder that had taken place just up the hill.

"Come on through," he said. "Believe me, it's worth seeing."

They entered the hangar and found themselves in a cavernous space that smelled faintly of ammonia. It was not dark inside, but coming in from the bright sunshine, it still took their eyes a few minutes to adjust. As they did, they could make out cage wire stretching down from the roof to the floor all around the sides of the building, about two metres out from the walls. Other wires ran off this screen back to the walls, creating a series of towering pens, each, Salter would have guessed, at least four metres high. Somewhere in each pen, a single falcon sat on a perch.

At a desk beside the rear door sat a young woman. She was short and small-boned, with delicate features and dark brown eyes that seemed to accentuate her pale face. Her short hair was the colour of straw. Pretty, decided Salter, but not the type of woman she had come to associate with Holland. Far less flash and brass. If she had been asked for a description, the anodyne "nice girl" would have been the constable's choice.

"This is Darla," Holland announced, moving over to stand beside her. "She looks after the Crown Prince's falcons. Feeding, care, stuff like that. Flies them, too, when he's not here."

Maik, also, had been appraising Darla Doherty. He approached, holding out his hand.

"Had a bit of a fright, Tony tells us," he said. The hand she offered looked tiny in Maik's gnarled paw. Even from a few feet away, Salter noticed it was still trembling.

"I feel so silly. I mean, it was probably nothing." She turned her eyes away from Maik. Her voice was small and girlish. *Barely a kid,* thought Salter. Tony would be the responsible adult in this relationship. As disturbing as the thought was, perhaps it was the role that he had been looking for, after all.

"The constable mentioned a cabinet. Mind if I have a look? See if it's worth getting the fingerprint boys in?"

She seemed to hesitate slightly. Holland saw it, too, and he shifted uncomfortably. "Sure, why not," he said.

The woman fluttered the kind of smile toward Holland that seemed to be looking for one of reassurance in return, and he obliged.

"Darla carries the cage keys with her," Holland told his sergeant. "Both the wire and the locks are high tensile steel. One look and anyone would've known they weren't getting in."

Maik nodded absently. "Unless they'd brought the right equipment along." He held up a sheaf of small green booklets that were stuffed untidily in a file. "What are these?"

"Passports … for the birds."

"There's a punch line coming, right?" asked Salter. She offered Darla a smile to show her she was on her side.

The girl shook her head. "Falcon owners from Emirati countries can apply to have passports issued for their individual birds. They often travel with them from country to country. With a passport, the bird can travel on the plane with its owner. Often, they will even buy the bird its own seat."

Despite her earnest delivery, Maik was still looking at Darla as if to check whether she was joking. He turned to Holland. "Had you heard anything about this?"

"Not until today."

"I suppose these documents would be valuable," said Salter. "Are any of them missing?"

Darla shook her head. "No, I checked them. Fourteen. One for each bird. They're all there."

Salter and Maik exchanged a glance. If so, she was the one who had stuffed them in the draw so untidily.

"So what d'you reckon, Sarge?" said Holland over-brightly. "Some local layabouts after a few quid and some ciggies?" He flashed a look at Darla to indicate he would appreciate Maik backing up the story he had already given her to appease her fears.

"Not likely to find any cigarettes with you two, though, were they?" asked Maik pleasantly.

"If you're all done with Darla, I'll drive her back home." Holland held a hand out to help her up from her chair.

Darla turned to Salter and then to Maik, but she couldn't quite seem to make her eyes meet either of theirs. "Thank you for coming. I didn't mean to cause any trouble."

Holland wrapped an arm protectively around her shoulder. "Come on." He looked back at them. "I'll only be five minutes, if you want to hang around."

They hadn't intended to, but it was so unlike Holland to cut short an opportunity to spend time with a girl, what Salter had heard him refer to on other occasions as *quality time*, that it was probably worth staying on to find out what was going on.

After they left, Maik picked up the falcon passports again and began idly riffling through them. Most hadn't been used in a long time, but a couple had fairly recent exit stamps.

"Well, the break-in has definitely scared her," said Salter.

Maik nodded. "Something has, at least." He returned the passports to the drawer and pushed it shut. Neither he nor Salter expected they would need the fingerprint team on this one.

Salter looked at the cages all around. The birds sat impassively on their perches, not a single feather stirring on any of them. She felt the cold stare of fourteen pairs of eyes watching her, gazing down from on high. If Danny Maik had not been beside her, she might have shivered. "I'm going outside," she said.

When Maik joined her she was staring in the direction Holland and Darla had gone, up past the compound to the main road into Saltmarsh.

"Better get your tux dry cleaned," she said. "If he carries on like this, we'll be getting wedding invitations before you know it. We could go together if you like. I'll get a nice new frock."

Maik smiled. He let his gaze linger in the same direction as Salter's, the direction of the trees. Of Wayland's murder. Salter noted his look and understood its meaning.

"Why did he have to go all the way up to Scotland, Sarge? Can this book really be that important?"

"He has his reasons, Constable," he said, though Jejeune hadn't shared them, or much of anything else, with Maik during their brief call that morning.

The news update Maik gave Jejeune had been short and to the point. No progress. No prospect of a meeting with Prince Yousef. A silence had followed, in which Maik fancied he could hear the distant bleating of sheep and the occasional rush of a passing car. "Then a senior executive, Sergeant, the highest member of the Old Dairy board available. Set it up, please."

And that was it. Maik had no idea if this new request was related to Jejeune's doubts about the prince's alibi, or some new approach entirely. All Danny knew for certain was that this was not heading in a direction he was keen to follow. The sooner the DCI returned to relieve him of his temporary responsibilities, the happier he would be.

Holland wasn't back in five minutes, but it wasn't much longer. He approached them, casting his gaze to the ground and nodding. "I know," he said, "she knows who it was. I suspect she realized as soon as she called me. By the time I got here there was a message on my phone telling me not to bother coming."

Both Salter and Maik waited in silence for Holland to get around to telling them. "It was her father."

"Are you sure?"

"He lives next door. They're not speaking. He objects to her hacking the birds — free flying them — over his land. I think she probably does it deliberately, just to wind him up. He was a harvester himself for most of his life. Falconer, hunter, fisherman, the lot. But now he's reformed, and, these days, he's all about protection and conservation. He's one of those leading the protests up the hill. Apparently, he's become a real zealot. Darla thinks he might have found God."

"I'll cancel that missing person's report then, shall I?" asked Maik dryly. "If it was her father who broke in, what would he have been looking for in that cabinet?"

"Keys. He told her he was going to release all the birds one day. He said they shouldn't be kept in captivity." Holland shook his head. "I dunno, magnificent animals like that, you see them flying, you think he might have a point." He looked up at Maik. "I know she shouldn't be wasting police time like this, Sarge. That's why I didn't want you to come out in the first place. But she's on edge. They all are around here. Leave it to me. I'll go and have a word with the old man." A thought seemed to strike him. "Here, d'you reckon the DCI would know anything about Gyrfalcons?"

"I'd imagine so," said Maik. "He seems interested in all kinds of birds."

"Perhaps I'll have a chat with him when he gets back, before I go see Darla's dad. If I can talk to the old man about falcons, a bit of common ground, you know. Can't hurt, can it? Maybe I can patch things up between him and Darla while I'm there."

Tony Holland, trying to broker a reconciliation between a father and his estranged daughter? Maik might have to dig out that tux after all.

Danny Maik sat in his Mini for a long time after Holland and Salter had left. Had she seemed reluctant to accept Holland's offer of a ride back? And what about that strange backward glance she had given him as she climbed into the Audi? Maik's car door was open, and he turned to take in the gentle swaying of the tall grasses on the hillside. Over the speakers, The Velvettes were telling him how hard it was to find a good man — *a needle in a haystack.*

He got out of the car and walked over to the high hedge-row that marked the boundary of the Old Dairy. From all sides, Maik could hear the sweet, insistent burble of birdsong, though the only birds he could see, crows, gulls and the like higher up the hillsides, were not making any sounds at all. He leaned on the gate and stared out over the untilled fields of Niall Doherty's property. The high sun dappled the land; a pattern of dark shadows lay across the rutted ground, as if tiny pockets of the night had been snagged during its retreat from the coming dawn.

A needle in a haystack. About right, he thought. Protesters, colleagues, acquaintances, even strangers who had crossed Philip Wayland's path. His killer could be anyone among them. It would be the DCI's haystack soon. But he had something to do before Jejeune returned. It wasn't something that he was particularly looking forward to, but then, that was about par for the course for Danny Maik these days.

11

Damian Jejeune's head snapped around and he turned back to Domenic. "Did I just see a surfboard on that car?"

Domenic checked the rear-view and nodded. "Apparently, the north coast of Scotland is one of the surfing hotspots of Britain, particularly the area around John O'Groats."

"Why not?" asked Damian sarcastically, "I know the first thing I think of when I see menacing skies and seas the colour of lead is 'surfing Mecca.' I'm surprised the Beach Boys never mentioned it." He looked across at his brother. "You're serious? I mean, what would possess them to go out on a day like today? Are they crazy?"

Domenic inclined his head. "They go out in all kinds of weather. And they spend a fortune on it, too. Surfers will travel hundreds of miles just to catch that one perfect wave."

Damian shook his head slowly. "I'm sorry, I just don't get it."

"Me neither," agreed Domenic, "but what can you say? Some people get a little obsessive about their hobbies, I guess."

He slowed down as they passed a series of large grassy mounds on their left, and wheeled the big Range Rover off the main road, following the narrow track signposted for Dunnet. It was already after noon, but neither man regretted the day they had spent driving along the north coast of Scotland. They had taken the route north from Ullapool, up through the high hill country of Lochinvar, where the towering black crags pushed through green skin of gently sloping foothills. Farther on, as they traced their way east along the coast road, a gradual softening of the landscape had begun to take hold. Fern-clad valleys and fields of bracken tumbled towards the northern shore, before the terrain levelled out still more, in a succession of wide, flat tidal estuaries; Tongue, Coldbackie, Bettyhill, that had led them finally to this tamer, cultivated area on the north-eastern tip of Scotland.

They had stopped only once, just outside Kylesku, in the shadow of a mighty column of granite that rose out of the foothills like a pair of praying hands, losing its fingertips in the blankets of cloud that seemed ever-present in those parts. Jejeune had pulled off the road to call the station, to let them know he would still be one more day. He turned off his phone just as Damian returned from exploring the landscape.

"Coping okay without you?"

"I should be there," said Domenic solemnly, "but to be this close to Dunnet Head and miss it ..." he shook his head. "They're a good team, they'll find whatever is there to be found," he said, as if trying to convince himself. He stared out over the landscape; this bleak, rugged terrain the guidebooks described as *barren* but was really anything but, if only you could be patient enough to wait, to watch: for the Linnets, the grouse, the eagles.

"You didn't mention the white Gyrfalcon," he said quietly.

Damian sat beside him and the two gazed out over the land. Somehow, it had always been easier for the two of them to talk like this, side by side, not facing each other. "I wasn't sure whether McLeod knew about it, but if he did, you needed to look suitably surprised. You never were the greatest actor, Domino. I think all good actors need a little bit of dishonesty in their souls, and you've never really had that, have you? Not even as a kid. Besides,

I could already tell you had a lot of respect for this McLeod. I thought it would be easier if you didn't have to lie to him."

"You think it came from Iceland?"

Damian nodded. "It's where most of the white ones are found. Icelandic Gyrfalcons don't normally migrate, but there's been a lot of volcanic activity up there lately, and it seems to have set some of them on the move."

"Do you think that's why De Laet was there?"

"I know it was. I think it may have even been the Gyr that knocked him off the rock face, especially if she had a nest up there. She's been on territory a while. It's possible. Can you imagine that?"

Nesting Gyrfalcons in Scotland. Domenic let his mind play over the idea for a moment. He realized his brother had gone quiet.

"It must have been hard to watch. They say talking about it can help sometimes."

"Did it help you?" asked Damian simply.

No, thought Jejeune, *it didn't*. But that had been different. In the case involving the Home Secretary's daughter, he could trace the death of the boy directly to his own actions. Damian wasn't responsible for this man's death, or at least he claimed he wasn't. He had merely witnessed it. But perhaps it was the connection with a death that really mattered, the proximity to it. Perhaps it was that which caused the guilt, whether you were responsible or not. "Come on," he said, standing up, "the birds of Dunnet Head are waiting for us."

A tour bus pulled up and disgorged its passengers, most heading directly for the Dunnet Head lighthouse built by Robert Louis Stevenson's grandfather. It was an attraction, certainly, but how could it compare with the magnificent cliffs just beside it, teeming with calling Kittiwakes and a circus of Puffins, as Skuas majestically carved the skies overhead?

"Some racket," said Damian. He and Domenic were sitting on rocks near the edge of the cliff, above a deafening cacophony of bird sounds — territorial calls, mostly, or the cries of returning birds trying to locate their mates in the cliff-side colonies. Both knew there were matters to be discussed between them, possibly *confronted* was a better word. But the wild, unmitigated beauty of this ragged coastline was not the place to trouble one's soul with such things, so they simply stared out in contented silence, watching the birds dive-bombing the wild seas as the crashing waves broke on the rocks in explosions of fine grey spray.

A harsh, guttural call alerted the brothers to the presence of a pair of Ravens overhead, and the men craned their necks back to watch the birds in their dazzling, exuberant courtship flight. Domenic drew his gaze away, warily eying the bus crowd, now milling around aimlessly in the car park. "We should probably be going," he said. As irrational as it was, he was concerned that with so many people around, someone might recognize his brother. Police cases he knew of had turned on such wild, coincidental sightings.

Damian seemed to understand. With a final glance out over the roiling seas and the vibrant, pulsating bird cliffs of Dunnet Head, the two men stood and turned reluctantly to begin making their way back to the Range Rover. They were halfway there when Damian broke into a sprint. A dark van was trundling slowly across the car park. From the far side, a woman with a baby on her hip screamed. Damian disappeared in front of the van, and then Domenic heard a sickening thud as the vehicle jerked to a sudden stop.

By the time Domenic got there, the woman was bending over Damian. In his arms was a young boy of about five. Alarm rose in Domenic as he saw the blood, but subsided when he realized it was from Damian's forearm, which had been scraped raw by the contact with the gravel car park. "He's okay," Damian told the mother. "Just a little scared, that's all. I'll take him over there for you." He nodded to a patch of grass near the stone wall and rolled to his knees, still clutching the boy in his arms.

The natural impulse to comfort her child compromised, the woman's shock morphed into anger instead, and she rounded on the van's driver, an elderly man wearing thick glasses. Her eyes were wild with fury. "You bloody old fool," she screamed at him through the open driver's window. "You should watch where you're going!"

"I didn't see him," said the man defensively. He sounded dazed, shaken. "What was he doing in the middle of the car park, anyway? You should keep better control over your young ones."

The woman hefted the baby up on her hip and squared herself to the car window, as if preparing herself for further confrontation. Some of the bus passengers had arrived by now, gathering in a small half-circle around them. From other parts of the car park, people were drifting over to see what was going on. The small crowd was beginning to build. There would be many mobile phones among them, Domenic knew. He stepped between the pair, blocking the woman's view of the driver. He locked her eyes with his own.

"Your son is safe," he said quietly, engaging her, taking her focus away from anything else. His voice was calm and reassuring. "He was crying because he's afraid, but he is unharmed."

"No thanks to this idiot." She was shaking now, trembling, the baby on her hip rocking slightly with the movement. "He could have been killed." She put her free hand to her mouth, and tears started to her eyes as the realization took hold. Her body seemed to melt slightly, and for a second Domenic was afraid she might faint. He reached forward to steady her. The crowd was watching them intently. No one had reached for a phone yet, but he knew he had only seconds before an electronic pulse of some kind went out from this scene: Instagram. YouTube. The police.

"Your son is safe," said Domenic again. "This man reacted quickly. We should thank him for that." His voice was soothing, calm, the voice of reason. He turned to the man now, still blocking the view between the two. "You did well, sir, to stop like that."

"I never saw the wee lad." There were tears in the old man's eyes, too, now, behind the glasses. "If I hadn't caught sight o' that man out the corner of my eye, going past the front of the van like that ..." He gripped the steering wheel tightly, staring out through the windscreen with unseeing eyes. Domenic realized for the first time that the van was still in gear. The man's foot must be on the brake. He reached in through the window and jammed the gear stick into neutral. The man didn't move. In the back of the van, Domenic saw an old chair, now lying on its back — the noise, he realized, the *thud*, the one he had thought was his brother, and the woman had thought was her child.

Domenic turned back to the woman. "I'm sure your son wants to talk to you about what happened, but I know you'll want to express your gratitude to this man for his quick thinking first."

Domenic stepped aside so she could see the driver now, his head bowed slightly, chin quivering.

"Aye ... well, thank you," she said grudgingly, uncertainly.

The driver turned to look at the woman. "I'm glad the boy is all right," he said, his voice almost breaking. He reached out a hand and unsteadily put the van into gear again, inching cautiously over the gravel at first, barely above walking pace, slowly gathering speed. The crowd watched the van navigate through the gap in the stone-walled car park and then dispersed in a cloud of low murmurings.

By the time Domenic and the woman reached them, Damian and the boy were lying on their backs on the grass, looking up into the sky. Domenic saw the woman's look of alarm. "It's fine," he said, "he's just showing him the Ravens."

As they approached, they could hear Damian's voice speaking to the boy as if to an adult. "Watch this now," he was saying, "the male will come alongside the female and then do a barrel roll, just like a fighter pilot."

The black bird executed a perfectly controlled dive out over the headland, twirling to fly upside down for a moment before swooping in at the last moment to fly alongside its partner again.

At his mother's approach, the boy stood up. The woman gathered him to her in a reassuring hug, smoothing the hair back from his brow delicately. The boy's cheeks were smudged with dried tears, but he managed a brave smile for his mother. She looked across at Damian, who had also stood up. "You've a nasty wound on your arm," said the woman. "Are you sure I can't do anything? Get you a bandage, perhaps?"

Damian looked down at the long bloody gash on his forearm, as if noticing it for the first time.

"He'll be fine," said Domenic quickly. He turned to Damian. "There's a first-aid kit in the car if you want to go and clean up."

Damian picked up on the cue. "Remember, '*caw*': crow, '*craaaw*': Raven," he said by way of a goodbye to the boy. He headed off quickly, barely stopping to acknowledge the woman's thanks as he passed. She hefted the other child up on her hip again.

"Thank you doesn't seem enough," she said, watching Damian leave. "But what else can you say to someone who has …" The thought of what might have been seemed to overwhelm her and she fell silent.

"Really, it's fine," Domenic assured her. "We're just happy everything turned out okay."

He was almost at the Range Rover when the woman called after him. "Excuse me, sir. His name. I should at least know his name."

"Jejeune," he said. "Domenic Jejeune."

12

The two men emerged from the thatched hide and stood on the dirt path, surveying the land around them. Senior snapped up his bins, but by the time Eric had started to follow suit, Senior was already lowering them again. He smiled. "Unwritten rule of north Norfolk birding, Eric. If you're not sure what it is, it's a Wood Pigeon."

The two men turned at the sound of gravel crunching beneath a measured military gait, and Senior's face broke into a guarded smile. "My, my, dear old Cley does seem to be attracting its share of non-birders these days." He turned to Eric. "Forgive me, Sergeant Maik. This is Eric Chappell, Miss Hey's editor at the magazine. He's in the early throes of birding, and frankly, I could think of no better place to start than here. Even in its much changed state, Cley's still a beautiful spot for a morning's birding."

Maik looked around at the sun-dappled landscape. He found it hard to disagree. The light seemed to lie with a particular softness on the quietly moving waters this morning, and the gentle crush of the grasses moving in the breeze provided a soundtrack for the birdsong that filled the air. Calls of other, distant birds drifted toward them from high above, where they rode the currents to glide effortlessly out over the marsh.

Senior continued to address Eric, as if a direct conversation with Danny Maik was something he might be wary of, though there was no reason Maik could think of for his caution.

"Though I would describe the sergeant as slightly more of an agnostic than Miss Hey in birding terms, I cannot imagine he has come here for our peeps and spoonbills." He raised his exuberant eyebrows in Maik's direction.

"Just out for a bit of fresh air."

Eric's face showed interest, Senior's more caution. A line of dark shapes trailed across the tops of the stunted grasses, wings beating fast. For once, Senior seemed disinclined to look. Perhaps he had already identified them. Or perhaps something else was occupying his thoughts. "Nothing to do with this dreadful business up on the prow at the Old Dairy, then?"

"Prow?"

"Public Right of Way. I trust your visit to Cley has nothing to do with that crime?"

Maik nodded in recognition finally. His only previous encounters with Quentin Senior had been when the birder was the focus of a pointed investigation into his possible motives and alibi in a murder. Though the line of questioning had been a justifiable one, Maik acknowledged to himself that he might have some way to go to earn back the man's goodwill.

"No, nothing like that," he said, sweeping his gaze across to include Eric in his assurances. "I thought I would see how the marsh was recovering. I'd heard that things were pretty bad down here after the storm." Maik continued his gaze past the men, taking in the Cley landscape again, the swaying grasses, the glittering cells of water. "I must say, it looks fairly healthy now."

If Senior recognized that showing an interest, genuine or otherwise, in another man's passion was a step towards reconciliation, his expression suggested he was ready to accept the sergeant's olive branch. He didn't strike Maik as a man who held grudges. You didn't get a face as open and friendly as Senior's if you spent a lifetime letting resentments fester behind it.

"The winter storm of '14 wreaked absolute devastation on the birding areas up and down the north Norfolk coast, as you are no doubt aware, Sergeant. But it seemed to save a particular wrath for Cley. The entire reserve was flooded with sea water. The original roof of that hide over there was found over two miles away. These other hides," he indicated the one behind them, "were flooded all the way up to their thatched roofs."

Maik looked around. In the soft sunlight, it seemed impossible to imagine such devastation. "I saw that photo of the seal swimming along the coast road, what is that, nearly a half-mile inland? But everything seems to be coming back nicely."

Senior shook his head ruefully. "To the casual observer, perhaps. Vegetation is certainly returning, but whether it will have the same species composition as before remains to be seen." Something approaching sadness flashed in Senior's eyes. With the human costs and property damage, Maik had not really stopped to think about how the storm-wrought devastation of these areas would have impacted the birds. Or the birders. Senior surveyed the outlying landscape slowly, seeming to gather it into himself. It was as if he drew something from it, thought Maik, something spiritual that filled his senses, something that completed him, perhaps, in a way Maik could only guess at, but that seemed real enough for all that.

"All that saltwater percolating into the ground must have had a tremendous impact on the soil invertebrates and root systems," said Senior quietly. "One suspects Cley as we knew it may come back in time, but for a long while, it will be different — different habitat, different species."

Eric nodded sagely. "Some of the veteran birders here have already been telling me the wader numbers are down this season."

To Maik's surprise, Senior managed to summon a soft smile. "Ah, complaints about numbers are a different matter, entirely, I'm afraid, Eric," he said with a slight tilt of his head. "As you will come to discover in time."

Eric looked puzzled.

"In truth, you are likely to hear similar complaints in all seasons in all birding locales. Nostalgia is as prevalent in birding as in any other area. Much as I'm told the sergeant here finds refuge in his music of a bygone era, the older we birders get, the better the birding used to be."

On another day, Maik might have taken issue with the *bygone era* comment, let alone *refuge*, but he was in the business of building bridges today and he let it slide.

Senior turned to Eric. "Nevertheless," he said, brightening with an act of will that was almost palpable, "still plenty to see."

"Got your bird guide at the ready, Mr. Chappell? No birder should be without one, I imagine." Maik turned to Senior for confirmation.

Senior took a moment to lift his bins and track a bird making a slow pass over the marsh. "Bar-tailed Godwit, Eric."

"On it," confirmed Chappell, without lowering his bins. He was getting the birding parlance down, anyway, thought Maik, even if he suspected the new man's skills wouldn't be quite there yet. He waited as the two men tracked the bird's lazy progress across the marsh.

Senior lowered his bins and smiled. "Forgive me, Sergeant, but a bird like that is not something that can be taken for granted out here. Remarkable species, though. Do you know, a female Bar-tailed Godwit was recorded as having made a flight from Alaska to New Zealand in nine days?"

"That's a distance of more than ten thousand kilometres, Quentin," said Eric, casting Senior a dubious glance. "That would be more than a thousand kilometres a day."

Senior nodded vigorously. "Non-stop, too. No food, no water, no rest. Birds can sleep during long-distance migration flights by shutting down one half of their brains at a time."

"Non-stop?" Even Maik felt compelled to question Senior's story, bridge-building or not.

"Tracked by satellite the entire way," confirmed Senior. He shook his head in wonder. "Every time you think birds have lost the capacity to surprise you, they come up with something new. But, to your earlier point, Sergeant, you are quite correct. We will have to make sure Eric here gets himself a good bird guide. We all have our favourites. Some birders like photos, while others prefer composite drawings. Then, as you progress in things, Eric, there'll be the specialties — immature gulls, migrating shorebirds, ducks in eclipse plumages. There really does seem to be a guide for every eventuality."

Maik nodded, trying to find a response that wouldn't charge the information with too much significance.

"Looks like you'll be buying new, Mr. Chappell. A good bird guide sounds like something a birder would want to hang on to. I wouldn't count on finding one in a used book store." To Maik, the casualness seemed forced, overdone, but if Senior noticed it, he gave no sign.

"It's possible," conceded the older man. "I attend meetings all the time where people have donated guides and bird books for one purpose or another. If, for whatever reason, someone considers a guide no longer relevant, then there is every reason to suspect it would find its way into a charity auction or a book giveaway of some kind."

Maik could see Senior readying himself for another contribution; a list of examples, perhaps, or a suggestion of one suitable for a birder of Eric's level. Either way, it would be further pursuit of a subject Maik now wanted dead and buried. He turned to Eric. "I hear Lindy Hey is up for some award. For a piece in your magazine?"

Perhaps not the smoothest topic change he'd ever engineered, but it achieved the desired effect.

Eric nodded. "As I never tire of saying, we are all very proud of her. She's a remarkable young woman, Sergeant, as you undoubtedly already know." He shook his head, almost to himself. "Whenever I assign her a feature, she always says the same thing. 'I'll do the best I can.' It's become something of a gold standard at the magazine. When Lindy Hey does the best she can, then the rest of us are inevitably more than satisfied, thank you very much."

Maik drew himself up for one final look around the marsh. He had done all he could to ensure the conversations about Cley and Lindy would airbrush the other topic from the men's memories in time. Perhaps he could have asked them to treat his casual inquiries about bird guides confidentially, but in his experience, few things fixed something in someone's mind as effectively as asking them to forget it.

"Well, I've kept you two from your birding long enough," he said. He left the men surveying the landscape with their binoculars, and turned to begin making his way back along the gravel path toward his Mini in the car park, where the refuge of his Motown songs awaited him.

13

The brothers paused for a moment to take in the invigorating scent of the surrounding pine trees that drifted toward them on the soft breeze. The valley below them was bathed in a pale blue-grey light that promised the approach of evening. They had come down through the Spey Valley to look for Crested Tit, a bird Domenic had long coveted. Though he wouldn't categorically rule out any bird appearing in north Norfolk, he was fairly sure he would never find a Crested Tit there. The conifer-clad hillsides on the lower reaches of the River Spey probably represented his best chance of seeing one, especially in the company of a bird finder of his brother's pedigree. But for once, even Damian's skills hadn't been enough, and after a couple of hours of intensive searching among the pines, they conceded defeat and made their way back to the car.

The argument started not long after they began driving again. Like many quarrels, its origins lay elsewhere, a related subject, perhaps, but no more than a gateway to the real conflict.

"Labrador, Iceland, Scotland. It seems pretty clear De Laet was after Gyrfalcons specifically," said Domenic. "Filling orders, you think?"

Damian shrugged and took in the passing scenery. "All I

know is, he was in a hurry to find them. The impression I got was that he needed one within a couple of days."

Domenic flashed a sideways glance at his brother. "That's a pretty tall order for catching any wild falcon, but a Gyr?"

Damian nodded in agreement. "And as much as I despised De Laet and what he did, he knew his trade. He would never have taken on a commission like that under normal circumstances."

A light breeze was moving the fields of golden barley on the hillsides. This was a different Scotland, a world away from the bleak ruggedness of the western Highlands, or the wind-scoured clifftops and pounding surf of Dunnet Head. This was a pastoral landscape, gentler, more tranquil. The scene seemed to mesmerize Damian and he continued looking at it for a long time. When he spoke, he did so without turning from the window.

"I took his day pack."

Domenic careened The Beast onto the road's gravel shoulder, rocking to a stop on the crest of a hill. The narrow road bent dangerously away from view in both directions, and an angry blast from a passing car protested the foolishness of Domenic's manoeuvre.

He spun on his brother. "Are you out of your mind?" he asked, unable to control his rising voice. "Not reporting what you saw is bad enough, but removing property from a dead body … It's a crime, Damian, an *actual* crime." He turned his intense gaze away from his brother and stared out through the windshield, rubbing his forehead.

Damian could see the tiny red blotches at the base of his brother's cheeks, spreading even as he fought to contain his temper. Damian hadn't thought about them in years. Whenever he had allowed himself to imagine a time when he saw his brother again, they hadn't been arguing.

Domenic turned to his brother, his eyes fixed on him, even as his mind was elsewhere, trying to find a way to undo the damage.

"Do you realize how serious this is? Where is the pack now?"

"I got rid of it, threw it off the dock in Ullapool. I didn't know if De Laet had stored my contact info anywhere. He deleted his phone calls, but I didn't know what police tech guys can do to get stuff like that back. There would have been calls from me ..."

"You destroyed evidence in a suspicious death?" Domenic pounded the steering wheel with the heel of his hand. "Why the hell would you do that, Dammy?" Domenic had not called his brother by his childhood nickname for many years. "What were you thinking?"

"I can tell you everything that was in there," Damian said defensively. "There were a couple of net traps, dho-gazzas they call them, a dead grouse for bait, two golf club covers, and his phone."

Domenic was shaking his head. "Even if you had held onto it until I came up ... You could have given it to me. I could have handled it."

"How? By telling the police what, exactly? I know you're the darling of the Free World, Domenic, but even you can't fix everything."

"I would have worked something out when I came. You know that."

"That's just it. I didn't know. That's the point, Domenic, don't you get it? I didn't know if you'd come."

They had been shouting at each other, half-turned to face one another, but now silence fell between them like a guillotine blade. Damian had left a message; a message both of them knew Domenic would understand. His fugitive brother was here, in Scotland. Had they really drifted so far apart that Damian was unsure whether Domenic would come? Did he really think Domenic Jejeune would hear his brother's cry for help and ignore it?

They were sitting on the terrace of a rambling nineteenth-century guest house, nestled on a densely wooded slope that climbed sharply from the road below. In the distance, the river was a rippling mercury ribbon that caught the light as it ran over the rocky stones of its bed. Damian was staring at it, transfixed.

After their argument, they had driven, unspeaking, following the river as it traced its way between fields until they reached the grey granite village of Aberlour.

"Food," Domenic had announced, pulling into the forecourt of the hotel. A drink with their meal had morphed into two, and then a decision to stay the night, giving them time to ease their raw nerves in the tranquility of the cool pine trees.

Domenic took a sip of his whisky, the smooth single malt swirling golden in the glass. He peered at his brother over the rim. *Why are you here?* he wondered. Because as genuine as Damian's love for birds was, and how great his desire to keep them from the clutches of a man like Jack de Laet, there had always been a strong element of self-interest about Damian, too. The man Domenic knew, used to know, would not have left the relative security of his home country and risked entering Scotland illegally unless there was a compelling reason for doing so.

Damian took a slow drink of his own whisky and surveyed the forested hillsides all around them. "New Scotland," he said. "Do you remember that area on the north shore of Lake Erie, around by Rondeau? That's what they called it — New Scotland. Billiard table-flat farmlands as far as the eye can see. Not sure where they were thinking of when they named it, but it doesn't look like any part of Scotland I've seen so far," said Damian ironically.

Domenic smiled and Damian let his look linger on it for a while. It was sincere, genuine; a once-familiar sight he had long missed. He toyed with his whisky glass. They would both be content to let their conversation stay out here, he knew, with birds and birding sites, letting the residue of their argument evaporate into the evening breezes.

Damian drained his glass with a flourish and looked around for their hostess for a refill. "Too bad you dipped on your Crested Tit. We could go back and try again tomorrow, if you like."

Domenic shook his head. "We have a long way to go. We need to get an early start." He gave his brother's empty whisky glass a significant glance. "And that means not hanging about looking for Crested Tits until the distilleries open."

Damian looked suitably sheepish. "You're sure you don't want to reconsider?" He spread out his hands, encompassing the entire valley in his gesture. "Speyside. This is the promised land for single malt lovers, Dom. Glenfiddich, The Macallan, Cardhu, all pretty much within stumbling distance of one another."

Domenic offered an apologetic smile. "You'll just have to pay your respects to the holy trinity some other time."

Damian sucked in a breath and shook his head in mock disapproval. "Such blasphemy. Madame Beauchemin would not be happy with you, young Domenic, though you would doubtless be forgiven unconditionally, while I was punished instead, for filling your head with evil notions in the first place."

"I don't remember it being like that."

Damian let out a derisive snort. "You're joking, right? Those teachers at our school carried on as if they all thought you had been born in a manger. I, on the other hand, was the spawn of Satan."

Domenic smiled. It had been a constant refrain through their childhood, Domenic leading his charmed life, while all the world's wrongs fell on his older brother's shoulders. In truth, it had always seemed to Domenic that life had treated them both pretty even-handedly. But then, in truth, it was always easier to notice life's injustices if you were the victim of them.

"So what's this I hear about you listing an Iberian Azure-winged Magpie in the U.K.?"

A sudden change of subject had always signalled that Damian was ready to move on. Often it had been from some uncomfortable situation in the present, but now, Domenic got the impression it might be the past Damian was so anxious to leave behind.

"I didn't find it," said Domenic. "I just happened to be there."

"Doesn't matter. It was a major sighting. And my little brother snagged it. Very proud to hear that, I was." Both men waited until it was clear Domenic wasn't going to add anything further. "I heard you were in St. Lucia, too," said Damian warily. "Any particular reason?"

"Lindy knew I had a friend down there. She thought I might like to see him, so she booked a vacation for us."

Damian nodded slowly. "And did Traz find you the endemics?"

Domenic tilted a hand. "Most of them. Not the parrot."

"You missed the St. Lucia Amazon? Jeez, Dom, all you have to do is stand on the Des Cartiers Trail and they'll practically come right to you."

"Like the chickadees at Lynde Shores, you mean? Maybe I should have just put some seed in my hand."

"Lynde Shores," said Damian wistfully. A quiet fell over them. For a moment, the two men were boys, wandering wide-eyed among the tall white pines, the path beneath them dappled with the filtered sunlight of summer. Or perhaps, still holding patches of late winter snow at the bases of the trees, as they peered up looking for owls or searched the woodpiles for Winter Wrens. Moments of such innocence, such connection. That two brothers could come from there to the wrath they had shared so recently seemed inconceivable.

Damian eased forward across the table, as if he had judged the mood between them, and found forgiveness in the returning peace. "I didn't tell you everything in the car."

Domenic pushed his glass away angrily, but when he looked up, there was no defiance in Damian's expression, no readiness for argument. Just a crumpled sheet of paper, torn from the bottom of a page of a cheap lined notebook, held between the fingers of a hand extended across the table.

Domenic carefully unfurled the paper. On it was scrawled a series of digits.

"There was one missed call on De Laet's phone, nothing else incoming or outgoing. From the time on the call log, he was dead before it came in. I took down the number."

Domenic stared at the paper for a long time. Most of the number was unknown to him, but the first few digits were ones he knew well: 01263. It was the area code for north Norfolk.

14

The sun struggled up a white sky, yet to crest the high yew hedge that enclosed the Old Dairy car park on all sides. Across the pink gravel, large patches of shadow lay like black pools. Danny Maik's Mini was already waiting when Jejeune arrived. The car door was open and the sound of two voices, locked in silky, seamless harmonies had the sergeant leaning back in his seat wearing an expression of quiet contentment as Jejeune pulled up alongside. Maik shut off the couple mid-song and eased himself out of the small car.

"Said your goodbyes to Sergeant McLeod, then," he said by way of a greeting. "He seemed a pleasant enough type on the phone."

Two seconds in, he thought, and here he was making sure his DCI knew McLeod had called, just in case the Scottish sergeant had forgotten to mention it himself. Was it his way of showing there were to be no secrets between them about what had happened during the inspector's absence? Was he asking for the same from Jejeune? Even Danny wasn't really sure. Either way, all he got in return was an easy smile and that same noncommittal expression as always.

"I thought there were supposed to be protesters here," said Jejeune, gazing back at the empty lane leading up to the gates of the compound.

"They're probably in rehearsals," Maik said contemptuously. "Prince Ibrahim is due to arrive any day now. I'm sure they'll be wanting to put on a good show for him."

"Not a fan of the democratic right to peaceful assembly, Sergeant?"

Maik moved his shoulders easily. Danny was all for protecting human rights, just as long as no human wrongs got protected in the process. "I daresay there are some that have genuine concerns about what is going on up here, but I get the impression a good number of these merchants are simply looking for something to do between sessions in the pub. This project has provided a lot of jobs for the people of Saltmarsh. It's provided a real boost to the local economy."

"While at the same time, posing considerable threats to the local environment, as I understand it." Jejeune gave Maik a loose smile. "Are you and I going to find ourselves on opposite sides of the barriers at some point, I wonder? Or should we take the novel step of actually informing ourselves of the facts before we make our stands?" Jejeune gestured to the high wire gate incised into the hedge on the far side of the car park, and the two men began walking towards it.

There was a security camera mounted above the gate, and as they waited for it to peruse them, Jejeune looked along the row of yews on either side. He realized the three-metre hedge concealed a high wire fence, part of a continuous barrier that encircled the entire compound. Whatever was going on inside this fence, somebody was taking the job of keeping it from the outside world very seriously indeed. The lock gave an electronic buzz and clicked open. The two men stepped through the gate and emerged on the other side of the hedgerow archway, stopping in surprise. It would have been hard to imagine a more incongruous structure on an old dairy farm in the middle of the north Norfolk countryside than the building in front of them.

It was an elaborate, ultra-modern design of cubes, perched on each other at odd angles. The frames of the cubes appeared to be steel, but by far the most prominent construction material was glass. Everywhere they looked, unbroken walls of windows reflected back at them like blind white eyes in the flat light of this overcast day.

The detectives entered the building through automatic doors of yet more glass. As the doors hissed closed behind them, all ambient sounds of the outside world were stilled. They found themselves standing in an expansive atrium that soared up the entire height of the building. A man approached with a purposeful, confident stride. He was of medium build, but muscular; his shoulders seeming to struggle against the constraints of the suit jacket he was wearing, despite its obvious expensive cut. "Gentlemen, I am Abrar el-Taleb. It is my honour to be project manager of the Old Dairy Carbon Capture and Storage Scheme." He had a hard face that seemed unaccustomed to greetings, but he had the grace to make his welcoming smile at least appear genuine, even if it never quite seemed to reach his eyes.

"You have had a long journey to come here, I understand, Inspector. The sergeant, I think not so far." It was clear small talk was as uncomfortable for Mr. el-Taleb as other courtesies. He seemed awkward in his role, uneasy. "Perhaps there are refreshments you would care to take?"

Boston, Jejeune decided; MIT or Yale. One of the Ivy League schools anyway, where the edges were rounded off accents when their owners spoke in English, leaving only the stilted cadences, like shadows of a former existence that had now been educated out of them.

El-Taleb waited until the men had declined his offer before delivering his news. "Prince Yousef regrets he cannot meet with you personally, and unfortunately I also have other encumbrances today, as do the other directors. We have arranged with your DCS Shepherd, however, that you may interview our senior researcher."

Jejeune looked around him, like a man searching for patience. Maik knew what he was thinking. It said something for the influence of those in control of Old Dairy Holdings that their formidable DCS would agree to somebody so far down the food chain being subbed in, when Jejeune had expressly requested a meeting with a senior executive. Maik wondered if Shepherd had pointed out that, in murder inquiries, people often took the trouble to rearrange their other "encumbrances."

"This senior researcher, that wouldn't be Catherine Weil, by any chance?" asked Maik. The sergeant made a face that saved him saying what he thought about this arrangement. Jejeune however, was quiet, taking in the information, looking for things, no doubt, that it might tell him about those who had made the decision — the absent prince, the present one, perhaps even Shepherd herself.

"Ms. Weil is knowledgeable in the subject of carbon capture, and in the aims of this project." El-Taleb seemed to be searching their eyes for a reaction to this information. He floated another cold smile their way, but this one found no place to settle with either detective.

Maik let his eyes trail around the high, bright atrium. A constant stream of people hurried back and forth across the marble-floored space — white-coated lab assistants with clipboards, shirt-sleeved clerks with files. But there was a noticeable absence of one category of employee.

"I'd have thought with all the protests going on up here, you would have had more of a visible security presence," said Maik.

El-Taleb smiled indulgently. "We are quite confident in our security arrangements, Sergeant. Besides, the protesters pose no actual threat." He raised a muscular hand slightly. "A noisy distraction, nothing more."

"Nevertheless, the protests don't show any signs of abating. Have you held any meetings with the protest leaders, to discuss their concerns?"

El-Taleb leaned his head forward slightly, as if to catch the sergeant's words. "Their concerns? That we leave? Or that we stay?" He used an upturned palm to show the impossibility of reconciling the two points of view. "Was it not Winston Churchill who said the greatest argument against democracy is a five-minute conversation with the average voter? I suspect with protesters, less than two minutes would be enough. But whatever their concerns," he flashed a mirthless smile Maik's way, "I can assure you, no unauthorized person can enter the compound without being detected."

"And there were no security breaches detected the night Philip Wayland died?"

The two men turned to the DCI. Whether it was a question or a statement, they all knew Jejeune would have already verified this. El-Taleb did not bother to answer.

It wasn't like the DCI to be so blunt, and Maik wondered if his attitude was a response to having his request for a high-level meeting so disdainfully ignored. But Jejeune seemed to realize his approach would be unlikely to bear fruit with a man like el-Taleb and he switched tack.

"This project is a considerable undertaking, Mr. el-Taleb," said Jejeune, looking around the vast atrium. "You assumed the role of project director quite recently, I understand."

"More than one year," said el-Taleb defensively. His eyes flitted between the men, like someone wary of an attack.

"Nevertheless, being project director must be a great responsibility."

Maik shifted uncomfortably. Abrar el-Taleb's ego probably got all the attention it needed from the man himself, and obsequiousness wasn't really Jejeune's forte, anyway. Besides, in Maik's experience, charm offensives like these rarely produced the results they intended, in this case, no doubt, a sudden re-evaluation by el-Taleb of his other encumbrances.

El-Taleb smiled modestly. "I have been here since the beginning. The project and I have grown up together, you may say. In many ways, I feel the role of director is more than an undertaking. This project has become like a partner over our time together. We have our differences, yes, but in the end, we always make our peace." The director gave them what Maik realized was probably as close to a genuine smile as they were going to get.

"Was your relationship with Mr. Wayland the same?" asked Jejeune. The business of massaging the project director's ego over, they were back to business now, noted Maik. But he noticed there was more subtlety in his DCI's tone, more caution. *Lesson learned,* he thought.

"Mr. Wayland contributed a great deal of valuable research to the project." El-Taleb paused, as if waiting to see whether this would be enough information. "It was not our decision that he should leave," he tagged on finally.

"But it was an amicable parting?"

Jejeune supplying an answer to a question instead of just asking it? thought Maik. *More surprises from the inspector today.*

"From our part, there was no animosity. But when someone no longer wishes to work for you, the matter is at an end." He raised his palms to show how the world was. El-Taleb leaned forward slightly to add sincerity to his next words. "I am saddened by his loss, as we all are at the Old Dairy project. Now, if you will kindly wait here, I will go to get Ms. Weil."

"I'd like to meet in her office," said Jejeune.

El-Taleb seemed to hesitate slightly. "I shall see if this is possible."

They watched him disappear across the marble-tiled floor of the atrium. Maik walked toward the centre and craned his neck back, looking up. Here, at the fulcrum of all the blocks, the open space soared above him all the way to roof. In the centre was an immense skylight that flooded the atrium with natural light. "Impressive," he said, "though I wouldn't fancy being the window cleaner for this place."

"Or a passing bird," said Jejeune. "They don't see glass. They see a reflection of trees, or the sky, but otherwise, from a bird's perspective, glass is invisible. Collisions with glass buildings are considered the second leading cause of non-natural mortality among songbirds." He drew his eyes away from the glass to find Maik looking at him. "I know somebody who studied it," he said simply.

"Speaking of birds," said Maik, "Now that you're back, Constable Holland is hoping to have a word with you when you have a moment. Something about birds of prey. Gyrfalcons, would it be? They've got some here, and he's dating the girl who looks after them."

Jejeune snapped his head around, then away again, as if try-ing to free himself from Maik's stare. While Holland's interest in birds had come about suddenly enough to be surprising, surely it wasn't enough to warrant the look on the DCI's face.

"I don't think it's a wind-up," said Maik uncertainly. "He seems genuinely interested."

"They have Gyrfalcons here?" To Maik's practised ear, Jejeune's voice held the deceptive disinterest of a man trying too hard.

"Not within the compound, but on the property, farther down near the coast. This prince, Yousef, has no interest, but the Crown Prince is a keen falconer, apparently. He likes to fly them whenever he comes over. Is everything all right, sir?"

But before Jejeune could give an answer, or avoid one, el-Taleb returned, a smile of any kind now noticeably absent. "Ms. Weil has agreed to see you in her office. Please come this way, gentlemen."

15

The men followed el-Taleb along a short corridor without speaking. Maik was used to his DCI's silences, but in a way he wasn't quite able to define, this seemed different somehow. He seemed genuinely distracted. Troubled even.

They arrived at a door and el-Taleb entered after knocking. "Ms. Weil," he announced formally, "the detectives from the North Norfolk Constabulary."

Catherine Weil stood up from behind a desk and came around to greet them. "Come in." She turned to el-Taleb. "You won't be staying, I take it?"

The frisson of tension between them was impossible to miss, and el-Taleb turned on his heel without speaking. As she watched him leave, Maik took the opportunity to take in Catherine Weil. Although she was almost as tall as the two men, she held herself upright, making no apology to the world for her height. She was very slim; skinny, Maik might have called it in his day, though there was probably a politically correct term for it these days. Her long red hair cascaded down to her slender shoulders in loose ringlets, framing a delicate face that drew its beauty as much from her bearing as her features. Like her one-time colleague, whose death they had come to discuss, Maik guessed Catherine Weil was probably somewhere midway between his own age and Jejeune's. It was a time of life that promised such wonderful rewards — years of education and life experience to guide you, and plenty of energy and enthusiasm still to apply them. In Catherine Weil's case, at least, Maik thought sadly, if not, any longer, in Philip Wayland's.

Weil closed the door on the sound of el-Taleb's retreating footsteps and turned to face them. Her ice-blue eyes were at once startling and hostile.

"I'm not quite sure how they think I can help you," she said curtly. "I already told Constable Salter everything I can remember about the night Philip died." She pointed out a window that looked onto the stand of trees beyond the fence. "I saw him on the public footpath. He was walking into the woods. It must have been almost exactly seven o'clock, because I finished my report right after and dropped it off at Taleb's office on my way out, noting the time on the front cover: seven minutes past seven."

She engaged the men frankly with her stare. Her directness was a quality Maik might have been able to admire if it wasn't tinged with this note of defensiveness. Did she think they were here to challenge her account? Perhaps they were, but not in the way she might have anticipated.

"We do already have your witness statement on file," said Maik easily. "Though, of course, if anything else about that night has come to mind, we would be interested in hearing about it. Your statement is of particular importance, since, as far as we can tell, you would have been the last person to see Mr. Wayland alive."

"I'd say that's highly unlikely, Sergeant, unless Philip's killer had his eyes shut when he attacked him." Catherine Weil didn't smile.

And that's what you get for using clichés on clever people, thought Maik. He flashed a look at Jejeune, who was standing beside him. If the DCI was paying attention to the proceedings at all, he was doing a good job of disguising it. He was staring out the window, in the direction of the woodlot. Wherever Jejeune's mind was, it was certainly too far from here to be of any use.

"We're actually here to learn a bit more about Philip Wayland's work," said Maik, in a tone that suggested he had already recognized he was going to have to frame his questions carefully. "Can you explain what he was working on when he was here?"

"Even if I was allowed to discuss it, which I'm not, I doubt I could cover it in the time we have," said Weil. "The overview is that Philip was leading a project to explore viable industrial-scale technologies for storing the carbon produced during industrial processes."

"As an alternative to having them released into the atmosphere. All this work you're doing here, then, it's all to do with climate change," said Maik.

"The methodology for capturing greenhouse gases has been around for almost a century," said Weil. "A chemical affinity exists between carbon dioxide and ammonia, for example, which can be exploited. But there are new processes, too, for improving the capture of CO_2. You can burn it in pure oxygen instead of air, or turn it into a mixture of carbon monoxide and hydrogen."

Maik looked at his DCI, to see whether he was taking this all in, but Jejeune's eyes remained fixed firmly on the great outdoors. Maik had fallen into the trap before of thinking his DCI wasn't paying attention, only to have him home in and seize upon something that had been said. But Maik sensed this wouldn't be happening this time. Somewhere between the car park and this office, something had taken hold of the DCI's mind and would not let go. Something beyond that window. Maik let his gaze drift out to the same distant point as Jejeune's. It was a soft Norfolk day, the kind of day when the subdued light playing on the fields could be mesmerizing. But even so, he could see nothing worthy of so much of the inspector's normally mercurial attention.

Weil waited patiently for Maik to return his gaze to her. "And this carbon capture, this was Philip Wayland's area of expertise, too?"

"No, Sergeant, that would be mine. Philip was concerned with what happens to the carbon once we've captured it. The storage part."

Maik looked across at his DCI again. This had gone far enough. Casual disengagement was one thing, but he had no intention of being the one who stood at the front of the interview room later to explain all this, being corrected every five words by Lauren Salter, or Tony Holland, or anybody else who had even a faintly better grip on this stuff than he did. Which, let's face it, would be just about anyone in the room.

Weil's eyes moved uneasily between the two men until Jejeune seemed to finally notice the silence that had fallen over the interview.

"The Old Dairy project is exploring methods of piping the carbon beneath the North Sea, I understand," said Jejeune, drawing his eyes from the window, with a noticeable reluctance, to fasten them on Weil.

"I can't go into the details, obviously, but yes, I can confirm the plan involves receiving the carbon into one central holding facility and then piping it into undersea caverns that exist from when the oil was extracted from them."

"Even though the international community has deemed this an unacceptable practice."

She inclined her head slightly, as if to acknowledge the inspector's familiarity with the subject. The movement set a ripple of light shimmering down her ringlets. "Wikipedia wisdom, Inspector?" she asked ironically. "The process is frowned upon at present, but until the various nations can get together and sort out the messy business of international maritime law, there's unlikely to be any binding restrictions against it. In the meantime, we are exploring ways to stabilize the carbon enough to store it this way. Believe me. It will happen."

"But surely, even if it does, the construction of the undersea pipeline necessary to transport the carbon out to those caverns would be catastrophic for the local marine environment," said Jejeune.

Weil nodded. "Philip was working on ways to mitigate the damage, but, yes, he was extremely concerned about that aspect of the plan. We all were … *are*."

Jejeune nodded thoughtfully. "I'm wondering where Mr. el-Taleb fits in, if carbon capture is your area, and storage was Mr. Wayland's."

"That's a fine question, Inspector. You're not the first to wonder what possible benefits a man with his background can bring to a project like this."

Both Maik and Jejeune stared at her. "He's not a CCS specialist?"

"Aeronautics. He came here as Prince Yousef's personal helicopter engineer." A look of amused contempt flashed in her ice blue eyes. "Done well for himself, wouldn't you say?"

"Any particular reason Prince Yousef would appoint someone with that background to run a project like this?"

Weil shrugged her narrow shoulders. "You'd have to ask him. I'm sure he has his reasons."

"I wonder why it isn't Mr. el-Taleb speaking to us today. He seems extremely proud of the Old Dairy project. People so intimately connected with something can rarely pass up the opportunity to tell others about it."

Weil eyed Jejeune warily. "He tries not to sully himself with the details of the day-to-day operations." She allowed a slight look of distain to brush her features. "He has other skills. It was felt best that I speak to you because I know most about Philip and the work he was doing here."

"You were working late, I understand, the night you report seeing Mr. Wayland enter the woods."

Report, noted Maik, with interest.

"A data set Taleb wanted," said Weil, her expression also showing interest in the DCI's line of questioning. "Last minute rush. Panic stations, as usual."

"Not much time for looking out the window, then."

The accusatory tone in Jejeune's flat delivery was impossible to miss. Maik managed to hide a look of surprise, but not without some effort. Jejeune was rarely anything but courteous in these interviews.

"The view from this office doesn't let you see the path approaching the woods. You would have a space of, what, five seconds between the time someone came into view and the time they disappeared into the woods? And at just that time, you looked up to see Philip Wayland."

Jejeune left a long, unblinking stare on Weil, while Danny Maik looked on with something approaching disbelief. What the hell was he playing at? Catherine Weil was a bright, accomplished woman. Surely Jejeune could see she wasn't the type to stand being pushed around like this.

Weil crossed her arms, holding them so high on her chest she almost seemed to be hugging herself. She would feel the cold, this one, thought Maik, irrationally. She'd be the type with a blanket wrapped around her when she sat on the sofa watching TV.

"I can hardly help the fact that mine is the only statement that gives Prince Yousef an alibi for the time of the murder, can I? I mean, it's your job to find corroboration, not mine." She looked at them both challengingly. "Look, you don't know me, so I'll spell it out for you. If you think I would say something to protect any of this bloody lot, then you are very much mistaken." She turned away and walked to the window, where she stood defiantly with her back to them.

"Did you like Philip Wayland personally?"

Something in Jejeune's tone made Weil turn from the window. "Yes," she said. "I did."

"You identified his body. Why was that?"

Weil gave another slight shrug, her arms still folded high.

"They said Xandria Grey wasn't up to it," she said simply. "I had met Mary and Jack, Philip's parents, a few times. They're nice people; they didn't need to see their son … that way."

Jejeune looked as if he might be ready to ask another question, but if he was, in the end, he decided against it.

"Thank you for your time, Ms. Weil," he said. "We'll be in touch when we need to speak to you again."

Not *if*, noted Maik. And he was fairly sure Catherine Weil had registered the word, too. But by now Jejeune had retreated once more into his thoughts, and it was left to Danny to wrap up the proceedings.

"I'll make a point of reassuring Mr. el-Taleb that you broke no confidences," Maik told her, earning a condescending look as his reward.

"That won't be necessary, Sergeant. He's well aware of everything that goes on here. Just in case you haven't already worked it out, Abrar el-Taleb is seriously, seriously good at what he does."

Just what that was, Maik couldn't have said. But although he had not known Catherine Weil long, she didn't strike him as the kind of person whose language would tend toward high drama all that often. If she was doubling her *seriously*s, it was her way of telling them that they would need to watch Abrar el-Taleb very closely. Possibly even *very, very* closely.

Maik was resting the considerable bulk of his frame on the front wing of his Mini, waiting while Jejeune returned to the building to leave a business card, in case either el-Taleb or

Prince Yousef found the time among their encumbrances to slot in a meeting with the North Norfolk Constabulary. From the car speakers floated the sound of Marvin Gaye and Kim Weston locked once again in the lighthearted back-and-forth duet he had terminated so abruptly earlier: *It takes two*. If it was investigating this crime they were referring to, he would have been hard-pressed to disagree. He would be the first to admit he had been making precious little progress on his own. But if this morning's interviews were anything to go by, for once the presence of DCI Jejeune didn't seem to hold the promise of much improvement. The oversight with the card, normally unthinkable, was par for the course for today. It had been one of Jejeune's less impressive performances, to put it mildly. There had been a number of missteps: this business about fawning over el-Taleb, or antagonizing Weil before finally reeling her back in. The DCI's normally assured questioning, too, had seemed awkward, abrupt even. But perhaps the one thing that bothered Danny Maik the most about today's performance was something that Jejeune had not done. Right from the moment he had revealed the presence of Gyrfalcons on the property, he had been waiting for his DCI to invent some spurious reason to go and take a look at them. But he had not. In fact, Jejeune had made no reference to the Gyrfalcons at all. And in a long list of questions about the DCI's behaviour since the call from Scotland, for Maik, this was perhaps the most puzzling of all.

16

Lindy didn't look into the living room as she came through the front door of the cottage. First, she laid her car keys on the small hall table, shrugged off her jacket and shoes, and gave her long blonde hair a good ruffle with her fingers. And perhaps this was why she was so startled; the fact that she had already been in the house for a time, doing these casual, private things, and all the while a man had been watching her, the man now sitting easily in the comfortable armchair, Dom's armchair, beside the fireplace. He made no move to get up, and offered her nothing but an awkward grin.

"Oh, hello," said Lindy, recovering herself slightly and deciding on nonchalance until she could get some sense of how some other, more strident response might play with this intruder.

"Hi, I'm … I'm a friend of Dom's, Domenic's. He's just gone down to the store. He said he wouldn't be long."

"I didn't know Dom had any friends," said Lindy, keeping it light, but feeling in her pocket for her mobile phone. Certainly no friends she had never met whom he might feel comfortable about leaving alone in their cottage. *Alone with her.*

Lindy kept herself between this stranger and the doorway behind her. He didn't seem threatening; in fact, he had made no move towards her at all. She thought she had pretty good radar for predatory behaviour, but all the same, it was obvious from his unease that this was no normal friend of Dom's.

The man seemed to pick up on her uncertainty. "I can leave if you want, until he comes back. If it's, you know, better."

There was something vaguely familiar about him, thought Lindy, as if she had seen him somewhere, like in an old photograph, perhaps. No, not that. Something more ethereal, more undefined … Whether this feeling would have been enough to stop her backing out of the house and going for help, she didn't get the chance to find out, because at that moment, the sound of Domenic's Range Rover pulling up outside fell between them like a guilty secret, leaving them staring at each other awkwardly in silence. And then, suddenly, Domenic was standing in the hallway, looking, perhaps, the most uneasy of them all.

"You've met," he said finally. "I guess we all need to have a chat."

The noise of the paring knife on the cutting board seemed over-loud. Lindy had retreated to her cooking chores, her safe haven when she was trying to work out difficulties, when even a walk along the clifftop path beside their home wouldn't be enough; when her troubles were so great even north Norfolk's famed coastal winds couldn't carry them away. Domenic was standing behind her, hovering, close enough to lay a hand on her shoulder, but knowing it would be the wrong thing to do. It would be interpreted as intimacy, a request for forgiveness. And he knew he wasn't entitled to that. Yet.

"So, any news on the award?" He tried to make the enquiry nonchalant, but in the taut atmosphere in the kitchen, it seemed awkward, crass even. To be blatantly ignoring the immense gulf that lay between them made Dom's attempt at small talk sound exactly what it was: desperate.

They were alone. Damian had gone to grab some north Norfolk air, as he had put it when he slipped out. So now it was just the two of them, Domenic and Lindy, and a graveyard of lies and deceit. Domenic looked out of the kitchen window, at the unbroken blue vista of the North Sea, stretching out beyond his field of vision in all directions. Was he hoping for something from it? A way to handle this? All it offered him was its gently undulating presence, its assurance that, no matter what turmoil their relationship was facing, the sea would remain constant, as unmoved by human frailties as it always was.

It had not been the words. There had not been many of those. It had been the look in her eyes, the one that told him she knew. That Damian was the real reason for his trip up to Scotland, perhaps the only reason; that he had known about it before he left but had failed to trust her, actively decided not to trust her. It was a look that almost made him wince with pain.

"I didn't want to do this without telling you. Any of it. It's just that it's—"

She slammed the knife down on the counter and spun around.

"Oh please, Dom, please don't say 'it's complicated.'"

The phrase had become Lindy's pet hate recently, so much so that she had even started to vent her frustration at the TV screen. "No, it's not, you halfwit," she'd told some hapless actor recently. "Quadratic equations are complicated. Having an affair with your best mate's wife might be a lot of things, but there's nothing 'complicated' about it."

Jejeune paused now, chastened. His opening gambit, and he had been so far off the mark. He searched around for a new beginning. Lindy leaned back against the counter and folded her arms. "You told him I'd agreed, or at the very least that we'd talked about it."

Domenic looked surprised.

"He was anticipating some kind of reaction from me. Delight, maybe hostility even, but something, certainly not surprise. He thought I knew he was coming, Dom, and I would have already prepared myself. But I didn't know. And he could see that. He could see you hadn't even talked to me about any of this. Do you have any idea how much that hurt me, that another man could see that you didn't even trust me that much?"

"It wasn't that," said Domenic emphatically. "It's this situation. There are ... circumstances."

"Your brother was in trouble with the law. I know that, Domenic. Your friend Traz told me when we were in St. Lucia. So you see, there was really no reason to keep anything from me." She turned away from him and picked up the knife again, ready to work away her anger.

Jejeune sat down in a chair by the kitchen table and spent a long time looking at the flagstone floor. "Is," he said eventually, so quietly that Lindy turned around to look at him again. "Not *was* in trouble with the law. He *is*, Lindy. Damian is a fugitive from justice. There's an international warrant out for his arrest." He felt adrift, unable to find a starting point for his explanation. He realized Lindy hadn't spoken, and he looked up. She was staring at him, her face a mask of astonishment. But her voice, when it came, had lost its harshness. Her calmness was almost a force, now, like a defence mounted to repress the panic welling inside her. She held up a hand.

"Whatever it is, Dom, whatever he's done, I don't want to know, okay? But he has to leave. He's got no right to put you in this situation. It's not fair. You'll have to deal with it. I don't mean you should turn him in, obviously, but he can't stay here."

Jejeune stood and moved to the window again. But the vast, heaving sea held no answers for him, no arguments against Lindy's relentless, measured logic. She joined him at the window and stood beside him, gently stroking his shoulder with the palm of her hand. "I'm sure he's already worked it out for himself. He knows what you do for a living. A quick word and he'll be on his way." A thought seemed to strike her. "Or I can do it, tell him, if it would be too difficult for you."

"It'll just be for a short time," said Domenic, as much to his own reflection in the window as to the woman standing beside him.

Lindy shook her head, drawing a breath to suppress her frustration in favour of a more reasonable tone. "You have to decide who you want to be in this, Dom, the policeman or the brother. Because you can't be both, and if you faff about trying to decide, the authorities will make your mind up for you. Even failing to report his presence is a criminal offence. He can't be here, in this house, under the same roof as you. Not even for a night."

"A few days, that's all I'm saying, a week at most. Just enough time to let me get to the bottom of all this."

"All what?"

"Damian came here for a reason, and I need to find out what that is. I think it may have something to do with Gyrfalcons, but I'm not sure."

"Gyrfalcons? Bloody hell, Domenic, this is serious. You can't risk everything we have over some birds." She looked around her with a kind of wild desperation, as if it all, this kitchen, this cottage, this life, might be taken away from her at any moment. "Harbouring a wanted criminal, it could mean prison. Do you have any idea at all what that could be like for an ex-policeman?"

The impact seemed to arrive only now, the truth of the risk they faced. Now, as she spoke it aloud for the first time, the effect of the ice-cold wave of realization on her was almost visible. "I'm sorry, Dom," she said, shaking her head, "he has to leave."

"There's a reason he came here," said Domenic, "I need to find out what it is."

"Then ask him, for God's sake, and send him on his way."

Domenic shook his head. "That's not the way it works with us. It never has. We need to work up to things. It's like we both have to keep manoeuvring around until we find a safe place, and then we can talk."

"We don't have time for you two to be playing musical chairs, Domenic. He's out there now, sampling the delights of the north Norfolk countryside. Who knows who's taking notes?"

Jejeune shook his head. "He's careful. He won't attract any attention to himself. I doubt anybody will even give him a second glance."

Lindy pulled away from him slightly and gave him a wild-eyed look, astonishment mixed with exasperation. "What village have you been living in? You can't get your front room decorated in Saltmarsh without it being the subject of the day at the fish and chip shop. If nobody knows he's here now, I can guarantee they will by the end of tomorrow. This lot makes the BBC look like they're still relying on the pony express for their news."

"The area is built on tourism. New faces show up here every day. One more won't raise any eyebrows."

"It will if they see the two of you out on the town together."

"They won't. I'll make sure we're careful."

He had won. He could see that the fight had gone from her eyes and been replaced by resignation. He had countered her arguments and he had won. She knew that whatever objections she raised, he would match them, until she had none left to offer. They had argued like this before — quietly, insistently, relentlessly — on other important topics, the ones that really mattered. And this was when they reached their resolutions, when one of them saw how vitally important something was to the other and decided that this was what mattered, the sheer overwhelming significance of it. It meant that Lindy was on his side now. Whatever misgivings she might have, it was their shared decision. All that remained was the fine print.

"A week?" She looked at him warily, distrustful almost, and Domenic recoiled from it. He knew he deserved such a look, had earned it, even. "That's all? And then he's gone? Even if he hasn't told you what he wants, and you haven't been clever enough to work it out? Even then, he leaves?"

Jejeune nodded. "A week. I promise." And he did, fully and unreservedly. The time had come to stop lying to Lindy. And it began now.

17

The pall of unease that had hung over the interview room since they had begun investigating Philip Wayland's murder was not lifted at all by the return of Chief Inspector Domenic Jejeune. Perhaps it might have been, if he had taken a position at the front of the room and locked them in with that intense stare of his, imperiously declaring that they had a definite lead or two; that there was a chance that he could now guide them, literally and figuratively, out of the woods and towards the light of truth in this case. But he did not. Instead, the inspector retreated to his customary perch on a desk at the back of the room, making only minimal eye contact on his way.

So it was left to Danny Maik to part the clouds, at least a little, by delivering the news that Philip Wayland's death was not quite as it had first appeared, after all.

"There is evidence of teeth marks on the neck tissue. According to the ME, the blow was enough to sever muscle, ligament, and bone to the extent that the head could later be detached by foraging animals. Foxes, he would suggest. He also confirmed the marks on the leather shoulder strap indicate the blade, whatever it was, skidded off it, meaning the initial blow probably wasn't aimed at the neck." Maik looked around the room significantly to make sure nobody missed the message, "In other words, Mr. Wayland was not intentionally decapitated by his killer."

The information was greeted with such relief, Maik would not have been surprised to hear a slight smattering of applause. In the strange world the detectives inhabited, it was an important distinction. The murder was a violent, ruthless act, certainly, but somehow less macabre, less inhuman now. In a way that none of them would have been able to explain, it made an important difference to know that their quarry had suddenly been downgraded to a more human prey.

There was other news awaiting them, too. Lauren Salter was gearing herself up to deliver it, primping a set of note sheets into alignment on her knee. She had taken to adding a touch of drama to her reports recently, and her preparations now were a signal that something significant was on its way.

"You know you asked me to do a bit of digging into carbon capture and storage? Well it's only relatively recently that governments and global organizations have begun paying any serious attention to it. But I think we could say they certainly are now."

"Could we?" asked Maik, playing along in order to get to the crux of her report as quickly as possible. "And why might we say that, Constable?"

"Because they've started doing what they always do with big global problems. They're throwing money at it. They've made a fund available — essentially a cash prize, I suppose you'd call it — for anyone who can come up with a viable method of capturing and storing carbon on an industrial scale."

"You're talking about the CCS Commercialisation Programme," said Jejeune from the back of the room. "I understood that had been cancelled."

Salter nodded. "The first competition was," she confirmed, "but it has been reinstated. This time around, they're providing something called competitive capital funding."

"Are we talking about a lot of money, Lauren?" Holland wasn't the only person in the room warming to this new information. As motives for murder went, money was pretty much your default setting.

Salter shrugged. "Depends on what you mean by a lot." She looked around the room, milking the moment. At the back, she could see that Jejeune already knew the figure. The others, though, were hanging on, exactly where Lauren Salter wanted them. Even Danny Maik was leaning forward slightly, as if ready to catch the number when she supplied it.

"How about one billion pounds?"

The announcement was greeted by a stunned silence. A billion pounds was a lot of money to throw at any problem. How and why this prize money was connected to Wayland's death might take some sorting out, but few in the room doubted there would be a connection somewhere. Most eyes turned toward Jejeune. Perhaps the inspector, with his processor-like mind, had already made a link. But if so, his bland expression gave no hint.

"The first contest, Constable," he said, "do we know why it was cancelled?"

"All the entrants eventually pulled out. Carbon capture and storage research is extremely costly, and with no guarantees of success, they found they simply couldn't carry on. You'd need almost unlimited resources to undertake a project like this."

"Enter Emirati princes buying up old dairies," said Holland. A thought seemed to strike him, and he gave a self-satisfied grin. "Which I suppose makes them milk sheiks."

"Although only officers who wanted to spend their careers giving bicycle safety tips to the children at Saltmarsh Primary School would dream of referring to them that way," said Colleen Shepherd from the doorway. No one was sure how long she had been there, but if she registered the atmosphere in the room at all, it came a distant second to her own agenda. She acknowledged Jejeune's presence with an uncertain smile.

"Welcome back, Domenic. And straight into the fray, I was glad to note. Catherine Weil was helpful, I take it?"

"To us, or to Prince Yousef?"

Shepherd decided to ignore the sarcasm. Perhaps it was a way of acknowledging that Jejeune had a point. Although he hadn't checked in at the station before heading out to the Old Dairy, they both knew she could still have got word to him that he wouldn't be meeting anyone in authority, if she had wanted to. "I'm sorry, but your request to interview senior figures at the Old Dairy could be interpreted as a sign that you consider them suspects. Perhaps even the prince himself."

Jejeune's silence could have meant anything, but Shepherd was taking no chances. "You're not saying he is, I hope. In case you had forgotten, the word *alibi* means 'in another place'," she said. "In the air, hundreds of feet above Saltmarsh, seems to me to be pretty bloody definitively 'another place' than a public footpath through a forest. Catherine Weil confirmed her previous statement, I take it, about seeing Wayland entering the woods around seven?"

"You'd hardly expect her to do otherwise, given that she was the person the Old Dairy executive hand-selected to speak to us."

"It was felt she was best-placed to answer your questions. I did take into account that she is the one who provided the prince with his alibi. And also the person who identified Wayland's body. I'm not completely oblivious to these things you know, Domenic. We did manage to get along here on our own, tie our own shoelaces and such, while you were off chasing around the Outer Hebrides." It was all lighthearted and pleasant, but the message was clear. Shepherd was not asking for forgiveness. She had come in here prepared to fight her corner when it came to protecting the Emirati family from Jejeune's investigations.

"Right, on to other things," she announced with customary briskness. "As you know, the Crown Prince arrives tomorrow. There are expected to be plenty of protesters on hand, so I want a full complement of detectives up there. Wayland's killer might well be among these protesters, so I expect you all to put yourselves about a bit and see if anybody knows anything."

A shimmer of unease rippled through the room. It was clear now that she hadn't yet been in the doorway when Salter delivered her bombshell. "It's possible the protesters might not be our primary focus now, ma'am." The constable's comment was delivered casually, but not enough to disguise its importance. Shepherd looked at Jejeune and then at Maik.

"Constable Salter has just brought us the news that, in the field in which Philip Wayland was working, someone is offering a one-billion-pound prize for the first one to come up with a viable solution," said the sergeant.

Shepherd shifted uneasily. "I'm not sure that constitutes a link to the Old Dairy project itself, necessarily," she said carefully.

Maik felt a stab of embarrassment for his DCS. If she acknowledged the link, she could hardly refuse Jejeune permission to follow wherever it might lead. But she was fooling no one by pretending she could not see where all this was going. He looked across at Jejeune. *It should be you doing this*, he thought. But he could tell the DCI wasn't going to respond, and, not for the first time, the dirty work fell to Danny.

"If Philip Wayland started making some headway on this problem, all of a sudden he would become a threat to all the competitors for the prize money. Including those he used to work for."

Shepherd was silent for a long time.

"A full complement of detectives, and plenty of uniforms up there, too. See to it, will you, Sergeant. Prince Ibrahim is a visiting dignitary. His safety is paramount, and I won't have it compromised by some mob of layabouts."

Not to mention the show of goodwill such a police presence would provide, thought Maik, *which might come in handy, if and when the North Norfolk Constabulary had to inconvenience Old Dairy Holdings with inquiries into the murder of a former employee.* The short beat of silence that followed Shepherd's orders suggested the others had picked up on her transparent motive, too, and as the meeting broke up, for the second time in a few moments, Maik felt slightly uncomfortable for his DCS.

Shepherd stopped Jejeune on his way out, waiting as the clatter of noise from the still-clearing room subsided. "I take it this Scottish business was resolved to everyone's satisfaction," she said conversationally. Her pause wasn't long enough for Jejeune to confirm or deny. "Though I see you couldn't quite manage to stay out of the spotlight, even up there."

Jejeune wasn't sure whether his look would have shown puzzlement or alarm. He felt both in equal measure.

"The press office has just informed me you've been mentioned in the dispatches again. Apparently the woman whose son you rescued writes a local blog. She thanked you in it."

Jejeune shrugged uneasily. "Right place, right time."

"Yes," said Shepherd. "The funny thing was, she described you as having a beard — a nice man with a beard, who talked to her son about Ravens."

Jejeune shifted, unable to keep his eyes on his DCS. "A couple of days' growth," he said, waving a hand vaguely in front of his chin. "She was busy looking after her son. She probably didn't get a good look."

At the man who had just saved her son? Even to him it sounded implausible. Shepherd tilted her face up to him slightly, and her eyes seemed to be searching his. Another time, perhaps she might have had more questions, pursued things a bit more. But for now, she had decided to move on.

"I've just been hearing on the radio about this award Lindy has been nominated for. I hadn't realized it was quite so prestigious."

Jejeune nodded vigorously, happy to be able to redirect the conversation. "I'm extremely proud of her. Obviously."

"And you've shown her this, I take it?"

The pointed question took him by surprise, and he gave Shepherd a blank look in lieu of an answer.

"You should arrange something, a small party, make an event of it. Whether or not she wins the award, it would be nice for her to have something to remember the nomination by."

Jejeune gave an indulgent smile. "I don't think she'd be that interested, to be honest."

Shepherd shook her head slightly. "You know, there are times when I find your ability to read people's inner thoughts quite astonishing." She paused. "This is not one of them. It *will* matter to her, Domenic, take it from me, regardless of how self-effacing she's pretending to be. Just because you're used to this sort of attention doesn't mean everyone else is. Recognition like this comes so rarely to most of us, it is something to revel in, if only for a short time. I'm not saying you should rent out the Saltmarsh Hunt Club, but a small gathering in that lovely little cottage of yours, a chance to celebrate this moment with a few of her close friends, it would mean a lot to her."

Shepherd had taken to wearing her gold-rimmed glasses on the end of her nose recently, perhaps to make it easier to peer over them intimidatingly when she needed to. "Do you want me to make it an order?"

She was eyeing him carefully. Was her earlier suspicion still lingering in her gaze? Domenic knew any further resistance might set her wondering, might send her mind rolling back over this business about the man with the beard. With a tilt of his head, he conceded defeat. After all, a couple of dozen people coming to his cottage, where his fugitive brother had taken up residence; what could possibly go wrong?

18

Jejeune didn't waste much time after the morning briefing. He wanted to get out to speak to Xandria Grey as soon as possible, and he asked Maik to accompany him, so the sergeant could fill him in on the details of his previous visit along the way.

Maik had told him everything; a slow, steady monologue that sound-tracked their route as Jejeune guided the big Range Rover along the narrow lanes. The sergeant gave his account unguardedly, though he would undoubtedly have felt more at ease about it if he didn't have the impression that Jejeune was listening for the messages behind the words, the parts left unsaid, undetected, perhaps, even by Danny himself.

Jejeune wheeled into the car park at the university's research facility. If he made no comment about the building, it was clear from his expression that he was no more impressed with its outward appearance than Maik had been. They walked along the putty-coloured corridors until they arrived at Xandria Grey's office. She looked up from a desk untidily strewn with papers as the two men entered. The neat bob of her hairstyle still framed her face, but it did nothing to hide the pallor of her skin.

"I hope we're not disturbing you," said Maik. "This is Chief Inspector Jejeune. He's running the investigation into Mr. Wayland's death." Ostensibly, the introduction was for Grey's benefit, but given Jejeune's recent performance at the Old Dairy, Maik thought it wouldn't hurt to remind the DCI of his role, either.

Jejeune took a step forward. "I'm sorry for your loss, Ms. Grey."

"You can call me Xandria." She flashed a look at Maik. "It seems to help when there are difficult matters to discuss."

"I understand it's hard for you to speak about things at the moment."

Grey held up a weary hand, as if to stop Jejeune. "I will try to answer any inquiries about Philip you may have, Inspector, no matter how troubling they might be."

There was an emptiness about her, a desolation, as if in denying herself access to her emotions, she had been unable to fill the internal spaces with any other feelings. Almost in front of Maik's eyes, Xandria Grey's personality was becoming a wasteland.

"I understand Mr. Wayland was an expert in the undersea storage of captured carbon," began Jejeune gently. "Is that what he was working on here?"

She nodded. "Though possibly not in the way you mean. Philip was looking at ways to promote CO_2 sequestration through the use of carbon-fixing algae. If you can create an algal bloom, you get large chains of diatoms, a type of phytoplankton. These use carbon to build shells for themselves, absorbing it from the atmosphere in huge amounts. Research shows that when these organisms die, they often sink as deep as one thousand metres. At those depths, the carbon they take with them could be safely and harmlessly stored in seafloor sediments and deep-water columns for centuries."

Perhaps because of his discomfort in previously having to stand at the front of the incident room with no new leads to offer, Maik now tended to view all information through a lens which had him presenting it to the rest of the task force. He was trying to imagine a scenario where he explained to them that the solution to global climate change, as proposed by one of the top thinkers in the subject, was to have microscopic creatures build themselves tiny shells of carbon and sink to the bottom of the ocean with them. As dutiful as Danny was, this could be one time when he might simply step back and insist that Jejeune leave his perch at the back of the room and handle the briefing himself.

Jejeune, though, didn't seem to share Maik's skepticism. "I assume he hadn't done any research on this while he was at the Old Dairy," said Jejeune

Grey shook her head. "Even if he did, any work he did there is considered proprietary. It would have all been protected under the confidentiality agreement he signed."

"Based on Catherine Weil's guarded responses to my inquiries, I get the impression it is particularly restrictive."

The comment took Maik aback slightly. In the first place, as he remembered it, they were *his* inquiries. More to the point, he was surprised to learn Jejeune had even registered Catherine Weil's responses, so preoccupied had he seemed at the time.

Grey stood up and crossed to a counter to pour herself a glass of water. She waved the carafe at the two men, but both declined. "I doubt Catherine Weil would have shared much with you whether she was bound by her agreement or not. They seem to particularly enjoy the covert side of things up there. Secrecy for its own sake, Philip used to call it. I'm sure it was one of the things that drove him to leave, finally. That and the opportunity to pursue this entirely new branch of research here at the university."

Jejeune had gone quiet. Possibly it was just one of his usual thoughtful pauses, but given the DCI's previous performance, Maik was taking no chances that this interview would sink into the desultory silences of the earlier one. "This new research, it doesn't involve piping the carbon out under the seas, then," he said. "Like they are planning to do up at the Old Dairy?"

"Like they are hoping to do, Sergeant Maik. You have no doubt been treated to Catherine Weil's breezy optimism on the subject, but I can tell you for a fact that unless they can find a way to stabilize the carbon first, the international community will never allow them to do it. Pumping captured carbon under the sea for long-term storage is fraught with dangers. Potential leaks, for example. And it will almost certainly make the oceans more acidic. There are a lot of people out there already looking to outlaw the practice completely."

"Secrecy for its own sake," said Jejeune like a man returning from a dream. "What did Mr. Wayland mean by that, I wonder?"

"That not only the research was restricted, but the raw data, too — even the simple things like measurements of tidal dynamics, meteorological readings. Philip always knew Old Dairy Holdings would own the findings he produced. I just don't think he ever expected that he would be denied access to his own data."

Jejeune set off on a small circuit of the office, an action Maik found strangely comforting. DCI Jejeune was starting to do the things he normally did — thinking, probing, wandering about all over the place. Could it be a sign he might finally be starting to get somewhere with this case? It was about time.

From the far side of the office, Jejeune turned and looked frankly at Grey. "Did you get the sense he felt he had been deceived, tricked into signing the confidentiality agreement in some way?"

She shook her head. "Philip understood how the world of corporate science worked. But he felt that the protections should only apply to the research, the answers they found in the raw data. He couldn't see how it could serve any higher purpose to keep a few tide charts and wind measurements out of the public domain. I always got the impression his insistence on keeping all these paper copies here was a reaction of some kind to what was going on up there. He wanted to show the world. If it had been up to him, the data at the Old Dairy would have been made available to the wider world, as it is here at the university."

For a moment, her eyes moistened and she seemed in danger of letting her memories overwhelm her. Maik saw her frame stiffen slightly, as if she was almost physically trying to force her emotions under control once again. The effort seemed to weary her. She looked spent, exhausted.

"I wonder," said Jejeune, "would it be possible to see this data?"

Grey looked up and seemed to draw herself together, as if aware her private sorrow had drawn her away from the men's presence. She set down her glass and grabbed a set of keys and a remote control device from her desk drawer.

The detectives followed her down a narrow concrete stairway and through a series of dimly lit corridors that seemed to switch back and forth upon themselves erratically. She stopped before a nondescript door and unlocked it. She fumbled for a switch somewhere on the wall and a bank of fluorescent lights blinked lazily to life, bathing the entire room in a ghostly pale-blue light. Across the far wall was a series of storage shelves stretching from floor to ceiling. The motorized stacks were pressed together at either end, with only a single opening between them. In the half-light, it looked like the entrance to a cave, ominous and forbidding.

She offered the console to Jejeune. "The motor and the emergency cut-off beams are activated by this remote device. The protocol is that only the person entering the stacks can hold it, and no one may enter them without it." Her voice was dispassionate, indifferent. *More self-protection*, thought Maik. He could not imagine the pain she must be feeling, the inconsolable sense of loss at being down here, so close to the nerve centre of her lost fiancé's work. Her willingness to offer more commentary startled him.

"Philip had the system set up as soon as he came. He spent a lot of time down here. He wanted to be sure he'd be the only one controlling the movement of the stacks."

Jejeune took the console and began edging his way down the narrow space between the shelves. Grey seemed to drift off towards inner thoughts as she watched him.

"Was Mr. Wayland close to a solution in this new line of enquiry?" asked Maik, more to dispel the uncomfortable silence that had settled between them than out of any genuine interest.

Grey stirred, seeming to free herself a little from the melancholy that had shrouded her since she first entered the room. "Philip was certain it was possible, and once he had convinced himself of that, he was willing to sacrifice any amount of time, conduct any amount of research, to find it. He would have found his viable industrial-scale process, Sergeant. I have no doubt of it."

Her emotions moved like water, thought Maik, flowing from her sadness into these tiny eddies of energy when she spoke about Wayland's work. If anything was going to save Xandria Grey, it would be this, continuing her ex-fiancé's research.

Jejeune emerged from the stacks with a number of manila folders. He crossed to a small desk and switched on a lamp, spreading the files out in front of him so that their titles and dates were visible. Tiny tabs of coloured paper protruded from the edges of many of the sheets in the folders. He selected two at random and scanned through their contents. He seemed oblivious to the presence of either Maik or Grey, both hovering uncertainly nearby.

"These sticky tabs," said Jejeune, looking up from the desk, "are they significant?"

"DNA markers." Grey's face softened a little as the memory brought back a smile. "Utterly unprofessional, let alone unscientific. Still, they seemed to work for Philip."

"*DNA markers*? I'm afraid I don't understand."

"His little joke," she said with another small smile. "It means 'Data Not Available.' He marked the areas where there were gaps in his research."

Jejeune's expression suggested he did understand now. A lot more clearly. He stood up and closed the folders, gathering them up and handing them to Grey. "Thank you. This has been helpful."

"It sounds like the Old Dairy project is going to run into a lot more resistance over their undersea storage pipeline than Catherine Weil would have us believe," said Maik, as the two men made their way across the car park to Jejeune's Range Rover.

Jejeune nodded. "Hardly what you want to hear if you've already focused all your efforts on it, as the Old Dairy owners have, is it?"

"On the other hand, there were a lot of those little tabs," said Maik. "It's hard to believe Wayland was as close to a solution as Xandria Grey seems to think he was, if each one represented an area where no research had been done."

"Oh, I don't believe that's what they said at all, Sergeant. You heard her. Wayland was a researcher from the old school. The good ones used to pride themselves on precision, in what they call "non-data ink" too. I'm pretty sure if there was no data, Wayland's tabs would have read *ND*."

Maik had gone quiet, and when Jejeune turned to face him, he saw that the sergeant's face had turned to thunder. He was angry with himself, furious, and Jejeune suspected he knew why. Under Maik's guidance, the investigation had made little progress, and while in reality that was no reflection on the sergeant's abilities, perception was rarely a faithful mirror of the truth. Now the sergeant was realizing that, in refusing Grey's earlier offer to look at Wayland's research, he had missed something significant, something that may have led the investigation forward in some way. Jejeune respected his sergeant too much to offer him any platitudes about it not being important, but he didn't need him dwelling on it either.

"You raise a couple of good points, Sergeant," he said.

"Glad to hear I got something right," said Maik tartly.

"It would be interesting to find out whether anyone at the Old Dairy shares Xandria Grey's point of view. If they felt their project was in trouble, and at the same time believed Philip Wayland was close to a breakthrough on an alternative solution, I can't imagine recent meetings of Old Dairy board of directors would have been a comfortable place to be."

"You know what else strikes me?" asked Maik. "We've now spoken to people involved in two projects that are competing against each other for a billion pounds, and no one has so much as mentioned the prize money. You don't imagine it's slipped their minds, do you?"

The sergeant seemed to be returning to the point where he wanted to start holding other people accountable for their actions, instead of just himself. Jejeune was pleased. The way events were unfolding, in this case and elsewhere, he had the feeling he was going to need the sergeant's support, possibly more than he had ever needed it before.

They had reached Jejeune's Range Rover, but instead of getting in, the DCI stopped and looked at Maik over the top of the vehicle. "*Troubling*, Sergeant," he said. "That was Xandria Grey's word. We could ask her questions, no matter how *troubling* they might be. Just what was it that she was expecting us to ask about Philip Wayland that might be troubling, I wonder?"

Jejeune opened the car door, but before he got in, he paused and looked back one final time at the washed-out facade of the research block. Whether it gave him any answers or not, the building held his gaze for a long moment before he finally slid behind the steering wheel and closed the door.

19

The low breeze sent gentle ripples over the dark surface of the water, the sunlight glinting off them as they lapped against the shore. The heads of the reeds tilted and rocked with an easy movement as the wind passed through them. Apart from a few dabbling ducks, nothing disturbed the quiet scene in front of the hide; but the men sat alert, ready for any flicker of movement that would prompt them to raise the binoculars clutched in their hands.

Damian and Domenic had decided to occupy opposite ends of the hide, so it was inevitable that anyone entering would sit between them and assume they were not together. Domenic had been prepared for the possibility that Quentin Senior might make an appearance that day, but certainly not that his closest birding acquaintance would be accompanied by another man the inspector knew very well.

The inspector's surprise at seeing Eric was genuine enough to overshadow any unease he might have felt.

"Eric?" exclaimed Domenic. "You're here, birding?"

"Just taken it up," he announced. "Quentin is being kind enough to show me the ropes. Anything interesting?" he asked, bending to look through the narrow viewing slat. "I'm hoping for Little Ringed Plover today."

The others recognized in Eric's comment the novice's desire for new species to add to his list, but Senior shook his head. "O, that way madness lies." He smiled at Domenic. "Forgive me, Inspector, I've been reading *King Lear* again, in light of your young lady's nomination. Wonderful stuff, truly moving." He turned back to Chappell. "But if not madness, Eric, then at least disappointment. You'll see one eventually, if you're patient enough, and dedicated enough. But in these early stages, it might be better simply to let the birding world show you what it wants to."

"Can't find you any Little Ringed Plovers, but there's a couple of male Ruddy Turnstones in full breeding plumage on the far shore," offered Damian. "Always a nice bird to see."

Eric raised his bins eagerly and began tracking along the shoreline until he located the birds. "Excellent," he murmured, not taking his eyes from the bins. "Thanks."

Senior turned toward Damian, studiously peering out through a slat, his face turned away from the group.

"It's simply *Turnstone* over here, Eric. The 'ruddy' rather tips your hand," he said to Damian amicably. "A Canadian accent, I would guess?"

Damian did his best to lean farther into the shadows at the far end of the hide. "I like to call myself a citizen of the world," he said easily.

It was the sort of fatuous statement that would put most people off, and Domenic suspected that was the point. Senior, predictably, took it with his customary good nature.

He nodded. "You see, Eric? People travel thousands of miles for the privilege of birding this magnificent north Norfolk coast, and here we have it all on our doorstep year-round. We really don't appreciate how lucky we are sometimes." Senior raised his bins, and tracked a small duck as it weaved in and out of view behind a curtain of reeds. "Garganey, female, over to the right." The men all raised their binoculars and followed Senior's directions to find the nondescript bird upending for weeds.

"A good duck, Eric," said Senior. "Especially for our North American friend. Friends, forgive me, Inspector. I sometimes forget you're from that part of the world too."

"I tend to consider myself a local now," said Jejeune, anxious to put any distance he could between himself and the North American at the other end of the hide. Though he was less than comfortable with the situation, he did not regret bringing Damian out to Cley. This was his home turf, some of the best birding habitat in the world, and it had seemed important, somehow, to share it with his brother. But he realized now that it had become dangerous for them to be here, and he was waiting only for a suitable pulse of time to pass before he could bid them all goodbye. Damian would pick up on the cue and make his own way from the hide a few moments later, linking up with Domenic at the car park, where he would have the Range Rover's engine running and the door unlocked.

At the far end of the hide, Damian had gone very quiet and was staring through his bins with an intensity that Domenic recognized well. Domenic raised his own bins quickly and watched as a gull made a final arc before swooping in for a landing on a mudflat. Damian withdrew his gaze and stared across the other men toward his brother. But Domenic knew what would happen. The need to identify, to share, was too strong for an ex–bird tour leader.

"That's a Franklin's Gull that has just come in with those Black-headed Gulls," said Damian in a low, measured voice. He seemed to realize that he was starting on a path with an uncertain destination, but as Domenic had known, he was unable to stop himself.

It was undoubtedly the casual nature of Damian's announcement that caused Senior to greet it with such low-key interest.

"Really, a Franklin's? Are you sure? I have to say, it would be a remarkable sighting if it was." Senior raised his bins. "Where are we looking, please?"

"Second group of gulls from the right. It's the fifth bird in, on the far side of the mudflat, slightly smaller than the bird in front of it, slightly darker back."

"I have it. Wind just ruffled its primaries, yes?" Senior sounded even less sure than before. "It's certainly darker, but has its head tucked under its wing, and its legs aren't visible. Conclusive diagnostics are impossible from here." He seemed to remember his manners and quickly corrected himself. "That is to say, they would be for me."

"I saw it come in," said Damian. "It had that narrow white band between the wingtip and inner wing." Domenic detected a touch of hesitation in his voice. *He's realized*, he thought. *Too late, but he's realized.* But Damian's tone carried the kind of assurance that caused Senior to lower his bins.

"Not the white wedge of the Black-headed?" He fixed Damian with a stare. "And of course, you would have seen enough Franklin's on your side of the pond, wouldn't you, to recognize one." There was rising tension in Senior's voice. He was warming to the possibility of it. Eric was sitting silently at Senior's side, watching with undisguised fascination as the drama of the discovery continued to play out.

"You really believe it is a Franklin's Gull?" It was as if Senior couldn't quite give himself permission to believe it, without one last confirmation.

Damian flashed a quick glance at Domenic.

"Yes."

"Well, this is wonderful," said Senior. "We must put the word out immediately. Eric, would you mind doing the honours? I'll let you know if it twitches so much as a feather." Eric withdrew his phone and began keying in his message. Senior looked up at Damian for a brief moment. "You'll forgive me if I ask Eric to note it as a *possible*. I'd be leery of an unequivocal declaration until I'd seen a field mark or two of my own."

"Be my guest. It doesn't look like it's going anywhere, so hopefully you'll be able to get your looks at some point."

Domenic shifted uneasily. In less than half an hour there were going to be upwards of fifty birders descending on this place. And Damian was going to be a thoroughly celebrated figure.

"There, done," declared Eric. He snatched up his bins and locked them onto the bird again.

"What a wonderful introduction to your birding career, Eric. Cherish this one. Many birders here wait years to see a Franklin's. They only pop up every ten years or so, and they hardly ever stay around for very long. Harry will be beside himself," he said, shaking his head and chuckling softly. He looked at Eric. "Our resident gull expert. Every birding group has one. I'm sure you'll run into him soon enough, though if he misses this bird, he probably won't speak to you for weeks." He smiled. "Well, this is a truly exciting, I can't thank you enough, Mr. …?"

"Damian," he said hesitantly, "John Damian."

"Okay, Eric, I suggest we settle in and watch this chap for a little while. There'll not be much doing until he stirs, but we might get a glimpse of the red legs, or the eye if we're lucky. Ready for a bit of a session, Inspector?"

Jejeune shook his head. "I have somewhere to be."

Senior looked genuinely disappointed. "Really? How sad. How about you, Mr. Damian, you'll join us, I hope, point out to Eric the bits he should be noting?"

"I have other plans, too, unfortunately," said Damian. He stood to leave.

"You will at least let us identify it as *Found by,* I hope?" asked Senior. "The local birders will be extremely grateful."

"Oh, that's okay, really," said Damian, reading the warnings in Domenic's stare. "I mean, you were on it, too."

With a birder less established, or more vain, it might have worked, but Domenic could have told Damian that Senior's integrity would have none of it.

"Not at all, I'd've barely given the chap a second look, to tell you the truth. And once he's roosted, well, no one could call a Franklin's now, not till he eventually pops his head up. No, this find is all yours, my friend. Please, I must insist ..."

Damian looked helplessly at Domenic, but there was clearly no safe way to refuse, especially under the watchful stare of Eric, who looked as if he may have picked up something between the two men, even if he was not quite sure what it was.

"Okay. Just *John Damian. Overseas visitor.* Something like that would be great. Thanks," said Damian, following Domenic's lead and escaping from the hide before Senior could unwittingly compromise them any further.

Outside, Domenic was covering the ground at such a pace that Damian had to half run to keep pace. "Come on, Dom, don't be mad," he said in a reasonable tone. "It was a Franklin's, for God's sake. Over here. You couldn't deny them a chance at that. You'd have called it if you'd seen it."

"I did see it," said Domenic.

Damian stopped on the path. "What, you want the credit? Let's go back, I'd be happy to give it to you, honestly."

"No, we need to get you out of here. Now."

By the time they reached the car park at the visitor centre, the first of the cars were pulling in. Birders hurried to extract scopes and jackets from their cars, readying themselves for the walk in to the reserve. Two or three of them recognized Domenic and hurried over for information about the gull's location. None gave Damian more than a passing nod. Senior obviously had higher priorities than having Eric assign credit for the find at the moment. But he wouldn't wait long. It wasn't in his nature to be anything less than gallant, and Jejeune was fairly sure the second wave of arrivals would come pre-armed with the news that they owed this coup to one John Damian. But by then, the man who had made the discovery would be long gone. And so would the man who had so recklessly brought him here.

20

Lindy pulled into the car park of the Old Dairy under a grey, uncertain sky. The size of the crowd surprised her. She had been led to believe there would be only a few protesters on hand, but this gathering was substantial, and growing. A steady flow of people were walking along the public footpath, joining the knot of individuals already there, milling and swirling around, collars turned up against a freshening breeze that tugged raggedly at the treetops.

Lindy made her way over towards the large wire gates of the compound. "Morning, Danny," she said. "Nice day for it."

Maik looked surprised. "Ms. Hey … Lindy," he said awkwardly. "The DCI didn't mention you would be here today."

"He didn't know." Lindy gave her long hair a toss and the wind swirled it around her head. "Nor did I, come to that. My publisher asked me to come down and cover the event. One of our reporters called in on a *sickie* — probably beer-induced, if I know him. He certainly knows how to attract a crowd, this prince." She nodded toward a throng flanking the approach road to the gates.

Maik's eyes drifted over to where a half-hearted chant had broken out; a warm-up, perhaps, for the main event still to come. Lindy saw Lauren Salter on the far side of the group and watched her carefully tracking Sergeant Maik wherever he went, as usual. And as usual, Danny Maik remained completely oblivious. *The course of unrequited love doth ever run untrue,* thought Lindy.

"You on security these days?" asked Lindy. There was humour in her tone, but faint concern, too. The Saltmarsh police department wouldn't waste a valuable resource like Sergeant Danny Maik on crowd control unless a crowd genuinely needed controlling. Maik understood and smiled reassuringly. "This lot will make a bit of noise, but we're not anticipating anything beyond that."

Lindy caught sight of Domenic, standing a good way inside the compound fence, with a group of people who were lining the road leading up to the glass-block offices. One person in particular took her eye, the one standing next to Domenic. "I see it has fallen to poor Dom's lot to interview that stunner with long red hair," she said. "Let me guess. She's single, an avid birder, and has a thing for Canadian detectives? Don't be too impressed with my psychic abilities, Danny. It's the kind of luck I get these days."

Maik smiled. "I don't think the inspector has paid much attention to Ms. Weil's appearance, to tell you the truth." He paused and cast a sidelong glance at Lindy. "He seems a bit, well, distracted lately, as a matter of fact. Nothing bothering him, is there?"

It was as close as Maik would come to prying, but Lindy knew him well enough by now to recognize the danger signs. Dom was off-kilter and Danny Maik wanted to know why. Nor was it an idle enquiry. The murder of Philip Wayland was an unsettling, brutal event, and no one would feel truly safe again until his killer had been brought to justice. That would take a Domenic Jejeune firing on all cylinders, and Danny Maik just wanted to make sure that version would be available if called upon.

Lindy shook her head casually. "No, I don't think so, Sergeant ... Danny. Nothing at all. Possibly this trip up to Scotland was a bit taxing, all that driving. But really, other than that, nothing comes to mind."

She turned away slightly, angry at herself. Perhaps it was okay to feel so guilty about deceiving such a kind, honest man as Danny Maik, but she could have probably done better than denying something three times in the same sentence. She knew it would be necessary to close down the subject before Maik could start to delve deeper. "I'd better get going. You've met my boss, I understand. So you'll know he's every bit as demanding and intolerant as yours." She treated Danny to one of her best smiles and threw a tiny wave in for good measure before melting away to join the growing crowd.

From inside the compound, Catherine Weil raised her hand in greeting to a small man on the other side of the wire fence. He was dressed in a ragged sweater and well-worn corduroys and seemed to be hovering slightly to the side of the main mass of protesters, as if unsure how closely he wanted to be associated with them. He smiled uncertainly and waved back. Jejeune watched the exchange with interest.

"There's been no harassment by the protesters of anyone working here?" Jejeune asked. "No personal threats aimed at any of the staff? Past or present?"

He saw in her eyes that she understood. Weil shook her head a little, her long locks dancing with the movement. "Most of the people who work here are locals, too. We've all known each other for years. I have never felt threatened or intimidated by these protesters, and I doubt any of the other staff have, either. Past or present."

She had accepted his presence beside her in the line without comment, and her tone betrayed no hint of hostility or defensiveness. What had happened between them was consigned to the past, she seemed to suggest, and she was a person of the present. Jejeune suspected Catherine Weil rarely spent much time on regrets or recriminations. She turned to look at him frankly. "The thing is, most of us understand their point of view. We can even sympathize with it, to some extent. The local people who work here love this coastline, too. But the simple fact is, if we don't do something about carbon capture and storage very soon, there won't be any coastline left to worry about. The storm of 2013 was only a foretaste of what is to come. The latest predictions are that coastal flooding will cost the world economy one trillion dollars by the year 2050. By then, there will be 150 million environmental refugees. That's not at some far-off point in humanity's future, Inspector, that's in our lifetimes. Yours and mine."

Jejeune was distracted momentarily by the sight of a woman who looked very much like Lindy milling around in the crowd on the far side of the fence. He strained to catch sight of her again, but the person, whoever she was, had been swallowed up by the mass of people and had disappeared from view. Jejeune let his eyes stay on the crowd for a moment. "Mr. el-Taleb mentioned a second set of protesters, ones who are keen to ensure the project does not leave?"

Weil gave a withering look of contempt. She nodded towards the man on the other side of the fence. "People like Niall Doherty have voiced a concern that if the project proves too costly, Old Dairy Holdings may just pull up stakes and walk away. It has happened with a number of other carbon capture projects elsewhere. All these people are looking for is some sort of commitment from the board of directors, a trust fund, perhaps, to ensure the employees aren't left high and dry if that happens."

"So there's no chance these conflicting points of view could develop into a genuine rivalry, then?"

"You mean civil unrest? Punch-ups in Saltmarsh Square?" Weil gave a light, derisive laugh. "I hardly think so, Inspector.

This is an environmental issue we're talking about, after all. I think people save that sort of passion for football matches, or the Boxing Day sales."

On the other side of the fence, the person who might be Lindy drifted into view again for a second and then was gone. Jejeune turned back to Weil, taking in her strong, uncompromising profile and her pale unblemished skin. Had they come far enough from their previous difficulties for him to get an honest answer to the most important question of all?

"Why did Philip Wayland leave the project, Ms. Weil?"

She seemed to consider the question for a long time before answering. "I suppose you might say it was a matter of respect. Philip never really seemed to have any, either for the project itself or for Yousef. I think Philip just saw him as some muppet with a chequebook."

The faint chatter of a blade chopping through the air arrived first, and everyone looked to the sky. To the west, the metallic glint of a small helicopter appeared, bucking slightly on the uncertain winds. It approached low, barely cresting the stand of tall pines on the far side of the property, before settling in a near-perfect touchdown onto a makeshift helipad in a field on the far side of the road. From either side of the wire fence, the assembled crowds watched as a tall, distinguished-looking individual dressed in a suit of immaculate cut ducked out from the helicopter, followed on the other side by another, slightly smaller man. For a pilot, he, too, seemed to be extraordinarily well-groomed.

"Prince Yousef," said Weil. "He makes it a point to meet his brother at the airport and fly him in personally. A helicopter pilot's licence is about the only thing he owns that his brother doesn't. Even then, the Crown Prince gets to travel around in his own custom-built jet, while all poor Yousef has is this dinky little thing to fly around in the local airspace."

For a moment, the appearance of Crown Prince Ibrahim seemed to take the protesters off guard, as if perhaps they had been expecting someone in the long flowing robes of the desert. The hesitation meant the noise built slowly, uncertainly, and by the time it had reached its crescendo, the prince and his brother were already ensconced in the Rolls-Royce Phantom that had been parked at the side of the helicopter pad.

"This is the part I love," said Weil sarcastically. "He funds a multi-million-dollar project to address carbon emissions, and drives a couple of hundred metres from the helicopter to the compound in a car that probably gets about one kilometre to the litre."

Jejeune acknowledged the comment with a faint smile, though it was becoming clear that the prince could hardly have walked the distance, not with the barrage of angry complaints the protesters were now hurling at the car. As it approached, the crowd began to surge forward; a roiling, organic thing, in danger of spilling out of control. A cordon of uniformed officers had been arranged in a semicircle, protecting the entrance to the compound, but as the protesters caught sight of the silhouetted figure behind the car's tinted windows, there was a concerted push, and one or two broke through the police line. As the car continued to inch ahead, reinforcements from both sides poured in, protesters piling in from the back of the crowd, only to be met by members of the prince's security staff, who had sprinted from the compound at the first signs of danger, and were now wading in with arms flailing. Scuffles broke out, wild punches and grabs and mis-aimed kicks. The noise had grown into an angry roar now, shouted insults drowned by cheers erupting at every small victory for the protesters. For a few dangerous seconds, the balance of power teetered between the two forces, until the combined efforts of the police and the prince's security detail could finally manhandle the crowd off the roadway and clear the way for the car to continue.

As soon as the Rolls was safely inside the compound, the gates were rapidly closed. Through the wire fence, Jejeune saw Maik, and behind him, Constable Salter. Their expressions spoke volumes. They had got lucky. The police had seriously under-estimated the mood among the protesters. Things could have become ugly if they'd been allowed to reach the prince.

Abrar el-Taleb emerged from the glass office building as the Phantom drew to a halt at the base of the steps leading to the front doors. He rounded to the far side of the car and opened the Crown Prince's door first, greeting him with a bow. Only when the formalities had been completed did he return to the near side to open the door for the patiently waiting Prince Yousef. Jejeune noticed a strange flicker of something pass between the two men, a faint quiver that continued even as they flanked Ibrahim at the bottom of the steps to await the stream of well-wishers which now descended to welcome him.

As the princes mounted the steps, el-Taleb came across to Jejeune, his dark eyes full of anger. "This is the result of your public right of way, Inspector. Private property should be private." He turned without waiting for a response and followed the princes up the steps and into the glass building.

With the targets of the protest beyond the reach of any further impact, the crowd beyond the fence began to disperse, milling about in a disorderly swirl of uncertain intentions. Only a few protesters continued to clamour against the wire, hurling comments and waving placards in impotent fury.

"It seems I was wrong," said Weil, looking at them thoughtfully. "There obviously are some people who feel quite passionately about this thing, after all."

She moved off, her straight-backed gait seeming to make her drift over the ground as she went. Domenic Jejeune didn't take his eyes off the departing figure of Catherine Weil for a long time.

21

They were sitting in the living room. Domenic had his back to the open window, sunlight streaming in over his shoulder and falling in pools on the polished hardwood floor. Facing him, Damian was lounging in an armchair. Lindy, for reasons only she knew, had chosen to lean against the mantelpiece over the fire, equidistant from each man. For once, there was no music. Damian had been introducing Lindy to an incessant stream of old Canadian songs and artists since his arrival, and Lindy, ever the willing student of other people's tastes, was showing a keen interest. For Domenic's own part, most were selections he had secretly hoped he had said goodbye to once and for all when he came over here.

All three had a can of beer in hand, the single survivor of the four-pack sitting on a coffee table wearing a necklace of plastic rings. In place of the dreaded musical "classics," the sound of birdsong drifted in through the open window. Somewhere just beyond the clifftop, a gull was announcing its flight over a glittering late-morning sea.

Domenic and Lindy had just finished a double act filling Damian in on the previous day's events at the Old Dairy compound. He had listened impassively, clearly interested but offering no comment.

Domenic shook his head. "It looked like DCS Shepherd might have been getting ready to sanction an interview with Yousef, but I can't see that happening now, especially while Ibrahim is in residence."

"I can't see why a prince would want to get himself involved in something like this," said Damian, "though I suppose he does have a lot to feel aggrieved about. It can't be easy being the second son in a social hierarchy that so heavily favours the first."

"Well, on behalf of the past couple of thousand years of disenfranchised women," said Lindy, "let me be the first to offer him no sympathy at all."

Domenic shook his head. "I can't see why, either, but he's being evasive, and his alibi is shaky. Plus, he has a lot of reasons to be worried. The project sounds like it's on the wrong track as far as carbon sequestration is concerned. It could cost millions in wasted R&D, money he's supposed to be responsible for while his brother is away."

Domenic needed to know where the Crown Prince's Gyrfalcons fitted into all this, too. Twice he had considered mentioning the birds to his brother, but each time he had found a reason not to. Until he knew what the Old Dairy connection was with De Laet, if any, he intended to keep that side of things to himself.

Damian noticed his brother's uncertainty, though he misinterpreted its cause.

"A stone unturned," he said, "and Little Domino was never very comfortable with those, was he?"

"Still, Shepherd's got good reason to tread lightly around this lot," said Lindy. "I would suggest the Saltmarsh police force probably needs to be very careful about taking on a family with virtually unlimited financial resources. It's not everybody who can dedicate millions of pounds to the building of an architectural pun."

Domenic looked puzzled.

She looked at Damian and nodded toward his brother. "You'll have to excuse him, he's a bit slow at times," she said. "I call him the original snail male. Transparency, Dom. It was the mantra, remember, all through the planning permission hearings. The authorities wanted assurances of transparency from the Old Dairy project. They all but asked for a plaque on the front gates agreeing to it. So Prince Ibrahim built the most transparent building possible, and then stuck it behind an impenetrable fence of security. You have to admire the man's sense of irony, if nothing else."

"If you like irony," said Domenic, "consider the fact that the building was given a LEED certification for being eco-friendly."

Damian shook his head sadly. "What's so eco-friendly about the wholesale slaughter of passing songbirds? I can only imagine what sort of carnage a building like that would cause. 'Harvesting by architectural design,' my university professor used to call it." He sipped on his beer thoughtfully. "I'm starting to get depressed here, Dom. Any chance you could break out the birdie dance? That always used to cheer me up."

A look of astonishment crossed Lindy's face. "Domenic used to do that?" she asked.

Damian nodded. "Quite the little mover, our Domino — YMCA, the moonwalk; he knew them all. Never a family gathering went by without Little Domenic standing up to take his star turn. Oh yes," confirmed Damian, nodding, "there's more than one reason Domenic was the favourite child."

Lindy's eyes were shining with delight. "Really? Oh my God, how adorable. I'll bet your aunties all just wanted to rush up and pinch your little cheeks," she said.

"Say," said Damian, holding a hand to his chest in a gesture of absolute insincerity, "I do hope I'm not embarrassing you with these revelations."

Domenic gave his brother an indulgent smile. "Not at all," he said pleasantly, "but there is a bus leaving Saltmarsh station at 7:00 p.m. tonight. I think you should be under it."

Lindy laughed and clapped her hands like a primary school teacher. "Now then, children." She started to move towards the kitchen. "I'll get started on lunch, while Damian sees if he can remember any more embarrassing stories about you."

An unfamiliar call drifted in through the open window, distinct from the background burble of birdsong. The two men froze, listening intently to the sweet melodious repeated notes, strong and clear.

"Nightingale," announced Damian.

Domenic shook his head. "Unlikely around here. Probably a Song Thrush. They do sound similar at times."

Damian inclined his head slightly, listening intently. "That's a Nightingale."

"And you know this from listening to all those Nightingales in Newfoundland?"

"Plenty of spare time on a boat trip through the North Atlantic," said Damian. "I spent a lot of it refreshing myself on British bird calls."

"Are you sure it's not a Skylark?" asked Lindy from the kitchen door.

In unison, the brothers turned to look at her.

"Wasn't it a Skylark that Juliet mistook for a Nightingale when she woke up next to Romeo?"

"I think we can put that down to dramatic licence," said Damian decisively. "Those two calls are so distinctive, I imagine even Domenic could tell them apart." The two men listened as the bird sang again. "I'm telling you, that's a Nightingale," he said. "I'll bet you that last beer. Go check it out. I trust you."

With a sigh of exasperation, Domenic rose from the chair and grabbed his bins. As they heard the door close, Damian smiled at Lindy. "You can hand me that beer, if you like. It's a Nightingale. I saw it fly in, just before it started singing."

Lindy passed Damian the beer. "He's not going to be a happy bunny when he gets back."

Damian shrugged. "I've done worse to him," he said. His face clouded slightly. "Far worse."

Lindy raised an eyebrow.

"Well, I saddled him with this career for one thing. I know he's a success and everything, but take it from me, he'd far rather be a birder. You can see it in his eyes, whenever he's out there."

"You know, it's strange he's never mentioned it," said Lindy with an irony so heavy Damian picked up on it immediately. He gave her a sad smile.

"Policing runs in our family," he said. "Most of the men on our mother's side are in law enforcement, one way or another. When I came of age, it was inevitable 'the gaze' would fall on me." He took a sip of beer. "But that was never going to happen. I suppose I just never really cared enough about making the bad guys pay. Suzette, our sister, was a non-starter, too; far too headstrong and focused to be told what career she would be following. And so, by the time they got to Dom, the pressure was well and truly on. He never really stood a chance." Damian gave his head another sad shake. "I guess you don't have to be a psychologist to work out why I spent so much of my life wishing I could have taken better care of him."

For a moment it seemed as if Damian might disappear into his regrets, but his mood lifted as his brother returned. Domenic saw the beer in his brother's hand and looked first at him and then at the window he was facing.

Damian raised the can in salute. "What can I say? Finely honed birding skills. Don't feel bad, I'm sure you'll win one of our bets one day."

Outside, the Nightingale unrolled its glorious, melodious song once more.

"You might want to take a look at it," said Domenic. "We don't see many anymore. There's been a massive decline, something like ninety percent in the past thirty years. Time was, there were places where a watch of Nightingales was reliable. Now the chances of seeing even a single bird are remote."

Damian set down his beer and stood up. "You're right, I suppose, we should go and take a look at it while we still can. Come on." He slapped his brother on the shoulder and they went out into the garden together.

Lindy watched them leave. Almost in spite of herself, she was starting to enjoy having Damian around. He had a healthy supply of his younger brother's natural charm, and his eagerness to show his appreciation for being allowed to stay was manifesting itself in delightfully overzealous, puppy-dog offers of assistance, in everything from cooking meals to helping with household chores. But more than that, she sensed it was important for Domenic to have his brother here, in ways that went far beyond their good-natured teasing. For so long, Lindy had wished for a friend for Domenic, someone with whom he could be less guarded, could escape the brooding loneliness that was so much a part of his existence as a celebrated senior police officer in a foreign country. Now, with the arrival of his brother, it was as if a gap in Domenic's life had been filled somehow, as if there was a new wholeness about him. And because of that, whatever dangers Damian's continued presence created, Lindy was prepared to risk them. For now.

22

Jejeune had been on his way home from a successful trip to see a Red-spotted Bluethroat at Blakeney Point when the call had come in. Damian had not made the trip. Many of the birders who had arrived to see the Franklin's, perhaps even Senior himself, would also be making the trek up to check the Bluethroat off their year list. The bird was not sufficiently rare for Damian to take the risk. Though he had never seen one in the U.K., he had long since stopped listing birds by country.

Maik approached the Range Rover as the DCI pulled up at the Old Dairy falconry. "One of the falcons has been injured, but there's no question of any crime. Holland's girlfriend saw it happen. Only, with the previous incident up here, the break-in …" he let his explanation trail off. The two men shared an almost pathological distrust of coincidence, and as long as the nearby murder remained unsolved, anything to do with the Old Dairy compound would cause a blip on the Saltmarsh police department's radar.

Jejeune got out of the car and followed Maik in the direction of a large patch of wheat stubble, near the boundary hedge, where Holland and Darla Doherty were standing shoulder to shoulder, looking at something on the ground. It took a moment to discern what they were staring at: a hunched grey shape nestled deep in the stand of wheat stalks.

As they approached, Darla began inching in slowly, turning her head at various angles to get a better look. She leaned forward and cautiously spread the tangle of stalks, pulling back and shaking her head. "It's not good. The stalk went right through the bird's upper wing as it landed." She looked at Tony. "I don't think I can get it free without some help."

Holland began folding back the cuffs of his shirtsleeves. He took off his watch and stuffed it into a pocket of his tight-fitting jeans. "Just tell me what I need to do."

"I'm going to have to use both hands to break the stalk before I can lift the bird out. I need you to hold these other stalks apart like this so I can get in. But you need to be really careful, Tony."

"I can see what she means," said Maik. "That beak looks vicious."

"I don't think it's the beak she's most concerned about," said Jejeune. "If the bird strikes, it will be with its talons. They're like meathooks. They can go right into the bone."

Holland stretched over the bird cautiously, trying to spread the tangle of stalks. The raptor flashed a lightning strike with its foot and Holland whipped his arm back sharply.

"Bloody hell," he said, rattled.

Darla gave him a look as if to reassure him that there was nothing personal in it. The bird was simply performing a role honed through the millennia: to strike, to tear flesh, to cause injury. "Okay," she said, "this is not going to work. Wait here. And don't go anywhere near the bird." She looked at him seriously. "I mean it, Tony, no heroics. It could end up badly for both of you."

She ran over to the nearby hangar and Maik's eyes tracked her as she passed. Speaking to Holland, her voice had the measured calm of a professional, concerned but in control. But watching her now, Maik could see worry etched deeply in her face. He looked across at Jejeune, to see if the DCI noticed it, too. Jejeune was clearly following every beat of the proceedings with keen attention, but there was something unusual about his interest. Maik couldn't help the feeling there was a kind of uneasiness, a disengagement that he had never seen before in his DCI when he was around birds.

Darla reappeared from the hangar and returned at a jog, her face still a mask of concern. And something else, too. Maik watched it melt into cool competence again as she handed Holland a coarse grey blanket. Whatever was on Darla Doherty's mind, Danny was fairly sure it wasn't solely to do with rescuing this bird. And it was clear she didn't want Holland to pick up on it, either.

"As I part the stalks, throw this blanket right over the bird. Try to cover it completely, but be sure to get the head. It should calm him down, and I'll be able wrap the legs." She looked into Holland's face, momentary concern returning to cloud her features. "You're sure you're okay to do this? You can say if you're not."

"Good to go," said Holland. He gave Darla a smile that was meant to be reassuring but, to Maik's eye, at least, didn't quite make it.

Darla spread the tangle of stalks as far as they would go, giving Maik his clearest view yet of the hunkering grey bird. He found its eyes almost hypnotizing; liquid pools as deep and black as oil. There was no panic in them, no fear. Only menace. It was a killer, he thought, every inch of the way. It disturbed him slightly that he could recognize the type even across species.

"Now," said Darla urgently. "Now, Tony, now." Holland launched the blanket and the bird thrashed around wildly as it hit its body. The Gyrfalcon squirmed and frantically tried to flap its wings, even the impaled one. The blanket had not quite covered the bird's head and it attempted repeated strikes with its powerful bill, struggling to free itself so it could get better purchase for that one final, telling blow. Timing her moves perfectly between strikes, Darla flipped the blanket over the bird's head. The struggling stopped instantly.

Reaching in with her other hand, she folded the blanket tightly around the bird's body and held it firm. It had taken a heartbeat for Holland to recover from the bird's flurry of panicked energy but now he reached in and snapped the stalk from the ground. Darla slowly lifted the falcon out, carefully pressing the bird's legs against its body, even though the shield of a heavy blanket now protected her arms from the talons.

Holland helped Darla to her feet, the bird still gently cradled in her arms. From his vantage point, Maik could see the wheat stalk protruding like an arrow from the top of the blanket.

"Will it be okay?" asked Holland.

"We need to get it to a vet right away. After the stalk is removed, they can get him to a rehab facility. If it can build up flight muscle again ..." She shrugged.

Maik didn't know much about bird anatomy, or a Gyrfalcon's powers of recovery, but it seemed optimistic to him, to say the least, to expect that this bird would ever fly again. And perhaps it was the same thought he could see now in Darla Doherty's unguarded expression. But there was something else there, too, that same look he had seen before. Only now he was properly able to identify it: fear.

At the far side of the field, where it met the adjoining property, a figure was leaning over a wooden fence, gesturing to be noticed. It was the man who had waved to Catherine Weil in the calm before the storm of yesterday's protests. At first, it seemed to Jejeune that it might have been the girl, Darla, whose attention he was trying to attract. Holland looked at Darla, but she made a point of deliberately ignoring the man. "As soon as I've got this bird in a box, would you mind giving me a lift to the vet's, Tony?" she asked.

As they walked away, the man continued to signal. Jejeune began to make his way over. As he approached, he assessed the man waiting for him. Niall Doherty had passed on his dark brown eyes to his daughter, and his slight build. But she must have come to him late in life, because he was old now, with feathery grey hair and a lined brown face that was gnarled with age. There was an openness to it, a peace that made Jejeune think he would be content to have reached this age living the life he had, even if there was a shimmer of pain behind the eyes. The estrangement from a child must cut deeper the older one became, thought Jejeune.

Doherty turned his watery eyes on the inspector as he arrived.

"It was bound to happen," said Doherty. "She was flying those birds too hard."

"You know about training falcons?" asked Jejeune.

Doherty inclined his head. "Did my share, as a younger man. Before I saw the error of my ways." He didn't smile. His lined face creased a little with disgust. "She was out here flying 'em day and night," said Doherty, "on a creance fifty yards long, at least. You can't fly these birds on a long leash like that, time and time again. They can injure themselves if they get caught up in it. Training should be gradual, not all at once. You need to have patience." He shook his head sadly. "My Darla knows that. She's been around hunting birds long enough."

"Why is she in such a hurry, do you think?" asked Jejeune.

"It's them up there," he said, gesturing to the Old Dairy compound with his chin. "The prince, or that el-Taleb. Rushing, see, to get them out hacking on their own. Same with this nonsense of having her wear a mankala instead of a gauntlet," He rubbed his left arm, where the fabric cuff used in the Middle East would be worn. I suppose they want the birds to be used to it when the prince flies them himself," he said. "But it's wrong. She needs a leather gauntlet. She has to have control of those birds during these early stages. My Darla knows better than to treat them lightly like this," he said, almost to himself. "Such beautiful creatures. They deserve better."

"Is that why you had threatened to release them?" asked Jejeune.

"Ah, just talk," said the old man, waving away the topic with a bony brown hand. "Keeping them penned in like that, barely able to stretch their wings, it's not right. They should be allowed to fly free."

Jejeune said nothing. He looked out over the landscape beyond Doherty's shoulder. It was a gentle day, calm, and on the hillside beyond the fence, Jejeune could see birds — crows, lapwings, gulls — roosting, feeding, flapping lazily. He could barely imagine the consequences for local wildlife if so many lethal hunters were released at the same time. The delicate balance of ecosystems could suffer catastrophically from even the best of intentions if actions weren't thought through.

Niall Doherty picked casually at a flake of wood on the top of the fence. "That business up at the gates the other day," he said, without looking up. "It wasn't meant to be like that. We emphasized that it was to be peaceful. 'No violence,' we said, but you can't always control who shows up to these things." It might have been an apology, or simply a statement of fact.

"Nevertheless, if you organize the protests, surely you must feel some responsibility for what goes on at them."

Doherty shook his head, his grey hair floating around him like a halo. "There were some bad elements, nasty. They don't understand what our concerns are. Not at all. They have an agenda of their own. You'd do well to be careful if you come up against them again, Inspector Jejeune. Them and the al-Haladins. You get caught in the middle, it could be unpleasant."

Doherty pushed himself back from the fence and walked away without another word. Jejeune watched him go, back up the hill toward his house. Whether the man's comment had been a threat or a warning, the inspector wouldn't have liked to say.

23

The figure was silhouetted against the bright sky as Jejeune crested the ridge at the top of the Old Dairy property, but the tall, lithe form would have been recognizable enough, even without the cascade of ringlets flowing down around the shoulders. Jejeune drew The Beast to a halt and lowered the passenger window.

"Fancy a chat, Inspector?" asked Catherine Weil. She cast a look over her shoulder at the glass office block. "Not in there. It's all a bit fractious at the moment." She gestured to the car park with a Styrofoam cup she was holding. "Park up and we'll have a stroll around the old cowsheds."

Jejeune pulled into the yew-fringed car park and got out. Weil began strolling across the pink gravel to the far corner, where Jejeune could see a second gate cut into the hedge. He fell into step beside her.

"A bit of excitement down the hill?"

"A bird was injured. One of Prince Ibrahim's Gyrfalcons."

"They send Major Crimes detectives out for that these days?" Weil took a sip from the cup and made a face. "The prince has got even more clout than I imagined."

"Is it often fractious in there?" asked Jejeune. Though their relationship had warmed considerably since their first meeting, he still suspected that if Catherine Weil was seeking him out for a chat, it wouldn't be about birds.

"It is when the Crown Prince is in town. He's not a man to suffer fools gladly, and I'm afraid he feels his younger brother fits into that category all too often."

Sometimes, Jejeune had learned, the worst thing you could do was ask a question when someone wanted to talk to you. He remained silent, the crunch of their feet on the gravel and the distant trilling of a Swallow the only sounds. They reached the corner of the car park and Weil swiped a card into a reader, opening the gate. Jejeune looked surprised. "The cowsheds are behind the compound's perimeter fence?"

"Not just any old cowsheds, though, are they?" asked Weil, mock-imperiously. "They house Ibrahim's stable of thorough-breds now."

They walked toward the cowsheds, passing Yousef's helicopter, perched on a concrete pad. Even close up, the lightweight model looked like little more than a toy. They entered an expansive cobbled courtyard, surrounded on three sides by low red-brick buildings. The battered, scarred walls and wooden doors of the shuttered pens showed the wear of many hard decades. The roof tiles had all been replaced, but an attempt had been made to replicate the original scalloped shapes. Though he could not see inside any of the pens, Jejeune knew the external appearance of old cowsheds held on to more than enough of their original identity to satisfy their English Heritage designation.

"I imagine there are some interesting bloodlines behind those doors," he said.

"You'd be surprised," said Weil archly.

"Is there any specific reason Prince Yousef incurred his brother's wrath today?" There was no point in trying to make the question sound casual. The two of them were alone in the centre of a cobbled courtyard, a safe distance from the offices. They hadn't ended up here by accident.

"It's couched in a lot of other things, but the central issue is that Ibrahim holds Yousef responsible for the lack of progress since Philip left. Of course, it should be Taleb carrying the can. He was responsible for bringing Philip on board in the first place. He should pay the price. But for some reason Yousef seems intent on making himself the lightning rod for Ibrahim's anger." Weil took a sip from her cup, tossing her head back slightly to let the breeze play on her pale face.

Jejeune watched a Swallow as it arced up under the eaves of the shed to a neatly constructed nest, where a brood of noisy nestlings awaited it. "Ms. Grey referred to a long-standing relationship between Wayland and el-Taleb, I understand."

Weil nodded. "Taleb knew Philip from his stint as a visiting professor at MIT years ago. When the researcher position became available, Taleb vouched for him. I think that's why Philip's defection, for want of a better word, must have been particularly galling for Taleb, especially after he had given his personal guarantees when the doubts arose over Philip's character."

Jejeune had been watching the Swallow again, swooping through the air with its rapier-like passes as it sought more insects for its hungry brood. He turned his eyes to Weil and she moved her narrow shoulders easily. "He was known to refer to morality as a personal indulgence. There was some talk that earlier in his career Philip might have borrowed sources that weren't strictly his to take. But whether there was anything to it or not, Taleb's endorsement won out in the end. Which is why I say it must have seemed like such a personal betrayal when Philip left to go to the university. I daresay Taleb felt his own honour had been tarnished in some way."

Weil fell silent, but if she was waiting for a response from Jejeune, she was disappointed. The Swallow delivered its cargo to its clamouring offspring and swooped out from under the eaves again to continue its aerial ballet in search of more food. But perhaps it was the meticulously restored roofs that Weil thought Jejeune was looking at. "We're all such hostages to our heritage, aren't we? Though I daresay amongst all the ill feeling, there was a sense of relief, too. I think Taleb was always secretly intimidated by Philip. Superior intellect, more charm, altogether better suited to a role as project director, you might say, than Taleb himself."

"You and Mr. el-Taleb don't see eye to eye yourselves. He seems uneasy around you."

She shrugged. "Perhaps he doesn't like redheads. I can't for a moment imagine it's my charming personality that puts him off." She smiled easily. "Of course, it could be the fact that I have a couple of decades' worth of experience in this area, while his background is mostly as a helicopter jockey for the rich and not-so-famous."

Jejeune's silence seemed to afford Weil's answer more importance than it should have merited. "Are you familiar with the area of research Mr. Wayland was working on at the university?" he asked eventually.

"Carbon Sequestration through Diatom Bloom Enhancement? Are you asking if I knew what it was, or if I have any expertise in it?"

Jejeune's questions rarely allowed room for such ambiguity. He could try to convince himself that it didn't really matter, but he acknowledged that he usually managed to do better than this.

"It sounds as if it could have a major impact on carbon sequestration practices."

"If it could be made viable," said Weil dismissively. "Which it can't."

"But if it could?"

"Well, for one thing, it would permanently consign ideas about storing carbon under the sea in abandoned oil caverns to the scrap heap of scientific thought."

"The technology the Old Dairy project has spent so much time and money concentrating on?"

"That'd be the one," confirmed Weil ironically.

"But you don't believe the idea is viable?"

Weil gave a cold laugh. "It's a dream, Inspector. Diatoms use atmospheric carbon. That's a world away from having them sequester captured carbon, let alone the logistics of how you would go about delivering it to them in the first place. My considered scientific opinion is that there is not a chance in hell anyone could ever make it work." She paused for a moment and Jejeune saw her eyes flicker towards the offices. "Look, I worked side by side with Philip. He was an extraordinary man, the kind of researcher who was convinced if he could only work hard enough for long enough, he could find his answers. But in this case, he would have been wrong."

"Can you think of any particular reason Mr. Wayland would take his new project to the university, over any of the other facilities competing for the capital funding prize?"

"Spoken like a true unromantic, Inspector. For love, of course. Xandria Grey must have convinced him that love would conquer all; *all*, in this case, meaning a severely restricted budget and vastly fewer resources. Love has such a way of blinding a person to the truth, doesn't it? Always assuming, of course, that Philip was told the truth in the first place."

Somehow, Catherine Weil never seemed quite able to suppress the mocking tone in her voice. But then, Jejeune suspected she didn't try overly hard most of the time, either. She took a final sip of her drink and looked around before issuing a deep sigh and depositing the cup in a nearby bin, shaking her head slightly. "Styrofoam cups, no recycling bins. We here at the Old Dairy project do intend to save the planet," she said wryly, "it's just that we want to make sure everyone else's house is in order before we start on our own." She gave him a lopsided smile. "Well, I suppose I'd better be getting back. We don't want Taleb docking my pay, do we? He can be quite vindictive when he wants to be."

Jejeune watched her go. *I'm sure he can,* thought Jejeune. But he doubted Taleb would be any match for Catherine Weil when it came to guile.

24

From across the room, Jejeune watched the people milling around his living room, engaging and disengaging from conversations with an ease that he had never quite mastered himself. This was usually Lindy's domain — the chat, the laughter, the casual intimacy of hands on forearms — but not tonight. However much she was putting into the evening, and it was plenty, Jejeune knew that inside she was no more carefree than he was.

She had hit Domenic with the news as soon as he had come through the front door, arms laden with bags of ice and a few other last-minute supplies she'd asked him to pick up. "He's still here."

In his alarm, Domenic had almost reacted aloud, until Lindy's eyes flickered their warning of the four people sitting near the fireplace in the living room.

"They arrived early," she whispered as she followed Domenic into the kitchen, ostensibly to help him unload his burden. "Damian was right by the door, ready to leave when the bell went. Ten seconds earlier and he would have flattened them on the path." She shook her head as she caught his expression. "It's not their fault, Dom. You know yourself you can never tell how long that trip up from London is going to take. It's just one of those things."

STEVE BURROWS

"Couldn't you have put them somewhere else, distracted them, until he got out?" Jejeune's hushed voice was tight with tension.

Lindy looked around the open-plan cottage, taking Domenic's gaze with her. "Where, exactly? Stick them in one of the bedrooms while I smuggle him down the hallway? I'm supposed to be hosting a dinner party, not a West End farce." Through the serving hatch, she saw one of her guests looking at her and flickered a smile back. "Be out in a minute," she called.

"He's in the guest room," she said, lowering her voice again. "I've locked it. Key's here." She patted the shelf above their heads. "'Renovations' is the story. Room's a mess, a bit unsafe even. Guests' coats go on our bed for tonight. Come on," she said, gathering up a tray of hastily arranged hors d'oeuvres, "let's pretend we're ready to host a party."

But Domenic wasn't doing much hosting. As the cottage had begun to fill up with guests, he had found himself gravitating more and more determinedly to a spot near the entrance to the hallway, where innocent wanderings toward the rooms beyond might be intercepted. True to her word, Lindy was doing her best to engage herself in the company of friends gathered to celebrate her nomination. And if she couldn't quite pull off the carefree buoyancy she usually managed at these events, even a Lindy with one foot on the brake was more than enough to entertain the masses. Domenic looked at her now as she made her circuit among the guests, greeting each with the sort of delight that would linger like a glow long after she had moved on. She had chosen her wardrobe with care: a simple thigh-length blue dress that followed her trim contours perfectly, highlighted with quietly elegant silver jewellery. The outfit, like the hair, which fell to her shoulders in a golden-blonde waterfall, and the restrained, carefully applied makeup, was designed to let Lindy shine through it, like a light behind a silken screen. *This is me*, it said, *on my very own night.*

160

Despite the underlying tension, it was all Domenic could do not to sigh with longing for her.

He watched her as she immersed herself in an animated, high-energy conversation with two of her colleagues from work. They were of a type— lithe, attractive young women with an air of easy, professional confidence, such as a position on the staff of Eric's prestigious magazine might confer. Jejeune suspected Eric had chosen carefully from the ranks when issuing the invitations for tonight's gathering. He would have wanted those who were genuinely pleased for Lindy's success; those least envious or threatened by it.

Jejeune watched as Quentin Senior approached the three women.

"Delightful gathering, Ms. Hey."

Lindy smiled her thanks down from her slightly elevated position. Her willingness to endure high-heels would have told all who knew her how much the evening meant to her, even if her other preparations hadn't. She introduced Senior to the two women from the magazine. Jen was Fashion, and Kate-Lynn was The Money.

"Makes me sound like I work in Accounting," said Kate-Lynn, with a smile. "I do the Business and Economy stories," she said, offering her hand.

"Despite all outward appearances of normality, Mr. Senior is actually a birder," said Lindy. "In fact, he's the one corrupting Eric."

"I supply the birds, and Eric supplies the pub lunches," said Senior, whose luxuriant white beard and impish smile seemed to have beguiled the women already.

"Blimey," said Kate-Lynn, "Eric must have taken a fair old shine to you. We're lucky if we can get him to put his hand in his pocket for a box of Eccles cakes for the staff meetings, aren't we, girls?"

"I take it neither of you are birders," said Senior.

"Not unless Vivienne Westwood is planning on coming out with a line of camouflage gear, right Jen?" asked Lindy. "And I'm afraid you'd have even less chance with Kate-Lynn."

"Well, a recent study did find the birding industry is worth $36 billion annually to the U.S. economy. That's billion with a *B*," said Senior, giving The Money a mischievous ivory-toothed grin.

"As opening lines go, Mr. Senior, you certainly know how to get a girl's attention. Would you mind if we had a little chat?" Kate-Lynn placed a gentle hand on Senior's arm and guided him away. Lindy watched them go. "Promise me you'll never get into birding, Jen," she said with a wistful smile. "Tell me you, at least, will stay with me, here in the real world."

With a start, Jejeune realized Colleen Shepherd had joined him. She was standing shoulder to shoulder with him now, staring out over the assembled partygoers.

"You could get a bit more involved, Domenic," she said good-naturedly. "After all, it's not you they're fawning all over for once. I would have thought you could have enjoyed this a bit, despite your well-known aversion to these things."

He smiled at his DCS, grateful that, for once, his ill-ease could be misinterpreted. "This was a good idea. Thank you." And despite the threat he felt throbbing like a physical force from the locked room behind him, he meant it.

Lindy's boss, Eric, ambled over to chat. Shepherd initially seemed pleased to see him approach, but it quickly became clear that he had come to talk about his new hobby with Jejeune. After two or three references to things she could only assume were birds, Shepherd made a valiant attempt to become engaged. "So you're enjoying it then?" she asked.

Eric nodded enthusiastically. "Tremendously. Though every time I think I'm making progress, I run into someone who reminds me just how much I still have to learn. That chap in the hide the other day, for example," he said, turning to Jejeune, "found us a wonderful bird. Terrific skills, even Quentin said as much. Canadian, wasn't he?"

"American, I think," said Jejeune. "I can't quite remember."

"*Can't remember*, Domenic?" Shepherd turned to Eric. "It must have been some rarity to fog the notoriously accurate recall of Domenic Jejeune."

"Franklin's Gull," said Eric with the novice's earnestness. "A great find for these parts. I've been very privileged to see one, so I'm told."

"Lindy was saying even the local Shakespeare society has complimented her on her article, Eric," said Jejeune, looking at Shepherd as if to suggest he was easing the conversation away from birding for her sake.

Eric nodded. "Indeed, she seems to have found support for her positions in a number of camps. Have you read the piece yourself, Domenic?"

"I'm hoping to," he said, "soon."

"Isn't there some controversy about whether Shakespeare even wrote *King Lear*?" asked Shepherd.

"Edward de Vere, you mean? Yes," said Eric dubiously, "I looked into that once. I'm fairly sure he didn't write it."

"I understand there are a lot of people who believe otherwise," said the DCS. She fixed him with a stare that suggested interest, rather than challenge. "What makes you so sure?"

"Well, mainly because he was already dead."

Shepherd offered a delighted laugh. "Well, I'd say that certainly introduces what we in our profession like to call an element of doubt."

Jejeune smiled. He had seen Colleen Shepherd at enough functions where enjoying herself came a distant second to trying to protect her career, or his. It was nice to see her in a genuinely carefree mood for once.

"De Vere died in 1604," continued Eric, "and it seems *King Lear* was first performed in 1607."

"Forgive me, Mr. Chappell, but it could have been written beforehand, surely? My experience," she indicated Jejeune, "our experience, compels me to point out that timelines can be manipulated in all sorts of ways."

"True," conceded Eric, as reasonably as before, "but if *King Lear* was written earlier, it wasn't by De Vere. It includes references to an eclipse that happened in 1605. And that, as I believe you people would say, seems to be the clinching argument."

"That's lawyers, actually. But it would undoubtedly be enough for me to inform the Crown Prosecutor that Mr. De Vere was no longer a suspect in this case."

In truth, Maik felt a pang of pity for his DCI. He had barely moved from the spot all evening, looking by turns uneasy and watchful, cradling a glass of red wine that must now be as warm as blood. Although policing could have a nasty effect on your social life, especially at the DCI's elevated level, surely he could still have formed a few closer friendships in these parts. From what Maik could gather, Jejeune seemed to rely exclusively on his girlfriend's acquaintances for his social interactions, resulting in nights like this, where she was comfortable with everybody and he was just that half-step removed. It came as something of a shock to Danny to realize he was probably the closest thing to a friend the DCI had in these parts. Even to him, their relationship seemed more akin to an iceberg bouncing off a granite wall every once in a while than to anything approaching genuine camaraderie.

And yet, even Lindy seemed a touch guarded tonight. Maik had seen her in full-flight at parties before, a whirlwind of unfettered joy and high spirits. Tonight she seemed apprehensive, reserved, as if the good time she was determined to have might all of a sudden be taken away. Perhaps she was uneasy being the centre of attention, but from what Maik knew of her, he would have thought she'd take this all in stride, have some fun with it.

She smiled uncertainly at Jejeune as she approached him. Maik saw in it some sort of veiled communication, but whatever it was, it was interrupted by Shepherd. "Lindy, Eric's been promising to tell us a King Lear story, but he was determined to wait until you could hear it, too."

Eric was at ease in his role of storyteller and took to his task immediately. "It concerns the time Garrick abandoned a performance of *King Lear* in Act Five, right at the climax of the play."

"But David Garrick is considered possibly the greatest Shakespearean actor of all time. Why on earth would he do that?"

"Apparently, some exceedingly wealthy patron had brought his dog to the performance — a huge Mastiff — and purchased a seat for it next his own, in the front row," said Eric. "The dog sat through the entire performance with its paws on the front rail, watching everything with the intensity of a drama critic."

"I can see how that might be a bit off-putting," said Lindy, "but surely Garrick had coped with worse. Those eighteenth-century theatres must have had all sorts of distractions. So what, he saw this dog and simply called off the performance?"

"Not at all." Eric eyed his audience, drawing them in with his skillfully measured pause. Even Maik edged closer. "Garrick manfully battled on, ignoring the beady-eyed stare as much as he could. But remember, those theatres used to get awfully warm, and by midway through the fifth act, the patron was so overheated he had to remove his wig. Having nowhere else to put it, he set it squarely on the dog's head. Garrick caught one glimpse of the bewigged pooch and he was done for. Rushed offstage and collapsed in a fit of giggles. Couldn't go back on for love nor money."

Danny Maik offered a rare, genuine smile. "I'm not much of a Shakespeare fan," he said, "but I would have paid a lot to see that performance. This *King Lear*, isn't that the one where the bodies all pile up at the end?"

Eric nodded. "About ten," he confirmed. "I don't think you could class it as one of the comedies."

Maik shook his head. "Can't say stories about people getting murdered would be my idea of entertainment. Still, it takes all sorts, I suppose."

But before anyone could concur, or otherwise, a loud crash at the far end of the hallway stunned the party into an ominous silence.

25

"What the hell was that?" asked Colleen Shepherd.

"Probably just one of Dom's feeders," said Lindy, over-casually. "Always getting blown over, aren't they, Dom? So, Eric, you were saying …"

"But it came from down the hall, surely?" said Shepherd, ignoring Lindy's efforts to kick-start the party again.

"Outside," confirmed Domenic. "This place is a bit of an echo chamber at times." He looked at Lindy for confirmation.

"It probably wouldn't hurt to check it out anyway," said Shepherd dubiously. "Budget numbers are tied to crime statistics, you know, Domenic. If we can get an attempted burglary collar, I might be able to buy you a new stapler."

It was pitched perfectly. Insistent enough to show Shepherd was taking it seriously, but with a tone that wouldn't even send a shimmer through the party atmosphere.

"I'll go and have a look around," said Danny Maik, setting his drink down on a side table.

Jejeune seemed to hesitate a moment before offering to accompany him. Maik declined the offer, but it became clear that it wasn't up for discussion, and with a quick glance back at Lindy, Jejeune joined him at the door.

"Go, we'll be fine," said Lindy, waving. "Eric's an ex-colonial.

He knows enough to shoot all us womenfolk if any rampaging hordes burst in and threaten our virtue."

Taking its cue from Lindy, the party picked up steam again as the men left, to the point that no one would have even noticed the worried looks she involuntarily flickered toward the hallway whenever she let her guard down.

Outside, an unnatural stillness seemed to hang in the darkness. From the surrounding fields came the hiss of silence. Apart from the muted sounds of the party in the house behind them, everything was quiet. Not a breath of wind disturbed the still night air. It was all well and good Lindy banging on about Dom's bird feeders getting blown over, but this night was as tranquil as any that Maik could remember out here on the coast. Whatever it was that had knocked something over out here, it wasn't the wind.

The sergeant moved stealthily along the side of the cottage, pressed in to the narrow shadow cast by the lights of the party inside. Jejeune followed closely behind, moving with the same silence, even if, it seemed to Maik, not at all the same caution. At the corner of the building, Maik crouched lower and paused, rocking slightly, steadying himself for an entry that was quiet, fast and low. He motioned with a hand for Jejeune to stay back, but by the time he had completed his spin around onto the rear porch of the house, his DCI was already on his way round.

Nothing. Maik looked out over the porch railing. The sea was out there, he knew, just beyond the cliff edge. But there was no moon tonight, and the dull black sky seemed to hunker low, so he could not see any horizon line, or even any light reflected from the dark water. From far below came the faint sound of the sea lapping against the shore. Still, not even the lightest of breezes disturbed the night air. Maik eased himself back from the railing and looked around the porch. Whatever had fractured the silence out here had gone now, leaving just a ringing emptiness.

He slowly let out a breath. "I don't see that feeder that fell over," he said. "These all look okay to me."

"Something else, then. One of Lindy's plant pots, perhaps. A passing animal ..." said Jejeune from behind him. "It's hard to tell in the dark. I'll have a look around in the morning."

"Unless you want to switch the porch light on now," suggested Maik. In the darkness, he couldn't see his DCI's face. But he could hear a voice untroubled by the same tension he had felt. Maik turned to face the cottage, all greyness and shadows, and froze for a moment. Jejeune was behind him and Maik couldn't tell which direction he was facing, but he had the impression the DCI had half-turned away from the sea, and had been looking back at the house, too, in the same direction he was. Above him, the two square glass eyes of the rear windows, somehow darker than the rest of the house, stared out blindly over the sea. The far one was the kitchen, he knew. This one? He stared at it and waited. Waited.

From the front of the house, faint strains of music drifted toward them, and now and again a voice was raised in laughter. "Time we went back in, I suppose," said Jejeune. But he seemed to be waiting, too, just that extra heartbeat, until Maik could drag himself away from staring at the window to join him. The two men made their way along the side of the house to the front door, and the party. Neither found anything worth saying on the way back.

"False alarm," said Jejeune as they came back in to the room, seeking out Lindy's face in particular to offer his reassuring smile.

"Glad to hear it," said Eric heartily. "Still, it never hurts to check."

To Maik's eye, Lindy's efforts to enter the party spirit had gone into overdrive while they were away. She was a whirlwind now, circulating, connecting, and pouring her bubbly personality into every corner of the cosy living room.

As the people began to break off from the crowd in small knots again, Shepherd drifted over.

"Everything all right out there?"

No. But yes. "There was nobody prowling around," said Maik simply. "It looks like the DCI is going to have to wait for that new stapler, after all."

Shepherd eyed him uncertainly. "Then I suggest you pick up your drink and get back into the party spirit. One senior detective looking ill at ease in social situations is quite enough, thank you very much. We don't want people thinking it's a departmental directive, do we?" She offered him a smile and went to rejoin a small group where Eric's booming laugh suggested he was still holding court.

Danny would do what he could. But looking at them now, both Jejeune and Lindy seemed to carry a kind of guarded relief that told him he may not have been wrong. In the darkened window of that room from the porch, that guest bedroom, Maik fancied he had seen, just for the briefest of moments, a faint flash of light. He had waited, but it hadn't reappeared, and in the darkness and shadows at the back of the house, there was no way to be certain. Besides, Maik was all but sure Inspector Jejeune had been looking directly at the window at the time, too. And if one of the most observant men Maik had ever known chose not to comment on anything he might have seen, then Danny Maik wouldn't either — not tonight, anyway.

26

Lindy and Domenic stood together in the doorway of the cottage, silhouetted against the lights of the living room. They watched as the last of the cars departed, the tail lights disappearing down the lane until they were finally swallowed up by the night. She turned to him and linked her hands behind his neck, stretching up to give him a kiss. "We can't do this again. I feel like I have been through a tumble dryer." She looked at him seriously. "I mean it, Dom. No more visitors while he's still here. I don't think my nerves could take it."

She seemed to be expecting opposition from Jejeune, though he couldn't imagine why. Surely she knew he had been every bit as much on edge throughout the evening. Lindy closed the door with her foot and started to move toward the kitchen. "Well, I suppose we'd better let the cat out of the bag," she said.

"You go on to bed," said Domenic. "You must be exhausted. I'll tell Damian you'll see him in the morning."

Lindy didn't argue, and padded away down the hall to their bedroom. Domenic took the guest room key from the kitchen shelf and went along the hallway. When he opened the door, Damian was sitting on the bed, propped up against the headboard with his knees drawn up to his chest. They were supporting a book, which he was reading by penlight.

"What did Mom tell you about that?" said Domenic, flicking on the light. "You'll ruin your eyesight."

Damian set aside the book: *King Lear*. He noticed his brother's look. "It was on the desk," he said. "It's been a while, so I thought I'd give it another go." He pulled a face and got off the bed. He headed for a whisky bottle on a nearby table, holding it by the neck and waving it at his brother. Domenic nodded, and Damian grabbed a second glass from a shelf and blew the dust from it before pouring two healthy shots.

Domenic picked up the book and set it on the top of an untidy pile teetering on the desk.

"I was going to ask you about that," said Damian. "Are you building a tower?"

"Lindy stacks them up like this to encourage me to re-shelve them, even though half the time I haven't finished with them. She thinks if she piles them up on the desk like this, eventually I'll get tired of the mess and cave in."

"It's obvious you haven't told her about your bedroom when you were a kid," said Damian. "Don't worry; I'll put them away in the morning for you."

"Don't do that, whatever you do," said Domenic in mock alarm. "I think she's only a couple of books away from her own breaking point. Any day now she's going to come in here and do it herself because she can't stand it any longer."

Damian handed his brother a glass and sat back down on the bed. "I never did get these head games that partners play," he said. "Maybe that's why I've never been in a long-term relationship myself."

"Could be," agreed Domenic. "Then again, it could just be because you're ugly and not very bright." He gave his brother a wan smile and settled in the room's only armchair.

"Good party?" asked Damian.

"Tiring. I had to take a walk outside at one point, too." He looked at his brother through the amber liquid in his glass.

"Yeah, I reached for the bottle and knocked the table over in the dark. Saved the English single malt though," he said with a grin. "I haven't had this before. It's pretty good."

And there, in a nutshell, was his relationship with Damian, thought Domenic. No enquiry as to whether his actions had caused a problem for his younger brother, because it simply didn't matter to Damian. Something had happened, Domenic had cleared it up, and Damian was ready to move on. *Ever it was, and ever more will it be*, thought Domenic wearily.

"That guy Eric sounded like he was enjoying himself. That's some laugh he has on him."

Domenic nodded his agreement. "Can you imagine what it must be like to be him just now, getting into birding for the first time? To see all those new birds, to get that feeling, that rush," he said.

"That's the thing, Dom. For me, that's how it is, still. Every time I see something special — a Painted Bunting, a Scissor-tailed Flycatcher — I get that same buzz I felt the first time I saw one."

Domenic knew it was true. He had seen it in his brother with the Franklin's Gull at Cley. Even watching the Raven's barrel roll at Dunnet Head; his wide-eyed enthusiasm had been every bit as much in evidence as the boy he was sharing it with.

Damian's face softened with sadness. "You probably think it's the big things I miss, being able to travel wherever I want, walk down the street without looking over my shoulder. But really, it's nights like tonight I miss the most, having friends over, being able to tell them the truth about who you are and what you do."

The truth? Domenic had spent most of the evening avoiding precisely that. But he let the comment pass. He knew what Damian meant. They sat for a few moments, sipping their drinks, thinking their thoughts.

Damian drained his glass and rose from the bed. "Another?"

Domenic nodded. "How did you manage to get the bottle, anyway?"

"Lindy brought it in for me when she locked the door." He poured the drinks and brought one over to Domenic, standing over him. He smiled. "I think I'm in love with your girlfriend, Domino."

Domenic smiled back. "She's easy to love."

"High maintenance, though, I'm betting."

"An entire department." He looked at his brother. "I'm guessing she's been making subtle inquiries about our childhood?"

Damian nodded, "Subtle, like an open-pit mining operation, you mean?"

"It's okay. She's just trying to build up a picture for herself."

"I read her article," said Damian. "She's a smart lady. I can see how she might have some problems with an arrangement where the older male child had claim to everything, though." He looked up at Dom. "Can you imagine if it still worked like that? All this would be mine." Glass in hand, he spread his arms to embrace the vast expanse of this three-metre-square bedroom.

"Lindy, too, I suppose," said Domenic.

"I'm not sure she'd take kindly to being classified as chattel. And I certainly wouldn't want to be the one to break it to her." Damian suddenly became serious and looked at his brother with an earnestness Domenic hadn't seen for a long time. "I love what you have here; your career, this cottage, Lindy. Live it well, Domenic. For both of us."

Domenic wondered if it was the whisky causing Damian's sudden lurches between moods. He sensed that it was close, the time when his older brother would be able to tell him the reason he had come, sought out Domenic with the siren call of that bird guide. *Close, but here yet?* He saw the dark square of the window over Damian's shoulder. Outside it was as still and quiet as before. In the house, too, nothing moved. The ticking of a distant clock drifted down the hallway, but otherwise there was silence.

"You have to tell her, Domenic," said Damian quietly. "She needs to know about the person she has staying in her house."

"Don't, Damian."

"You can't let it go any longer."

"I'll, it'll be …"

"It'll be what? It'll be fine? It'll be taken care of? Or it'll be the end of your relationship with her, if she finds out what her boyfriend's brother has done?"

"Stop, Damian. Okay. Just … I'll deal with it."

"Just be sure you do, little brother. I've messed up enough people's lives already. I don't want any more sorrow on my conscience." A wave of melancholy seemed to sweep over him.

"Why did you come here, Damian?"

Damian looked up from the bed and smiled, greeting the question like an old friend he had been waiting to arrive. "Simple, Domino," he said. "You're the only person I know who might be able to keep me alive."

He gave his brother a lazy smile. "Just words, Dom. I'm fine. Really. It's late. Get some sleep. We'll talk later."

Domenic had stepped into the hallway before he paused and looked back. But Damian was already engrossed in *King Lear* again. He didn't look up.

27

Colleen Shepherd was waiting in the car park of the police station, leaning against one of the patrol cars when Domenic wheeled the Range Rover in. He looked at her curiously, and then noticed her white cross-trainers.

"Fancy a walk, Domenic? Do you good after all those full Scottish breakfasts. I'll bet it's been a while since you had a nice stroll in the sunshine."

Except strolls didn't usually involve elaborate stopwatches, like the one Shepherd was now withdrawing from her pocket, as she made her way to the starting line of the car park entrance. She held an arm aloft and dropped it like a falling axe, setting off along the street at a brisk pace. Jejeune caught up to her, and they walked side by side in silence for a few moments, shuffling into a comfortable rhythm. The weak sunshine bathed the streets in a gentle light, giving a soothing, almost ballet-like quality to the comings and goings of the people. Jejeune envied them their anodyne tasks, their daily chores, while his own life seemed to be constantly lurching from one potential catastrophe to another. He felt so weighed down by all he had already faced, all he still had to face. The last thing he needed today was a speed-walk through the streets of Saltmarsh. He redoubled his efforts to keep up with Shepherd, who showed no sign of slackening her pace.

"No new leads among the protesters, I understand," she said, as he came alongside. "Though I'm not sure I'm quite ready to write them off just yet."

"Wayland's new plan would allow for carbon storage without the need for offshore pipes or massive underground storage caverns," said Jejeune. "Okay, it involves pumping large amounts of iron into the sea to induce the algal growth in the first place, but I would have thought the protesters would have found that a far more acceptable solution than destroying the coastline."

Shepherd nodded to herself. "If they understood the difference. It's still carbon capture and storage, and it's still a hot-button topic out here. It may be another approach, but truly, when have you ever heard of a mob doing nuance, Domenic? As lead researcher at the Old Dairy, Wayland was the poster child for all they are protesting about. Old hatreds don't always die with a change in the facts."

Shepherd condescended to look each way before stepping off the curb to cross the cobbled high street, though in truth, Jejeune doubted it would have made very much difference whether there was any traffic coming or not, such was the DCS's determination to maintain her steady pace. While he wasn't exactly struggling to keep up with her, he found himself hoping this would be over soon.

"So if not the protesters, where do we go with this?" She seemed to have mastered the art of locking on sideways eye contact while maintaining her pace.

"When Catherine Weil spoke to me, she did everything she could to put Abrar el-Taleb on our radar," said Jejeune. "She couldn't have laid out his potential motives any more clearly with a process chart."

"Does she have any particular reason for not liking the man?"

"He has a job she would like for herself."

He steeled himself for the response he knew would be coming. Shepherd cast him a withering sidelong glance, barely managing to keep up her pace as she did so, but her reaction was far more sanguine than he had been anticipating. Perhaps this exercise regimen was having an effect on the DCS's temperament, too.

"And what, you think she's willing to provide Prince Yousef with a false alibi on the premise that once we railroad the hapless Mr. el-Taleb into twenty years at her majesty's pleasure, she'll get a promotion? Really, Domenic, even for you, that's a bit weak."

Jejeune made an extra effort to stay alongside the DCS. His point needed to be made on an equal footing, not from half a step behind. "Weil's testimony is the only thing that stops us from saying Wayland was already dead by, say, 6:30, long before the prince ever took off in his helicopter."

"But do we have a *why* in all this, Domenic? Why would Prince Yousef want Philip Wayland dead in the first place? I'm not even prepared to accept el-Taleb as a suspect just yet, but there's a hell of a lot stronger case to be made for him than for Prince Yousef. Let me tell you where I see you heading with all this, shall I? Taking el-Taleb out of the equation and substituting the prince instead, it goes something like this: Wayland abandons the project, and this reflects very badly on the man who is supposed to be running things at the Old Dairy, particularly in the eyes of his brother. Prince Yousef, therefore, decides to dispatch Wayland, almost a year after the fact, to avenge his personal humiliation." Without breaking stride, Shepherd called upon one of her special expressions to convey her contempt with an eloquence no words could match. "Revenge for dishonour? It's all a bit archaic, isn't it? Not to mention it is leading us down some very dubious us-and-them cultural paths. Prince Yousef is a modern, sophisticated man, Oxbridge-educated. The idea is more than offensive, Domenic. It's downright insulting."

Jejeune didn't say anything. He had all but made the left-hand turn back to the station when he realized to his dismay that Shepherd was continuing on, instead, heading down toward the waterfront. Returning to the station via this route was going to involve considerably more strolling than he had bargained for.

The walk along the quayside was one Jejeune had often enjoyed with Lindy. But they usually did it at less than a quarter of this pace. The clanking of lanyard rings and the gentle flapping of canvas in the breeze mingled with the calls of wheeling Herring Gulls, filling the air with the music of the seaside. Small encampments of commerce were emerging on the quay; cafés setting up for lunch, stores putting out their wares. A pair of early browsers stopped suddenly in front of them, forcing them to walk around. The tourist season was beginning to build, and although Saltmarsh didn't see nearly the numbers of other places up and down the coast, in another month this waterfront area would be too densely packed to allow the DCS to maintain a steady pace along here, regardless of how much determination she showed. The thought gave Jejeune a glimmer of guilty satisfaction. The Boatman's Arms appeared on the horizon.

"They should be open by now," said Jejeune casually. "Perhaps we would be better discussing this over a drink."

"Why not. We can have a pie while we're at it." Shepherd shot him a look of exasperation. "The idea is a sustained period of exercise, Domenic, though this regimen would undoubtedly be a lot more popular if you could add a couple of glasses of Chardonnay in at the halfway point." She shook her head. "We'll be on the home stretch soon, but if you feel you can't keep up, you can have a rest, and I'll wait for you at the station."

The gauntlet thrown down, they crossed another street without breaking stride and turned a corner. Jejeune welcomed the cool shadows that lay behind the high walls of a row of former maritime warehouses, long ago converted into small stalls and waterfront apartments. A greengrocer was bent over a chalkboard, listing today's specials — samphire, chard, onions — all at prices so low it was hard to see how anybody could make a profit from their sale. Shepherd let her look linger for a long time on the signboard as they passed.

"The al-Haladins move in a world mere mortals like you and I can't even imagine, Domenic. Look at these birds, for example, these Gyrfalcons. I understand they're worth tens of thousands of pounds each, and the Crown Prince has, what, fourteen of them, standing by waiting, in case he might just find the time to fly them during the couple of visits a year he makes to the U.K.? Now, does all their money put them above the law? Of course not. But it certainly puts them above the day-to-day workings of police divisions out in the wilds of north Norfolk. Especially when we have no evidence — none whatsoever — that they have been involved in anything illegal." She managed another full-pace sidelong glance. "Unless there's something you're not telling me? Something that brings us closer to a genuine motive for Prince Yousef to kill Philip Wayland?"

Was there? Did Philip Wayland's new research, as incomplete as it was, pose enough of a threat to the Old Dairy project to warrant killing him? A billion pounds in prize money was at stake. Even Emirati royalty sat up and took notice of sums like that. But Jejeune had nothing yet, nothing he could present to DCS Shepherd. He knew he was only going to get one chance when the time came, one grudging agreement to arrange an interview with the prince. He needed to have everything in place before he made his final appeal. And he was a long way from that yet. A very long way indeed.

They returned to the station in silence. Shepherd skipped up to the top step of the entrance and paused to look down on Jejeune, who was leaning against the iron railing, trying to draw as much breath into his lungs as possible without appearing to breathe heavily.

"Prince Yousef is off-limits, Domenic. I'm not going to pretend I'm hiding behind some higher directive here. This is coming from me. I'm sure I don't need to remind you that avoiding any diplomatic incident here has to be our number one priority."

Jejeune looked up at her. He felt it might be slightly churlish to point out that, in a murder inquiry, the number one priority was usually solving the case. But as he watched her disappear through the door, he wondered if DCS Shepherd had, in fact, meant exactly what she'd said.

28

There was no doubt in Maik's mind that the DCI had been set on going out to the Old Dairy again this morning, despite Shepherd's objections. Jejeune felt there was something there. Maik could sense it in his DCI's attitude, a restlessness that usually signalled he was closing in on something. But the news awaiting Jejeune on his arrival at the station had changed all that. Prince Yousef had agreed to a meeting. Jejeune and Maik were to go to the Palm Court Hotel tomorrow at noon, where they could speak to him over lunch. As welcome as this response to his earlier request was, it left Jejeune searching for a new direction to channel his nervous energy while they waited for their audience. He had settled on the university.

The fact that there was no genuine reason Maik could see for them to be heading out there seemed to make the prospect of visiting a soul-destroying building, where only the inconsolable sadness of Xandria Grey awaited them, even less appealing. In response, Maik had chosen The Temptations to raise his spirits. *I Can't Get Next to You* was upbeat enough to brighten anybody's mood, and with his preoccupied DCI staring obliviously out the Mini's window at the high hedgerows blurring past, Danny even treated himself to a little extra volume.

"Tell me, Sergeant," said Jejeune without taking his eyes from the fields, "you've been inside that Gyrfalcon facility at the Old Dairy. How would you describe it?"

Maik considered the question for a moment. "Not what I expected, to be honest. It was quite a bit larger, and brighter. The cages went from floor to ceiling."

Jejeune seemed to think about Maik's answer for a moment. "So the Gyrfalcons had a lot of room. You wouldn't say they were cooped up?"

Maik shook his head.

"Your report said Darla thought it was her father who had broken in, but I don't think he has ever been in there. He doesn't seem to know the conditions the birds are kept in. Like a lot of uninformed objectors, he just assumes the worst."

A momentary cloud passed in front of the sun, sending a dappled shadow over the land. "She's scared of something, that girl," said Maik. "The break-in, and the accident with that bird, they've got her shaken-up. You don't think it's connected. This business at the Gyrfalcon facility and Wayland's murder?"

"It's hard to see how," said Jejeune. "Unless Xandria Grey mentioned any interest Wayland might have had in Gyrfalcons?" He looked across at Maik.

"I don't remember it coming up in conversation," said Maik drily. "Perhaps you can ask her yourself when we get there."

"Perhaps," said Jejeune. "Oh, and Sergeant, if you are going to play that old music all the time, I wonder if we could dial down just a little on the volume."

When the detectives entered the room, Xandria Grey looked up from behind a desk piled high with papers, though to Jejeune's eye, the workload was not much diminished from the last time they were here. Perhaps she was using the activity as a shield, a place of refuge from her sorrow. She was not achieving anything, likely not even trying to, but the simple act of being here, in this office, with its panacea of familiar tasks and duties, was like a blanket that she could gather about her, as a barrier against the awful reality of the world outside. Jejeune wondered if he could ever draw such solace from his own work? In truth, he had never had much need to find out. Though he sometimes tired of hearing what a charmed life he led, blessed, as his brother and others kept reminding him, he knew, too, there was an element of truth to the claims. Only once had the world wounded him beyond healing, dealt him an unbearable sadness. And where did he go when those memories gathered and threatened to engulf him? Where did he seek his escape from the desolation that crept in, so frequently in those early days, and now, perhaps not so often, but still, at times, with devastating intensity? To wild open spaces; to wind-ragged heathlands where he might see a Kestrel balancing on the updrafts, or to blustery coastlines, where gulls rode onshore breezes and issued their keening cries. To woods, alive with birdsong, or wetlands with their stillness and their stealth. To places where he would find birds to snatch away his gathering despair and pour their light into the spaces that remained, filling him with hope again, reminding him of the pleasures that life could hold. But never work. He never turned to the business of murder and motives for his solace. His police career, Domenic Jejeune knew, would never offer him that.

"News?" asked Grey, half-hopefully. But there was a guardedness to her optimism, as if even news of progress might bring more pain.

Jejeune shook his head regretfully. "More questions, I'm afraid," he said, "about Mr. Wayland's work. The idea of using phytoplankton to sequester captured carbon, it's attractive to climate control experts on a number of levels, I imagine."

Grey nodded. "Cost, for one. And it's far less environmentally invasive. Most important to Philip, though, was that, once established, it would be an easy technology to export to other parts of the world, where the need to control carbon emissions is going to be even greater than in the West."

Grey's face was drawn and ashen, like someone who hadn't been out in the daylight in a long time. Jejeune had seen the same pallor in prisoners. But then, he thought, this woman, too, was being held captive by something.

"I'm sure if you have spent any time with Catherine Weil, you will realize she is utterly convinced none of this can ever work," said Grey frankly. "Here, Philip found a team of believers, people who had faith in him, a group who shared his belief and his optimism that he could achieve what he set out to."

Jejeune was still standing by the window, but now he crossed to the far side of the office, trailing a hand over a row of journals arranged on a low bureau. Not a complete walkabout, but enough to show he was looking for a way to approach a difficult topic. Jejeune looked across at the sergeant. But Maik's expression suggested he had already brought his share of pain to Xandria Grey. He would leave it to his DCI to bring her any more.

"It's been alleged that Mr. Wayland felt personal morality shouldn't necessarily get in the way of looking for answers."

Grey's face darkened with anger. "What a truly ugly thing to imply," she said with dangerous control. "I would have expected more, even from Catherine Weil. I know Philip had a high regard for Catherine, and until now, I have always tried to see the best in her, even if, frankly, I did always feel she was largely riding on Philip's coattails. The work she's pursuing up there, it's all based on studies that Philip set in motion before he left, you know that?"

"But did Mr. Wayland ever suggest anything like that to you? That the ends may have justified the means, if it served the interests of his wider research?"

Jejeune's face showed no expression. It hadn't been his most subtle approach, but he didn't have the time, or perhaps even the will, to couch things in softer terms these days, not even to a woman who had so recently lost the man she loved.

Grey paused for a long moment, as if deciding something, and took a deep breath before answering. "Philip believed that with the fates of millions of people quite literally at stake, it was wrong to hold a competition that encouraged corporate secrecy, when really a global problem is going to require global co-operation. Hoarding valuable research data so your competitors can't get to them is not what we were brought up to believe scientific research was all about."

Jejeune thought for a moment, taking in the information. "I wonder, the material Mr. Wayland marked with his tabs?"

Grey managed a brave smile. "His *DNA* markers?"

"Yes. Were there any plans here at the university to do the research he needed to get that data?"

Grey shifted her body slightly, and Jejeune recognized the unspoken language of evasion. He continued to stare at her, waiting patiently for a response.

"The start-up costs for a new data-gathering project are often where the major expenses lie," she said finally. "These projects would all be major undertakings, any one of them alone quite possibly beyond the resources of the department." She paused for a moment. "You know, I've often wondered what it must be like for the people who work at the Old Dairy. It must be strange to work for an organization for which money is literally no barrier. What would it be like to operate in a climate like that, I wonder? Absolute freedom from all sorts of restraints that the rest of us have to deal with. Would it still be possible to make moral decisions under those conditions, responsible decisions, which put the planet first? Or would you have a different perspective?"

Jejeune suspected Grey wasn't looking for an answer from him. Which was okay, because at that moment he wasn't sure he had one.

"If I needed to review the material in the vaults," said Jejeune, his tone softer now than at any time during the interview, "take it away for a few days, I presume that wouldn't be a problem? It wouldn't interrupt any of the work you are doing at the moment?"

She nodded faintly. "I'll clear it with the oversight committee. Just let me know when."

Jejeune smiled his thanks. And with that, the two detectives left Xandria Grey to the quiet world of her grief.

"I might as well tell you, sir," said Maik as they made their way along the bland corridor toward the car park, "this business with the tabs. I'm not sure that makes much sense to me. *ND, DNA*. Whether there was no research done, or it had been done but the results weren't available, doesn't it amount to pretty much the same thing?"

Jejeune paused for a moment. "No, Sergeant, I don't believe it does. But perhaps the bigger question is how Wayland could be so sure that the research had already been done, and even more interestingly, how he could know the data it produced would be relevant to his own studies."

Maik allowed himself a smile of understanding, finally. "Because he was there when they were doing it, you mean? The data he needed comes from the research he was involved in at the Old Dairy before he left."

It was Jejeune's turn to smile. "I think Wayland specifically used that *DNA* designation for data he knew already existed at the Old Dairy. And much of it, possibly all of it, would have been extremely relevant to his current studies. Recent, and from exactly the same stretch of coastline he was studying now. It would have met his needs perfectly, I would imagine."

"But all that data is under lock and key, protected by who knows how many layers of cyber security. Given el-Taleb's hostility towards him for leaving the project high and dry when he walked away, Wayland must have known he was never going to release any of that data to him."

Jejeune stopped. In the washed out fluorescent light of the corridor, Jejeune's skin took on the same pallid colour as Xandria Grey's. But there was a lot more brightness in his eyes. "Yes, Sergeant," he said. "I'm fairly sure he did."

29

The Palm Court was the kind of place most people in Saltmarsh had been to once or twice. It was a favoured destination for wedding receptions and corporate functions, and over its century and a half of existence, its elegant dining room had witnessed all manner of marriage proposals, birthday celebrations, and heartfelt apologies. But that was in the public section. Towards the back was the Palm Court's private wing. And the great unwashed of Saltmarsh didn't get to venture down here on their once-in-a-decade visits. The word *exclusive* on the Palm Court's brochure was used in the literal sense.

The wing had its own private entrance and it was from the interlocking-brick forecourt that Jejeune now surveyed the formidable structure. A semicircular portico shielded the extravagant double doors, and above it a grey block of ivy-clad granite soared up four storeys. The facade was flanked by twin turrets punctured with small, discreet windows. A colony of house sparrows had taken up residence in the ivy and Jejeune was watching their constant movements and interactions with interest when he heard footsteps behind him. He turned to find Maik, looking neat and well-presented. Clearly, the opportunity to no longer be *excluded* from the Palm Court's private wing was a powerful draw even for the sergeant.

"Ever been in the presence of royalty before?" asked Jejeune.

Maik shook his head. "The only prince I know is that Nigerian one on the internet who's having trouble claiming his fortune."

"I don't think this one has had any such problems," said Jejeune. He tugged at the collar of the pale blue shirt he was wearing and loosened the knot of the equally new tie that Lindy had insisted would be a perfect match.

"You obviously can't go to meet a prince wearing that rubbish you usually knock around in," she had told him. "He'll think you've come to do the flower beds."

Damian had watched with unabashed delight from an armchair, offering comments that could best be described as unflattering, as Lindy unpacked a bag from the local tailor's onto the living room couch and paraded Dom through a series of shirt-and-tie combinations before settling on this one. Uncomfortable at the memory, or perhaps the shirt collar itself, Jejeune gave it one final tug and stepped to the door.

The carpet felt like a cushion of air beneath the detectives' feet as they made their way into the Grand Hall. The room shared the trait of all truly great things down through the ages: it didn't try too hard to impress. Instead of overwhelming visitors, the Grand Hall let them come to its elegance, to discover it, to marvel in each small detail as it unfurled: the perfectly formed finial on the end of a curtain rod; the delicate, immaculate swirled plaster patterns on the ceiling. Sensation built on sensation in a subtle procession until both men, in their own way, came to the gradual realization that they had been utterly seduced by the room's splendour.

"I could get used to this," said Maik. "If I get that raise the DCS is always talking about."

Either the hotel staff or the prince's own advance team had been hard at work preparing the room for his arrival. The walls had been draped in rich fabrics, brocades of exotic patterns bearing an elaborate medallion at the centre, and along one side of the room was a long table covered in a dazzling white cloth. On it was an array of gleaming silver platters. Jejeune could see and smell the assortment of exotic Middle Eastern delicacies. At the far end of the room, light flooded in through a majestic picture window that soared three storeys and provided a view of the hotel's immaculately tended gardens beyond. In front of the window was a table of perhaps the same length as the buffet. It was adorned with numerous silver centrepieces and lavish arrangements of fresh flowers, no doubt from the gardens outside. There was only a single place setting, and at it sat Prince Yousef. When he noticed that the detectives had arrived, he rose to come around the table to meet them. From nearby, two men in suits watched carefully but made no move to approach.

The prince was taller than Jejeune had expected, which meant, he realized, that his brother, the Crown Prince, must be very tall indeed. Yousef wore an expensively tailored pearl-grey suit with a lilac handkerchief of the same material as his tie protruding from the breast pocket of his jacket. In his lapel was a tiny red carnation. At first sight, he might have been mistaken for a theatre manager, or a sales clerk in a high-end jewellery store. But there was a lean intensity to his features, and an assured self-confidence about his movements that suggested the concerns of others would never be this man's first priority. A strong waft of cologne reached the detectives like an advance party for the man himself.

"It is fortunate I find myself in Saltmarsh today," he said, making no move to offer a handshake. "You have been asking to speak with me. Now this may happen." He swept an elegant hand toward the buffet table. "But first, you may eat, if you wish." Yousef's courtesy had a brittle quality to it, as if it was a lesson learned somewhere, but not quite remembered. He called over one of the suited men and leaned in to murmur something into his ear. There was no consideration for his guests, no apology for interrupting their conversation.

Neither Jejeune nor Maik felt inclined to break off the meeting to visit the buffet table, so they remained resolutely standing before the prince, waiting for him to finish his covert conversation. Jejeune regarded Yousef carefully. His skin shone with a glow the detective had not seen before, as if it had been polished, almost, burnished to this smooth, perfect shine. If there was a treatment someone could use to produce this effect, Lindy would likely know what it was. Jejeune didn't particularly want to undergo the procedure himself, but he would be interested to find out just what could cause such impressive results.

"I trust the Crown Prince and yourself can appreciate the situation with the protesters at the compound was not something we could have anticipated," said Jejeune, when Yousef finally turned his attention back to the two detectives.

The prince's dark eyes seemed to glitter with a cruel amusement as he dismissed the idea with a brief brush of his hand. It was clear that the incident was not the reason Jejeune's request for a meeting had finally been granted. Nevertheless, Jejeune couldn't shake the impression that there was some reason he had been summoned here today.

Another wave of cologne drifted toward the two detectives as the prince swept his gaze over the detectives once more. "You have asked repeatedly to speak with me. You have questions you wish to ask?"

There was no warmth to the man, thought Jejeune. In fact, there was very little of a man, of a person, at all, in Prince Yousef. This was a product, he thought, a manufactured artifact. Second prince, redundant, a nothingness. He had rarely seen such vacancy in a person. But it was not benign. Such a disconnection from humanness could be dangerous. It would disconnect you, too, from the normal constraints; polite behaviour, empathy, impulse control.

The man in the suit returned and leaned in to whisper something to the prince. He nodded, and as Jejeune watched, he realized what it was that had been bothering him about this scenario. From his understanding of the infrastructure at the Old Dairy, he would have put this role of personal confidante down as el-Taleb's.

"I don't see Mr. el-Taleb here today," he said casually.

"He has remained at the compound."

Jejeune nodded in understanding. "His role as project manager must be very demanding."

The prince nodded economically. "The project makes many demands of us all. Mr. el-Taleb is but one functionary among many. It is unwise for an employer to give too much responsibility to any one employee." Yousef touched his immaculately manicured moustache briefly, but whether it was some sort of confiding gesture or an unrelated reflex, Jejeune couldn't tell.

"Would notifying the authorities of the Crown Prince's visit be among Mr. el-Taleb's duties, I wonder? We usually receive notification well in advance, you see, but this time, we only received word at the last minute."

"The visit was arranged at short notice," said Yousef flatly. "Sometimes it is so; the Crown Prince's schedule is not always easy to predict. But it is not the duties of Abrar el-Taleb that you have come here to discuss today." The prince's delivery made the comment a statement, rather than a question.

"I was wondering what you thought of Philip Wayland's departure to work on a new project at the university," said Jejeune. Behind him, Maik suppressed a nod of approval. Plenty there to tempt an unguarded answer — the departure, the project, the university. Yousef settled on the middle point. "I cannot speak of this project. I know nothing of it. I was not given the chance to consider it."

"But you would agree the loss of Philip Wayland was a major blow?" Again, the DCI had provided an invitation for the prince to interpret the question as he wished; personally, in terms of the project, or as a wider philosophy about the death of a human being. Once again, Yousef's choice might tell Jejeune far more than his answer. The DCI seemed to be returning to top form, thought Danny. And about time, too.

"Philip Wayland was an intelligent man," said Yousef, "but perhaps not as intelligent as he believed."

"Still, at least now with the Crown Prince here, you'll be able to address some of the challenges caused by his departure," said Jejeune brightly.

Yousef let his stare linger on Jejeune for a moment. "It is my responsibility to deal with the challenges the project offers," he said coldly. "The Crown Prince visits to receive updates only."

"I see," said Jejeune. And watching from the sidelines, Danny Maik had the distinct impression that DCI Jejeune did. Or at least he was beginning to. Maik got the feeling it might be a good time to lead the conversation off in another direction.

"Helicopter pilots I know tell me the crosswinds can be a bit tricky in these parts, but I was there when you flew in. You didn't seem to have any trouble."

The prince tilted his head slightly in appreciation of Maik's comment. "Flying is my great passion, and this landscape from the air …" He touched the fingertips of one hand together, but seemed to check himself from getting drawn too deeply into his subject. "But I have many duties I must attend to, and I am sure, you too, have many other people you need to interview."

As dismissals went, it was not the most abrupt the detectives had ever received. But it carried a finality that few others had before.

Thinking about it later, Maik realized the panic hadn't erupted suddenly, as it might after an explosion or gunfire. It was a

slow-building crescendo of small moments. Phones simultaneously withdrawn at silent signals, puzzled looks, followed by
understanding, then alarm. Movements across the room, slow,
hesitant at first, and then urgent, to and from, between people,
quiet murmurings, insistent gestures. And then, a man, perhaps
the same one who had approached the prince earlier, speaking
urgently in his native tongue, showing the prince something
on his smartphone. And the realization, immediately from
the prince and then radiating outward, as if everyone in the
room, except for the two police officers, got the message at the
same time. They were all allowed to believe it now, allowed to
respond. It was real, it had happened, was happening, still.

The prince gestured toward Jejeune and the man brought
over a phone with a large screen. It showed a field, then treetops on angles, a fence, perhaps, or a gate, with white patches
on the ground behind it and the brown blur of dry grasses in
front, and images of the base of a hedgerow that was jumping
in and out of view, as the person holding a phone ran across
the field. There was the sound of breathing, laboured, coming
in short bursts. And then there was the green-grey mound,
lying on the grass, with a smaller grey one beside it, both getting larger as the person approached. Jejeune could hear the
camaraman's voice now as he shouted his panicked, breathless
commentary into the phone while he ran.

"It is Abrar el-Taleb," said the prince, as Maik gathered
behind Jejeune to look at the screen. "There has been an accident, at the Gyrfalcon facility. We must go there now."

As the prince turned to one of the suited men to make
arrangements to have his car brought round, el-Taleb had
finally got close enough for the detectives to make out the
green shape on the ground. And the red colour that they
hadn't seen before but now seemed to be all around. El-Taleb's
voice was raised in anguish. Both men recognized what they

were seeing at the same time, but it was Danny Maik who was the first to voice it.

"Darla Doherty."

He and Jejeune were halfway to the doors of the Grand Hall before any of the others had moved.

30

They had received updates as they raced along the narrow lanes toward the Old Dairy property; reports from Abrar el-Taleb, direct to Prince Yousef, translated over a phone to the detectives by an unknown voice, possibly one of the suited assistants. So by the time they arrived, they knew. It had been less than thirty minutes since they had seen the video of Darla Doherty lying on the ground. And now she was dead.

Holland was waiting for them when they pulled up on the gravel pad in front of the Gyrfalcon facility. He was so distraught he could barely speak. "He won't let her go, he won't let me have her," he said. "He's destroying the crime scene." He looked helpless, disoriented, close to tears.

"Who won't?" asked Maik gently.

As Holland moved aside, Maik could see Niall Doherty sitting on the ground, the upper body of his daughter cradled in his lap. Doherty was rocking back and forth, his head bent low over his daughter's limp form. They had heard nothing of Doherty on their updates. He must have appeared recently, in the small window between the last of the messages and the time they had pulled up. The detectives went over to the scene, crossing the uneven field at a jog. As they got nearer, they could hear Doherty's voice. He was speaking to his daughter in a low, hushed tone. Maik wondered if it might be a prayer, but when Doherty heard the detectives approaching, he looked up. Tears were running unchecked down his lined, weathered cheeks. "She's still alive. Please help her. I can still feel her breathing. Help her."

But they knew they couldn't. Maik called Salter quietly over to one side and asked her to set about the task of removing Niall Doherty from the scene. "Gently, mind, and take as long as you need. But we need him away from here. Even if the scene of death is already shot as far as evidence is concerned, there may be things we can still salvage."

Salter moved off and Maik went over to where Jejeune was standing, near the prince's Rolls. In the distance, Maik could hear the alarms of other emergency vehicles approaching. At least one ambulance; no one had told them that there would be no need for a siren.

Jejeune stirred as el-Taleb finished giving his report through the open window of the prince's car, and readied himself for the other man's approach. The expression on the project manager's face suggested he knew he was going to have to give his account all over again, this time in English. He reached Jejeune at the same time as Maik, and the sergeant could see that he was still dealing with the shock of what he had witnessed.

"It is not possible to believe," he said. "She was standing over there by the hedgerow when I came down the hill. She was twirling the lure and I saw the bird come in for a strike. I was too far away to see what happened. I thought she had stumbled at first, but then I saw the bird on the ground beside her, and I realized something was wrong."

"Was she still alive when you got to her?" asked Jejeune.

"I do not know. I did not approach her." El-Taleb looked down, as if ashamed by his failing. "There was so much blood. I did not think it would be possible for a person to survive this."

Even if he had not told them, it would have been obvious to the detectives that he had ventured nowhere near Darla Doherty's body. The girl's clothing was soaked in blood, as was the surrounding ground, and the Gyrfalcon's talons. But on Abrar el-Taleb's sand-coloured suit, there was not a speck.

"Who moved the Gyrfalcon?" From what Jejeune could tell, it was at least five metres farther from the body than the video had shown — the video he had seen less than half an hour ago, in the plush comfort of the Grand Hall.

"The leash was lying free, so I tied it to the hedgerow, to prevent the bird from flying off. But the leash was long and the bird stayed next to the ... woman. It was too close; it seemed to be ... guarding her."

Jejeune nodded. *Mantling*, they called it, the classic behaviour of a bird of prey, defending its kill.

"I wished to move it away, but these birds ... I am not comfortable around them," said el-Taleb, casting his eyes down in disgrace again. He looked up and indicated Niall Doherty, now being led away gently by Salter, the blanket around his shoulders held in place by the constable's embrace. "This man climbed over the fence and moved the bird to where it could not reach the woman. It seems he knows of these things."

The men looked over as one of the uniformed officers cautiously approached the bird, which was still tied to a branch in the hedgerow by its long creance. The bird shuffled, ruffling its feathers and swaying its body slightly away from the officer's approach. It had that same dark, malevolent dead-eyed stare Maik had seen in the other bird taken from here only a few days earlier.

"And you left your phone on the entire time? You never turned it off after you dialed for help?"

El-Taleb shook his head dumbly. "I don't know. I do not remember." He seemed to think of something. "Yes," he said firmly. "I turned it off only when Prince Yousef arrived and I went over to speak to him."

"With your permission, we will need to get that footage." Maik held out his hand, but el-Taleb seemed hesitant.

"We'll try to get the phone back to you as soon as possible," said Jejeune.

"There is sensitive data on there, project data," he said uncertainly. "But to help you to understand this terrible incident …" El-Taleb handed over the phone.

"We would need a warrant to access anything else on there. At the moment, we have no intention of seeking one." Jejeune seemed to be mulling something over. "Mr. el-Taleb. I may have to testify at an inquest that your phone could not have been compromised by any other electronic devices you have on you. Can you just give me a brief account of what else you are carrying?"

The word *may* covered a lot of territory, but Maik couldn't ever remember such a question at an inquest, and he would bet the DCI couldn't either. But in his distraught, distracted state, such considerations were beyond el-Taleb. He patted his pockets absently, withdrawing only a wallet, a set of keys, and a handkerchief. If Jejeune found anything of interest among the contents of Abrar el-Taleb's pockets, he gave no indication.

Jejeune turned to Maik. "Can we see if there is a transport cage in the facility? Let's try to locate an experienced handler, too. If the ME decides he needs blood samples from the talons, we will need someone who can control the bird while he gets them." He looked at el-Taleb. "We may have to ask Prince Ibrahim, even, if there is no one else."

El-Taleb nodded again, as if the information was unimportant. He wandered over towards Yousef's car, presumably so he could inform him that his brother's services may be needed.

Jejeune and Maik went back over to the body. Salter was just returning from having shepherded Niall Doherty off to a newly arrived patrol car. He was now sitting in the back, with the engine running, even though it was a warm day.

"Neither one of them can have been anywhere close when it happened, Sarge," said Salter as she approached. "The blood from the severed artery sprayed in a wide arc, at least a couple of metres in all directions, based on the pattern on the grass. She must have twisted as she fell, probably thrashed about a bit. If anybody had been anywhere in the vicinity at the time, they couldn't have avoided being hit. But you saw el-Taleb's clothes, that pale suit, there's not a mark on it. And Niall Doherty's coveralls, they're soaked from where he was holding her in his lap, but there's no spray pattern on them at all."

Maik nodded. He could see a small piece of bloody meat lying on the ground at the end of a leather lure. Bait. The morsel the bird would receive as its reward for its strike. Salter came up next to him and pointed to the mankala Darla Doherty was wearing on her left arm. "Doherty just kept on saying how dangerous it was for her to have used this. You need to be really strong to hold a bird on there." She thought for a moment. "I don't know if it could have contributed to what happened."

Maik saw Jejeune looking at the area immediately around Darla Doherty's body. The area had been heavily trampled by both el-Taleb and Niall Doherty, but on the periphery there was no evidence of disturbance. There were no scuff marks or dragging, no broken wheat stalks, no trail between them through which a body might have been dragged. Maik could see the dark stains of blood on the soil where Darla Doherty's body had lain until her father scooped her up. Small pools still lay on the black soil, but there was one larger spot, where her unconscious form had settled finally, and the blood had continued to pump out and seep into the soil until it could pump no more. From everything the evidence was telling them, the victim's body definitely had not been moved. Darla Doherty had been attacked here, and this was where she had died.

And the weapon? There was little doubt of that either. The deep tearing of the wounds he had been able to make out on the victim's neck seemed to match the bird's blood-stained talons. As unlikely as it seemed, all the indications were that this could only be a tragic case of a falconer having been struck by the bird she was flying.

Maik could see Tony Holland a little way off, standing motionless, staring out over the horizon like the man on the prow of a ship. He followed the direction of his gaze and walked across the rutted, uneven field towards him. They strolled away shoulder to shoulder, pausing to rest on the fence that separated the Old Dairy property from Doherty's next to it. Maik gazed out across the green unkempt fields. A group of birds were resting peacefully up on the hillside. He looked back over his shoulder at Jejeune. He would register the birds, thought the sergeant, if he was here, perhaps even search around for correct collective noun for them, whatever they were. Even in this moment of crushing grief for Holland, and the sadness and the turmoil of Darla Doherty's death, he would note the birds, even if he would no longer announce them to Maik or anyone else. But Tony Holland, looking out over the field, did not notice them. He was not seeing anything.

"What crime, Constable?"

Holland stirred and looked at his sergeant, desolate, uncomprehending.

"You said it was a crime scene. To everybody here, it just looks like an accident, a terrible one, but there are no signs of foul play that I could see."

"She was scared, Sarge. I mean, really scared. She told me she had got herself into some trouble. She tried to make it sound like it was a long time ago, but I don't think it was. She said she wanted to clear it up, put it behind her now ..." he faltered, "now that things between us were ..." He snapped his head away, and Maik gave him time. He had seen many men's tears in his time, but he had never met a man who was comfortable crying in front of another.

"She said she wanted to get it sorted, and get on with the rest of her life," Holland said finally.

"The kind of trouble a detective constable couldn't help her with, you think?"

"I think it was about these birds. Every time I brought up the falcons, she would change the subject. It was subtle, but it was there once you started looking for it."

Maik nodded to himself. Despite his rawness, Holland was a good policeman. Over his shoulder, Maik saw the ambulance draw to a halt. Salter was walking towards it to give the crew directions. With a severed carotid, he thought, Darla Doherty had probably been dead before he and Jejeune had even reached Palm Hotel's car park, but he knew they wouldn't be able to move her until the ME had examined the body and pronounced death. By then, he hoped Holland would be long gone from here. But for the moment, Danny would do his best to preoccupy him, to keep him from realizing that the vehicle had arrived that was going to be taking away, for the last time, the person he had known. From now on, Darla Doherty would become something else — a victim, the subject of an inquest, but not a person. Not anymore. That part of her existence would cease when she left this place, the place her life had ended.

"I liked her ... you know," said Holland to the fields beyond the fence. "I know it sounds ridiculous, I've only known her five minutes, but I really ... liked her."

"I know you did, Constable," said Maik. He knew too that things would change from this point on for Tony Holland. Things that once seemed important would pale into insignificance, while others, the throwaway moments, those little mementos of memory, he would learn to clutch those to his heart and cherish them. But such realizations wouldn't come to Tony Holland yet. He was a long way from quiet reflection like that. He was still in the throes of grief for someone he had cared for, someone who was barely more than a stranger, but whose loss he would carry with him forever.

31

Damian came into the laundry room holding the kitchen utensil like a weapon. "I don't think much of this spatula, Lindy. It's too thick to be of much use. I suppose it's better than nothing, though."

She looked up from folding the clothes. "I've got a man like that," she said. "I wish Domenic was as handy with one of those."

"He's not?"

She shook her head. "I think it was his cooking that put the 'hospital' in hospitality."

She picked up something from the dryer and held out her hand to Damian. "I threw your jeans in to wash and these started rattling around."

She opened her hand to reveal two coins.

"Two bucks, my life savings," said Damian. He saw that she didn't understand. "Those are loonies. One-dollar coins."

She held one of the multi-edged gold coins up between her finger and thumb and studied it carefully. "I'm guessing the Canadian government designed this one specifically so people would be able to remove it from Domenic's grip with a spanner?"

It was Damian's turn to look confused.

"A wrench."

"Oh." He shook his head. "He's still careful with his money, is he?"

"That's one word for it." She smiled, but it was no more than a disguise for her thoughts. He had come from Canada. Across the high Arctic, on a ship, studying bird calls. Even if she didn't know much else about him, she knew Damian Jejeune was a fugitive from Caribbean justice. Canada would have been a safe haven for him. Only something important could have been worth the risk of leaving it and coming here. What that could possibly be, she didn't know. But she suspected Domenic might. Now.

"I guess you and Dom chatted for a while the other night after I went to bed?" she said, letting the act of folding a shirt claim all her attention.

Damian looked uneasy. The laundry room door was open, and a glorious sunny day was unfolding outside. Farther out, a calm blue sea stretched out to the horizon, its surface glinting as it gently heaved under slow waves. He wants to be out there, thought Lindy, away from my oh-so-casual scrutiny. But did she want to let him off that easily?

She knew the brothers had spoken because Domenic didn't tell her. He didn't tell her there was nothing new, as he had every morning since Damian's arrival, as he kissed her and headed out the door to the station. The day following the party, he hadn't said anything, and his eyes hadn't quite met hers when they kissed. But looking at Damian now, at the uncertainty in his face, the fear almost, she decided it wasn't up to her to ask. They would come to her, one of them, or perhaps both, when they were ready. In the meantime, she would give Damian some respite.

"I like who he becomes when he's around you," she told him matter-of-factly, still methodically folding the laundry. "He has to take a stand on positions, instead of just wafting around in the breeze, as usual. He has to make a bit more effort to define himself, because you challenge him. It's good for him."

"He's always been that way," said Damian simply. He leaned back against the washer, letting the sunshine from the open doorway paint his left side with its warm, alluring light. "He's a good guy, but I think his problem is that he's never known exactly who he wants to be. We talked about it once, before … a long time ago." Damian jangled the coins in his hand. "I told him nothing can measure up to a vague idea of a perfect life. Everything is going to be found wanting if you don't have definite ideas of what you're looking for."

Lindy was quiet for a long time. How important it would have been for Domenic to have had his brother around when he was going through some of the times he had faced. How he must have missed him.

She nodded at the coins Damian had continued to roll around absently in his hand. "Does your family know you're here?"

He shook his head. "They know I'm okay." He gave her a lopsided grin. "Not dead, anyway. I think Suzette may have known I was in Newfoundland." He looked down to the floor. "I got drunk once and called her, all maudlin and full of self-pity. I don't remember what I said. She told me I couldn't call her house again. I remember that part. It's okay," he said, seeing Lindy's expression. "Her husband's a nice guy. I wouldn't want to put him in a situation where he needed to make a decision about whether he should call the authorities on me or not."

Though it was okay to put Domenic in that position, she thought with a momentary bitterness. But she understood. It was different. Suzette had made a separate life for herself and her family, apart from her brothers. Lindy didn't know her; they exchanged Christmas cards, but other than that they had never had any contact, save for one brief phone conversation, when she had called looking for Dom. She had been polite, but no more. Lindy had always imagined her living on the periphery of Dom's life, as her own sister did with hers. They would both be equally delighted if one made the effort to contact or visit the other. But somehow, neither of them ever did.

"You said it was your mother's side of the family that were police officers. So not your father?"

Damian shook his head. "Furniture-maker. Woodworker, he calls it. More like a miracle worker. You should see the wedding gift he made for Suzette and Roy; a rosewood dining room set. It was an absolute work of art."

"Perhaps I should have a word with Dom. We could use a new dining room set," said Lindy. She closed her mouth abruptly, but not quickly enough. She turned back to her folding as the silence settled around them. Damian's softening expression showed he shared her embarrassment.

"He wouldn't mention anything like that to me, Lindy. Something as big as his plans for the future, what they were, who they involved. He would keep those things as close to his chest as possible."

"Sure," she said, still unable to turn around and face him fully. Damian let her have her silence, her time. She picked up the clothes and made her way into the bedroom to begin putting them away. Damian trotted along behind her like an obedient puppy.

"So tell me," she said, facing the closet, "what's Newfoundland like? I'd love to see it. How could you not be interested in seeing a place they call *The Rock*."

He was willing to follow wherever her path out of her discomfort led them. "I think it must be what heaven looks like," he said. "Not that I'll ever know, sinner that I am. But you sit on a grassy clifftop looking out at the sea and the sky and the land all around you, and you find yourself thinking that it's so wild, so perfect, it's hard to imagine there could ever be anywhere better."

"Dom says it can get a lot of snow," she said, still busying herself meticulously hanging up clothes. Lindy Hey, award-nominated columnist, turning to the safe harbour of the weather as a topic. She still couldn't quite bring herself to face him, and he felt a pang of sympathy for her humiliation.

"You know what I like about snow?" said Damian. "Its stealth. You can be sitting there in front of a fire with a whisky and a good book, and look up a few hours later and snow has covered everything, completely blanketed the landscape for as far as your eyes can see, possibly even moved on by then, and you never sensed it coming or going." His efforts to drag the conversation back to the light side were almost tangible. But Lindy wasn't ready to join him there yet. She turned and lingered for a moment longer with the discomfort of her earlier comment. He saw her expression and knew they had both exhausted the small talk.

"What I said, earlier," he said awkwardly, "you shouldn't read anything into it. He guards his feelings from everyone. Even this kid who died. Even something as big as that, he has never talked to me about it."

"Then you'll need to get to the end of a very long line," said Lindy, not even pretending that the laundry held her interest anymore. "The thing that people don't realize is that it wasn't all good, that time. I mean, I know he was genuinely elated to be able to return the Home Secretary's daughter to her family. My God, who wouldn't be? But there were other things going on. There was talk of this promotion, some award he was going to get. The media wouldn't leave him alone. There was even some stupid bird sighting that got everybody bent out of shape."

Damian nodded. "Iberian Azure-winged Magpie. He doesn't seem to want to talk about that either."

Lindy shook her head. "I think it's all mixed up with everything else that was happening at that time. He can't separate out the good bits without bringing back the not-so-good memories. I don't know if he ever will. Come on," she said, brightening, "let's see if you can work some of your wizardry in the kitchen. I'll let you make me more of those beaver tails, if you like." She gave him a brave smile, and Damian rewarded her efforts with one of his own.

"All I can tell you is I've never seen him happier, Lindy. Ever."

Lindy turned back to pick up the empty laundry basket. Whether Damian's praise was enough didn't really matter. For the foreseeable future at least, it was all she was likely to get, so it was going to have to do.

32

They were in the car park of the station, the three of them, gathered in the sunshine beneath a cloudless blue sky. Holland was idly pushing mud off one of the Audi's wheel wells with his foot. Salter saw that he was smoking again.

"Hardly matters now, does it?" he said ironically.

"If Darla talked to you about stopping smoking, Tony, it was for you, not her. She wanted you to care about your health, because she cared about you."

He looked at the glowing end of the cigarette, but didn't extinguish it. "So which one do you fancy, Yousef or Taleb?"

It may have been misdirection, but it was a topic they would have normally discussed anyway, out here in the car park like this, before they headed out for the day, having received the considered wisdom of Domenic Jejeune, via Danny Maik's presentation, on the progress of the case so far.

Salter shook her head. "We've gone from no suspect to two viable ones in the blink of an eye." Holland shot her a glance and she reddened, but it was too late. No one who knew Danny Maik would have described him as thin-skinned, but there was no doubting the fact that any reference to the lack of progress under his temporary leadership still struck a nerve.

"At the very least, I think we need some sort of explanation as to how some rotary-blade cowboy like el-Taleb rises above a bright woman like Catherine Weil to head the project," said Maik.

"Perhaps you're overlooking the obvious, Sarge. A woman in a heavily male-dominated environment." She offered a half-hearted smile. "Or perhaps she's just not as bright as everybody seems to think. After all, we only have her own word for how clever she is."

Maik shook his head, missing the undercurrent. "Even so, the couple of times I've seen her, she's seemed about as straightforward as anybody you're likely to meet. I have no reason to doubt her account of what she saw that night," said Maik.

And in her long flowing locks and her lithe dancer's body, a couple of very good reasons for believing her, Salter's tart look seemed to say. "Catherine Weil's statement can't be corroborated by anyone else," she said, with particular emphasis. "The prince is her employer. He provides the funding for her to continue her research, a well-paid position with access to the best facilities and equipment money can buy. She has a lot to lose if he's found guilty." Salter cast a sidelong glance in Maik's direction. "You know, there's always been something about her attitude towards the Old Dairy project that doesn't sit right with me. You're that unhappy somewhere, you leave. End of."

Maik inclined his head. "Still … Now el-Taleb, on the other hand. That, for me, is a possibility."

"Motive?" asked Holland, not entirely interested. "This personal honour thing?" His expression told Maik what he thought of the idea.

Maik shook his head. "Perhaps not. The DCI seems pretty sure that, one way or another, Philip Wayland intended to get his hands on the research data he knew existed at the Old Dairy. In his eyes, it belonged to him, never mind that he had signed an intellectual property agreement. Perhaps he demanded it back from el-Taleb. Perhaps he had other plans for acquiring it and el-Taleb found out. All we know for sure is that el-Taleb wouldn't have been prepared to let that data go under any circumstances. Just how far he would have been willing to go to protect it, though ..."

Holland stirred slightly. "No matter how many safeguards and firewalls you put on electronic data, there's always someone who can hack around them, with the right amount of expertise."

They all fell silent with their thoughts. Danny Maik's, at least, revolved around the idea that somebody like Philip Wayland didn't have that kind of expertise. If he was going to go that route, he would have needed help.

"You know," said Salter, emerging from her own ruminations, "that sign Wayland was found under, PRIVATE PROPERTY. Read one way, it could be a message of some kind."

Maik sighed inwardly. Why did people feel the need to constantly keep seeking some sort of symbolic significance for death, to keep looking for other explanations, for other, parallel universes to tie these tragic events to? Was it perhaps to soften the terrible reality of what it was, the signal of the end of civilization, the point at which we ceased to be humans, taking the life of another member of our species, not for protection, or defence, but merely for gain? A motive like that did not deserve the dignity of metaphor or symbolism, only the harsh light of reality shining on it, on the killer, on us, as humans, reflecting what we truly were, and what we were capable of.

The silence that followed Salter's comment lasted a long time. It was still intact when Jejeune appeared in the doorway at the top of the steps.

"Ah, Constable Holland. I thought you should know that the ME's report has just come back. Dr. Jones's conclusion is that there is no evidence that Darla Doherty's death was anything other than misadventure." Jejeune was suddenly uncomfortable to be delivering news from up on high like this. He descended the steps and joined the group. "She appears to have pulled the lure too close and the falcon struck her, over her shoulder, from behind." The news was greeted by Holland with silence. "She wouldn't even have seen it coming," Jejeune added lamely. "It would have been very quick."

"Bleeding to death from a severed carotid usually is," said Holland. Maik gave him a look that seemed to help him remember who he was talking to, and Holland dialed down his tone. "About the bird, sir …"

"I don't know if it will be euthanized. DCS Shepherd has been pushing for it, but there is no precedent anyone can find. I have to tell you, it does look like the prince would challenge any attempt to have the bird put down. The Assistant Deputy Commissioner has already heard from his legal team, asking if he knew what the ruling was likely to be."

"I'd like to request not, if I have any say." Both Salter and Maik looked surprised, Jejeune less so. "It's not what Darla would have wanted. She loved those birds. She would just stand there and watch them, soaring, diving, swooping in. There was this kind of look on her face …" Holland seemed to gather himself a little. "Anyway, I just know she wouldn't want the bird to be put to death, that's all. Tell me," he said, drawing on his cigarette and looking at Jejeune frankly, "this Taleb, are we also looking into any possible role he might have in Darla's death?" He rested his gaze on Jejeune, but it was Maik who shook his head in answer.

"Tech has confirmed there's no break in the iPhone footage at all, Constable. Mr. el-Taleb was seen leaving the building less than two minutes before the recording started, and in keeping his phone recording throughout, he has inadvertently proved conclusively that he couldn't have been involved."

"It was an accident, Tony," said Salter reasonably. "Nobody could have left from there after killing Darla without being detected, unless they went across Doherty's land or arrived by boat and came up from the shoreline. Nobody has come up with any sightings. We've asked."

There was something in the way Holland angrily drew on his cigarette that suggested however ready he might be to exonerate the bird, he wasn't prepared to grant the same privilege to humans just yet. He shook his head. "This wasn't an accident; there's more to it."

"Sometimes it seems that way," said Salter, trying, in her own gentle way to make him see just where the boundaries of logic lay. "Perhaps we even want it to be that way. If there is a reason, then it's not so senseless, not such a random twist of fate. But that's what it was in this case, Tony. Honestly."

He was adamant. "No, this is not what it looks like. She was genuinely afraid."

"They all were," said Salter. "There was the murder up there, and then that break-in recently…. But however much you would like to think there is something more sinister behind this, there isn't. We've looked at it, all of us, and there is no way any third party could have been involved in this. Mansfield Jones is an excellent ME, not to mention the most cautious human being you will ever meet. If there was anything there to suggest it wasn't how it looked, that the scene had been staged, or the evidence manipulated in some way, he would find it. You know he would."

But Holland seemed not to hear. "You know the last thing she said to me? *I'm scared, Tony*. And I told her not to worry. Like it was all going to be okay, like I was going to be able to protect her. And now, she's lying on a steel table in a mortuary. How's that for protecting somebody?" he asked bitterly, flicking his cigarette away in disgust.

"It's not your fault, Tony," said Salter gently. "You have to let this go."

Holland shook his head. "I don't think so. Not yet. I did some internet research about these Gyrfalcons. Turns out there's a very healthy underground trade in smuggling them. Some birds were recovered at Moscow airport a few years ago. You know what black market value the officials put on these Gyrfalcons taken from the wild? Fifty-thousand U.S. dollars each."

The personal investment in this case seemed to have given Holland an edge. There was intensity to his tone, a righteousness none of them had ever heard from him before.

"The thing is, some countries have a particularly dodgy rep for this kind of thing — Russia, China, Indonesia — so I went and checked with local tourism registrations. It turns out there is only one visitor here in Saltmarsh at the moment who's travelling on a passport from any of the top five countries involved in Gyrfalcon smuggling. A Kazakh national, Tamilya Aliyev."

Jejeune had already been reeling from the news that Holland wanted to look into the Gyrfalcon angle when the constable delivered the news that he now had a solid lead. Jejeune had no idea what connections he might uncover, to Jack de Laet, or beyond. Perhaps there were none to be found, but the longer this case went on, the less he found himself believing this. He knew he would either have to shut down Holland's investigation or get to the evidence before him. But at this point, he had no idea how he would be able to do either, especially with Sergeant Maik so ready to praise the constable's initiative.

"Impressive work," said Maik. "I presume you have plans to go and talk to this Kazakh national. Do you want me to come along when you see him?"

"Her, it's a woman. I'll go on my own first. She's been off somewhere for a couple of days, but she's booked back into the hotel again for tomorrow. Let's wait and see what she has to say for herself. If I don't like her answers about the day Darla was killed, maybe I can ask you to come along and we can make things a bit more formal."

"Answers to what, specifically, about that day?" asked Jejeune. He had recovered enough to consider correcting Holland, the day Darla *died*. But the constable was right; she had been killed, though not by any Kazakh tourist. Jejeune was all but certain of that.

"Aliyev arrived here the day before the break-in, and she left on her mystery trip the day after Darla was killed."

Killed. Holland's use of the word was a result of the guilt he felt, Jejeune realized, like all this activity, this misplaced suspicion, his conviction that there was more to Darla Doherty's death. Holland believed he could have saved the girl, and the DCI knew only too well what came next; the terrible sinking hopelessness, the remorse, the self-recriminations. If only he had done more, Holland was thinking. She had complained about feeling unsafe and he had done nothing. He could have saved her, but he had not.

Jejeune looked sideways to find Maik staring at him. Did he recognize it, too, and perhaps believe this brand of guilt was the same as Jejeune's? It wasn't. Holland's was grief, nothing more. He could not have done anything else, and in time he would come to realize this. Peace, of a sort, would visit him again. But Jejeune's guilt was grounded in the facts. It *had* been in his power to act, and he had not done so. And as a result, the boy had died. As heart-breaking as Darla Doherty's death was, there was no one to blame for it, no one to be held accountable. No matter how much Tony Holland was willing them all to see it otherwise, her death had come as the result of a terrible accident, a tragic, freak event, but an accident nevertheless. Jejeune was convinced of it.

33

The creamy globe of the moon had been cut in half by a cloud drifting in front of it, leaving only the lower section visible as a perfect semicircle.

"Look at that, Dom," his brother urged. "In all my travels, I've never seen anything like it. Every day is something new here. Every night, too. It's magical."

"Now you're getting the picture," said Domenic.

He took his coffee and joined his brother at the rail, the porch perched like an open-air stage on the edge of the cliff behind the cottage. The reflection of the moon laid a liquid trail on the dark waters, like a pathway to a promise. On the horizon, a bank of dark grey clouds sat low. The early-warning signs of a coming night storm ran a gentle ripple through a wind chime somewhere close, and Domenic felt a momentary buffeting of the wind coming in from the sea. On the water, two lights burned bravely against the gathering gloom. Fishing boats, approaching Saltmarsh from different directions, each eager to reach the safe harbour before the storm came.

"How did you get here, Damian?"

Damian's safe response had always been the flippant one, and he sought its refuge now.

"You brought me, remember, Domino. In that ugly old beast of yours."

Domenic waited. Not getting exasperated, or punching his brother on the shoulder, or storming off to tell their parents. Those days had gone, lost to time, like so much of the past between them. Together, the brothers watched as the scudding clouds swallowed up more of the moon, leaving only a ghostly, translucent light shining through.

"You don't need to know, Dom."

"I do."

Damian sighed. "When a foreign vessel comes into port, the coastguard can issue shore passes for the crew, as long as a local escort, usually a volunteer of some kind, accompanies them through the port facility. It gives the sailors a chance to go shopping, maybe, or just have a poke around the town." He paused. Even though Domenic was still looking out over the sea, Damian knew his brother was absorbing every word. More, he was examining the information for its nuances, the tremors that ran beneath its skin.

"When the sailors are ready to go back on board, the volunteer escorts them back onto the ship." Damian shrugged. "Now if the volunteer's mind is on other things, like maybe counting some bills in an envelope, maybe he forgets to check whether the number of people accompanying him back on board matches the number of passes the coastguard has issued. And if the captain doesn't report anybody missing ..."

The younger man's eyes stayed resolutely on the water, but in profile, Damian could see Domenic's jaw muscle tightening.

"You can't plug every gap in every system, Domenic. If people want to break the law, they will find a way. And if there aren't any gaps, they'll make some. That's how the world is. You do what you can, but you're not going to stop every crime or catch every criminal."

"You need to tell me everything you know about Gyrfalcons and Kazakhs, Damian. Everything."

Damian paused for a long moment, as if something out on the sea had caught his attention. The two boats? Their lights were drawing together slightly across the vast expanse of darkness, as they headed for the harbour. Was the left one closer to land? Perhaps, but it was impossible to tell, really.

"You got there," said Damian finally. "You're obviously as good as they say you are."

Domenic didn't give any credit to Tony Holland. He needed Damian to be in awe of his skills, his ability to find the truth. It would make him think twice about holding things back.

"Jack de Laet hired me to guide him to some Gyrfalcons. He had buyers in Kazakhstan, people who would take the birds and wouldn't particularly care where they came from."

Damian paused. A long time ago, Domenic wouldn't have needed any reassuring that he wouldn't be involved in wild bird trafficking. But now, he wasn't sure where the boundaries of their relationship fell. Like the distance between the boats on the dark surface of the water, they seemed uncertain, undefined. Now, he felt the need to hurry into an explanation.

"I thought the best way to prevent him from doing any damage was to be close to him. So I agreed to lead him. He was offering good money, and it seemed a pretty safe bet that we'd never find one anyway."

"I thought Gyrs reused their nests forever?"

Damian nodded. "If they're not disturbed. Researchers have carbon-dated some nests in Greenland to over a thousand years of continuous use. One has been used for two and a half thousand years. But I know of some old sites that have been out of use for a long time, even though they look good. And if I ever saw a Gyr carrying food or nesting material, we would head in the opposite direction."

"You didn't think De Laet would catch on?"

"You're good at what you do, Dom. Give me a little credit, too. Even if we had trapped a bird, it would have escaped, somehow. Do you really think I would ever have let him take a bird from the wild?"

Domenic took a sip from his coffee, now barely warm. He thought for a while. "What's De Laet's connection with the Old Dairy facility?"

Damian shrugged. "I never heard him mention Norfolk. As far as I understood it, he dealt with the Kazakhs directly."

"How?"

"Email draft box. Communication method *du jour* for international criminals. You set up an email account, give somebody else the sign-in details and then just leave messages in the draft folder. They can be written and read by either person, but nothing is ever sent. It's untraceable."

Domenic stared out over the sea thoughtfully. The cloud had begun to gather and the once-radiant moon was now no more than a memory of light, the faintest suggestion of translucence behind a curtain of deep grey. So what brought De Laet here, he wondered silently. And what did it have to do with Philip Wayland's death?

"It was all pretty leisurely at first," said Damian. "We're out in Northern Labrador looking for birds. If we don't get one today, we'll get one tomorrow. And then everything changes, and we're off to Iceland, to find a white Gyr as fast as we can. We're halfway there, and De Laet gets a message. A white bird has been spotted in Scotland, and it seems to be on territory. So it's full steam ahead, and Scotland, here we come."

"And if you weren't able to get it, this white Gyr?"

"We didn't talk about that possibility much," he said. "But it was the only time I ever saw Jack de Laet worried, about anything."

"So he went from a leisurely pursuit to a panic on the basis of this one message. And as soon as he lands he gets a call from a pay phone in Saltmarsh."

Damian shrugged, his eyes still watching the drifting ballet of the clouds across the dark night sky. The lights of the boats didn't appear to be moving, and yet they seemed closer to shore, as if they were somehow dragging the land out across the vast black expanses of nothingness to meet them. Damian seemed unable to draw his eyes away from the scene before him.

"I can't go back to a Colombian prison, Dom," he said quietly.

"Can you be a fugitive for the rest of your life?" Domenic asked sadly.

He fell silent, but Damian was shaking his head, smiling, to show even in his silence that his little brother had it all wrong, as he always seemed to, when they were together. "I'm not looking to get out of this. I'm guilty. I need to pay for it. But for what I did, they would send me to La Tramaćua, perhaps even La Modelo. A foreigner in there? Carrying my kind of baggage? There are times when the phrase 'a fate worse than death' is not hyperbole, Domenic, believe me."

Domenic let his look linger on his brother, the grey-black curtain of the clouds behind him. He felt moved almost to weeping by his helplessness.

"You would get segregation. They wouldn't want the hassle of a foreign government bringing up human rights issues." But perhaps there was something in his tone that told his brother even Domenic recognized the hollowness of his response.

Damian shook his head. "Foreigners are like currency in those places. Someone would find a way to get to me. It would be worth a couple of months' extra rations, maybe a carton of cigarettes. You have to understand, Domenic. If you let them send me there, it's capital punishment."

The wind chime jangled suddenly in the freshening breeze, startling them both. The cloud was rolling landward now in great swirling bands. The moon's silky trail had gone, and the only lights on the water were the tiny pinpricks of the two boats. "I want you to broker a deal for me, Domenic. I want to do my time in a country with no possibility of extradition to Colombia. I figure I'm looking at a few years in a reasonable criminal system. Culpability but no intent."

Domenic listened without speaking. This was vintage Damian. Setting the agenda, telling the justice systems of the world what was fair, what they should be allowed to charge him with, what he was prepared to pay for his crime. "And St. Lucia? Is that off your list of preferred destinations, too?" he asked with something approaching bitterness.

Damian shook his head. "None of that is true. I never hurt anybody. The guard was lazy. He needed a story to cover himself with his superiors."

"Did anybody else interview him?"

"You don't understand, Dom," said Damian earnestly. "I'm not trying to find a way out of this. I'm guilty. I did it, what the Columbians are saying. And I'm prepared to pay the price. I just can't do it the way they want me to." He turned from the sea and leaned his elbow on the railing. The wind tousled his dark hair. He looked at Domenic now, his eyes burning with intensity. "I've thought it all through. We can spin it that you talked me in. It would be a coup for you." He held up a hand. "I know that doesn't matter to you, but the point is, you wouldn't be compromised. This time here, it never happened. I contacted you out of nowhere. You convinced me to turn myself in and I did. To you. The Colombians would have to accept it, if they knew there was no chance of ever getting me back. I would still be in prison. They could still claim it as a victory for their judicial system. Justice for the victims."

Yes, this was the old Damian, thought Jejeune sadly, working the angles, looking for the 'spin,' trying to make something from nothing, to make explanations appear out of thin air. As if he believed people could be made to see things his way, the world according to Damian Jejeune, by sheer force of will, because he wanted it to be so, needed it to be so. Perhaps they could.

The two boats had finally made it into the harbour. The one that had been farthest out had arrived first, but there was really nothing in it. It had not even been a contest. The competition had not existed anywhere but in one distracted man's imagination. Jejeune looked at his brother in the ghost of the moonlight. He believed Damian was sorry. He was always sorry for the trouble he brought, for the turmoil and the disquiet. But that didn't mean that he wouldn't be bringing more.

34

It was as if the sun's rays had shattered on the canopy, spilling only tiny shards of light down through the treetops onto the forest path below. The filtered light gave the glade a strange, unearthly quality; dappling the pathway like a trail of gems that led away into the shadowy interior of the forest. On either side, a dense green curtain of undergrowth gripped the edges of the path, clinging on as it traced its serpentine route. A soft vesper of wind tousled the tops of the tall pines, but there was no other sound beyond the soft rush of air through the branches. There was no birdsong, no chattering of squirrels or chirping of insects.

Domenic Jejeune's footfalls were muffled by the carpet of pine needles. He walked along the pathway without haste, noting the common birds that flitted amongst the shadowy undergrowth — Robin, Chaffinch, Blackbird. A Greater-spotted Woodpecker flew lazily across the path and landed on a dead snag. He paused to watch it for a moment, not even needing to raise the bins from his chest to see it wheedling its way through the bark; in it, around it, under it. He smiled. It was such a common sight now, this bold, busy bird, but still one he found rewarding.

Far back through the screen of trees beyond the bird, he could see the high fencing of the Old Dairy compound. He knew the Gyrfalcon facility was off down the hill on the far side of the path, though he could not see it from here, or from anywhere in this stand of trees. It seemed inconceivable now, with all that he had learned, that Jack de Laet's death was not connected with Darla Doherty's in some way, but he could not find a link. Nothing he could think of, no pathway he could trace, brought the two events together. Even if both De Laet's and Doherty's deaths were accidents, as he believed they were, there would be something, some tenuous thread tying the two realms together; he remained convinced of it. And he'd find it, if he had enough time. But that, he knew, was by no means certain.

He watched the shifting patterns formed by the filtered light on the ground. He was in Ullapool again, sitting across the breakfast table from Iron McLeod, watching the patterns on the tablecloth as the sun streamed through the lace curtains. The Scottish detective was filching his breakfast toast while he wondered idly whether there was deeper significance to the book, something Jejeune had forgotten to mention. There hadn't been then, and there had been a kind of innocence to Domenic's denial, even if there were shadows of doubt behind it. But not now.

And suddenly it was DCS Colleen Shepherd doing the asking; Jejeune standing uncomfortably in front of her doing the explaining. He had been approached in the bar at Ullapool. He had convinced Damian to give himself up and he had agreed to come back to process it in Norfolk.

"And why not in Scotland, Domenic?" the ghost of Colleen Shepherd asked him now, over her gold-rimmed spectacles.

Because he wasn't certain about the legal system up there; perhaps there were provisions that could create difficulties.

"And the side trip to Aberlour, where you and your brother were seen taking the air at the Craigellachie Manor, living it up over a curry and a couple of single malts?"

One last fling of freedom before he brought him in.

The phantom Shepherd treated him to a steely gaze from beneath those exquisitely manicured eyebrows. But she would let it go. She would let it all go up to this point. But not beyond.

He could not help his brother. Domenic had tried to come to terms with it, tossed through a sleepless night, but he knew he could not. And that meant Damian would be on the move again, soon. He thought about what would happen if Shepherd found out Damian had been here, in his home, and had managed to slip away, fade into the ether whence he came, without the police of the North Norfolk Constabulary ever being able to lay a glove on him?

There would be silence, then a call to a couple of uniformed officers to escort Domenic to an interview room. Shepherd wouldn't want to do it herself. She wouldn't want anything more to do with him. There would just be a look of devastation in her eyes as he left, at the betrayal of her senior DCI; the person she had indulged so often, into whom she had invested so much, poured so many of her own career hopes and dreams. But there would be no forgiveness. Understanding, maybe, of the primordial ties between siblings that could cause someone to do such a thing. But not forgiveness. That would come only from Domenic's family; his aging parents back home in Ontario and his sister, Suzette. And Danny Maik? He would want to handle the arrest, as difficult as it would be for both of them. He wouldn't want Domenic Jejeune subjected to the accusatory glances, the contempt of the other officers. So he would process the arrest himself. That would be a form of forgiveness in itself, Jejeune supposed.

The cracking of a twig in the undergrowth seemed overloud in the heavy silence of the forest interior, and it startled him. Jejeune casually raised his bins and scanned the area but he detected no signs of movement. He listened to the ringing, ponderous emptiness of the forest. But there was something else, a suppressed idea that reached him, like a distant echo, across the stillness;

something about time, about Swallows, about Gyrfalcon nests, about a leather satchel. Something that was there, yet not there.

Out of the corner of his eye, he saw a shadow of movement. A figure, a human, tall and moving away, about to disappear around the bend at the far end of the path. Something about the person was familiar. The height? The build? He began moving towards the figure, even as it continued to draw away from him. The gait? The clothing? The satchel slung over the shoulder? What was it that was so recognizable? And then he realized: Wayland. The person he was looking at was Philip Wayland.

He quickened his pace along the path. He was about to call out, but for some reason thought better of it. The figure seemed to sense his approach anyway, even at this distance, and turned towards him slightly. Now Jejeune did call out, and the man froze. But he did not turn back. He risked a flashing glance in Jejeune's direction as the DCI called again, but then he took off and began running away down the slope, abandoning the trail for deeper cover. Jejeune crashed after him, scattering the fronds of thigh-high bracken as he headed up over a rise to cut off the man when he rounded a bend in the trail. Too late. He crashed through the undergrowth, mirroring the other man's awkward, loping gait to compensate for the uneven ground and the dense, tangled foliage. The man broke off into deeper cover still, plunging down a steep hillside, farther into the darkness of the forest. Jejeune was closing now, pursuing him at full speed. The other man redoubled his efforts, both men half-falling down the steep slope, urged on by their momentum as they hurtled downhill. Jejeune found the breath to shout for the man to halt, identifying himself as a police officer, but that only seemed to spur his target on. Jejeune hit the bottom of the ravine seconds after the man, too late to lunge for his ankle as he fought for purchase on the steep, wet slope on the far side.

Jejeune followed him up, scrabbling for hand holds, dragging himself up the slope by exposed tree roots, even as the soles of his city shoes slid from beneath him. With one last lung-bursting effort he crested the slope and collapsed to his knees at the top. He looked up to see his quarry in the same pose a couple of metres away. Now it was about recovery. Jejeune raised himself to one knee, the breath still pounding in his chest, his lungs fighting for air as he lunged forward from his half-crouch, reaching out for the man just as he began to rise. Again, Jejeune missed his grip, but the force of him striking the man's legs sent him crashing to the ground again, where he slid and tumbled back into Jejeune. They grappled as the man tried to get back past Jejeune, striking the detective full in the face with his leather bag, sending him flying, spinning back through the debris and undergrowth. Jejeune felt the salty wetness of blood on his lips. He reached out a flailing arm to trip the man as he passed, knocking him sideways into the ravine again, Jejeune holding on this time, even as he was dragged along. They both slid back down the steep bank, skidding and tumbling until finally they came to rest with a jolt at the bottom. The man was on his back, Jejeune half-lying on top of him. The DCI peeled himself off the man, leaving him red-faced and gasping for breath, both the fight and the flight now knocked out of him.

It wasn't Wayland. In truth, the wide-eyed man lying on his back staring up at the forest canopy bore little resemblance to the carbon storage researcher. The similarity was in the build, the height, even the clothes, the same olive green coat and dark trousers. It was the appearance from a distance that might fool someone, that had fooled Jejeune.

"I didn't know I was doing anything wrong," said the man, sitting upright finally. "I only came to see the site where that man Wayland was killed."

Jejeune said nothing. He sat with his elbows on his knees, letting his chest rise and fall rapidly as he tried to bring his breathing under control, picking absently at brambles and twigs caught in his clothing.

"I was just curious, that's all. I mean it could've been me."

Jejeune stilled his laboured breathing. He looked across at the man, waiting for an explanation.

"I was here, that night, at about the time they're saying Wayland was killed," he said. "For all I know, it might've been me who got topped instead."

The man stared at Jejeune, awaiting a response that never came. Instead, beneath the mud and grime on the detective's face, a slight glimmer of satisfaction was beginning to emerge.

35

"So, who the hell is he?"

Colleen Shepherd was standing at the front of the incident room with her hands on her hips. She was dressed in a matching blue jacket and skirt and a starched white blouse. It would have been the epitome of professional business attire, were it not for the white cross-trainers that she had clearly forgotten she was wearing. On another day, the people in the front row might have allowed themselves a sly smile at this incongruous detail. But they were well aware that DCS Shepherd was not in the mood for smiles of any sort today, much less ones at her expense. The meeting had barely convened when she had entered, fixing, in turn, Danny Maik and Domenic Jejeune with her steely gaze.

"A hiker." The simplicity of Maik's answer seemed to annoy the DCS. "He's part of a tour group from South Africa."

Shepherd shifted uneasily. "I hope nobody is going to tell me this is a coincidence."

"He was dating Wayland's ex-wife Carla for a while. It ended some time ago, but she was always going on about how wonderful the north Norfolk scenery was, so he decided to come over and see for himself."

"He wasn't disappointed, apparently," added Salter, earning a ferocious stare from Shepherd.

The DCS passed a hand through her hair in exasperation. "And there's no possibility he could have been involved in Wayland's murder?"

"His friends dropped him off near the Old Dairy and picked him up about twenty minutes later at the far end of the forest."

"We've verified this with them, these friends?"

The fact that she was straining so hard to check on the obvious was another sign of Shepherd's agitation. The cause was clear enough to everyone in the room. If the person Catherine Weil had seen in the woods could have been this man, and not Philip Wayland, then Prince Yousef al-Haladin's only alibi for the night in question had just evaporated like the morning mist over Saltmarsh harbour. And that meant Detective Chief Inspector Domenic bloody Jejeune, sitting so impassively on his desk-perch at the back of the room, was well within his rights to ask for permission to pursue him now as a viable suspect. Shepherd could have no grounds to deny him. For the foreseeable future, Colleen Shepherd's life was going to consist of ducking irate messages from people very much higher up the food chain than she was — unless she could find a whisper of doubt in any of this.

Maik tried an even tone that he hoped might rein in some of Shepherd's ire. "The friends say when he got back in the car there were no signs that he had done anything other than have a nice stroll through the woods. No weapon, no blood."

No hope, in other words, of tying him to the murder in any way. Shepherd sighed with frustration. An angry red welt down the inspector's cheek triggered another thought. "Why on earth did he run from you, then," she asked, "if it's all as innocent as he claims?"

"Apparently he was unsure about what a public right of way meant," said Jejeune simply. "He thought he might be trespassing on the Old Dairy property."

"That bloody Highways Passage Act," said Shepherd, shaking her head. If she could find nothing else for the brunt of her anger, then archaic British law would have to do. But there seemed to be something more behind her response; something beyond her discomfort that she would need to broker access to a member of a wealthy, privileged family so her DCI could question him about his role in a man's murder. There was a sense, too, perhaps, that other agendas were at play, concerning whirlwind Scottish trips, and Gyrfalcons; things of which she knew nothing, but of which her DCI seemed to know plenty. And of shadowy Kazakhs moving around the countryside, *her* countryside, out here in north Norfolk, without her knowledge or understanding. A case which had never seemed entirely straightforward was now threatening to spin out of her control, in directions she could neither predict nor prevent. And leaving Domenic Jejeune alone to operate in a landscape like that filled her with unease.

"I don't suppose it would hurt to know a bit more about this turbulent history between Wayland and his ex-wife," said Maik evenly. He stared at Tony Holland in a way that was meant to engage him. Holland had been sitting sullenly at the front of the room thus far, contributing nothing, and seeming to prefer some place in his mind as unconnected to the incident room as it was possible to be. He stirred slightly under Maik's gaze, but made no move to volunteer his services.

Salter moved in to fill the void. "They were just kids," she said. "No mortgage, no children. It's hard to imagine what they'd have to fight about, unless one of them was sleeping around." She seemed to realize the others in the room might imagine they were listening to the voice of experience, and she coloured slightly as she fell silent.

"Still, we know she was keeping tabs on him — that Facebook thing," said Maik. "If she discovered he was getting married again and was the type who found it hard to let go …" He shrugged. "Some messy divorces have a way of staying messy long after the parties have gone their separate ways."

At the back of the room, Jejeune was shaking his head slightly. "I don't know," he said. "The tribute she posted on his Facebook page. '*Philip always tried to do what he thought was right.*' It sounds like someone trying hard to find something positive to say. If she was involved in his murder, I would expect her comment to have been a lot more flattering. After all, it's easier to be complimentary if you don't really mean it."

Shepherd's expression suggested she agreed with Jejeune, even if she wasn't particularly impressed with herself for doing so.

"I'll tell you what we should be checking out," said Holland suddenly. "How Darla Doherty happened to get killed in a field less than four hundred metres from where this bloke had his wander through the woods."

"Doherty?" Shepherd looked puzzled. "But her death was an accident, surely? The coroner has already ruled on it." She looked around the room as if for confirmation.

"Yes, ma'am, it was an accident," said Salter, rushing in protectively. "It's just that there are a few loose ends Tony would like cleared up. You know, for his own peace of mind."

"Loose ends? What loose ends?" Shepherd looked down the room at Jejeune. "Does this have anything to do with the Wayland case, Domenic?" she demanded. "Is there any connection?"

"None at all." Jejeune had stood, and was now walking rapidly to the front of the room, to a spot where his body would be between Shepherd and Holland. "The constable is looking into a couple of things on his own." He offered the DCS a glance laden with significance. *Grief*, it said, *sorrow, regret.*

Shepherd shifted uncertainly. "Yes, well ..."

"Things like the fact that this has never happened before," snapped Holland from behind Jejeune's back. "Ever. Check it out online. I did. In the annals of falconry going back as long as anybody can find, there's no record of a Gyrfalcon attack on a human resulting in a severed carotid artery. Ever," he repeated.

He looked around, but the incident room had become a silent, still place, filled with uncomfortable people who did not want to meet his gaze. "Or things like the fact that there's a birder out there who nobody seems to know anything about. Found some spectacular bird for them down at Cley, but then buggered off before they could thank him. And nobody has seen hide nor hair of him since."

Jejeune had half-turned away from Shepherd when Holland had begun speaking again, ready to deflect any further comments he might offer. Whatever expression flashed across his face, he knew he had not been able to suppress it. Had Shepherd seen it? Had Maik? He realized he had missed Holland's question, and turned to face him full on, fighting to control his internal panic.

"I said," Holland enunciated with exaggerated care, "isn't that suspicious behaviour for you lot? Don't you usually like to get credit for the birds you find?" From his seat, Holland was looking up into Jejeune's face, penetrating, searching. Jejeune felt as if they were the only two people in the room. The rest were nothing more than a grey blur surrounding them; a backdrop for the drama he and Holland were playing out between them. Holland's eyes continued to rest on him, probing, questioning. *He doesn't know anything,* realized Jejeune. *He's asking.*

"It depends," he said, weakly. "There are circumstances. Some people ..." He faltered to a stop.

Shepherd took a moment to look at Holland, as if assessing something. He would need watching. He was a good officer, for all his wildness. She'd heard only the briefest of accounts of his involvement with Darla Doherty, but it hadn't sounded like his usual nonsense. It seemed as if he really cared for this girl, this *young woman*. And his attitude was not one of someone whose judgment was being clouded by grief, either. Despite what Domenic Jejeune seemed to be implying, Holland's questions seemed well worth asking. She just wondered why Domenic Jejeune had so far failed to ask them himself.

36

Eric snapped up his new EL Swarovisions and lowered them again just as quickly. "Wood Pigeon," he said, not quite succeeding in keeping the note of frustration from his voice. He seemed to realize it himself, and smiled at the other two men in the hide. "I do try to appreciate every sighting of every bird, as Quentin suggests," he said, "but I'm afraid I'm not quite there yet. After about the hundredth time of getting my hopes up, only to have them dashed by just another Wood Pigeon with some eccentric flight pattern, I'm afraid I can quite see why some people are willing to shoot the damn things."

Although he never voiced such feelings aloud, Jejeune did have a certain sympathy for Eric's point of view. Back in southern Ontario, the first Yellow Warbler of the spring was always a welcome sight. By the fiftieth, however, when the flash of yellow could potentially have been a much more highly prized sighting, Domenic would have been quite happy to forgo any further views of the small bird for the entire year.

Eric crouched down behind a tripod and looked through his scope, while Senior gazed on with a faintly amused look on his face. Jejeune saw that Eric had acquired a full range of top-of-the-line gear since their last meeting, and it was all arranged in front of him on the shelf of the hide: phone with bird call app, laminated tide chart, tablet loaded with an electronic bird ID catalogue. It was perhaps a natural impulse for a man of means who was embracing a new pastime as enthusiastically as Eric, but Domenic still felt a momentary shimmer of something approaching envy at the stunning Swarovski spotting scope Eric was now crouched behind.

Domenic raised his glasses and took a slow sweep of the area in front of him, scanning the reed beds for flickers of movement. He tracked the movement of a distant bird flying erratically across the water. Wood Pigeon, he decided. Perhaps Eric had a point.

"I was wondering if either of you had heard anything on the wires about anyone with an interest in birds of prey," he said casually, without lowering his bins, "possibly someone from central Asia?" He seemed to consider whether to continue. "Kazakhstan, perhaps."

Senior stroked his beard thoughtfully. "Lots of interest in falconry in that part of the world. Sadly, the new wave of affluence over there means it's no longer just a sport for the elite. Women are becoming competent falconers, too."

From behind the scope, Eric sounded shocked. "Sadly? Another bastion of male-only sport gone, Quentin?"

"No, sadly because the more people who are involved, the greater the demand there is for birds to be taken from the wild. Magnificent creatures like that should fly free."

"So you've not heard anything?"

Jejeune's persistence alerted Eric and he straightened up from his scope to look at the DCI. "Are we talking about people with a legitimate interest, Domenic? Forgive me, but with your line of work …"

Jejeune inclined his head to acknowledge Eric's remark. Quentin Senior was quiet for a moment, chewing thoughtfully on a sandwich he had withdrawn from his day pack.

"I only know of one possible source of falcons in this area, Inspector." He looked at Jejeune significantly. "I have to say, Gyrfalcons would be highly prized in central Asia. Normally, they prefer wild birds, of course. Training them themselves is a point of pride with many of the old falconers out there. But I imagine the sort of bloodlines the prince's Gyrs must be supposed to have would also create considerable interest."

He looked across and, seeing that Jejeune would be drawn no further on the subject, switched gears smoothly. "Found that Rose-coloured Starling yet, Eric?" He looked at Jejeune. "Got a report yesterday, vaguest of the vague, so I didn't bother posting it. Eric and I took a run up to Tilden's Barns, where it had been reported, but a nomadic species like that …" He shrugged and offered upward turned palms. "It might be anywhere by now. Let's face it, if Eric's new toys couldn't locate it, what hope is there for a poor, unplugged birder of the old school?" He slid a sly grin and a wink toward Jejeune. "It's an unlikely sighting, I grant you, Inspector, but I urged Eric to remember our adage."

"Birds have wings, but they don't have calendars," recited Eric dutifully, straightening from his tripod once again and smiling. "I was being reminded to expect just about anything at any time of year out here."

"And how wonderful that is. Don't you agree?"

Eric nodded vehemently. "I do, though I have to say, there's something to be said for reliability, too. I mean, look at the Spoon-billed Sandpiper in Hong Kong. April 18th, isn't it?"

Senior had begun a slow turn to rest his gaze on Eric. He found Jejeune's already there when his arrived.

"My birding friends used to circle the date on the calendar," said Eric cheerfully.

Senior had made the complete half-turn of his body by now, the sandwich in his mouth suspended in mid-chew.

"We're talking about one of the most sought-after birds in the world, Eric," said Jejeune reasonably, "You're telling us your Hong Kong friends could predict to the exact day they would see it?"

"Well, okay, they always go there a couple of days early, just in case, but it showed up at Mai Po between the fifteenth and the nineteenth of April every year I was there. And every one since I left to come here, too, I understand. So what's that, the past dozen years or so, at least?"

"I can't tell you how envious I am," said Senior sincerely. "I wait year after year in the hope that one will show up here in North Norfolk, but I've never been lucky enough to see one, and here's you, still wet behind the ears in birding terms, and you already have a 'Spoony' under your belt."

"Oh, I've never seen one," said Eric casually. "I could never seem to drum up the enthusiasm to go out with them. As I said, I wasn't a birder back then." Senior's face had morphed into a mask of horror, and Eric at least had the good grace to look remorseful. "Probably a bit of a blunder, as it turns out."

"Then we must go," said Senior decisively, "you and I. Next year. I always wanted to go there. You don't think of Hong Kong as having a lot of birding spots, but there are over five hundred species, apparently, all in an area a little over half the size of Greater London. So it's settled, then. Hong Kong, Mid-April. Care to join us, Inspector?"

Jejeune made a face that suggested he might have difficulties committing to a trip so far in the future. Unlike Senior, he wasn't retired, and unlike Eric, he wasn't the head of his own company. Work would undoubtedly intervene in any plans he made, if Lindy didn't get there first. Their last trip had been an "ornitholiday" as she called it. The next one would almost certainly not be.

"I'm beginning to wish I had just said I'd seen one," said Eric. "No one would have been any the wiser, and I could've saved myself a fortune."

Senior smiled to show he knew Eric had been joking, but he seemed compelled to offer a comment anyway. "A question of integrity, though, isn't, Inspector? With no one to police us but ourselves, we must be scrupulously honest."

A troubled expression flashed across the inspector's features for a moment, but it was gone as soon as it appeared. Eric raised his bins to watch a pair of ducks as they rose from the water, silhouetted against a white sky. "Light's awful today," he said, shaking his head.

"Then we must resort to other tools: size, shape, habitat, even behaviour. They can all give us clues as to what we're looking at."

Jejeune looked at Eric carefully. He hoped Senior wasn't overcooking it. A man with Eric's influence and resources could be a valuable ally in local environmental issues if he decided to become a serious birder. He seemed to be taking it all in, wanting to learn, but as Jejeune knew first-hand, Senior's astonishing range of birding skills could be a daunting prospect to measure yourself against.

Jejeune considered Senior, too, chewing his sandwich contentedly even as he scanned the waters with his bins held in one massive paw. On another day, Jejeune might have waited just that little bit longer, but time seemed in such short supply these days.

"I was wondering, Quentin," he began casually, "you have a lot of experience seeing hunting birds on your trips to Asia. Have you ever seen one trained to hunt a non-natural prey?"

"I once saw a Golden Eagle used to bring down a full-grown deer in Mongolia, which I could hardly imagine is a natural occurrence in the wild," said Senior. "Not a spectacle I would wish to see again, if I'm honest, but I had expressed disbelief to my guide and I was thus somewhat obliged to watch the demonstration." His face took on a look of concern as the connection to their earlier conversation registered, as Jejeune had suspected it might. "Is this about that dreadful business at the Old Dairy? Surely you don't think someone could have trained a Gyrfalcon to kill that poor girl deliberately."

"Are you saying you don't think it was an accident?" asked Eric, alert as ever for a story.

"I *do* think it was," said Jejeune definitely. "It's just that I would like to continue doing so."

Senior gently gathered his beard in a fist and drew it through his grip. "I highly doubt you could ever get a habituated bird to attack a human in that way," he said. "I suppose you might find enough ferocity in a bird taken from the wild. Though, of course, the prince would never permit a wild bird among his collection."

"It would unsettle the captive ones too much, you mean?" asked Jejeune.

Senior nodded. "Plus of course, there is the risk of infection. A wild bird might bring in all sorts of diseases. That reason alone is enough to encourage any falcon breeder to steer well clear of wild stock."

"It looks like a formidable creature," said Eric, consulting a picture of the bird he had called up on his tablet. "I think I'd want full body armour before I went anywhere near a bird like that."

Jejeune nodded. But Abrar el-Taleb wasn't wearing any body armour when he found Darla Doherty's body. And the constant stream of video, coupled with a meticulous search of the field later, meant that he couldn't have got rid of one. Or anything else he might have been carrying, like a falconer's gauntlet, or even a golf club cover that could have doubled as a makeshift hood for the bird. And that meant the question of whether the Gyrfalcon could have been trained to kill a human or not was moot. Abrar el-Taleb could not have been anywhere near the bird when it killed Darla Doherty. And, as much as he disliked the idea, that left Jejeune with only one conclusion: Darla Doherty's death had been an accident.

37

B ehind them, the north Norfolk countryside bent away to the horizon, the landscape dotted with only a few signs of human habitation: a church spire, a couple of isolated cottages, the ruins of an old abbey. But it was towards the sea that the three men were facing. From their vantage point high on the hillside, the vast unbroken sweep of the North Sea glittered beneath the morning sun like a carpet of jewels. Along the ragged edge of the coastline, a string of golden beaches stretched out; pristine, unsullied, unpeopled.

"They're going to destroy it all, you know," said Niall Doherty, with a small shake of his head. "They'll dredge it out, tear up the sea bed to lay their pipes, build their maintenance facilities along the shoreline. By the time they've finished, there'll be nothing left of the coastline we're looking at."

Neither Jejeune nor Maik said anything. They knew that it was true, at least in part. Even if the carbon was captured farther inland and transported out here to the coast, there would need to be a processing centre, to prepare the gas for its journey, via a vast pipeline network, to the storage caverns offshore.

A light wind tousled Doherty's thin grey hair as he cast another sad look over the coastline. "It's not just the present they'll destroy, either, or the future. It's the past they'll be taking away from us as well. This was a place of prosperity once. Shipments of Norfolk wool went all around the globe from those wharves down there." Doherty pointed at a cluster of buildings just visible in the distance, huddled along the banks of the Saltmarsh River as it wended its way across the flat estuary to the sea. His gnarled hand betrayed the slightest of tremors. "What will be left of that heritage, once they've finished? It can't be allowed to happen," he said quietly. "It won't."

There was a thread of steel in Doherty's voice, a blend of reason and indignation. It was the sound of quiet, determined opposition, of a willingness to resist.

"There's another protest planned in a few days, I understand," said Maik. "Perhaps, after what happened last time, it would be safer if you were not there."

Doherty shook his head. "They'll have moved on, the troublemakers. No more interest in this coastline than that lot over there." Doherty flung his bony hand in the direction of the Old Dairy, barely visible atop the sun-gilded fields that swept down the slope just the other side of the boundary hedge.

"You have a perfect view of the surrounding area from this vantage point, Mr. Doherty," said Jejeune. "How long had you been out here?" He didn't need to stipulate when; neither Doherty nor Maik would misinterpret the question.

Doherty shook his head slowly. "At least twenty minutes. What I can say for certain is nobody went up and down those hills. Not until I saw Mr. Taleb appear from over there."

"Did you make a point of being here when the prince's Gyrfalcons are flown?" asked Maik.

"Those birds, their flights, it was the only contact I had with my daughter since she left to work at that place." He shook his head. "You can't see the mews itself. It's too close to the hedgerow, kind of tucked-in, like. But I could see the birds flying every so often, most days, so I'd know my Darla was down there."

A blur of movement flashed across the field far below. It could have been a bird, but if it was, it was the fastest one Maik had ever seen.

Doherty seemed to read his thoughts. "Over a hundred and thirty miles an hour, Sergeant. The fastest bird in the world, in straight flight."

Maik looked first at his DCI and then back to Doherty. The older man was of an age to be confused by the U.K.'s half-baked efforts at metric conversion.

"Would that be kilometres, sir?" he asked politely. "That's quick enough, but a hundred and thirty miles would be well over two hundred kilometres an hour."

"Miles, Sergeant," said Jejeune, not taking his eyes off the aerial acrobatics below.

"It'll be the prince himself who's flying them," Doherty said, "now that my Darla's ..." His jaw twisted as he fought for control.

As Doherty had said, neither the handler nor the facility itself was visible from this position, both hidden in the area where the ground dipped down to the hedgerow that marked the boundary between the two properties. Only the Gyrfalcon could be seen, a grey blur scarring the air with its flight, twisting, arcing, setting itself each time for a scintillating horizontal pass. The three men watched in silence as the Gyrfalcon built its momentum, until finally everything merged, millennia of evolution climaxing in a flight of such power and precision and speed that Maik could do nothing but shake his head in wonder.

"*Yarak*," said Doherty, "that's what they call it in the Middle East, when the bird's in a perfect flight."

"If it makes you uncomfortable, sir, I could go and have a word with them."

"Leave them be, Sergeant. Those birds need to fly," said Doherty, still watching. "It was instinct, that's all. If there is something bad in all this, and I don't say there is, not for certain, but if there was, it'd be people you'd be looking at, not birds. People who got my Darla to fly them day and night."

"Why would they do that?" asked Jejeune.

"No reason I can think of," said Doherty, with a sad shake of his head. "You might try to train a wild one that way, but the prince would never have wild birds in his cast. Falcons are like people. The high and mighty don't much care to mix with the riff-raff." He shook his head again and watched the bird make a final pass before it disappeared beneath the hedge line, its flight done for the day.

"You want to see a sight; you should come up here when the white one is flying. I haven't seen it recently, mind you," he said, "but the way Darla would get it to bank. Caught the light something wonderful. Like a white angel, it was. It would take your breath away."

"I can imagine," said Maik. He had expected a contribution from his DCI, but when he looked over, Jejeune was staring at Doherty with a strange, troubled expression.

"The prince has a white Gyrfalcon in his cast?"

Doherty nodded. "Beautiful bird. Pure as the driven snow. I've seen it down there plenty of times, though, as I say, not lately."

"Since when?" Neither Maik nor the other man could have missed the urgency in Jejeune's question.

"I couldn't say." Doherty shrugged. "A couple of weeks anyway."

Jejeune thought for a moment. "Did Darla ever mention a man named Jack de Laet to you?"

"We weren't talking, Inspector. Not for months." There was regret in Doherty's voice.

"You've never heard the name, or heard Darla talk about people from out of town, foreigners, interested in the birds?"

"Kazakhs?" asked Maik, just to show that, however determined Jejeune might be to keep him out of all this, he was not prepared to go quietly.

The inference was clear. No one could pursue an interest in the prince's Gyrfalcons without Darla Doherty's co-operation. Niall Doherty shook his head firmly. "My Darla thought the world of those birds. She would never let anybody near them that wasn't supposed to be there."

"I'm told this De Laet could be a persuasive man, Mr. Doherty," said Jejeune softly. "I know it's difficult ..."

But the older man was emphatic. "You're wrong, Inspector. My Darla would never be a party to anything like that. Never."

His vehemence swept over the detectives like a wave. There was a certainty to the denial that was compelling.

When Maik turned back to Doherty, the older man was staring down at the coastline. "We used to gather samphire from down there, Darla and me, when she was a girl." He called it *samfer*, in the local way. "There used to be an old man who would come by and collect it, too, with a horse and cart. He'd sell it in newspaper cones. Had a song — 'Samfer, long and green.'" Doherty sang softly, his thin voice wavering back across the years. He continued to stare out at the sea for a long time, at the mercantile past of the north Norfolk coast that had been swallowed by the centuries, at the generations lost to time, as the rest of the world moved on, without even noticing their passing. "They'll walk away, one day. You know that? Tear up our shoreline and then, when it no longer suits them to be here, they'll be gone."

"The Old Dairy project has invested a lot of time and money in this operation," said Maik. "What makes you think they won't be in it for the long haul?"

"Mongstad, in Norway. You've likely never heard of it, Sergeant, but it was the largest carbon capture and storage facility in the world at one time. It's closed now. Abandoned. Longannet, in Scotland, too. If they can walk away from projects as big as those, it will happen here, too, eventually."

Jejeune looked at his watch and motioned to Danny Maik. Fishing, the inspector had called it. Go out to see Niall Doherty and drop a line in the water, see if anything bit. *Had it?* wondered Maik, letting his look linger on his DCI. *Perhaps.*

Doherty was looking across the hill on his property, at an invisible place, far beyond the lapwings and gulls and crows gathered there. "I'll spread her ashes here," he said, as much to himself as the others. "She may have left me once, but as the folks round here say, Norfolk chickens always come home to roost."

They left Doherty on his hillside, staring out over the sea. Jejeune was quiet as they made their way back to their cars. The silence confirmed he was on to something, but that knowledge didn't help to quell Danny Maik's anger. But he would hold his tongue for the moment, in case the DCI had anything to tell him, after all.

"You saw those birds in the facility, Sergeant," said Jejeune eventually. "Any one in particular stand out?"

Why the hell can't he just ask what he wants to know? thought Maik. Why did he always have to go around things like this, as if he didn't quite want you to know what he was thinking? In his frustration, Maik decided to match his DCI's obtuseness like for like. "I'm no expert, but they all looked the same to me. If I had to guess, I'd say they were all the same species."

He tired of the game, and added. "And colour."

He looked at Jejeune as they walked across the uneven ground, challenging him to ask. Could he have missed it? Was he colourblind? Something in his look seemed to get through, and his DCI nodded, accepting the report. There had been no white Gyrfalcon in the mews when Danny Maik was there.

They walked in silence again for a long time. Maik realized Jejeune wasn't going to offer him any information. If he wanted to know anything, it would be up to him to ask. He stopped as they approached the parked cars and turned to Jejeune.

"Jack de Laet," Maik said. "If I was going to be pulling names out of the air, I'd probably start with something a bit less exotic. Was this the man from Scotland? You said he could be persuasive, as if he might not be anymore."

Jejeune nodded slightly to acknowledge Maik's perceptiveness.

"I think De Laet recruited Darla Doherty to help him get a falcon he intended to sell to somebody from Kazakhstan. I believe De Laet had an order for a wild white Gyrfalcon, but he couldn't capture one, so he convinced Darla Doherty to supply the white bird from the prince's collection instead."

Maik nodded to himself but said nothing. If Jejeune knew the name, knew this Kazakh connection, why didn't he say anything to Holland? Why shut him out like this? Why shut all of them out?

"I'm just wondering, sir, how we came up with the name, how we know he's tied in to anything down here?"

There was a long pause. Maik could hear birds in the trees, and the faint hum of traffic from the road that ran past the front of Doherty's property. Still, Jejeune waited. He seemed torn, struggling within himself, wrestling with a decision he needed to make. It was a long time before he spoke. "There's nothing official, Sergeant."

It was the first time he'd ever fallen back on the phrase, and it resonated with Maik in a way few of the DCI's comments had before. "Nothing official," confirmed Maik quietly.

"There seems to have been a phone call made to De Laet … from Saltmarsh. It makes sense that it would have come from Darla Doherty."

Maik said nothing as the two men walked to their separate cars in silence. He watched Jejeune drive off, but sat in his Mini for a long time, not even turning on his music, for once. In his mind, he was replaying the phone call from Iron McLeod, the

DCI's reference check, as he had jokingly put it at the time. There was plenty in McLeod's gravelly accent that might have been difficult to make out, but not the words Maik was thinking about now. They rang out as clearly as when he had first heard them. "I know your man's got a stellar reputation," McLeod had told Danny over the miles, "but if he pulls anything out of this one, he's going to have to be a bloody miracle worker. The body has nothing on it to give us any clues at all. No documents, no wallet. No phone."

38

Xandria Grey was halfway down one of the stacks, working busily through the files, when Jejeune entered the room. His appearance seemed to startle her slightly.

"Forgive the intrusion," he said. "I did knock, but there was no answer."

"You can't hear anything when you're down in these stacks," said Grey. "It's one more reason I dislike being down here. But the work must be done," she said determinedly. "It must be completed, for Philip's sake."

As dreary and oppressive as it was down here, thought Jejeune, it was quiet. It would be a good place to be alone with your thoughts, even as you absently arranged files on the shelving racks. It would be easier to pretend the rest of the world did not exist, to hide from the pain it could inflict.

Jejeune waited for her to emerge into the room, but it became clear she wasn't going to. Instead, she continued stuffing files into the built-in buckets on the shelves with a vigour that suggested she would brook no resistance from them. He eased down the narrow gap on the other side of the stack so he could see her.

"It's a lot of material," he said, looking up and down the shelves.

"Data was Philip's currency. He was eclectic, willing to take anything from any source as long as it was useful to him. It's what made him so good at what he did. And, as I told you, he was very old school. He liked his data in print, in his hands. He said he found reading electronic files made his eyes tired, especially with the amount he consulted."

"I wanted to let you know there has been a development in the case."

Grey continued to stare blankly at the shelf in front of her, not letting her eyes drift toward Jejeune's face, half visible between the files, a few inches away.

"A development?" she said guardedly. "About Philip?"

"Specifically, we have to revise the timing of the last sighting of him," he said. He paused, as if he might be awaiting a reaction. Grey offered none, though she did stop working with the files.

"So she was wrong, then, Catherine Weil," she said quietly, as much to the shelf in front of her as to Jejeune.

"The man she saw in the woods that night may not have been Mr. Wayland. It means the last verified sighting we have of Philip was much earlier, when he left here that day. You would have been the last person to see him."

Jejeune had thought returning this moment to her may have made a difference. She now possessed the last minutes of her fiancé's life, instead of having them belong to some other woman. But Grey did not seemed moved by the information, standing motionless instead, deep in thought.

"I wonder," he said, "can we step out into the room?"

"Claustrophic, Inspector?"

"Home cooking," he said, trying a smile as he sucked in his stomach to ease himself sideways along the rack. Grey matched his progress and emerged from the stacks next to him. She clicked the remote and the shelving units rolled along their tracks with a deep chest-resonating rumble. Jejeune watched the slow, inexorable trundle of the stacks with fascination, until the end one closed on the others, pressing them together and sealing them all shut with an echoing shudder.

She looked down and began brushing the dust off her clothes.

"You said Mr. Wayland spent a lot of time down here," said Jejeune. "Why was that, do you think?"

She looked up at Jejeune, her face pale in the subdued light of the room. "When Philip felt he was on to something, he was willing to dig through any amount of files, put in whatever effort was necessary. Finding a workable solution for carbon storage really was the most important thing in his life. He was close to a solution, and he thought it may well have lain within the research that had already been conducted. Data hold many answers. Often, it is in the way you interpret them that gives you the ones you are looking for. Shall we?"

She gestured to the door with her hand and Jejeune followed her from the room. They mounted the stairs and emerged into the corridor. In contrast to the stifling, almost sinister atmosphere of the vault, this grey hallway now seemed a place of light, of life, of hope, even. Perspective, thought Jejeune, what a strange power it had.

Grey flicked on the light as they entered her office, revealing a desk piled high with paperwork. "Forgive the mess, departmental admin," she said, pushing it aside and taking a seat.

Jejeune wondered why so many academics took on administrative roles within their departments. Arrogance, he decided. Not in a negative sense, but it was simply that they spent so much time being the brightest person in a room, they could not understand how anybody else could do the job better. Any job. Still, it was unnecessary, surely, for her to take this on. It was another example of Grey burying herself in her work.

She was staring at a picture of Philip Wayland on her desk. She reached out and touched it tenderly with her fingertips.

"How is it possible?" she asked finally, looking up at Jejeune. "How could Catherine Weil have made a mistake like that?"

Jejeune thought he might have an answer, even if he didn't want to share it with Grey just yet. Or anyone else, for that matter.

"A man who looked a lot like Mr. Wayland was in the glade about that time," he said. "If she only had a fleeting glimpse of someone entering, at dusk …" He tilted his head.

"But you're not certain she was mistaken?"

"Not certain, no. But …" *But yes*, his expression told her. He picked up a paper from her desk, riffling idly through it. "The more I read about biochemical carbon sequestration, the more it seems unlikely that the problems can be overcome."

Behind the desk, Xandria Grey seemed to stiffen slightly. Without Philip Wayland at the helm, she recognized Jejeune had meant. "It is a matter of when, Inspector, not if. Philip left us an astonishing legacy of research data. It's only a matter of time before we unravel it and find our solutions."

"Time, and money," said Jejeune. He walked to the window but the world outside didn't seem to hold much interest for him today. Instead, he turned abruptly and looked squarely at Grey. "I wonder if Mr. Wayland realized the full extent of the limitations he faced when he left the Old Dairy project to come here to the university."

"Did I mislead him, you mean?" Grey raised her eyebrows and tilted her head slightly. "Did I beguile him into coming here under false pretenses?" She managed a faint smile. "Really, Inspector, you're embarrassing yourself. Or to be more precise, I suspect Catherine Weil is once again doing it for you." She took a deep breath, as if steadying herself, drawing in protections against welling emotions. "Money, respect, and support, Inspector, three pillars of any researcher's palace of dreams," she said. "You're wondering why he left to come to the university, if he had all that at the Old Dairy."

Jejeune's silence told her that he was.

"Because he was missing the fourth pillar there — freedom. The phrase he used most was 'philosophical differences,' but the philosophy was pretty simple really. He wanted to pursue this branch of research. He was given the opportunity to do so here, Inspector, the chance to look for a viable solution to biochemical storage of captured carbon. Philip was one of the most intelligent men I've ever known. He understood the constraints he would be working under. He took a leap of faith. His conviction should be something to celebrate, not used as a weapon to attack his character." A strange look of contempt seemed to spread across her features. "I would suggest the truth of it is that Catherine Weil can't bear the thought that Philip knew exactly what he would be facing, and had the courage to leave the Old Dairy anyway. Which is something, I might add, that she doesn't seem quite able to do herself."

"You said he was eclectic, willing to take anything from any source, whatever he could find."

Grey sat up straighter in her chair, seeming to rouse herself slightly, as if only now realizing the full import of Jejeune's deceptively casual comment. Jejeune waited patiently. Truth? Or loyalty? He knew only Grey could resolve the conflict roiling within her, and only time, and his silence, would let her. Tears leaked from the corners of her eyes, as if escaping from some vast underground reservoir of emotions she was keeping hidden. Perhaps they were shed in frustration at having to defend her fiancé against such suspicions, perhaps at the betrayal she felt from Catherine Weil. But Jejeune wondered if something else might have been there, too. Could her sorrow be for the memory of a complex man whose global conscience might have been so much at odds with his personal one?

"Philip was so committed to his cause, Inspector," she said eventually. "With a global crisis looming, did he believe that personal constraints, moral objections, can start to seem like a bit of an indulgence, if they stop you from getting the answers you need? Possibly." She nodded her head emphatically. "Philip wanted to solve the carbon storage issue, desperately, more than anything, but he was intelligent enough to come up with answers on his own. He had no reason to look elsewhere. Not when he was convinced the solutions were already here, somewhere in those vaults."

Perhaps, thought Jejeune, *but what if they weren't? How far would Philip Wayland have been prepared to go to get all the data he needed, then?*

39

On another day, Lauren Salter might have considered Tony Holland and his conspiracy theories a bloody nuisance. But it was hard to feel that way today, sitting in the *Diana*, hand on the tiller, with Danny Maik facing her and only the calm blue waters of the sea around to witness it.

It was a soft day, with faint wisps of mist rising from the water like smoke. A gull drifted gracefully overhead, wheeling effortlessly on breezes that eased the clouds into a gentle dance across the skies. In fact, about the only thing that wasn't relaxed and laid back and soaking up the pleasant ambiance of Saltmarsh morning on the water was Danny himself. Judging by his expression, he might well have come down in favour of the view that Tony Holland was a bloody nuisance after all.

"You can relax, Sarge, I do know what I'm doing, you know."

"I'm sure you do, Constable," said Maik uneasily. His tone suggested Salter's competence wasn't entirely the issue.

"Not a fan of the water?" asked Salter.

"I used to swim for the school team," said Maik. "I don't have any problem being *in* water."

"Just *on* it. I thought I heard you say you liked working on boats — painting them, that sort of stuff."

"Oddly enough, most of the time I've painted boats, we've both been on dry land," said Maik tersely.

"My dad was raised on the water," said Salter breezily, "and he made sure his kids were, too. We were on boats before we were on bikes. The other boaters down at the marina used to call us the water babies. Now he's doing the same with his grandson. Takes him out with him whenever he gets the chance. Max is turning into quite the little sailor."

"Good for Max," said Maik gruffly.

They were taking their second leisurely pass offshore from the Old Dairy, scanning the coast for a place someone might have come ashore in a boat, or, more importantly, left in one. Salter had volunteered to helm the *Diana*, and with Jejeune and Holland both off to parts unknown, the role of able seaman had fallen to Maik.

A small group of round, shiny objects broke the surface, and submerged again, almost before Salter could remark on them. "Seals," she said. "The colony out on Blakeney Point sometimes ventures up this far. It's a pity we aren't going farther out. There are dolphins and even whales out there at times."

"The seals mean we're out far enough for me," said Maik. He shifted uneasily in his seat, bringing the camera up to eye level to test for focus. On the first pass, Salter said she thought she may have seen a slight inlet along the craggy coast that might make a suitable landing spot. Maik had missed the area she was talking about, so they were now on their way back for a second pass.

"Fancy a sandwich? There's beer in there, too." She pointed to the large hamper she had prepared that morning — ham sandwiches, pork pies, a couple of kinds of cheese — all his favourites. She had brought music, too, Motown. Smokey Robinson was easing his way through "Cruising" even now, and if it didn't seem to be doing much to relax Danny, Smokey's smooth-as-silk vocals were at least earning an appreciative smile every now and again.

"I'm fine, thanks," he said dismissively.

He's seasick, she realized. Danny Maik, a man who you could sometimes believe capable of breaking another human being apart with his bare hands, was all wobbly in the tummy over a few waves. The poor love. She averted her eyes, so he wouldn't feel he had to hide his weakness from her any longer. For a moment, the only sound was the lapping of the water against the side of the boat and the gentle putter of the engine ticking over. "The DCI, Sarge," began Salter tentatively, "do you think he's been a bit off lately?"

Maik said nothing. His look, though, wasn't one of the ones he gave when he wanted to discourage her from continuing.

"I mean, he normally approaches things in a bit of a strange way, but he's usually razor sharp. On this case, though," she shook her head, "he just doesn't ever seem to have become fully involved. There's been no clever insight, none of that roundabout thinking that still seems to get him to the centre of everything. It's as if there's something else constantly on his mind, distracting him. Has he said anything to you?"

"Hardly likely, is it?" asked Maik. But was there evasion in his tone?

Salter hesitated before continuing "He asked me to do something for him, Sarge …" Salter's eyes were focused on the gently moving water beside the boat, "in confidence."

"Then that's the way he wanted it, Constable."

"But it's to do with this case in some way, I'm sure of it." She turned to look at Danny, seeking his permission. He hesitated, and that was enough. "He gave me a phone number to check out. It's was a public call box on the high street."

Still, it seemed as if Maik couldn't quite bring himself to stop her. "I asked for the date of the call he was interested in, and the time. I offered to check the CCTV cameras for him. There's good coverage of that box. But he said no. The thing is, I'm pretty sure he's checked the footage himself. I saw the log the other day."

Maik tilted his head slightly, as if to acknowledge that the trouble with working with good detectives was that they were always good detectives. "There's still a way you can keep his confidence, Constable," he said eventually. "If you don't tell anyone else, and I don't. Whatever he's up to, he'll have a good reason. Now, is this about where you thought it was, that landing spot?"

"Just up here." Salter pointed and swung the tiller hard.

Maik stood up, bracing his calf against the low wooden seat, as Salter cut the throttle to idle, holding the boat against the slight current. He raised the camera and began filming. What they might miss here from the bobbing water surface could still appear when they reviewed the video footage back at the station.

Whether Salter saw the grey shape a split-second earlier than Maik did, she never knew. But it seemed in her later memory that she was already calling out as the water surface broke like shattering glass in front of him. The glistening grey back of the seal arced out of the water, disappearing as quickly as it had breached. But the damage had been done.

"Bloody hell," shouted Maik. He reeled back, lurching to his left as the wake from the seal's re-entry nudged the side of the boat. It was enough. Salter watched in horror as Maik's centre of gravity shifted before his legs could compensate, and she knew with the certainty of a water baby who had been on boats before she had been on a bike that Danny Maik was going over the side.

The splash rocked the small boat dangerously and Salter was thrown back into her seat from the half crouch she'd been in. She scrambled around desperately trying to fasten the tiller and get an anchor over the side, as the boat lurched and pitched. By the time she got to the side and looked over, she couldn't see him anywhere.

"Danny!" she called.

From the far side, there was a choking, gurgling noise and she swung her body around, resting her hands on the side of the boat as she scanned the water. He had gone under again. As she shifted positions, her foot caught on a taut rope. Her eyes followed it as it disappeared over the side of the boat, and she realized what had happened just as Danny surfaced again, gasping and sputtering for air. "Leg's caught, cut me loose," he managed before he disappeared again beneath the oily green surface.

Frantically, she scrambled around, upturning the hamper, sending everything scattering onto the bottom of the boat. But there was no knife. In desperation, she grabbed the taut rope, hauling back on it, even against the weight of the man and the water below. Her fingers chafed and bled and her knuckles slammed into the gunwale until she could hold the rope no longer and, with an anguished sob, had to release it.

She had just kicked off her shoes and crouched into a position to launch herself into the water when suddenly the side of the boat tipped violently towards the water. She almost lost her balance, but she recovered reflexively and fell back, striking her head against the wooden seat. Reeling, she pulled herself upright. And that's when she saw Danny Maik's beautiful, calloused hand grab on to the side of the boat.

She threw herself to the side and looked over. Danny's head was all but submerged still, but his face was out of the water, breathing air in huge, grateful gulps, so large they forced his eyes shut. She clamped her hand on his wrist, as much to let him know she was there, that she was not going to let him go under again. He was not going to drown.

"Bloody thing's round my ankles," he managed between gasps. "I can't move my legs."

"I'll hold you, Danny. I'll hold your arm here. Can you swing your other hand around and grab onto the side? I can come in and help, if you need me to. Just say."

Maik took a deep lungful of air, and then, with a massive effort, he twisted his body around and reached his free hand for the side of the boat. He missed on the first attempt, but on the second, scrabbling for purchase with an effort that left his nails bleeding, he managed to grab on to the gunwale.

"It's all right, my love, I've got you. It's all right, you're safe. I won't let you go."

It seemed to Danny as if he had been lying in the bottom of the boat for ages. He wondered if he had passed out. He remembered the lung-bursting effort of trying to haul his body back up into the boat, Lauren Salter at once stretching out to help him and pressing back against the far side of the boat to counterbalance his efforts. He remembered the point at which his chest crested the side, and he slumped forward, his legs still tangled in the rope, to crash face-first into the bottom of the boat among what seemed to be spilled food and beer cans. But then, his next memory was the sunlight in his eyes, and his legs free and the soft, cool feel of Salter's hand on his forehead, stroking it in time with her words, her rocking motion echoing that of the small boat as it eased over the swells. She was kneeling beside him, leaning in close, her other arm wrapped across his sopping shirt.

He made an effort to sit up, and Salter loosened her grip slightly before gathering him into her chest once again. "We need to keep you warm," she said. "There's a blanket in the locker. I'll get it." But she didn't move. She simply stayed there, kneeling beside him, hugging him, holding him close, telling him over and over again that he was all right, he was safe.

She stayed that way for a long time, murmuring gently to him, stroking his wet hair away from his forehead, so reluctant to let him go he even felt a tiny tug of resistance when he pulled free finally to sit fully upright and untie the remains of the rope from his legs.

"Come on," she said, suddenly, "let's get you back." Her tone was brisk now, efficient. It sounded like the voice of another person. "We need to get you out of those clothes. Into some dry ones, I mean." Her smile was brief and held no humour. She handed him the blanket and he draped it around his shoulders.

Neither of them spoke on the journey back. Salter silently performed simple tacking operations with a crisp, focused efficiency, while Danny huddled with the heavy blanket around his shoulders, lips blue and teeth chattering slightly.

Maik stared at the passing coast, the same thought circling through his mind, refusing to be shaken off. What would have happened if she hadn't been there? Would he have been able to haul himself back into the boat, with it pitching and rolling towards him so violently? By the time he had grabbed the side, he was spent, finished. He knew he had no more strength left for another try if his effort had failed. Would he have died out there?

He looked at Salter, at once studious and troubled in her silence. He wondered if she was thinking the same thing. How else to explain this business of clinging on to him, clasping him to her like that, even when it was clear he was safe and his ordeal was over? She was thinking how she would have felt if it had been her little boy, Max, he decided. Imagining the emotions she would have experienced, the terror she would have felt if it had been someone she loved.

Maik shivered slightly beneath the blanket. He felt the throttle ease and snapped his mind back to the present just in time to see the Mini hove into view around the point. Salter silently guided the boat to the shore, to the spot where they had embarked on this trip such a short time, and so many millions of emotions ago. "Here we are," she said, "terra firma. At last."

40

As Jejeune pulled up in the car park of the Old Dairy compound, the noise that came in through the open windows of The Beast was startling. All through the country lanes on his drive here, the skies and hedgerows had been filled with exuberant birdsong. Most of it, he had recognized, though there were one or two snippets he had needed to puzzle over, and a couple of others that had, frankly, defeated him. But here, despite the extensive stand of yews around the car park, and magnificent beeches and pines beyond, there was nothing. No birdsong, no sound. Above the yews, he could see the top edge of the glass office block glinting as it caught the morning sun. If it was the cause of this ominous silence, it was, in the detective's opinion, a terrible price to pay for its ultra-modern design.

Danny Maik joined him as he emerged from the car. The sergeant would not have noticed the absence of birdsong, he suspected. Danny's ears would still be ringing from the Motown he would have been playing on the way over here. Even with his windows down, it was unlikely, to say the least, that he would have been paying attention to any bird calls along the way.

Together, Maik and Jejeune walked across the car park, past the glass office block and on to the second gate, the one that emerged onto the cobbled courtyard of the old cowsheds. On all sides, the doors of individual bays stood open, revealing glimpses of the prince's stable of thoroughbreds: a Bentley Mulsanne, a Jaguar XJ220, an Aston Martin Vantage.

The Rolls-Royce Phantom sat in the sunshine, its coachwork glistening from a recent wash. Beside it sat Prince Yousef's helicopter. Abrar el-Taleb emerged from the cockpit with a cloth. He was wearing white overalls.

"I was not aware that you were coming here today," he said. It was not the friendliest greeting the two detectives had ever experienced, but then again, it was some way from being the most hostile, either.

"I would like to speak to Prince Ibrahim," said Jejeune evenly.

"The prince is not here," said el-Taleb.

"When will he return?"

El-Taleb wiped his hands on the cloth and tucked it neatly through the handle of the helicopter door. "This is not known. I suggest if you wish to discuss matters concerning Philip Wayland, you do so with me."

Jejeune seemed to consider this. Maik bought him more time, while he decided. "Nice selection," he said, indicating the cars nosing out of the refurbished cattle stalls. "I don't remember ever seeing any of this lot out on the local roads. Surely some lucky devil has to take them out for a spin every now and then. Get the fluids circulating, keep the tires supple. That'd be your job, I suppose?"

"These vehicles are the property of Prince Ibrahim," said el-Taleb simply. "No one else is permitted to drive them."

"Not even his brother?"

El-Taleb looked uneasy at the question, but before he could answer, the throaty roar of a 3.5-litre V6 engine turned their heads. Prince Ibrahim, in dark wraparound sunglasses, wheeled a canary yellow Lotus Evora 400 into the courtyard. Another ninety grand to the Lotus assembly plant just outside Norwich, thought

Maik. At a push, you could even argue that this was further evidence of the positives this Old Dairy project was having on the local economy. The prince reversed the vehicle into an empty bay on the far side of the tiny helicopter and climbed out. He walked toward the group of men purposefully, removing his sunglasses with a flourish as he approached. He was wearing a blue silk shirt and casual cream-coloured trousers, with exquisite leather loafers that Maik estimated at more per toe than his monthly salary.

"Excellency, Detective Chief Inspector Jejeune and Sergeant Maik," said el-Taleb.

The prince nodded down at them from the full six and a half feet of his height, but he did not offer his hand.

"You have come to ask more questions about this dead man who was found on my property, the researcher, Philip Wayland?" said the prince. He exuded the kind of assured calmness that came from the knowledge that you had the right blend of personality and resources to control the situation, whatever it might be.

"He was found on the public footpath that runs through your land," said Jejeune. "Your staff were under orders to ensure that Philip Wayland did not enter the compound under any circumstances, I understand. Can I ask why that was?"

"This man Wayland took my money, made me promises. I bought him equipment, hired staff, gave him everything he requested. And then he betrayed me."

"Philip Wayland wanted to be the person who achieved the breakthrough on carbon storage," said el-Taleb. "He sought a new place to achieve his dreams of glory. He did not want to give us the time to consider his new approach. He took it elsewhere." El-Taleb flicked his eyes at the prince's darkening features, as if realizing he had already given the detectives too much information.

"This sort of disrespect cannot be tolerated," said Ibrahim simply. "This is why he was not permitted to return."

"And if Wayland was trying to recover what he felt was his intellectual property, data that was still here at the Old Dairy, how would such an attempt have been received, I wonder?" mused Jejeune.

Something flashed in Prince Ibrahim's dark eyes, but instead of anger, a small smile spread across his face. "The results of Philip Wayland's research belong to the Old Dairy Carbon Capture and Sequestration Project. Mr. Wayland signed a legally binding document to this effect. For those who respect the rule of law, the question is closed. For those who do not …" The Prince spread his hands, palms up, to show the infinite range of possibilities this situation might involve.

"I think someone has stolen one of your Gyrfalcons," said Jejeune suddenly.

El-Taleb seemed ready to rush in to address Jejeune's remark, but the prince held up a hand, stilling his intervention. "You come here to talk about my birds?" He sounded incredulous. "You are wrong, Inspector Jejeune. This is not possible."

El-Taleb was already withdrawing something from his pocket when the prince beckoned him forward. He made a subtle forward motion with his downturned index finger, like a hunter setting a hound after its quarry. El-Taleb tapped the screen of his phone and pulled up an app. It showed fourteen pulsing green lights and a small chart on the left with a list of tag numbers and the current GPS locations of the signals for each one. They all read the same; the coordinates of the Old Dairy.

"These falcons are valuable animals, Inspector, cherished possessions. Do you not think I would protect them, or be able to locate them if they should fly off? Each bird is fitted with a satellite transmitter. The signals are independently monitored by a tracking station. Had any birds left the facility, for any reason, we would have been alerted immediately." He turned his eyes to el-Taleb. "We have had no such alerts?"

"None, Excellency," said el-Taleb, though everyone in the courtyard knew such confirmation was unnecessary. The prince already knew the answer. "The complete range of signals continues to come from the facility, and have been doing so, uninterrupted, since His Excellency's last visit."

Prince Ibrahim turned back to Jejeune. "This you will verify independently," he said, though whether it was a command or simply a question, neither detective could tell. But the prince's next statement was less equivocal. "When you have done so, you will trouble us no further."

"I'd like to take a look at the Gyrfalcon facility," said Jejeune flatly. The insulting inference of the request could not have been clearer, but Jejeune did not seem at all abashed to be questioning the prince's honesty. Maik was annoyed. Did Jejeune not think the sergeant could tell a white bird from a grey one? Did he not think he could count, or had looked around thoroughly enough, through the documents, the passports, the contents of the desk and filing cabinets? The unease and distrust of earlier days was beginning to take hold, he realized, colouring Jejeune's every action for him, his every comment.

"This will not be permitted," said Ibrahim coldly. "Do you think we are fools? Do you not think we know that these falsehoods are just an excuse to come here and question my brother about this researcher's death, now that Catherine Weil's statement has been challenged? My brother has not developed into the kind of man it is easy to take pride in. Nevertheless, it is my duty as the head of the family to protect its honour, its dignity. This I will do."

He turned without another word and stalked off in the direction of the research compound. The three men watched him go. Jejeune saw the Swallow fly under the eaves to the same nest as before, its beak laden with insects for its hungry brood. How many times had it made that same journey since he was last here? he wondered. The lengths we are willing to go to, the sacrifices we are ready to make for our families, to nurture them, to protect them, to keep them from harm.

"This was unwise, Inspector," said el-Taleb evenly. "Prince Ibrahim will make his displeasure known. I would suggest you do not come back onto this property."

But far from looking chastened, to Maik's surprise, Jejeune smiled indulgently. "The only reason I would need to come onto this property again, Mr. el-Taleb, would be to make an arrest."

Maik had never thought of his DCI as a man to be cowed by threats, but even so, Jejeune's demeanour as they walked back to the cars seemed a bit more sunny and carefree than he might have expected. The inspector seemed almost buoyed by his exchange with the Crown Prince, and actually smiled as he turned to the sergeant in the car park.

"So, Sergeant, how did you think that went?"

"I think it's about time I had a change of career anyway," said Maik flatly. "The prince moves in influential circles. I doubt if even the overwhelming charm of DCS Shepherd is going to prevent some sort of involvement at a higher level."

"Possibly, but we have some answers. I don't believe there's still a white Gyrfalcon at the facility, Sergeant. But there are still fourteen signals here. So somebody must have removed a transmitter from the white bird to disguise the fact that it was gone."

"De Laet," said Maik. "But I can't see how he can have done that without the assistance of Doherty."

"Nor can I," said Jejeune, "and I am betting anyone else who knew about it felt the same way."

So he hadn't wanted to check up on Maik. He had asked to visit the Gyrfalcon facility because he wanted to see the prince's reaction, to prove the point he already knew — that the prince would not let him look around, even if fourteen signals were still beaming from there. There were times when Maik got fed up with trailing around in his DCI's wake, feeding off the scraps of information tossed his way, being kept in the dark all the time, as if perhaps he couldn't quite be trusted with things. It wasn't much of a way to conduct an investigation, in Maik's opinion, all this secrecy and guardedness. Because even plodders like Danny Maik came up with nuggets of wisdom every now and again. And where would the investigation be, where would his inspector be, if Danny decided to start keeping things to himself as well? But he wouldn't do that, would he, loyal Danny? He would keep trotting along behind his inspector, trying to shove the square pegs of the evidence Jejeune collected into the round holes of police procedure, and sharing any of his own snippets of evidence that he picked up along the way.

"Those Gyrfalcons, sir," he said, "they might not have left the country since the prince was last here, but a couple of their passports have."

41

Tony Holland was worried; worried that things wouldn't be the same again. He had liked Darla, and had experienced feelings for her he hadn't known before. Feelings of protectiveness, a sense that he wanted to make things better for her. She was gone now, and he was coming to accept that, but whatever they had been, these feelings, they were still with him, occupying his thoughts, driving him on to follow his leads.

But something else was new, a strange disconnection from women, in that old sense. The one he was looking at now, for example, on the far side of the coffee shop. She was, in the vernacular of the Tony Holland of old, an absolute belter. Her trim figure had all the right curves in all the right places. Long blonde hair framed a delicate, pretty face, with skin so clear and light there was almost a translucent quality to it. She was wearing an expensive-looking outfit that combined with her air of measured confidence to tell you that this was a woman of both means and taste. It was, in a word, a package that would have had previous editions of Tony Holland trampling all over the other patrons in the coffee shop for the chance to sit next to her. And yet, here he was, sitting as far away as possible, trying not to look interested, and feeling something that he could only identify as guilt. Darla was still with him, and even if he had no intentions of acting on his interest in this woman, it was as if even acknowledging her beauty was an act of betrayal somehow. So, Tony Holland was worried. Whatever it was he had felt for Darla, she was not coming back. He would need to move on. And for him, that meant feeling the right sort of attraction to women like this again. If he ever could.

He watched the woman over the rim of his coffee cup, seeing her glancing at the large clock on the wall and checking her iPhone several times. Whoever it was she was here to meet, they were late, and our little Kazakh beauty was getting nervous. If her appointment didn't show soon, as cool and as confident as she seemed, Tamilya Aliyev would be gone.

Holland didn't know who she was waiting for, but he was as certain as he could be that it wouldn't be one of her contacts from the world of international finance. The hotel where she was staying had a lavishly appointed lobby that would have been far better suited for a business meeting than a nondescript, out-of-the-way coffee shop like this. There had been something in her demeanour, too, as he tracked her here, a furtiveness that belied the confident, rolling, shoulders-back gait with which she had sashayed through the streets of Saltmarsh. It was subtle, but it told an experienced watcher like Tony Holland that she was on her way to a meeting that had hidden cadences.

A dispute at a nearby table took his attention away from the woman momentarily. One of Saltmarsh's elderly dowagers, of which a small place like this seemed in Holland's view to have far too many, was making a fuss because the waiter had delivered the wrong order. "I ordered a Victoria Sponge," she enunciated slowly, as if getting her order wrong might be evidence of some mild form of brain damage in the unfortunate young man. "This is a Viennese Swirl."

An irrational rage built within Holland. Darla Doherty was dead and this woman's world was falling apart because she'd received the wrong pastry. *It's a cake, for God's sake,* he thought irritably. *Shove it in your face and shut up.*

When he turned back, there was someone sitting beside Aliyev. Holland was angry that he hadn't seen the man arrive, that he hadn't been able to pick up whether he had just come in or whether he'd been sitting in the coffee shop all the while, biding his time. It would have been an important point. It would have told him whether Aliyev's guest was waiting to see if anybody was watching her, whether he was expecting surveillance, alert for it. But the man sitting beside her now was not looking around, not scanning for anyone paying particularly undivided attention to them, so either way, he wasn't aware of Holland's interest. The constable forgave himself a little and settled in to watch.

The couple shared smiles, and Holland recognized in the man a practiced ease in his technique. He had clearly spent some time perfecting the art of "the pull," like Holland himself, and was comfortable in situations like this. It crossed Holland's mind that it could even be just that. Aliyev was a stunner, and she had been sitting alone. Perhaps this guy was just an innocent punter who fancied his chances. But Holland could detect something between them that was not a part of the normal joust and parry of a casual pickup. They shared something already, these two, and he became convinced, as he risked a longer-than-safe glance at them, that they were here to discuss something about which they already had a past connection. If it was Gyrfalcons, and Holland thought it was, then he needed to take in as much information about this man as he could.

"He was tallish, with dark hair," said Holland. "Full beard, but neat. I suppose some women would find him not too bad looking."

Salter looked like she was about to contribute something flippant, but Holland, understandably, hadn't been much disposed to banter these past few days, and at the last moment, she seemed to think better of it. DCS Shepherd was leaning casually against the jamb of the incident room's open doorway with her arms folded. Her presence, too, might have had some influence on Salter's decision. Despite the DCS's casual attitude, there were no white trainers today. This was the Colleen Shepherd they all knew, in full battle regalia, high heels and silk blouse open to the second button.

Maik was standing in his usual spot in front of the assembled group as Holland gave his report. At the back of the room, Jejeune was sitting on his desk, but he was hunched forward much more than normal, as if trying to commit every detail of Holland's description to memory. His stone-faced expression suggested he wasn't in the mood for humour either.

"And you're certain they were talking about Gyrfalcons?" asked Jejeune earnestly. "It couldn't have been something else? An innocent meeting between two friends, for example?"

Holland looked at the DCI questioningly, and both Shepherd and Maik joined him. It was the second time in as many contributions that Jejeune had wondered aloud whether the meeting might have been less than Holland was imagining it to be.

"I heard the word *birds*," said Holland flatly. "I couldn't get too close, obviously, but I risked one pass right by them, as if I was going to the toilets. And on the way back, I heard a name, too: Jack."

Maik looked at Jejeune for signs of a response. If there was one, an expression that seemed to flicker in Jejeune's face for a moment, before he could rein it in, Maik couldn't read what it signalled. But it was obvious the DCI wanted to keep his reactions to Holland's news under wraps, at least for now.

"Was it this man's name?" asked Shepherd, unfolding her arms and easing herself up from the jamb to an upright position. "Jack, like she was addressing him?"

Holland shook his head. "Definitely third person, ma'am." He seemed to hesitate for a moment. "This man she was meeting, though, I think his name might be John Damian."

Had there been a faint shimmer of movement from the back of the room? By the time Maik looked at Jejeune, he was motionless, intense, focused.

"He fits the description of that birder I told you about. John Damian told Quentin Senior he was over here on holiday, but there's no record of him at any of the hotels or guest houses in the area. I know, I checked them all."

"All, Tony?" Salter was the first to voice her astonishment, but the others in the room all shared it. "Bloody hell, that's a mountain of work. There must be literally hundreds of holiday rooms out here. It would have taken you hours. Why didn't you ask? Some of us could have helped."

Holland simply shrugged.

"That's a commendable effort, Constable," said Colleen Shepherd. "A pity you couldn't have followed him from the coffee shop, to find out where he was staying."

"I did," said Holland.

Now it was clear. It was alarm that DCI Domenic Jejeune had been suppressing. The sudden tensing, the agitation, the flitting gaze, as if he couldn't find a safe place to rest it. The eyes of everyone else in the room were on Tony Holland now, but it was a couple of moments before Danny Maik could bring his own to join them.

"When they finished, they went their separate ways. I didn't follow the woman, because I already knew where she was staying," said Holland practically, "so I stayed with this bloke. Only I lost him on the north Norfolk coastal path. He was heading down to your neck of the woods," he said, casting an off-hand look Jejeune's way.

"No suspicious-looking characters slinking past your place, by any chance, Domenic?" asked Shepherd with a grin.

"I couldn't say," said Domenic, forcing a smile. "I wasn't home."

But Maik wasn't smiling. Tony Holland hadn't said when it was that this mystery man, this John Damian, might have been passing by his house, so it was hard to understand how DCI Jejeune could be so certain he wouldn't have been at home. Shepherd and the others, though, had already moved back to Holland's report.

"John Damian," Shepherd said, rolling the name around in her mouth. "It's an unusual name. So why does it ring a bell with me? Sergeant? Anyone? You seem to have almost total recall of things like this, Domenic? Any suspects with that name ever cross our paths since you've been here?"

"It's never come up," he said, with a firmness that seemed to Maik's heightened sensibilities to go some way beyond certainty. "But this part of the world is a popular holiday destination; it's not unusual for out-of-towners to be wandering around. Saltmarsh's economy would pretty much crumble without them, as I understand it." He shifted his position slightly on the desk, a precursor to a shift in emphasis. "I wonder, Constable, were you able to determine the exact nature of Ms. Aliyev's business here in Saltmarsh? I mean, is there any reason to suspect she isn't also just here on holiday?"

"What, other than her putting down *business* on her hotel registration as the reason for her stay, you mean?" Holland eyed Jejeune with undisguised contempt. "There's the Kazakh connection to Gyrfalcons for a start."

Jejeune shook his head. "I don't know. There are markets all over the world for Gyrfalcons, many of them much bigger than Kazakhstan's," he said, with a quiet insistence that seemed to have eluded most people. *Most* not including Danny Maik.

"Are you saying you're not even interested in talking to her? To either of them?" asked Holland incredulously. "You're brushing all this off, just like that?"

Maik saw Shepherd shift uncomfortably. In truth, in the past, it wouldn't have been entirely unlike Jejeune to do just that, if he felt they were unproductive leads. But with Tony Holland a good deal beyond merely engaged in this line of enquiry, and Jejeune, for reasons all his own, as nervous and edgy as Maik had ever seen him, this standoff had the potential to get personal in a way few had before. Shepherd seemed to sense it, too, and flicked a glance at Maik, signalling him to move in.

"That's not the case at all, Constable, but there is no evidence that either one of them have committed any crime, is there? And I take it you've already done background checks that show neither of them as having any criminal record. So it's hard to see how we can justify bringing them in."

"Agreed," said Shepherd. "We have no grounds. If there was evidence of any connection between Darla Doherty's death and the Philip Wayland's murder, or even with the Old Dairy compound itself …"

"She died on the property, for Christ's sake," shouted Holland in exasperation.

But Shepherd was in a forgiving mood. "If either one of them crosses our radar again, we can most certainly invite them in for a chat, but until then, I'm sure what the sergeant is saying is that there are areas we can employ ourselves more productively, solid leads we can follow. We are all aware of your loss, Constable, and we are all deeply sorry for it. Truly. I understand your need to reconcile yourself to it, to get some answers, and I give you my word, if they are out there, we will pursue them. But for the moment, there's more than enough to be done in trying to find Philip Wayland's murderer."

Unable to contain his rising frustration any longer, Holland gave an exasperated snort and stormed from the room. Like the others, Maik watched his departure in silence. Once, all you had to do to turn Tony Holland off an investigation was to make it sound like hard work. But this was a different Holland now, one pursuing his own agenda, charged with an urgency and a rightness of purpose that was unlikely to be quelled by a little thing like an unenthusiastic response from his superiors. Whatever it was that Domenic Jejeune didn't want Holland looking into, Maik was pretty sure this approach wasn't going to prevent it.

42

Lindy entered the cottage with her customary post-work relief and shrugged her shoulder bag onto a chair.

"You birders have a lot to answer for," she said in a tone that Damian was unsure how to interpret. He looked up from the book he was reading with a puzzled expression.

"Taking a nice, well-balanced, rational man like Eric and turning him into a raving lunatic," she said. "He's talking about going to Hong Kong to see some bird, only he claims he has to go on 18th April. He is joking, I take it."

Damian shrugged. "When we were kids we had a Baltimore Oriole show up on the same bush on the same day three years in a row. 8th May." He smiled at the memory. "I wonder if Domenic remembers that. He was so excited by the third year he kept asking me every day when May the eighth was coming. He was so small then, he couldn't even read a calendar properly. What bird is it?"

"A Spoon-bellied Sandpiper? Does that sound right?"

Damian laughed. "Now, that's a bird I would like to see, but I think Eric will be going after a Spoon-billed Sandpiper." He inclined his head. "It's a good bird."

"But you wouldn't travel to Hong Kong to see it?"

"What, me? No. You kidding? That's crazy."

Lindy regarded him suspiciously for a moment. "Because you've already seen one, right?"

"A couple," admitted Damian sheepishly.

She slumped into a chair opposite him. "So what bird would you travel halfway round the world to see, I wonder?"

Damian gave it some thought. "There's a few, but probably top of the list would be the Floreana Mockingbird."

"Never heard of it," she said.

"Few have, which seems a little unfair, considering it's probably the single most important bird in the history of modern science."

Lindy's eyes widened and she sat forward slightly.

"It was the Floreana Mockingbird that led Darwin to the first step on his theory of natural selection," said Damian simply.

"But that was the Galapagos finches, surely? I mean even I remember that from university."

Damian shook his head. "Darwin saw the finches, but it was the difference between the mockingbirds on the Galapagos island of Floreana and a nearby island called Chatham that he suspected undermined the 'stability of species' as he called it. Of course, if anybody ever comes up with a sighting of a Spoon-bellied Sandpiper, I'm on the next plane. In fact, I think I'm going to make that my new Twitter handle."

Before Lindy could comment, they heard a car door closing outside. A look of relief crossed her face. "Thank God. He said he might go up to the Old Dairy compound again, but it looks like he changed his mind."

Damian was puzzled.

"It was a strange mood up there last time," said Lindy. "Ugly. There were some nasty undercurrents with those protesters. I worry about him going up there again, about what might happen if things get out of control. Somebody could get hurt."

Domenic opened the door, but for once there was no smile

for Lindy. For anybody. He looked directly at Damian. "Fancy a walk?"

"Not particularly," said Damian, turning his eyes back to his book. Whatever it was that had Domenic seething, Damian seemed to know what it was.

"Damian's been telling me about the Floreana Mockingbird," said Lindy innocently, trying to dispel the tension. "Did you know about this?"

Domenic nodded but it was clear he wasn't going to buy into any distraction. "We should talk," he said to his brother.

Lindy could see now that there was going to be no way of derailing the confrontation. She picked up her bag and swung her car keys around her finger. "I'm just going to pop out to the shops for a few things. I shouldn't be more than about an hour," she said, giving the men a timeline. As soon as the door closed behind her, Domenic rounded on his brother.

"Are you out of your mind?"

If Damian was going to protest ignorance, or innocence, Domenic was in no mood to give him a chance. "You were seen, Damian, talking to Tamilya Aliyev. Seen by a police officer."

Panic creased Damian's features and he involuntarily flashed a glance out the window, in case an arrest team had followed Domenic, or perhaps even accompanied him.

Domenic read the signs. "I can't protect you, Damian. If they find you here, I'm going to be in the next cell. Do you know how much harm you could have done?"

"To what, your pride? I was trying to help," said Damian simply. He wasn't defensive, but there was no contrition in his statement either.

"I don't need any help."

"You do, Domenic. You're completely on the wrong track. About the girl, about the birds, everything."

"What, so now you're an expert in police investigations, too?

Why did Aliyev agree to talk to you anyway?"

Damian shrugged evasively. "Maybe she got the impression through a draft email that I could help her get some birds." He didn't smile. "They weren't stealing the prince's Gyrfalcons, Dom. The Kazakhs are only interested in wild birds. They don't want captive ones."

"They seemed happy enough to take the prince's white Gyr."

Damian shook his head. "No," he said. "White Gyrfalcons are not what they want. Black. That's what they're after, the darker the better. Why do you think we were up in Labrador? That's where the dark Gyrs are."

Domenic considered this news, the information taking the edge off his anger.

"Then why the sudden need for a white one?" he asked. "Iceland. Scotland. You said he intended to bring that bird to north Norfolk. What was that all about? Unless De Laet had more than one customer."

Damian tapped his lips with his forefinger. "I can't explain that. He wasn't in touch with anybody except the Kazakhs, as far as I know. But Aliyev said they would never pay the premium De Laet would want for a wild white Gyrfalcon." He paused and looked at his brother. "It's about passports. De Laet some- how convinced Doherty to provide them, so the Kazakhs could transport the wild Gyrs he got for them into their country. As soon as the birds arrived safely in Kazakhstan, the passports were returned to the Old Dairy, and no one was any the wiser."

"So what went wrong?"

"The Kazakhs paid for two birds, but there was a foul-up in the delivery schedule, and De Laet had to hold onto them for a while. Eventually the Kazakhs gave him the green light, but the birds were never sent. Aliyev came over to find out why." He paused significantly. "This is a dangerous business, Dom. The places some of these people come from, they're like the Wild West. They don't have a lot of respect for law and order. They don't see an unarmed police force as some quaint reminder of an earlier, more innocent time, they see it as a sign they have the advantage."

"Thanks, Damian," said Domenic sarcastically. "I have travelled a bit you know."

"Yeah, but seeing the world through the windows of the local Sheraton is not quite the same as being on the ground in these places."

It was the kind of remark that would have sent Domenic into a tailspin when they were growing up, but now, despite his anger, he was able to see Damian's words for what they were, a manifestation of his older brother's genuine concern for him.

Damian's tone softened. "I'm just saying you need to be careful, that's all. There's a lot of bad money out there, money from sources you don't even want to think about. I think the Kazakhs have taken the soft approach so far because this is dream arrangement. Trapping wild birds is the easy part. It's smuggling them across borders that takes the real work. To be able to waltz birds through Almaty Airport on a passport, that's an arrangement worth protecting. But as soon as they find out De Laet's gone, and their chances of getting any more birds have gone with him, they're going to have nothing to lose. If they start throwing their weight around to get what they've already paid for, people could get hurt."

"Perhaps they already have."

Damian shook his head slowly. "Aliyev didn't kill that girl, Domenic. I know what that feels like ..."

"Stop, Damian."

"I know, Domenic, and I'm telling you, she's not carrying that around with her. I could see it in her eyes."

He was silent for a long moment.

"I don't know how we got here, Domenic, you and I.

Sometimes, our past, those days we spent as kids, it all seems so far away it's like it never even happened." He shook his head. "I was telling Lindy about that Baltimore Oriole that came back to our garden year after year. Remember?"

Domenic nodded and seemed to peer into the past. "May ninth, three years in a row."

Damian didn't bother correcting him. It wasn't another argument he was looking for, merely a return to an earlier time, a time of innocence, when they had both been facing the world from the same side, before life and its labyrinthine ways had come between them. "A miracle of timing, Mom called it. Remember?"

"Timing," said Domenic, nodding slightly to himself. And then again, more significantly, "Timing."

And then, Damian knew his brother wasn't back in their childhood garden anymore. Domenic Jejeune had just closed in on a killer.

43

Lindy was sitting in the living room, her feet tucked beneath her on the couch as Domenic came in. She surreptitiously stashed her reading material away, but she knew he had seen it and she smiled guiltily. Her article, reread for the umpteenth time. Despite her ongoing protestations, he knew it meant a great deal to her to win the award. It would be a justification, of sorts, that she had made the right choice. Following the glare of public recognition that had accompanied her coverage of Domenic's case involving the Home Secretary's daughter, Lindy had been offered a number of high-profile positions. Her decision to abandon the frenzied world of national newspaper journalism for the opportunity to do more in-depth pieces with a smaller magazine had surprised most, and outraged some, and the lean years that had followed had often left her squirming with self-doubt about her choice. Though this nomination had raised her profile nationally again, Domenic knew that, in the competitive world of journalism, only winning the award would truly establish her place once more among the industry's elite.

"Okay if I turn this off?" He crossed the room and consigned another vapid Canadian one-hit wonder to silence.

"Damian?" he asked, to spare her the effort of acknowledging her reading material.

"Out for a walk. I feel so sorry for him at times, cooped up in here. You can see him almost pacing back and forth to get back out there. It's like he's in captivity. By the way, 'Disturbing Mental Image Alert'." She splayed her fingers out at him like blinking neon sign. "I think my boss and your boss may be hooking up sometime soon."

Jejeune's eyes widened. Lindy nodded in confirmation. "Eric sidled up to me and asked in an ever-so-casual way whether you might be able to get him Colleen Shepherd's phone number."

"Could it be about a story for the magazine?"

Lindy gave him an exasperated look. "Since he's the senior editor of one of the country's leading magazines, I think we can assume he'd know the police department has a Press Office to handle requests like that."

"I've always thought of Eric as a man who seemed more comfortable in the company of attached women," said Domenic.

"Some men are like that. Perhaps he's always just enjoyed the comfort of knowing he doesn't have to try, if they're already taken. In truth, it's unlike him to take such a direct approach. Like his birding, he seems ready to get serious in a hurry. Perhaps he's reached that stage of life where he realizes he might only get one more shot at things."

She could only smile at the look of anguish on his face. "Cheer up, Dom, I sincerely doubt they'll wile away their evenings talking about us. It may come as something of a shock to you, but the world doesn't entirely revolve around DCI Domenic Jejeune." A thought seemed to strike her. "Isn't it funny how she always seems drawn to the same kind of man — confident, powerful, charming?"

Jejeune nodded sadly. "And it always seems to turn out so badly for her." He paused for a moment. "Do you think that's always the case, that a person tends to be attracted to the same type of partner? That after one relationship, they might move on to somebody else who is similar in a lot of ways?"

Lindy let her beautiful eyes rest on Domenic in a long, unblinking stare. "My, what an interesting question, Inspector Jejeune! Santayana said those who do not remember the past are condemned to repeat it. Is that what you're afraid of? Damian hasn't covered the chapters on your love life back in Canada, in case you were wondering — at least not yet. Or have I got this backward? Should I be worried that you're going to leave me for a younger and more beautiful version of myself?"

"I'm hardly likely to leave you for an older, uglier version, am I?"

Lindy pressed her forefinger to her lips and then wagged it at Domenic. "There are right answers, Inspector Jejeune, and there are wrong answers," she said archly "And then, there are *wrong* answers." She looked up and saw that something was troubling him. He sat in a chair opposite her. It was what he did when they needed to speak, and Lindy recognized the signs. She deliberately didn't change her relaxed pose; the less formal she was, the less guarded he was likely to be.

"He's asked you, hasn't he? Damian. What he risked coming from Canada to ask, on a boat across the North Atlantic?" She smiled to let him see how pleased she was with herself at having been able to piece so much of this together already.

Jejeune turned to look out the window. The tree where the Nightingale had been was dancing in the breeze, but there was no bird among the leaves today.

"He's asked. But I can't help him."

"You must. Whatever he did, whatever kind of a mistake he made, it shouldn't be allowed to ruin someone's life to the point he has to skulk around indoors like this, not even able to let his family know where he is, or even that he's safe? Whatever it is he's asking you to do, can it be worse than that?"

She looked at him, torn by what she took to be his turmoil at having to choose between his duty as a policeman and that as a brother. She suspected he had never held anything but the strictly legal point of view and was tormented now by the knowledge that he had to abandon the principles he had held dear for so long. The agony she felt for him was almost like a physical pain. "It's an awful choice, Dom, I know. No one should ever have to face it. But he's your brother, and he needs your help. You can't let him down. I understand, I really do."

But he knew she didn't.

"He wants me to broker a deal for him," he said quietly, staring into the space between them, "to save him from being extradited to Colombia."

"Extradited?" Lindy unfurled her legs and sat forward intently now. "They don't do that for bits and pieces, Dom. Extradited on what charge?"

"Manslaughter. He's wanted in connection with the deaths of four people."

He reached out for her, but she rushed past him, tears seeming to have come from nowhere. The front door smashed open as she fled. He left it swinging wide, too crushed to go after her, too crushed even to rise.

Jejeune paced in their narrow kitchen and checked his watch again. He glanced out the window, at the blue expanse of the sea, stretching out to infinity. He had determined to give her five minutes before venturing after her, but now that time was up, he decided on two more. He watched the time disappear second by second, refusing to move until the second hand swept past the twelve. It was a tiny, pathetic display of resolve, as if the extra few seconds might make the difference, might bring back the Lindy he may have lost. Forever.

She was on the cliff path looking out to sea, where he knew she would be. It was where she went for solitude, for comfort, perhaps for certainty, too. He came up beside her tentatively. She didn't turn her head, although he knew she'd sensed his approach. He stood beside her for a moment, silent, uncertain, before reaching down for her hand, fearing the rejection that would burn his skin like acid. But she let him take it and he felt the kind, precious warmth of her fingers as they entwined his own.

"I'm so sorry," he said.

But for what? For the deceit, or for the callous, cruel revelation of it? For the pain he had caused her? Or for being himself at this moment, when he felt she might have preferred the presence of just about anyone else by her side?

Lindy said nothing. He risked a glance across at her and saw traces of tears still on her cheeks. Was she waiting for the onshore winds to dry them? Or was she waiting for Domenic to make them go away, by telling her that none of it was true, that it was all just some nightmare, and the innocent, blissful life the two of them had built in this windswept hilltop was still intact, as pure and as perfect as before?

"He led a personalized tour into an area designated as off-limits by the Colombian government. The man was sick. Damian's group made contact with a small band of indigenous people, and four of them died later from contracting the illness."

Lindy stared out resolutely over the sea, but something in her changed, a slight relaxing in the tension. "You can't call that manslaughter."

"It's what the Colombian government calls it. Foreigners were expressly forbidden from visiting that area. Damian had even applied for a permit and been denied one. He entered the region anyway. And he did it for money. The man died shortly after from his illness, and the local guide is nowhere to be found. Damian was the only target the authorities had left."

It was getting cold now and Lindy had no jacket on, but neither made a move to go back to the cottage. It was as if they both sensed that they could not return there now, to the life they used to have, until they had discussed this thing that threatened to take it away from them.

Lindy shook her head. "This doesn't sound right. It's such a massive over-reaction. As heartbreaking as the deaths of these poor people were, surely anybody could see that this was completely innocent." She shook her head again. "It isn't manslaughter in any sense that I understand the word."

"It was just months after the Colombian government had issued a very public apology to the Witoto people, acknowledging their horrific treatment at the hands of the rubber barons in the early days of the rubber industry in that area. The government undoubtedly saw the chance to prosecute an unscrupulous foreigner as a heaven-sent opportunity to prove they were taking Native rights seriously, and actively trying to protect them."

"It sounds like the trial would have been a foregone conclusion," said Lindy. "I can't imagine how terrifying it must have been for Damian to go into a courtroom knowing the verdict had already been decided."

Domenic shook his head. "There was no trial. Damian got wind of the charges and fled the country. He's smart, he's resourceful; he knows the culture and the language in that part of the world. He made it all the way to St. Lucia, but he was found there and arrested. I heard he confessed to his crimes when they picked him up."

She turned to him, incredulous. "You heard?"

"I hadn't seen him since this all happened, until a few days ago. But I know he escaped from custody before the St. Lucian government could extradite him to Colombia. There's been a warrant out for his arrest since then."

Lindy was quiet for a long time. A blustery wind picked up off the sea and brought its coolness over the clifftop. "He confessed?" she said finally.

Jejeune nodded, but he could find nothing more to say.

"You have to do it, Dom. You have to help him."

Did he? Jejeune said nothing. His brother had spent a long time running from the knowledge that he was responsible for the deaths of four people. But Domenic was fairly sure that, one way or the other, his days of running were coming to an end.

44

"Sergeant Maik," said Catherine Weil with undisguised pleasure. "I thought I might be seeing you here, now that you've been given the old red card from the property. *Persona non grata* these days, I hear."

She was wearing figure-hugging blue jeans and a loose cotton blouse of dazzling white. With her cascade of red curls draped over her shoulders, she cut a striking figure.

"I think it's the DCI who's non grata," said Maik, "I'm what they refer to as 'collateral damage.'" He gave her a small smile to show he was going to be able to live with the disappointment, and stepped into the hallway as she stood aside for him.

She crossed to the sink and filled the kettle without asking. An ex-army type, of Maik's age and sensibilities? He could forgive her for being presumptuous. It gave him the chance to look around the flat. It was very small. The sparseness and frugality in which some people lived never ceased to amaze him. The apartment was immaculately clean and tidy. He would have expected no less from a woman with such a meticulously ordered mind and crisp, no-nonsense demeanour. He couldn't imagine much tolerance for clutter, physical or intellectual, in Catherine Weil's world. But there was little evidence that any personal investment had been made to turn the tiny living space into a home, no little touches that claimed it from the anonymity of a dwelling space and marked it as Catherine Weil's own. Maik would be the first to admit that his view of the world could be somewhat dated, at times, but it looked to him like the living quarters of a woman waiting for the man of her dreams to arrive and carry her off to somewhere better.

On a shelf above the built-in washing machine, Maik saw a small pile of neatly folded laundry. Weil turned in time to see him avert his eyes from her underwear. She smiled as she handed him his tea.

"Don't worry, Sergeant, nothing to get your pulse racing. More like Queen Victoria's Secret, these days, unfortunately."

"No time for romance?" Maik had no idea where the question had come from, and it seemed to distress him far more than Weil. She simply rolled her narrow shoulders easily.

"You've come to tell me once again that I was mistaken about seeing Philip that night in the woods. That nice Constable Salter of yours has already had a bash." She took a sip of her tea. "I wasn't. It was Philip I saw."

"The other man is very similar," said Maik reasonably. "In build, general appearance. He was even carrying a similar leather satchel. It does seem likely …"

"It was Philip. I worked closely beside the man for over a year, Sergeant. I identified Philip's body at the mortuary. It was him I saw entering those woods that night."

Maik shrugged his shoulders. Jejeune had told him she would insist, and that he shouldn't push it. In fact, he had the distinct impression he had been told to come here and ask more for form's sake than anything else.

"We can go out onto the balcony, if you like," said Weil, without the slightest hint of lingering offence. It was how she was, thought Maik, she dealt with something and brushed it aside, moved on. She stepped out onto the narrow balcony and leaned against its waist-high railing. Even from this modest height, barely one storey above street level, Saltmarsh took on a different perspective. With its trim front gardens and clay-tiled roofs, it looked like a village from a postcard. If you stood beside Maik up here and told him Saltmarsh had never seen a crime, he might almost have believed you. Up on a hill in the distance, he saw a faint glint of light. Concealed as it was behind its bank of dense yew trees at ground level, he hadn't considered the Old Dairy office building would be visible from other vantage points.

He turned to see Weil looking in the same direction, her hand held up at her brow like a visor against the high sun.

"Forgive me, but, it strikes me you're not particularly happy up at the Old Dairy."

"Not particularly, Sergeant. No."

"Then why do you stay? I mean, Philip Wayland found a way to make the move. Could you not have followed him?"

"To the university?" She let out a delighted laugh. "I have to say, I don't think Philip's fiancé would have cared much for that."

"Is that because of your own previous relationship with Mr. Wayland?"

She snapped her head around, as if to deny it, but then seemed to resign herself to something and simply smiled.

"You had met his parents," said Maik simply, "you knew them well enough to want to spare them the sight of their son's body. It was a caring thing to do. A brave one. The sort of act that might go beyond friendship."

"It was something that happened," she said matter-of-factly. "Sometimes a physical attraction is the first link in the chain of intimacy, sometimes it's the reverse. Shared interests, experiences, hopes can lead you there."

Maik nodded. Though Jejeune had suggested she wouldn't deny it when he told his sergeant to ask, Danny had been quietly hoping that for once, his DCI might have been wrong.

"Had it ended by the time Mr. Wayland left?"

She nodded. "God, yes. Long before. Months. Professional differences, I suppose you could call it, but in reality, we had just drifted apart. After he moved on, Philip just thought it was better if we kept it quiet. He was getting engaged." She shrugged. "It didn't really matter to me one way or the other."

"But if not the university, then surely you could still find a job somewhere else. I mean, you're a bright woman … person," he said awkwardly. If this was how he was going to conduct himself at interviews from now on, he thought, it might have been better if Salter hadn't dragged him back aboard the boat after all. "I'm just wondering why you would stay there if you're so unhappy."

She met the question head on, frank and seemingly not offended. "The simple answer, Sergeant? Money. Filthy lucre. I'm not under any illusion that the project can ever be successful, not within the parameters they have set, but if someone is willing to pay me to prove it, then I may as well get as much as I can for wasting my time. We'll get there with the capture, eventually, but we're still miles away with the storage challenges. Abrar el-Taleb is no Philip Wayland, and it's his expertise that would be needed to make any undersea carbon storage plan work." She leaned her elbow on the balcony rail as she turned to look at Maik directly. "Just in case you're wondering, though, I'm not completely mercenary. I have voiced this opinion a number of times."

"And they weren't willing to listen?"

She turned away from him. "It was politely pointed out to me that my opinions are exactly that, and while they graciously acknowledged that I was perfectly entitled to have them, the Old Dairy board of directors sees no reason to share them."

Maik leaned on the railing and drank in the scene before him. There were so many things he found to dislike about his job at times, and the obvious deception and evasiveness of a DCI he had come to trust and respect was high amongst them these days. But a sunny morning tea break with a woman like Catherine Weil could do a lot to restore you enjoyment of your job. She was such easy company, so open and honest, with a disarming frankness that took on a much more appealing quality when she wasn't bristling under the slights, perceived or otherwise, of the Old Dairy executive or DCI Jejeune.

"Niall Doherty thinks the al-Haladins will walk away at some point?" said Maik, still looking at the glass building. "Do you think he's right?"

Weil shook her head. "Prince Ibrahim has a personal stake in this."

Maik looked confused. "Forgive me, but how exactly does a ruler from an inland desert kingdom have a personal stake in global temperature increases?"

"With the warming in the Arctic and the melting of the polar ice caps, which creatures do you think are going to be most vulnerable?"

"Those that live there," said Maik. He nodded, understanding. "Like Gyrfalcons."

"Men like the prince need a project big enough to fit their egos, important enough to be worthy of their resources, and the animals of the polar regions are under the greatest threat of any creatures on Earth from the direct effects of climate change. But when you have the resources to put your support behind just about any cause you want to, I think there has to be some spark, some glimmer of personal interest. Prince Ibrahim could have any hunting birds he wanted, even eagles. And yet he chose Gyrfalcons, exclusively. I think he truly loves those birds, Sergeant. Perhaps they represent a freedom, a spirit that even he, with his vast fortune, still can't control." She shrugged. "So no, I don't see him walking away."

In the cobbled street below, people passed by utterly unaware they were being observed from on high. They continued with their tics, their traits, their unturned collars and hitched up skirts. So much of humanity's foibles were there to see, thought Maik, if a person wasn't aware they were being observed. He finished his tea and looked around for somewhere to set the empty mug. "Best be off," he said. Weil held out her hand and he passed the mug to her.

"Sergeant," she said, as he turned to go, "this brilliant DCI of yours. Is he going to catch Philip's killer, do you think?"

"Any day now, we expect," he said, returning her smile. "Well, hope, anyway." But there was something in the way he said it that made Catherine Weil think that hope wasn't a commodity Danny Maik had in particularly strong supply these days.

45

The music, so often a balm on their drives together, seemed to miss the mark today. Whatever Maik had managed to dig out of the Motown archives, it was setting Jejeune's teeth on edge. With evenings at home now a steady diet of tunes from his darkest past, the DCI was rapidly tiring of musical nostalgia. And now Maik was apparently intent on subjecting him to more rubbish from half a century ago.

"For God's sake, doesn't anybody listen to music by people who can still chew their own food?"

Despite the music, the silence in Maik's Mini was deafening, and Jejeune regretted his outburst immediately. "I'm sorry, Sergeant. Bad day at the office. Several bad days, as a matter of fact." He rubbed his forehead and tried an ingratiating smile. It didn't really come off, but Maik was in an indulgent mood.

"I'm sure Mary Wells has heard worse." said Maik evenly. "Eddie Holland would have approved, though. He always had an ear for a good line." He leaned forward to turn down the volume, but Jejeune held up a hand.

"No, Sergeant, leave it. It's fine."

He turned to look out the window at the passing countryside. Maik knew the outburst wasn't really about Mary Wells. But then again, he doubted it was about a bad day at the office either. The

DCI had experienced bad days before, without ever showing this kind of reaction. Plenty of them. They both had. In fact, Maik was hardly going to put a circle around today's date on the calendar himself. Solicitous questions from DCS Shepherd into his well-being had a way of making Danny's day turn sour in a hurry.

"You're sure you're okay, Sergeant," Shepherd had asked earlier that morning, her concern genuine, but no less annoying for all that. "No need to talk to anybody about what happened? I can book you an appointment if necessary."

"I got a bit wet, that's all. It was nothing. I'm fine."

"But you have a fear of boats, I understand. It must have been traumatic for you."

Maik had sighed irritably. This was how rumours got started. "I don't particularly like being on boats, but I'm not afraid of them. I don't much like the current Norwich City lineup either, but I wouldn't say it scares me. Mind you, that defence they've got at the moment …"

But Shepherd wasn't buying levity. This was her element, caring for her staff, showing compassion, making sure they were fit for the job.

"It's just you've been in the wars a bit recently. The head …" She touched her own. "Everything still okay there, I take it?"

"Still got just the one," said Maik. He had recently had stitches removed from a severe gash near the crown of his head, received when he tried to arrest a suspect, and Salter hadn't been the only one surreptitiously watching Danny Maik's gait and speech for signs of lingering effects.

She nodded. "And the other business?" she tapped her fingers delicately against her sternum, the protector of the heart. Against external threats, anyway.

"Still just the one of those, too."

Maik's pleasant smile indicated that he wouldn't be answering any more questions about a heart condition that it took all of his willpower to even acknowledge, let alone discuss. To her credit, Shepherd read the signal immediately.

"Well," she said, switching gears, "all I can say is thank God you had the good sense to take another officer with you. I need hardly point out how this reinforces the importance of having backup on these kinds of operations."

But hardly needing to point something out was Shepherd-speak for telling him she would be soon be giving them all a lecture about the importance of staying partnered up whenever they went out on a call. Maik had felt another sigh building. As if he didn't feel bad enough, now he was saddled with the knowledge that he would be responsible for inflicting one of Shepherd's pep talks on them all.

"So what are we going to be doing up here?" Maik asked, as casually as he could manage. It took Jejeune some time to turn from his examination of the fields.

"Chancing our arms, Sergeant. Trying to see if we can make something happen."

There were probably responses that could have made Maik feel worse, but just at the moment, he couldn't come up with any.

"It's the inconsistency. I'm not getting the same story from the people at the Old Dairy. Prince Yousef claims never to have seen Wayland's proposal, and yet Catherine Weil appears to know a great deal about it. El-Taleb claims they were not given the time to consider it, not the *chance*, Sergeant, the *time*. You see my problem?"

"Still, sir, el-Taleb's English, as fluent as it is, it's an easy mistake to make."

Jejeune made a face to suggest he wasn't convinced.

Maik drove for a moment in silence, the music turned so low only the heartbeat of the rhythm section was audible.

"The person playing bass on this track, it's a man named James Jamerson," he said.

Jejeune looked less than interested.

"He was Motown's top bass player in the sixties. I mean, widely acclaimed as being one of the best there has ever been. He played on a lot of great songs." Maik paused and looked at Jejeune for emphasis. "A lot. Around the same time, though, there was a top-flight session musician by the name of Carole Kaye, and she claimed she had played bass on some of these same songs."

"Awkward," said Jejeune, perhaps more interested than he expected himself to be. "So who was lying?"

"Neither of them. It turns out Carole Kaye played on recordings of some tunes to be used on shows on the West Coast and Jamerson played on the recordings for the tracks in Detroit. Of course, the story goes a bit deeper than that. You can only have one original recording. But the thing is, essentially, sometimes there are versions of the truth. Perhaps each person at the Old Dairy is only stating the version they know."

Jejeune thought for a moment. "Then I'd say we need to get up to the Old Dairy compound as quickly as possible, Sergeant."

Maik sighed. It was typical of his luck that introducing a harmless topic like the Motown bass controversy had now, in some strange way, led to this urgency for them to get to the Old Dairy, in direct contravention of DCS Shepherd's directive to him that morning.

"Everything fine with the inspector?" The segue from the value of partners had not been subtle, but then, Maik doubted Shepherd had intended it to be. "He doesn't seem a little bit guarded to you, secretive?"

"More than usual, you mean?"

He had given her as innocent a stare as he could manage.

She had returned it with a casual smile. "He does so like his obtuse angles," she said.

"They say he's at his best when he's thinking laterally."

Plain-speaking Danny Maik reverting to reportage might have been a sign of something, even if neither of them seemed sure quite what it was. Shepherd had picked up a paper from her desk, as if she might want to diffuse the directness of her next question. If so, she had thought better of it at the last moment, laying it down again and fixing Danny with a look from over her glasses.

"You don't think he's distracted by anything?"

"Anything?" Maik shifted his eyes a little from Shepherd's gaze, as if he was trying to will the conversation to another place. But this morning, DCI Colleen Shepherd was not for turning.

"This business with the Kazakh woman, and this man, the birder. He seems to want to not pursue it. Any idea why?"

"No," said Danny. There were a couple of half-formed thoughts, perhaps. But nothing that Danny Maik would classify as a fully-fledged theory.

"Do you think he needs some time off?" Shepherd was staring at him when he finally looked up again.

"I think he needs some answers."

She had treated him to one of her special looks, as if suspecting behind all these short responses a desire to avoid telling her something more. "You know he wants permission to go back up to the compound? He doesn't have anything, does he? Anything firmly tying Prince Yousef to Wayland's murder?"

"No ma'am, he doesn't."

Shepherd mulled this over for a few moments. "I want you to stay close, keep him out of trouble."

"What kind of trouble?" Maik had asked warily.

She looked down at her desk and then back up directly into his eyes. "He's a wonderful detective, Sergeant, but he doesn't always seem to understand where his own best interests lie. If he even looks as if he's about to go up there and accuse the prince of being involved in Wayland's murder, I expect you to do something about it."

Shepherd had a way of ending interviews sometimes that left Danny Maik wondering if there was any more to come. He hovered uncertainly for a few seconds before making his way to the door.

"By the way," she said, not bothering to look up from her correspondence, "in case you were wondering, we won't be docking your pay for dropping an expensive piece of police kit in the drink."

Maik had toyed with the idea of telling her that he knew exactly where the video camera was, if she fancied going to retrieve it. But instead he just left her office, her instructions still ringing in his ears.

Jejeune's studied silence as they drove unnerved Danny Maik. The DCI often sat beside him without speaking, scanning the passing countryside for any birds that might be up and flitting about. But this was different. There was an edge to this quiet, a brooding, troubled intensity that went beyond Jejeune simply mulling things over. He had seen the DCI like this before, and it meant he was close to something. But what?

Maik didn't like babysitting jobs at the best of times, but this one Shepherd had saddled him with had the potential to go wrong on so many levels that he found it easier just to push the possibilities to the back of his mind. Even with a normally functioning Jejeune, matters were never quite as straightforward as you might like them to be. The DCI's erratic attention span and wild theories often led them into territory where they had no right straying. Maik had the scars to prove it. But trying to intercept a Domenic Jejeune in this distracted, unpredictable mood from embarking on his latest attempt at career suicide was going to be doubly difficult. DCI Jejeune was, in Maik's considered opinion, teetering on a tightrope these days. And the high winds were blowing.

As Maik negotiated a tight left onto the narrow single-lane road that led out to the Old Dairy compound, he tried the same nonchalant vein he had struck earlier. "I just wanted to confirm, sir, we haven't come across any evidence tying anybody up here to Philip Wayland's murder?"

Having given Shepherd a bulletproof assurance a scant few hours ago, Maik thought it might be nice to find out whether it was true. But far from reassuring Maik, the strange, almost disconnected way Jejeune delivered his answer left him feeling more uneasy than ever.

"Not yet. But we haven't quite finished looking."

46

Later, Maik recalled the steely determination in Jejeune's face. That should have told him something about how the DCI intended to go about matters. A confrontation was his guess, a full-frontal assault on Prince Yousef that might shake something loose. If he failed, this gambit was likely to have diplomatic consequences beyond DCS Shepherd's worst nightmares. A call to her would be Maik's first act when he parked the car at the Old Dairy compound.

"I don't like the look of this," he announced, as he turned off the road onto the driveway leading up to the Old Dairy's gates. A large crowd of protesters had gathered at the entrance to the facility, but there was no aimless milling around, no sporadic chants, feeding off each other, morphing into an almost festive, party-like atmosphere. Instead a mood of uneasy stillness hung over the crowd, a menacing hush, as if they were marshalled in anticipation of something, like gunpowder packed into a barrel, waiting for a spark. Maik swung the Mini into the car park and nodded at the fence. "I'll call for support. I'll meet you in there."

Jejeune made his way through the crowd and flashed his badge at the guard manning the small pedestrian gate.

"The Crown Prince is leaving," the man said. "He returns home today." Jejeune turned as the crunch of car tires on gravel announced the arrival of the Phantom behind him. As the gates swung open, the crowd surged forward and the wire fence heaved with the crush of bodies. Jejeune was swept along with the movement, but as he passed the car he caught a flash of a second silhouette in the back seat: Yousef. Prince Ibrahim was going to spirit his younger brother out of the country with him, denying Jejeune the chance for an interview. Jejeune spun from the fence and tried to force his way back through the crowd, making for the roadway. He looked above the sea of heads for Danny Maik, and saw him approaching at a jog, but still too far away to hear a call over the noise of the angry crowd.

The protesters began hammering ferociously against the side of the car as it inched through the crowd, rocking it on its suspension. From somewhere, a wooden stake emerged and smashed violently against the roof, splintering on impact. A demonstrator draped herself across the radiator grille, forcing the driver to stop. A team of expensively suited bodyguards moved in to remove her, and the crowd crushed in around them in protest. Jejeune inched his way to the car and pressed his warrant card against the window. To both his and the crowd's astonishment, the door opened and Crown Prince Ibrahim got out. He gazed imperiously around at the gathering, looking not in the least bit intimidated. His bearing stilled the mob to silence and they backed off slightly.

"I need to speak to your brother, Your Excellency."

Prince Ibrahim's calm was unnerving. Jejeune had known other powerbrokers, but their power lay in their associations, their positions, their possessions. Stripped of these, they were just people, and every one Jejeune had known was still afraid of something, some force or entity greater than themselves. The prince had the same attributes of these other men, but if he had any of their demons, he kept them very well hidden. There was a cold, composed, self-assurance about this man that suggested he knew the full range of his powers, and he would have no hesitation in using them.

"My brother is accompanying me to a business meeting. His legal representatives will contact you in due course."

"I have questions for him regarding a murder inquiry. He cannot leave this country until I have spoken to him." Jejeune's tone was urgent, compelling. He realized this was the only chance he was going to get. Everything hinged on these next few moments.

"We have many things of importance to deal with. I can give this matter no more consideration." He turned to re-enter the car.

But Domenic Jejeune wouldn't allow anyone to treat murder victims as inconveniences. No one had enough power, enough influence, enough wealth, to step over dead bodies and continue on with their life unconcerned.

"Three people are dead, Excellency," he shouted angrily, loud enough even for people farther away in the crowd to hear, "and you and your brother *will* afford them the dignity of your consideration."

"Three?" The prince tilted his head to one side slightly. "I know of only two, a woman who did not work at the project and a man who was passing through my property."

"A man who used to work for you. Your brother has no alibi for the night Philip Wayland died. No one seems able to tell us where he was the night a man who abandoned your project in favour of a rival one was murdered."

A strange light seemed to flicker for a moment in the prince's dark eyes, a hint of something Jejeune didn't recognize.

"You have a reputation as an excellent detective, Inspector, but I wonder if you always understand *why* a person acts the way they do. In this case, particularly, I think, you do not."

"Was Philip Wayland's defection just an act of betrayal? Or was it something more pragmatic. His departure compromised your project, didn't it? Possibly even gave the edge to someone else? I can't imagine the House of al-Haladin taking the potential loss of a billion pound project lightly. Some might even see Philip Wayland's actions as worthy of vengeance."

The prince's face darkened with anger. "I will listen to no more of your insults." He spun on his heel and began to make his way back to the car.

From the periphery of the crowd, Maik had watched the exchange warily. There was desperation in Jejeune's face, a recognition that if he allowed these men to leave, it would all be over, his case, his search for justice in Philip Wayland's death. Somebody needed to rein the DCI in, but Danny was too far away, on the far side of the crowd, with thirty bodies between him and Jejeune. Maik noticed a bearded man behind Jejeune beginning to sidle closer to the confrontation, looking more intense than the rest of the protesters, more focused.

Perhaps Jejeune was not the first to move towards the prince. Perhaps there was a slight surge to crowd in around him as he turned to get back in the car, and the detective was simply carried forward by the other bodies. Amongst all the jostling, it was hard to tell. But it was Jejeune's hand that reached out for the prince's shoulder. Maik was sure of that. The action seemed to explode in slow motion. Maik saw the prince's muscular bodyguard reach around the DCI's throat and fasten him in a chokehold. He saw the inspector's knees buckle and watched him sink to the ground.

Maik flailed his arms, pushing bodies frantically out of the way in an effort to reach his DCI, but the crowd was packed so tightly, the people had nowhere to go. He shrugged his arms high to swim through the mass of bodies, but he made no headway and was carried away by the ebb of the swaying crowd until he, too, lost his footing and stumbled back into the people behind him. Maik heard a sharp crack and the sounds of a scuffle. A rush of alarm rose; cries and shouts. A car door slammed and the sound of an engine revving at high speed caused further panic, as people dove away from the moving vehicle. By the time he was upright again, Maik could see the scarlet of blood and hear the gasps of horror. He put his head down, burrowing through the crowd, parting them now with an irresistible force, to get to his DCI.

The blood had forced everyone back a step or two, and there was a small space around the two men. Jejeune was on one knee, holding a hand against his throat. Beside him, the guard who had grabbed him had sunk to the ground. Blood was streaming from his eyebrow and nose. A second bodyguard arrived at the edge of the circle at the same time as Maik. He reached under his armpit and withdrew a pistol. Maik lunged for him, both hands reaching for the gun arm and stretching it into the sky. He stomped a vicious kick into the inside of the man's knee and snapped an elbow back into his jaw, twisting the gun away from the guard's hand as he crumpled to the ground.

The sight of the gun caused panic in the crowd and people recoiled, stumbling as they fell back, spinning off each other in a desperate rush to get away, only to meet the wall of others crushing in.

"Stay where you are. We are police officers. You are not in any danger now."

Maik's bellow seemed to freeze them all in their tracks. Holding the gun low in one hand, he grabbed Jejeune's arm and helped him to his feet. The two bodyguards lay on the ground. Neither made any move to get up. The Rolls was already out of sight, a faint haze of dust and distant hum of a rapidly retreating engine its only legacy.

"Please move back over to the fence," said Maik in a tone of authority that brooked no argument. "Do not leave. We will need to speak to all of you as witnesses. Other officers will be here shortly. We will not detain you any longer than necessary."

But some had sloped off already, and others sidled away now, unwilling to have their names associated with a protest that had got so dangerously out of hand. One in particular, Maik noticed, was missing now, the taller man with a dark beard, who had been close to Jejeune, very close indeed, when the inspector and his assailant had gone to ground.

47

By the time DCS Shepherd arrived on the scene, most of the witnesses' names and addresses had been gathered. Maik had taken those closest to him at the time, and Jejeune had assured him he had recovered enough to handle the rest. Only a small knot of people remained, standing around uncertainly, waiting to be dismissed, or directed, or merely hanging around watching the wrap-up of the operations.

Jejeune sat in the open doorway of an ambulance; the rear doors swung wide to reveal the racks of supplies and equipment. A young paramedic was gently running her fingers along the sides of his Adam's apple, murmuring questions only Jejeune could hear. He answered them all with a small shake of his head.

"Right," said Shepherd briskly, "in an effort to make sure we all still have jobs in the morning, I'm going to find out what happened here before someone higher up asks me. Danny?"

Maik looked first at Jejeune and then back at the DCS. "It's hard to say."

"Then I suggest you rise to the challenge, Sergeant."

Maik told her what he had seen of the altercation and of the ensuing melee, making it clear, without actually pointing it out, that it was more difficult to have an objective view of such situations when you were in the middle of them, trying to restore order.

Shepherd nodded her head as she listened, like a person processing the information with a view to fitting it all into a report. She nodded shortly again now, at the end of Maik's report, though neither man was under any illusion it was in approval of what she had heard.

"And you got all the witnesses' contact information."

"All that stayed. I know one in particular who didn't though. A tall bloke with a beard who was standing fairly close to you, sir. You didn't notice him?"

Jejeune shook his head dumbly.

She turned to Jejeune. "You're not hurt?"

Jejeune apparently felt disinclined to answer. Maik looked at his watch. The prince's private jet would be airborne from Norwich any moment, if it wasn't already. He knew they needed to have DCS Shepherd order it back before it left U.K. airspace, if they were to have any hope of ever speaking to either of the princes again. But at the moment, with his DCI sitting in the back of an ambulance massaging a sore windpipe and Danny himself doing his best to tap-dance his way around Shepherd's withering interrogation, the prospect of even raising the subject with her seemed remote, to say the least.

"And the injured parties? They're both at the hospital now, I take it?"

Maik nodded. "The one has a nasty cut above his eye and I think his nose is broken. My guess is he'll get patched up and be out again soon. The other one." Maik shrugged. "Knee ligaments, the medic said, and a suspected broken jaw." There was no contrition in Maik's voice, no hint of remorse, or a wish that things had happened differently. For a flickering moment, Shepherd had a glimpse of the man who had seen so much action on the field of battle, when any damage you could inflict on your opponent simply meant there was less chance he could harm you in return.

"This business with the gun?" she asked.

"He was pointing it up in the air. I don't think he intended to use it. Just wanted to show people he had it, I suppose. I'm sure he has a concealed weapon carry permit."

"Not so he can wave it around in my bloody jurisdiction. Where the hell did he think he was, the OK Corral? Thank God you didn't let him actually discharge it, Sergeant. We would have been up to our necks in paperwork for the next six months. I'll advise him we won't be pressing charges for withdrawing a loaded weapon in a public place, and that should be that. As for the first one, I daresay he's going to be looking for answers. No one got a good look at the person who assaulted him?"

Maik left Jejeune to field that one, but again the DCI seemed disinclined to answer.

"I assume you've impounded all the cameras and mobile phones?"

"I asked, but no one was filming, so ..."

Shepherd looked at Jejeune dubiously. "You didn't get a good look at him yourself?"

The DCI shook his head, causing Maik to give him a long stare.

Shepherd gave another brief nod of her head, as if deciding on a course of action. "Okay, Constable Salter will go to the hospital and have a word with the victim. She will tell him we will pursue it of course, if he wants us to, but our initial investigation suggests it was an unidentified citizen, just some member of the general public, that assaulted him, *overpowered* him, let's use that word. And we'll see whether a top-flight personal security guard really wants us to take it any further and put it on the record."

She looked at them both, daring them to smirk. "The bigger challenge is going to be squaring this with the Professional Standards bunch. I seriously doubt the al-Haladins themselves took the time to lodge a formal complaint before they left, but you can rest assured the idea of foreign citizens getting hospitalized after brawling with senior officers of the North Norfolk Constabulary is going to capture someone's attention."

Maik was quietly impressed by the deft, professional way Shepherd was going about all this. With other superior officers he had known, a temper tantrum wasn't beyond the realm of possibility. Nor was hanging the men out to dry. But Shepherd's own efforts at protecting herself and her division seemed first and foremost to include bringing Maik and Jejeune under her umbrella. He knew that the DCI wouldn't have missed this either, and he had no doubt Jejeune appreciated it as much as he did.

A low chirrup signalled an incoming text message. Shepherd withdrew her phone and a look of frustration crossed her features as she read the screen. "And right on cue ..." she said. "Investigators from the Professional Standards Department would like to know whether you two would be free to join them in my office in an hour." She looked from Maik to Jejeune and back again. "I assume you have somewhere you need to be? Pursuing a lead, an extremely promising lead, shall we say? Somewhere far away, possibly even out of phone contact, while I sort all this out."

Maik knew of a pub in Brancaster that had rubbish phone reception in the back room. It seemed as good a place as any to keep their heads down. He knew he would get no argument from Jejeune. The adrenalin had started to drain away, but a settler or two in a quiet place where they might be able to gather their thoughts definitely wouldn't go amiss. The sound of a light aircraft passing overhead caused them all to look up. It was clear that the same thought was visiting them all. Their only real lead, extremely promising or otherwise, would be heading out over the North Sea by now. And flying away right along with it was just about the only chance they had of bringing anyone to justice for Philip Wayland's murder.

Maik returned from the bar with two pints of Greene King. He set one in front of Jejeune and took a seat opposite him. They were tucked in a corner at the back of a dimly lit room, where the stale smell of beer seemed to linger. As promised, no one was chatting on a phone. Instead, the low hum of discreet conversation hung in the room like smoke.

Maik took a drink and followed it with a slow survey of the room. It was likely Jejeune had been on the opposite side of a pub table from him enough times now to recognize the signs. The sergeant was about to give him a theory. Jejeune seemed to shift a little in his seat.

"The split eyebrow, the broken nose — it looked like a head butt to me."

Jejeune took a drink, wincing a little as he swallowed. He wasn't going to offer any alternative theory, then, thought Maik. He turned his glass quietly in his hands, staring down into the dark liquid.

"Being held round the throat from behind like that, with both of you facing the same way, I'd have thought anyone approaching to head butt that guard would have been right in your line of sight." He picked up his pint. "Still, if you didn't see anything, you didn't." He took a long, slow drink, the kind designed to give his DCI the time to think. Or speak, if he wanted to. He didn't.

Maik accepted the silence. "You think the DCS will get this sorted?" he asked conversationally, to show the other topic was behind them now.

"I'm sure she will. I don't see anyone wanting this to go any further."

Maik nodded. "The third person you told the prince about, that would be this De Laet, up in Scotland? Was he also murdered? Is he a part of this?" He eyed his DCI, careful to keep any look of disapproval from his expression. It was information he wanted from Jejeune, not defensiveness.

"I think his death was an accident, but he is connected to all this in some way. I'm sure of it."

"The prince didn't bite, though."

"No," said Jejeune, "he didn't. He said he knew of only two deaths."

"To deny something that quickly. That's either somebody who's telling the truth, or somebody who's very good at doing the opposite."

Jejeune nodded. "But which is it, I wonder?"

He lifted his glass and took a drink, wincing once again.

"You should probably get that checked out," said Maik, nodding toward the DCI's neck. "It could be a bruised windpipe."

Jejeune offered his sergeant a smile. "Thanks for the concern, but I'm sure I'm going to be fine."

Danny Maik took a long drink of his beer, deep in thought. Not for the first time recently, he wasn't entirely sure he could agree with his DCI.

48

The coming evening lay like distant smoke in the sky to the east. Domenic leaned on the Range Rover while he waited for Lindy to get out, drinking in the beauty of the landscape that stretched out before him. Lindy joined him and together they made their way down the steep path and out toward the heathland of Dersingham. A towering stand of pines flanked the path, and above them, Wood Pigeons soared in, joining those already roosting amongst the tall trees, ready to add their voices to the refrain of soft coos. From the undergrowth, the manic, staccato trills of a herd of wrens sounded harsh and out of place.

They walked slowly along the path, hand in hand, pausing only for Domenic to occasionally raise his binoculars and track some flitting shape across the landscape. The woods on each side of them were alive with birdsong, as they always were at this time of day, as if the birds realized this was where they must make their last stand on territory before the coming night poured its darkness into the forest.

As the trees petered out, the path opened onto a wide expense of uneven mounds and tussocks. A pheasant flushed as they passed, rising from the gorse-clad hillside with its customary heart-stopping explosion of wingbeats, leaving Lindy breathless but smiling. They did not speak until they were on the boardwalk that wound its way out over the boggy ground, disappearing into the gloaming that was beginning to settle over the land.

"Bird, small, moving left." Lindy pointed and Domenic tracked it; a Stonechat, bouncing its flight through the air until it lit upon a grassy stem, showing beautifully, less than five metres away.

"It's ringed," murmured Domenic. "Too hard to see the colours in this light, though."

Of long practice here at Dersingham, Lindy had automatically withdrawn a notebook when she saw the bird, ready to record the colour sequence of the rings so Domenic could call them in later to the study group. She even knew the species to look out for; this pretty one, the Stonechat, and the other one that sang so beautifully but looked so drab to her; the Woodlark.

Domenic raised a hand and massaged his throat. He had done it a couple of times recently, when he thought she wasn't looking. Damian, too, had a nasty bruise forming on his forehead, but neither one was saying anything about it. Had they fought, she wondered, physically scrapped, when she left them that day? She thought about the atmosphere when she got back, quiet, subdued, a lingering residue of something, perhaps, but not combat.

She leaned on the railing of the boardwalk and looked out over the land. There was a curious quality to the light tonight, as if the flat, faded green of the landscape was clinging on to it, unwilling to let this place slide into the darkness that would so soon render it featureless and silent. Domenic scanned the grass for birds for a few moments longer, while Lindy stood by, patiently waiting.

"You still haven't read my article, have you?"

"Not yet. Work," he said lamely. He wouldn't read it. Not until after the judges' decision had been announced. Lindy always wanted him to be scrupulously honest with her about her work, and more to the point, she could always tell when he wasn't. Despite all her affected indifference about the nomination, he knew it would break her heart if he couldn't discover in her article the same magic everyone else seemed to find. For now, it was much better to make excuses, and let her bask in the moment. Life had a way of bringing you back to earth soon enough as it was.

She was silent for a long time, watching as the grey light of evening slipped over the landscape, embracing it into its shadows. A thought seemed to come to her on the night breeze. She turned away from the land, facing Dom across the boardwalk, elbows resting on the railing behind her. "Have you decided?"

They both knew it had been coming, since they first got in the car to drive here. It had been in the studied silence as they walked, side by side, along the pine-lined path out towards the heath, in the unusual patience Lindy had shown as he scoured the landscape for his Stonechats and Woodlarks. But Lindy wanted the discussion before they headed back to the car, and the topic got more difficult to broach with each passing mile that brought them closer to the cottage. And Damian.

"I said I would ask," she said gently.

Domenic stirred towards anger. "He has no right, using you as a go-between."

"He's just trying to make it easier for you. He's trying to help you."

"Really?" said Domenic, still angry. "Because I thought the whole idea of him coming here was for exactly the opposite reason."

"It always is, isn't it? That's just the point, you never seem to want help, never seem to need it. But what he's asking you is massive. Do you think he doesn't realize that? It will be seen as helping him to evade the justice he deserves. And it will make things difficult for you professionally. Your career may suffer for it. He knows all that, and it's killing him to ask you. But you can't deny him, Domenic."

Jejeune was less angry now, but still raw from being forced to confront the subject he had been avoiding in such a beautiful place at such a beautiful time. He wondered if this moment would tarnish this place for him forever from now on. "There was a time when you didn't want me to get involved."

Lindy shifted her elbows on the railing and shook her head to free a strand of wind-blown hair from her face. "It's a woman's prerogative to change her man's mind, haven't you heard?" She tried a smile. They were past arguments, it said. They were friends again, and this thing wouldn't divide them. But it needed to be talked out, completely.

The horizon had already disappeared into the gathering gloom; a grey smudge of treeline all that was visible now. The bird calls had faded, too. Only the soft murmurings of the roosting Wood Pigeons drifted towards them. Soon, they too would stop, and Domenic and Lindy would be alone in this landscape, in the middle of nothingness, surrounded by shadows and uncertainty, with only each other to remind themselves that anything had ever existed here at all.

"I don't think I can, Lindy."

"You don't get to choose on this one, Domenic. You have to do what's right. You know you do. You are one of the most principled men I've ever met. But principles are guidelines for the way you should live your life, not laws. What good is integrity if it costs you your humanity?"

Jejeune shook his head. "I can't be a party to putting him in prison, any prison. It would kill him. Even if he survived, physically, there would be nothing left of the man who went in there. You've seen him. The wild coasts of Newfoundland are his idea of heaven. What do you think his idea of hell would be? Even being cooped up in the cottage is too much for him.

'Captivity,' you called it, and you were right. If he didn't take his daily strolls down to that coffee shop, I think he would go crazy. Literally, I mean. Ten years in a cage would be more than he could bear."

"He killed people, Domenic, or, at the very least, he was responsible for their deaths. He wants to do what's right, to pay for his crime, so he can get on with his life. You can't expect him to run forever. You can't ask that of any man."

"It was an accident, arrogance motivated by greed, or more likely defiance, knowing Damian, not wanting to be told where he could go and what he could do. But it wasn't manslaughter, and I can't let them put him in prison for it." Jejeune shook his head. "I can't."

She could sense the struggle within him. She knew what it was costing him to even consider this point of view, and she loved him so much for it. She reached out and touched his arm.

To do what's right. But how could brokering a prison term for his brother be the right thing to do, when it was wrong on just about every level he could think of?

49

The manicured lawns behind the café sloped gently down to the water's edge, leaving most of the picnic tables arrayed across it tilting slightly, as if poised to tumble into the man-made lake.

Only one other person was outside when Maik stepped out into the sunshine; a man, sitting at the table nearest the water. He was sitting on the table top, his feet resting on the bench. He was leaning forward slightly, elbows on his knees. The pose gave him a look of hunched intensity, as if he might be scrutinizing the ducks that glided across the surface of the still water, studying them for something specific.

"Mind if I join you?" Maik rested his hip against the other end of the picnic table and raised a cardboard cup in salute as the other man looked across. He glanced at the lawns as if to suggest there might be other tables, any other table, Maik could have chosen.

In the end he gave a small shrug. "Sure."

Maik climbed up and sat on the table; a bookend to the man on the other end. "They tell me this is the best place in town for a decent cup of coffee," said Maik, indicating the cup cradled between the man's clasped hands. "Is it any good?"

The man looked down into his cup a moment before answering. "Not bad, unless you're a coffee connoisseur."

"Me?" Maik gave an easy laugh. "No, I'm a tea man. My boss, though, he likes his coffee. He's from Canada."

If Maik hadn't been looking for it, the slight tensing would have been easy to miss. The two of them sat for a moment in silence, sipping their drinks thoughtfully and staring out as the ducks went about their business, completely unconcerned by the scrutiny of the men perched above them.

"Beautiful colours, those on the right," said Maik. "Shelducks, aren't they?"

"Shovelers. There are some Shelducks here, though, over on the far bank."

Maik nodded. "And those with the white stripe on their heads?"

"Eurasian Wigeon." The man corrected himself. "Wigeon."

"Some life they've got, pottering about all day, find a bit of food, have a rest now and again. Not a care in the world, I should imagine. Pity we can't all have lives like that, eh? My name's Danny, by the way." He leaned across the table and extended a hand in a way that left the other man no opportunity to refuse it. He received a hand in return, but no name to go with it, until his own lingering grip made it uncomfortable.

"John," said the other man. "Nice to meet you, Danny, but I must be going."

"My boss, this Canadian bloke, he likes to sit like this, up high," said Maik, as if John hadn't spoken. "I never realized what a perspective it gives you until now." He turned to look at the man in a way that stilled his move to rise.

"You're Canadian, aren't you?"

"North American. Canadian, yes," said Damian finally, relenting under the other man's questioning stare. Over Maik's shoulder, Damian eyed the doorway to the café, as if he might be regretting his decision to sit at this table so far away from it, especially now that the formidable frame of Sergeant Danny Maik had settled himself in between.

"Forgive all the questions," said Danny amicably. "Can't help myself sometimes. It's my job, see. I'm a police officer."

Damian Jejeune must have spent large parts of his recent life controlling his reactions to uncomfortable situations. "A detective?"

"On my good days," said Maik with an easy smile. "You know a lot about birds. You wouldn't be the one who found that rare bird they're all talking about — the Franklin's Seagull?"

"Gull." Damian shrugged uncomfortably. "Sometimes you get lucky."

"I'm sure you do." Maik nodded, as if recalling some dim memory in his past when he had been lucky himself. "It certainly seems to have caused a flap." Comedy wasn't Maik's forte and his apologetic smile seemed to acknowledge as much. The other man, though, seemed to have little time for humour anyway. He looked wary, guarded, ill at ease. Maik recognized the signs. It was the look of a hunted man.

A silence fell between them, but Maik was relaxed. This man wasn't going to run. If he took a stand, he might be a handful. He had a nasty bruise on his forehead that suggested he had seen a bit of action recently. And Danny knew exactly where. But his years of experience told him the man wasn't going anywhere. He was too clever, too experienced. He would be looking for another way out instead of making a run for it.

"This boss of mine I told you about, this Canadian, he's a detective, too. Chief Inspector, as a matter of fact. He's a good man. I've got a lot of time for him."

Danny waited, but the other man seemed unable to find anything to say. He continued staring straight ahead, at the water, and the ducks, and the idyllic man-made landscape.

"I'll tell you the kind of man he is," said Danny. "Not all that long after he came here, I was taken ill on the job. Fine now, thanks," he said with a terse smile. "The thing is, at the time, it was touch and go whether I would be able to keep my job. I knew I was still up to it, but the brass don't always see things the way you'd like them to, do they? Certainly not in my line of work."

Perhaps Danny was asking what the man's occupation was, perhaps he wasn't. The Shovelers drifted off nearer the far shore and the man's eyes tracked them. But Danny was fairly sure he still had his attention.

"In the end, it all came down to the inspector's word. And he made it his business to see things worked out all right for me. Now why would he do that, I wondered? As I said, we'd only just met. But that's the way he is, see? When push comes to shove, he'll put himself on the line for you. Loyalty. It doesn't seem as easy to find as it used to be. Certainly not like that. I'm from an army background, myself. You learn to value the people you can rely on in that way."

Something in Damian's expression had changed. The concern was still there, but the alarm, the look of panic, had gone, replaced by something else. Sadness? Regret? Danny wasn't sure. But he knew it was time to close in.

"So, as I say, I've got a lot of time for this Chief Inspector of mine. And if he wants to tell me he doesn't know any other Canadians who happen to be visiting, other birders, I've got no reason to think otherwise. The thing is, he's not been his normal self lately. I think something is bothering him, and I don't think it's his work. I wouldn't like to think it was because somebody he knew was putting him in a difficult situation. The thing about loyalty like his is, it would be easy to take advantage of it, if you know what I mean."

Damian was silent so long Maik thought he had resolved not to speak at all, that he was waiting until he was sure Danny had said his piece before deciding what his next move would be. But Damian finally swivelled around and looked at him directly.

Maik realized this was not Domenic Jejeune's face he was

looking into. This man had been down a long, hard road. Not as long and hard as Maik's own, perhaps, but enough of one that it had left its scars. The man facing him now wouldn't be inclined to take anybody's advice. Not unless he wanted to. For a long moment, the uncertainty hung between the two men like a physical force.

"This boss of yours," said Damian quietly. "I guess he has no family over here?"

Maik eyed Damian warily. "None that I'm aware of, sir."

Damian nodded slowly. "The world can come at you from a lot of different directions, Danny. It must be difficult for his family, I imagine, him being so far away. I'm sure they care about him, too, and they'd want to watch out for him if they could. But maybe they can't, for whatever reason." He looked out over the water again and then back to Danny. "If that was the case, if they couldn't be around for him themselves, I'm guessing they would be very grateful to know there was some-body like you out here, looking out for his best interests. It would make them feel, you know, better about things."

Danny Maik sat in silence for a long time. He was looking at the water, at the ducks gliding over its surface in what seemed to him to be such aimless pursuits, but were, surely, full of pur-pose for the birds themselves. He drained his now-cold tea and crushed the cup in his powerful hand. "I'd better be going," he announced, climbing off the table. "Enjoy the rest of your time in the U.K., John. Going to be a long stay, is it?"

Damian shook his head regretfully. "I'll be moving on soon." He looked out over the lake and the soft green lawns surround-ing it, dappled by the faintest pockets of shadow from the high, wispy clouds. "Pity though. If things were different, I'm pretty sure I could get to like it here."

50

When Domenic wandered past the kitchen, he heard the sounds of food preparation, plates being laid out, something frying in a pan. Domenic didn't look in. He knew Lindy would go in to help Damian make the breakfast as soon as she finished her shower.

Domenic went into the study and sat behind his desk, drawing a file towards him. Work, a refuge from the problems of the world, as it was for Xandria Grey, perhaps? Only it wasn't working for her. Would he have more success? His mind was churning, a whirling vortex of Swallows and Gyrfalcons and Edward de Vere. Of canvas bags and satchels and thousand-year-old nests. But he couldn't stop any of it long enough to grasp it clearly, and he was terrified it would all spin away into nothingness before he could make sense of it.

He heard footsteps coming along the hallway, but it was not the usual barefoot padding of Lindy bringing him his coffee. He hadn't realized how much he missed that sound, how much it meant to him, how much it had become a part of their morning ritual. Damian appeared in the doorway. He set a mug on the corner of Domenic's desk. "Breakfast in about twenty. How was the walk last night? Any Nightjars?"

Domenic shook his head. There was no point in describing the wild, desolate beauty of Dersingham Bog to his brother, who would never have the opportunity to experience it for himself. There was furtiveness about Damian this morning, he noticed, the same kind of guarded attitude that Danny Maik had shown the day before, when he returned from a short unexplained trip. Somewhere local, based on the time he was gone, but beyond that Jejeune had no idea what could have called his sergeant away so urgently. And Maik apparently had no intention of telling him.

"I think I know what happened to the Kazakh's Gyrfalcons," said Domenic to his brother quietly. "I believe they're at the prince's facility."

Damian sat in a chair across the desk from his brother. "I thought you told me there were only fourteen birds up there, the number the prince has always had. And they were all satellite tagged."

Domenic nodded. "But I think only twelve signals are from live birds. I believe De Laet and Doherty had to store some wild birds in the Old Dairy facility at some point, and two of the prince's falcons got infected and died — one white and one grey."

Damian pulled a face. "It's possible. Those wild birds could have carried any number of parasites to which the captive ones would have had no resistance."

"If the dead falcons were buried in very shallow soil near the facility, their tags would still transmit, and the signals would still come from the same coordinates," said Domenic. "I thought you might like to know, given your interest in all this."

Music came from the kitchen. "Hallelujah," one of Lindy's favourites, telling them she was up and ready to assume control of breakfast. Damian listened for a moment. "I'll probably have them play Leonard Cohen at my funeral," he said. "That way, I won't feel quite so bad that I can't be there."

Once, the brothers would have shared a laugh at the mischievous slight, but now Domenic met it only with a sad expression. "None of it was ever a coincidence, was it Damian? You coming here? Your connection to Jack de Laet?"

"The first part was," said Damian quietly. "Meeting Jack in a bar in St. John's and him telling me he was looking for Gyrfalcons. But after that, after the liquor got talking and he told me he knew how to smuggle birds into the U.K." Damian shook his head. "I went home that night and thought about it. If he could do it with birds, he could do it with people. And if I could just get over here to see you again, to talk to you … No, by that time, it was a plan. I became Jack's best friend in a hurry, a bird guide who could find him his Gyrfalcons, somebody who would be happy to accompany him to Labrador, Iceland, hell, even to the U.K."

In the kitchen, Lindy had cranked up the music, perhaps to let them know she would be staying out there, keeping herself busy with toast and eggs and bacon, leaving the brothers to speak in here. Privately.

But they didn't speak. Damian couldn't find a way to ask, and Domenic seemed incapable of breaking the silence himself. Damian picked up the copy of *King Lear* from the corner of the desk and riffled through it idly. "This case you're working on, do you think the younger brother ever wonders what life would have been like for him if the birth order had been different?"

Domenic looked down at his desk for a moment, as if looking for an answer in the swirling patterns of the dark wood grain. "We all want somebody else's life, I suspect, or a better version of our own, at least. But it's probably easier to take if society has already conditioned you to your fate. It's not always the hopes for another life that disappoint us, so much as the failure to live the one we expected."

Damian smiled at his brother. "You always were able to see the world in black and white. I admired that about you. Envied you a bit, too, I suppose."

Domenic was silent for a moment. He gave his brother a sad smile. "I'm glad you came, Damian. It's been good to see you. I just wish the circumstances were, you know …"

"Yeah, but, let's face it, if the circumstances were different, I probably wouldn't be here at all."

Domenic looked away, and Damian knew his brother was going to refuse him. They had shared the unspoken communication of siblings when they were children, and now, when it mattered most, it was as strong as it ever had been. Despite his disappointment, Damian knew he needed to spare his brother from the pain of guilt.

"It's okay, Dom. Really. I'll get out of here as soon as I can."

"There's no rush. Stay a couple more days. Till the weekend, at least."

Damian laid down the book and picked up a photograph from the desk, grateful for somewhere else to rest his eyes.

"Evidence?"

Domenic shook his head. "Loose ends. It a screen grab from the phone of the man who witnessed the Gyrfalcon attack." The small talk, the unrelated matters, this was where they would find their safe harbour now.

Damian tapped the photo against his fingertips and then looked at it once again. "Gyrfalcon," he said, "such a beautiful bird. The ultimate hunter. Raw power, wrapped up in a lethal package."

Domenic nodded. "That grab was taken about five seconds after the bird struck that woman. Look at it, no remorse, no regret, no concern at all for what it has just done." He shook his head slightly.

"You sure?" Damian held it closer to his eyes and stared at it intently.

"A guy called el-Taleb starting filming seconds after it attacked. The bird had just landed after striking the handler."

"I don't think so," said Damian uncertainly. He came around the desk and stood next to his brother, holding the photograph in front of them both. "Take another look."

Domenic stared hard at the photograph, as he had done many times. But he saw nothing now he had not seen before. He half-turned to his brother and looked up at him, shrugging.

Damian leaned forward and tapped the photo with the finger of his other hand. Not the principal part of the image, but off to one side, in the background. "These white patches on the ground, beyond the hedgerow," he said.

"That's Niall Doherty's property. A crop of some sort, maybe."

"I don't think so," said Damian again. And now, looking closer, neither did Domenic.

51

Colleen Shepherd looked around the dark interior uncertainly. "This is the first time I've been in one of these," she said. "Is there anything in particular I should be doing?"

"You mean crossing yourself and genuflecting?" asked Eric with a smile. "I suppose you could if you wanted to. Most people just sit down and open one of the slats, though."

"Hide etiquette consists mainly of sitting still and keeping quiet," said Senior. "These days so many people seem to twitter on about things — new birding software and apps and such. I can remember when people in hides just talked about birds, if they talked at all." Quentin Senior seemed to realize his *faux pas*, and hurried into an apology. "Forgive me, Superintendent. I was speaking in general terms. I'm delighted you've come to join us."

Shepherd smiled. She might have asked him to follow Eric's lead and call her Colleen, but as long as she had known Quentin Senior, he had possessed an almost religious reverence for official titles, and she suspected she would remain "Superintendent" to the older man whether she wanted to or not.

"First Sergeant Maik, and now our distinguished DCS dropping in on us," said Eric playfully. "The wonders of Cley Marshes are clearly starting to register with the North Norfolk Constabulary. Do we have Inspector Jejeune to thank, I wonder?"

"Danny Maik was here? He never mentioned it."

Senior nodded, drawing his eyes away from his survey of the waters long enough to look at Shepherd.

"Some time ago, yes. Though not to watch birds, I regret to say. Some tittle-tattle about this and that. Said he was wondering how Cley was recovering after the flooding."

Said, registered Shepherd. For all his country duffer affectations, Quentin Senior, she knew, remained a remarkably astute observer of things besides birds.

"Can we assume the same is true of you, Colleen?" asked Eric. "Or might one dare to hope that you are taking an interest in birds yourself?" He smiled gallantly, in a way that made Shepherd glad he was here. It went some small way to mitigating the unease her real motive was causing her.

"Please, do take a seat, Superintendent," said Senior. "I trust you can at least stay for a few moments to savour the beauty of a sunlit morning on the marshes?" He waved a hand toward the letterbox landscape beyond the viewing window. Shepherd peered at the wooden bench in the half-light and toyed with the idea of brushing it off first, but feeling both men's eyes on her, she daintily stepped over the bench and took a seat between them.

The sunlight was playing on the water with such intensity, it took her eyes a moment to adjust from the dim interior of the hide. Gradually, shapes of birds appeared; on the water, in the reed beds, on the mudflats on the far side of the cell. There seemed to be a huge variety, some she recognized, some she may have noticed once or twice in passing, and a couple she was fairly sure she had never seen before.

"The beaks are upturned on these ones at the front here," she exclaimed. "These black and white ones."

"Avocets," offered Eric.

"Are they rare?"

"I had never seen one either until I started coming here, but now I see them almost every time I come."

Senior nodded. "They're residents here, though they're scarce elsewhere in the country. One of the area's many natural treasures. Marsh Harrier, Eric," he announced, "coming in from the right." Eric snapped up his bins dutifully, leaving Shepherd to stare out at the grey-green landscape on her own for a moment. The birds lifted from the muddy spit as the shadow of the harrier drifted over them, and began a slow, languid circuit over the reed beds before settling roughly where they had been before.

"So you don't wander around looking at the birds then? You just sit here?" It was a question that held no judgment, and the men took no offence.

"In other places, we'll walk around. Here at the marshes, movement along the berms and water edges would disturb the birds too much. They would still have to feed and roost, but they would do so much farther back, likely out of view. Sitting here like this, we can allow them to approach us. The looks can be spectacular."

"Would all birds of prey cause that response I've just seen?" asked Shepherd. "If there was a flock of Lapwings, say, something like that. They'd all go up if a bird of prey went over?"

Both Senior and Eric turned to look at Shepherd, but it was Senior who answered. "A deceit, Superintendent," he said carefully. "It's a deceit of Lapwings. And yes they would."

Shepherd was silent. *A deceit*. How could it be anything else, with what she was doing here, behind the back of her most trusted DCI?

"Forgive my impertinence," said Senior, fixing her with brilliant blue eyes that seemed to burn into her from the darkness, "but can I ask why you're here?"

She thought for a moment, as if considering what she wanted to tell them. "In truth, I came to verify some information. About birds."

The silence sat between them uncomfortably. Eric was the wordsmith, but Senior, too, would recognize the significance of the word. *Verify*, as in confirm information you have already received from another source, another birder, in this case. Senior's expression left her in no doubt that he knew who this other source was. She could not bring herself to look at Eric, although she knew that he, too, would be staring at her now, with an intensity that matched Senior's own.

She withdrew an iPad Mini from her bag. "Can I ask you to look at something, Quentin?" She retrieved an image and zoomed in on a small section on it. Eric craned in for a look and she shifted the screen slightly to include him. It was the screen grab from Abrar el-Taleb's phone, enhanced so that the quality was clear and bright.

"Can you identify these?"

Senior looked across at Eric, as if offering him the challenge, but something in the uneasiness of Shepherd's demeanour seemed to register with both of them. The importance of the answer to Shepherd was obvious, and Eric deferred to the older, more experienced birder.

"Those are your Lapwings," said Senior decisively. "Nothing else locally they could be." He looked at Eric significantly, and then at Shepherd. "There's many a birder around here that could have identified those for you, Superintendent." Including one in your own department, his lingering gaze seemed to say.

"What are the chances they'd be roosting like that if a Gyrfalcon had just flown over?"

Senior's eyes opened wide in surprise. "A Gyrfalcon? Here in north Norfolk. That would be most unlikely, to say the least."

"Nevertheless, if one had."

"The Old Dairy," said Eric quietly. "A bird from the prince's collection, you mean?"

Shepherd had given up all pretense of couching her enquiry in idle curiosity now. She swivelled on the bench and looked at Senior directly. "What are the chances, Quentin? It's important."

Senior took a moment to peer outside through the window slat and Shepherd followed his gaze. Out there, the intensity of the sunshine seemed to infuse everything with such a clarity, such certainty. The shadows of this dimly lit interior seemed only to intensify the doubt she was feeling, the conflict, even as she drew inexorably towards her conclusion.

"None in a million."

Shepherd looked at him to see if he was being flippant. It seemed unlikely in the circumstances, but she needed to be sure.

"It's the survival instinct, Superintendent. They don't get to cast an eye up and decide they can't be bothered fleeing today. It's hardwired into them, a raptor passes overhead, and up they go."

"Every time?"

"Every time. Unless a bird is very ill or injured."

"And they couldn't have missed it somehow, a passing Gyrfalcon?"

Senior indicated the photograph. "How many birds are there in that field? Ten? Twelve? That's a lot of pairs of eyes to all simultaneously miss the single most important threat in these birds' universe."

On the other side of her, Eric seemed to be holding his breath, sitting motionless, mesmerized by their conversation. A thin band of light fell through the window and settled on the ledge in front of them, but whatever was happening outside this hide at the moment seemed to have faded into insignificance, rendered irrelevant by the exchange going on within.

Shepherd readied herself for the payoff, the moment she had been leading up to. Senior seemed to sense it, too, and leaned in slightly, intimately.

"So if I told you that screen grab was taken seconds after a Gyrfalcon flew in ...?"

"I'd say it wasn't," said Senior flatly.

As Jejeune had, when he had stood before her desk that morning, showing her the screen grab and explaining things just as assuredly as Senior. She had distrusted her DCI, distrusted his motives, because there was something else in all this, something she didn't understand, even now. But he had been right, as he so often was. About these birds, and about Abrar el-Taleb. Darla Doherty's death could not have happened the way the project manager said it did. And regardless of what else was going on, that meant el-Taleb was guilty of lying about the circumstances of a suspicious death, at the very least. She was ready now to let her DCI bring him in and question him.

There was a small sound from Eric, who had been peering out over the water, and Senior raised his binoculars. A pair of Spoonbills had concluded a lazy swirling spiral with a landing near the back of the cell where they were now resting, dazzling white against the tawny grasses.

"It's a pity John Damian isn't here for these," murmured Eric, still observing the birds through his glasses. "It would be nice to give him something back, albeit nowhere near as spectacular as the Franklin's he found for us."

Shepherd was grateful both mens' eyes were at their binoculars so they did not see her reaction.

Holland's voice was a faint whisper in her ear. *Tamilya Aliyev met a tall man with a beard. Fits the description of a man named John Damian.*

She steadied herself for a second before she would trust her voice. "You two know John Damian?" To her, the question sounded so forced and insincere, she half-expected them both to lower their bins and stare at her. But the lure of the Spoonbills was proving strong, and Senior answered without taking his eyes off the bird.

"I've only met him once. First-rate birder, though. I can tell you we would have never got onto the Franklin's without him. Do you know him?"

"I don't. What's he like?" she asked smoothly.

This time Eric did lower his bins, though there appeared to be no suspicion in his eyes when he turned them on Shepherd.

"Nice chap. Canadian, did he say?" He turned to Senior. "From Domenic's part of the world, anyway."

Shepherd had developed an impressive poker face during her misspent youth. But she hadn't slow-played a hand like this for a very long time.

"An old friend of the inspector's, was he?"

Eric shook his head. "I don't believe so. I got the distinct impression they had just met."

Danny Maik's voice was roaring through her head like the sound of steam. *A tall bloke with a beard. Standing fairly close to you, sir. You didn't notice him?*

She drew a shallow breath, pausing until she could trust her voice once more. "I'm surprised Domenic hasn't tried to get in touch with him again. Fellow Canadian, and a birder, too, you'd think they'd have plenty to talk about. But perhaps he doesn't know how to reach him."

Senior stroked his white beard thoughtfully. "I couldn't say." He turned to the other man. "Eric?"

"I wouldn't know, I'm afraid. There was quite a bit of excitement about the gull that day. I was texting the rare bird line, Quentin was hanging on to it for dear life through the bins. I do remember Domenic saying he couldn't stay, that he had to be somewhere else, but whether they swapped contact info …"

He shook his head. "I'm sorry, Colleen, I simply couldn't say for sure. As I say, there were some pretty important things going on just at that moment."

Indeed there were, Eric, thought Shepherd. Indeed there were. By now, Colleen Shepherd's poker face had long since been replaced by a mask of polite disinterest. But behind it, yet another voice was ringing in her head. Her own. "*The funny thing was, she described you as having a beard,*" she was telling Domenic. "*A nice man with a beard, who talked to her son about Ravens.*"

52

There had been many fractious meetings held in the incident room at Saltmarsh station; many times angry words ricocheted around the room like truth-seeking missiles, searching for explanations, of actions, of timelines, of details. But there had never been an atmosphere like this, where facts were jealously coveted, and contributions went through filters to be judged against motives, agendas, and personal interests. It was a dangerous, toxic environment of guarded words and furtive glances.

"It's a matter of the timing," said Jejeune. "I believe Darla Doherty was involved with a man in a scheme to use falcon passports to transport wild-caught Gyrfalcons to Kazakhstan."

"Does he have a name, this man?" asked Holland. "It wouldn't be John Damian, would it?"

"He wasn't involved in Darla Doherty's death. In any of this," said Jejeune with certainty.

"What is it with you and this bloke? Why can't you see how much he's tied up in all this? Is it because he's a Canadian? Of course, if anybody could find him, perhaps we could ask him ourselves about his involvement. Talk about dropping off the face ..." Holland looked around the room accusingly. "I told you, we should have pulled him in when we had the chance, but no, you all knew better."

The discomfort, previously an ambient background noise, ratcheted up to new heights. Maik stirred slightly, as if he might desert his post on the very edges of the discussion to intervene. "The girl's gone, too," said Holland. "Tamilya Aliyev checked out of her hotel room, and boarded a plane for Almaty Airport via Munich less than twelve hours after she met with Damian." He turned to Jejeune. "Are you going to tell me that's a coincidence?"

"How does the timing of Wayland's murder come in to all this, Domenic?" asked Shepherd. Her tone assured Holland she had taken note of his comments, but it carried enough authority to move the discussion forward.

"I believe wild birds they stored in the Old Dairy facility infected two of the prince's falcons. A grey Gyrfalcon died, and a white one. The plan was to have Darla Doherty train one of the wild birds as a replacement for the grey one, but the white one was a problem. If anyone went to the facility, they could easily tell it was missing. Yousef had no interest in the birds, so while Doherty was the only one working with them, her partner still had a chance to trap a wild white bird as a replacement. But then Philip Wayland was murdered, and they knew it would bring Ibrahim over. Even if he didn't fly any of his falcons, he would certainly visit the facility. It was only a matter of time before the absence of the white bird was detected. Yousef was responsible for protecting his brother's cast of Gyrfalcons. I think he was shamed by Ibrahim into an act of revenge when he found the white falcon had gone."

The others in the room turned their eyes to Shepherd for her response. She shifted uncomfortably. "There's evidence that the timeline around Darla Doherty's death was manipulated. It revolves around the fact that some birds were in the vicinity — Lapwings. I must admit, it seems compelling."

Holland's face twisted with fury. "She asked me to protect her," he said bitterly. "And I couldn't. And nobody will ever pay for this, because the al-Haladins are gone, and bastards like that are too rich to face justice."

"Perhaps," said Jejeune, "But if I'm right, Yousef al-Haladin must have had an accomplice."

"El-Taleb," said Salter. "But why would he help Yousef?"

"It is the end of a very long, tangled chain," said Jejeune. "I think that Wayland did go to them with the biochemical project, no doubt through el-Taleb, but the Old Dairy had already invested millions in R&D for undersea carbon storage — driven by Weil, I believe — and Yousef couldn't bring himself to face his brother's wrath, knowing that he had wasted all that money on the wrong track, so he rejected Wayland's proposal out of hand. Only, it turns out later he has let Wayland walk away with a potential solution that might lose them the prize money. His only recourse is to claim to Ibrahim that he was never given the chance to consider it."

"But el-Taleb knows different," said Salter, nodding, "and unless he becomes project director, so will Ibrahim." She chose to look at Danny, rather than at Jejeune, for her confirmation.

"And as we know, Constable, any sort of arrangement based on that sort of quicksand is going to suck both people under eventually. When Yousef needed somebody to help him stage the girl's …" Maik flicked a look at Holland, "… *Darla's* death, el-Taleb was in no position to refuse."

The room fell silent as everyone digested the information. Simultaneously, Salter and Holland seemed to stir towards the same idea, the idea that appeared to already be resting with the three senior officers in the room. It was Salter's thoughts that found voice first. "Anybody else wondering if this was their first go-round?" she asked cautiously. "That perhaps they both wanted revenge for Wayland's betrayal, as they saw it, and killed him, too?"

Shepherd shook her head. "Not for revenge, Constable. I still don't think that's a strong enough motive." She glanced at Jejeune. "But if somebody came to me with an idea about getting a rival out of the way in a race for a billion pounds in prize money, I'd be willing to listen to that. We plan to ask Mr. el-Taleb as soon as we bring him in."

Maik followed the DCS's eyes to Jejeune's face, but the expression he found there wasn't confirmation. Jejeune was quiet, in a way Danny had come to recognize. It didn't fit. Perhaps Shepherd's theory made sense, but something troubled Jejeune about it. Danny believed he knew what it was. Because, for once, he felt like he and Inspector Domenic Jejeune were on the same page about Philip Wayland's death. And neither el-Taleb nor Prince Yousef was on it.

"I can go and pick el-Taleb up now," said Maik "I assume you'll want to come with me, Constable Holland?"

Shepherd glanced at Jejeune. "No. The inspector and I will go."

"Given the connections this family had, still have in this country, this will need to be handled delicately. We'll have uniforms on standby if necessary, but if we can get Mr. el-Taleb to come in with us voluntarily, it will be much better for everyone."

Shepherd's explanation had been so hollow, it had left a ringing buzz of unease in the room long after she and Jejeune had left.

"Any chance I can have five minutes with Taleb when he comes in, Sarge?" Holland was seething that he wasn't allowed to be part of the arresting team for the man involved in his girlfriend's murder. "If he played any part in Wayland's death, it wouldn't take me long to find out."

Salter eyed Holland warily. With his emotions teetering on the edge of control, keeping him as far from el-Taleb as possible seemed the sensible course. Maik's look appeared to confirm her thoughts.

"Do you think it was el-Taleb who killed Wayland?" she asked.

Maik shook his head slowly. "I don't think so." He paused for a long moment. "I think it was Catherine Weil."

No one moved. Danny Maik's announcement, in the aftermath of all the undercurrents of distrust and evasion, cut through the charged atmosphere of the room like a laser.

"She and Wayland had an affair. She said it ended before he left to go to the university, but let's say it didn't. He's moved on, taking any hope of success in the Old Dairy project with him, and the next thing anybody knows, he's engaged to Xandria Grey, as close to a professional rival as Catherine Weil has."

"He had been gone a year, though, Sarge," said Salter. "That's a long time for anybody to wait for payback. Weil has got a temper on her, I'll grant you, but she doesn't strike me as a slow-burner."

"I agree, and she may have even made her peace with it all. But then he did something else, recently, that sent her over the edge. He asked her to steal data from the Old Dairy compound for him."

"He was asking her to steal information so he could work on it with the woman he had abandoned her for? As if anybody's ex would ever agree to that." Lauren Salter looked around the room. She would have searched out Shepherd, another woman, to support her point of view, but she was no longer there. "Just what sort of hold did Wayland imagine he had over Weil? Why would he even ask?"

"Professional differences," said Holland. "When you asked her the reason she and Wayland split up, that's what she said, wasn't it? But what bigger professional difference is there than you believing in something as much as Wayland did, when the woman who works right beside you every day thinks it's all a bunch of crap."

"So you're saying Wayland thought it would be easier for Weil to give up something she never really believed in in the first place?" asked Salter skeptically.

Maik nodded. "He saw her disaffection, her disillusionment, and he thought that meant she would be willing to help him. A man with morality like Wayland's — flexible, convenient, easily abandoned when the circumstances called for it — I don't think he understood how she could disrespect her employers, consider the work on carbon storage a waste of time, yet still be prepared to protect it, simply because it was the right thing to do. It must take a special kind of integrity to do that —"

He stopped short and was quiet. The rest of the team waited a long time for someone to venture into the space he had left. In the end, it was Holland who broke the silence.

"But why murder him? She could have just refused to help him."

"It was the fact that he asked her," said Salter. "Wayland couldn't have told her any more plainly that he had no regard for her — no respect, either personally or professionally — if he'd flown a banner over the Old Dairy from the back of Yousef al-Haladin's helicopter. Catherine Weil is no fool, and she wouldn't stand for being treated like one."

"So those little tabs things you were going on about, the one he called his DNA markers," said Holland. "He was getting his material ready so he could just slot the stuff in as soon as Weil gave it to him?" He shook his head. "He was certainly confident enough that he would be able to convince her. Talk about misreading somebody."

"I think he misjudged Catherine Weil, on a lot of levels," said Maik. "But then, he's not on his own in that regard."

53

There was an aura about Colleen Shepherd that Jejeune had never seen before. She shifted uneasily in the passenger seat of the Range Rover, greeting all attempts at conversation with monosyllabic, distracted responses, until he eventually stopped trying, sensing correctly that she would lapse into silence the moment she could. It might have been nervousness, perhaps, venturing out into the field for the first time in as long as anyone could remember. And certainly, el-Taleb was well-connected enough, even in the absence of his royal protectors, to warrant special care in handling and processing. But nervousness had always manifested itself in Colleen Shepherd as energy, or a constant fretting and fussing over details she had already confirmed a thousand times. Now there was only a dark edginess, as if she was entering a place she didn't want to go, a haunted house that held who-knew-what horrors.

Jejeune spent the rest of the journey on his Bluetooth, confidentially confirming el-Taleb's location, first with the receptionist at the Old Dairy and then with a worker at the helicopter maintenance shed at Cromer. He pulled the Range Rover off the dirt track and bounced up into the ragged, untilled field where the makeshift helicopter pad was located.

"I'll park here," Jejeune said unnecessarily, for something to say. He put The Beast into reverse and tucked it neatly in beside a bramble hedgerow. "When el-Taleb comes in, we can drive across to pick him up." Jejeune looked at his phone and then at his watch. "He should be landing soon. He's already on his way, and flying time back here is only about ten minutes."

"Does he know that we'll be here? Or why?"

Jejeune shook his head. "He'll think he's in the clear now that Yousef has gone. His guard will be down." He paused and took a moment to look at the surrounding fields, bathed in gentle sunlight. It was a clear day, with faint trails of white clouds high in a pale blue sky. The birdsong came from the skies, too, from Skylarks and Meadow Pipits. Jejeune watched one spiral up, piping its beautiful rolling trill as it descended again.

"You're sure it was the prince who killed Darla Doherty, Domenic? It wasn't el-Taleb?"

Jejeune shook his head. "He couldn't have. He had no gauntlet, no protective gear. No one could control a Gyrfalcon without them. I think Yousef hooded the falcon to subdue it, before dragging its talons across Doherty's neck. A surprise attack, most likely, while she was turned away, distracted. Then el-Taleb flew him to the Palm Court in the helicopter while he changed clothes and got rid of the falconer's equipment. Everybody assumed Yousef had gone there by car because the helicopter was here, but I think el-Taleb flew it back after dropping him off. He had keys with him, in the field. They must have been from the helicopter."

Shepherd nodded. "And then he reports having witnessed her accident, knowing there is nothing at the scene to tie him to the crime in any way, and he can have an ongoing, unbroken video record to show he couldn't have got rid of anything." She shook her head in what could have been admiration, of a sort.

"It was all planned in advance," said Jejeune. "It was why we were granted our audience with Yousef at the Palm Court. What better alibi could he have? Not only was he in another place, he was with two senior police detectives at the time."

Shepherd looked across at Jejeune. She seemed sad, tired. "Domenic, I need you to tell me about John Damian."

Jejeune gripped the steering wheel in both hands and stared out through the screen in front of him. This was why she was here. Shepherd, out on a field operation, with Maik and the others, Holland, Salter, left behind to do … what? Anything. Nothing. Just something that would keep them away from Domenic Jejeune as his world collapsed around him, as the dust and rubble of the lies and half-truths and evasions finally poured in, ready to bury him, suffocate him, swallow him whole.

"I know …"

The noise from blades sounded so close, they both flinched. The helicopter skimmed the top of the hedgerow, barely missing the Range Rover. It was the cavalier flying of someone who had done this many times, someone free of controls and constraints. The flight of a man with nothing to fear.

Until he saw the vehicle.

"What the hell's he doing?" shouted Shepherd as the helicopter lurched wildly to the left.

"He's seen us. He's trying to get away." Jejeune fired up the Range Rover and slammed it into gear. The helicopter, still low to the ground, was close to righting itself as it sped away across the field.

"I thought you said he wouldn't know why we were here."

The only reason I would need to come onto this property again, Mr. el-Taleb, would be to make an arrest, thought Jejeune, burning at the memory of his own bravado. "We have to stop him before he gets over the treeline. If he stays low, air traffic won't be able to track him and we'll lose him."

Shepherd reached for Jejeune's radio as the Range Rover

shuddered over the uneven terrain. "I'll have uniforms get cars along the coast road."

The helicopter was closing in on the far stand of trees. Jejeune sped along beneath him, looking up, watching every dip and swerve as el-Taleb fought for altitude. The trees were approaching fast, hurtling towards them both. The helicopter seemed to falter, and then with a final heaving effort, rose almost vertically and crested the treeline. It had made it to safety, to freedom. But at the last moment, it tilted. The left-hand runner clipped the top of a giant beech, the tallest tree in the stand. For a moment the giant metal bird seemed to stall in the sky. Then it eased over on its axis, driven by the rear rotor into a cartwheeling spin that drove it down on the far side of the trees. From behind the screen of foliage came an earth-shaking explosion and an orange fireball that swelled and heaved into a cloud of thick black smoke.

Jejeune slewed the Range Rover to a halt and sprinted to the boundary hedge, hurtling through it, oblivious to the scratches and snags as he passed. But he was driven back, forearm raised to his face, by the intensity of the heat and the flames arcing out as the sizzling metal cracked and spat in front of him.

Somewhere through the roaring of the flames, he heard his name being called. He backed away from the wreckage, unable to drag his eyes away from the carnage of the burning helicopter until he reached the hedgerow. He turned to see Shepherd through the tangle of branches. She was searching his eyes, for hope, for a miracle. He offered her nothing, but his sloping shoulders told her what she already knew. There would be no miracles today.

The acrid smoke was making his eyes water as it drifted towards him. He could hear the first sounds of the sirens racing along the coast road. Shepherd, from his car phone, he thought dimly. He looked at his DCS, standing forlornly in the field behind the hedgerow, the one that he had so easily crashed his way through just a few moments before. Now it seemed such an impenetrable barrier, barring his way back to the other place, to where his life had been before he crossed over to this side. His thoughts were coming irrationally, and one of them was whether he would ever be able to cross this barrier again, ever go back to where he used to be. He turned away from Shepherd and wandered back toward the wreckage, standing for a long time, watching as the orange-yellow flames continued to reach up, licking the carcass of the helicopter like a hungry animal. He was sitting down on the grass now, he realized, unable to remember when he had done so. The heat from the flames was less intense here, but still reaching him. He stared at the burning wreckage, unable to move, unable to help. He was still there when the first of the fire engines pulled up and two fire fighters came over to escort him to safety.

54

This time, there wasn't any playfulness in Catherine Weil's ice-blue eyes when she opened the door. And Constable Salter suspected that there wouldn't have been even if Danny had come here on his own.

They stepped inside the small flat and stood before her formally. A woman of Weil's intelligence wouldn't need to have the situation explained to her, but Salter did it anyway. She told her they were conducting the interview as a precursor to obtaining a warrant for a search of these premises: her flat.

"A warrant? What on earth are you looking for?" Weil turned her eyes on Maik, but Danny looked as if he would rather be anywhere else in the world than this tiny, over-neat flat. That was okay. Salter would do what needed to be done.

"We will come to that, Ms. Weil. We are now prepared to accept that the man you saw in the woods that night was Philip Wayland."

Weil looked to be readying herself for a triumphant response, but at the last moment, seemed to check herself.

"You knew it was Mr. Wayland, because you had arranged to meet him there."

"No," she said quickly. She lowered her eyes. It was the first time Maik could ever remember her failing to meet anyone's gaze; the first lie, the crack in the dam. The rest of the deceit, the evasions, would follow now, spilling out before them like blood, filling the room with their rancid odour. How much he hated this job at times. But the old soldier in him was still on duty, reminding him to stand up straight, stare ahead, and show no emotion. And like the good soldier he was, Danny Maik obeyed.

"He had asked you to meet him, and you suspected you knew why," continued Salter. "But you went along anyway."

"No!" shouted Weil, so abruptly it made Maik start. "No, I didn't."

"You did," insisted Salter. "He was going to ask you to steal his research from the Old Dairy databases. And you were prepared to go along with it."

"No," she said again. Weil dropped her eyes and a single tear escaped down her cheek. "Yes," she said softly. "He was going to ask me to give him his research, so he and his girlfriend could work on it together. *Meet me, Catherine*," she recited, "*it's for the greater good, Catherine, for the benefit of so many. Personal morality and considerations shouldn't come into it. We should be above all that.* As if he was ever going to get anywhere working with Xandria Grey, whether he had the Old Dairy data or not."

"What happened when you met him?" asked Maik softly.

Weil shook her head. Her red hair was like a veil, cascading down over her, shrouding her. She looked so frail, so broken. Salter was sure it was all Danny Maik could do to stop himself from reaching out a hand to her.

"I didn't. I was on my way to meet him, but at the last moment, I realized I couldn't do what he wanted me to. Philip could be so persuasive. His passion about his project, it overwhelmed you. I knew if I let myself talk to him, I wouldn't be able to say no. I knew I couldn't allow myself to meet him."

Salter was silent for a moment. Danny had gone walkabout. Nothing on the scale of the grand tours Jejeune undertook, but enough to distance himself from the spectacle of Catherine Weil, shattering like glass before his eyes.

"But you didn't leave, did you, Ms. Weil? You stayed on, and waited. Waited until Philip arrived."

"I wanted to see him, as he made his way down there, to where we were supposed to be meeting, by the sign. I just wanted to see if there was any hesitation, any contrition, any indication at all that he felt badly about what he intended to ask me to do. Or was it just the same old Philip; project first, everything else nowhere." She flashed her eyes at Maik, "Collateral damage, isn't that what you called us, Sergeant, the by-product of other people's thoughtlessness. I just wandered around for a while in the woods. I couldn't think properly. And then I left."

Inspector Jejeune was so measured, so careful in his approach. He constructed his case block by block, allowing the suspects to supply the mortar with their own mistakes, their inconsistencies, until they suddenly realized they had built a wall around themselves from which they could not escape. But this was Lauren Salter, doing the heavy lifting because Danny Maik was standing as far away as he could manage in this small flat, as animated as a tailor's dummy. So Danny and the DCI and the whole bloody lot of them would just have to put up with Lauren Salter making the best fist of things she could.

"You killed him, Ms. Weil. You followed him and you killed him. And you thought you'd left no evidence. But there may be some."

The statement was so surprising Maik snapped his head round to look at Salter.

Weil looked shocked, puzzled.

"Philip Wayland was carrying a shoulder bag when he died. We have it and we're testing it for your fingerprints."

Weil shifted uncomfortably. "This is ridiculous," she said, but the defiance was gone from her now. She was nervous, afraid.

"He's had that bag for years. We worked side by side. Of course my bloody prints could be on it. But it would be from months ago, years."

"Unfortunately, unless they're overlaid with others, there's no way to tell how long fingerprints have been on an object," said Salter. "If we found a clean set of your prints on the bag, Ms. Weil, Catherine, it would be up to a jury to decide how long they'd been there. Why don't you tell us what happened?"

"Philip had his bag with him that night?" Weil retreated into silence again, but it was more thoughtful now, more measured. Not at all the sullen defiance of earlier. Maik watched the expression on her face with interest.

"It's not looking particularly good for you," said Salter. "You have motive, opportunity. You've admitted to being at the scene, seeing Mr. Wayland there, even. Following him."

"I don't want to tell you your job, Constable." Weil's sarcasm had an edge to it. From somewhere she had rediscovered her fire. "But unless you have some actual evidence, I don't believe there is any reason I should let you stay."

Salter looked across at Maik, still staring thoughtfully at Weil. Even he should be sensing the turning of the tide. Weil was no longer on the defensive, no longer cowed, vulnerable. It was time for him to step in. But he didn't move.

"We will return with a warrant to search your flat, your car, your work area. We know what we are looking for and we won't stop until we find it."

The weapon, perhaps, she meant, or a fragment of blood-stained wood chip from the path that had clung to Weil as she left the scene. Anything.

Weil shrugged easily. "Whatever you find," she said, boldness fully restored now, "I can assure you, it will not connect me to Philip's murder."

"Any DNA might be enough for a jury. A long red hair, even,

with Mr. Wayland's blood on it. Would you be willing to gamble there would be nothing? If we find anything at all, there'll be no further need for any co-operation."

"I'll take my chances." She turned to Maik, who had watched her metamorphosis back to her old assured self with something approaching wonder, and was standing there now wide-eyed and uncertain. "What do you think, Sergeant Maik? On the off-chance the constable's pie-in-the-sky wishes don't pan out, do you think you have enough to charge me?"

"No," said Danny.

Salter stirred, half-turning to him in anger. "Sir, it would only take a couple of hours to get a warrant. I could organize the search of this place myself."

But Maik wouldn't stop staring at Weil.

Salter shook her head in anger and frustration. In the long series of missteps that had dogged the Saltmarsh Police Department in this case, this was the worst of all. And she was unable to stop it.

"Sarge, I believe we have enough reasonable suspicion to hold Ms. Weil, at least for a short time."

"No, Constable." Maik shook his head slowly. "Not enough. Not reasonable."

But there is Danny, thought Salter, sadly. *If only you dared to see it. If only you wanted there to be.*

She said nothing as they left the flat, nor even as they approached the Mini. Without a word, she carried on past the car. Danny watched her leave, feeling more alone than he had felt for a very long time.

55

Tony Holland drove. In the end, that was what it came down to. Holland drove, and Maik sat in the passenger seat. Whether it would have been any different if they had taken the sergeant's Mini, whether there would there have been less suffering, less damage in the end, Maik couldn't have said. But when Shepherd dispatched them to Jejeune's house as fast as possible, it was inevitable that the two men would have chosen Holland's Audi. He had the tires squealing out of the car park before Maik even had his seatbelt on.

Flashes of the north Norfolk countryside hurtled at them through ragged gaps in the hedgerows. Holland drove with a confidence born of long practice on these roads, anticipating the corners and expertly changing down in anticipation of the waiting straights where he could open up the 4.2-litre V8 engine to full effect. Maik sat beside him in silence, eyes resting on the grey blur of the road surface disappearing beneath the car. At this rate they would be there soon. Too soon?

Less than thirty minutes before, Maik had been sitting at his desk, taking in the enormity of what had happened to DCI Jejeune and DCS Shepherd at the Old Dairy, and wondering if it had thrown enough of a shadow over his interview with Catherine Weil to hide his own failings. Just as the acrid after-taste of smoke and burnt rubber no doubt still clung to Jejeune and Shepherd, the stench of Maik's own error filled his senses. He had let Catherine Weil go free. It had been the wrong thing to do. And he had done it for the wrong reasons.

If he needed any confirmation, Jejeune's panicked tone, when he had informed him, provided it.

"It's that satchel, sir," Maik had told him. "It must be the key. We're having it checked again for evidence, in case we missed something first time around." He shook his head, even though his DCI couldn't see the gesture. "There was something about it. Her attitude changed completely when we mentioned it."

"You told her about the bag, and then you let her go?" Jejeune had sounded alarmed. "Where is Weil now?"

"At work, I imagine. I can confirm that, and let you know when you get here. Will that be soon, sir? Only DCS Shepherd wants to see you the second you walk through the door. I got the impression earlier would suit her even more."

But there was no response. And so he had no answer to give DCS Shepherd when she burst into the room moments later.

"Where the hell is Inspector Jejeune going? After we wrapped things up at that terrible scene last night, I specifically told him first thing tomorrow, my office. And now I hear someone has just seen him making a U-turn less than five minutes from here and heading away as fast as he could go."

"What's he playing at?" asked Holland from the sidelines. "The sarge just told him you wanted to see him as soon as he got in."

She looked at Maik. "You told him that. Utmost urgency?"

Maik's lowered eyes gave her the answer.

She turned to Holland. "Find out where Jejeune is now. Ping his phone."

No *Inspector*, no *DCI*. Maik had reached for the phone and dialled a number, half knowing what was unfolding, even as Holland stared blankly at Shepherd, shocked by her tone and her terse use of the DCI's surname.

Shepherd turned to see Maik with the receiver in his hand and her eyes widened with alarm. She made a throat cut gesture with her hand.

"No contact." She looked at Holland. "You either. Just his location. On second thoughts, the two of you get to Jejeune's house now. Right away."

Maik leaned forward to cradle the receiver, brushing a button on the console as he did so, so softly it could have been unintentional.

Holland looked puzzled. "I don't get it, why don't we just wait till he gets back here?"

She looked at him incredulously. Then she turned her eyes on Danny. But all he could do was lower his own eyes and seek refuge for them in the phone console on his desk. And it was then that she knew. Danny Maik already knew.

Shepherd turned back to Holland.

"You're not going to his house for Inspector Jejeune, Constable. You're looking for John Damian."

For a moment Holland sat in stunned silence. And then he stood and hurried to the door. As Maik stood up to join him, his hand brushed the button on the phone again.

"Wouldn't it be faster to turn off here and cut down through Winscaston village?"

Holland flashed Maik an incredulous look. "You're joking, right? It's market day. Traffic down there would add another ten minutes. If we stay on here we'll be there in seven, eight minutes, tops."

The trill of Maik's phone ended any further discussions about the routes to Jejeune's. It was the inspector. "Sergeant, where are you?"

Maik signalled to Holland and the constable stopped the

powerful vehicle opposite a gateway. Holland drew out his phone and texted Shepherd: *J on line.*

"I need backup immediately," said Jejeune without waiting for an answer. "Get to the university as quickly as you can. Catherine Weil is not at the Old Dairy or her home. I think she's going to see Xandria Grey."

Holland waited, engine idling. Maik mouthed "requesting backup," and Holland texted the words. In his rear-view mirror, he saw a tractor trundling slowly toward them. It filled the lane, brushing the hedgerows on either side with its yellow mass. The university was behind them, down this lane in the other direction. The only turning place for the next two miles was opposite them right now. Holland could manoeuvre the Audi into the narrow space, let the tractor pass, and head back the way they had come. If Maik wanted him to.

"You need to call in and have them dispatch an arrest team, sir," Maik told Jejeune.

"There's no time. A team will be at least ten minutes behind me. We need to get there before Weil gets to Grey. She's in danger."

Holland looked at Maik and looked at his phone. Behind them the big tractor was inching closer, filling more and more of Holland's rear-view mirror. The gap beside him was still there.

"Are you still there, Sergeant?" Jejeune's voice was strained, urgent. "You need to head over there now. Right away."

Holland looked down as a single chime came from his phone and read the reply. Maik looked at him. Holland shook his head.

"I can't do that, sir," said Maik. "Go there and wait. I'll be there as soon as I can."

There was a moment of silence, as if perhaps Jejeune realized. "I don't think I can, Sergeant. I don't think there is time to wait. I'll go in. Just get there as soon as you can."

Holland had not moved. He sat, the car still in neutral, the big engine thrumming idly. The tractor was right up behind them now, waiting patiently. Waiting, while an eternity of small moments ticked by. There was silence on Maik's phone now, and on Holland's. Maik knew all it would take was a word from him. One word, and Holland, however much he disliked the idea, would make his manoeuvres, would turn around into the gateway, facing towards Jejeune, away from Damian. Maik stared out the window, while the breeze tousled the grasses in the fields beside them, and the easy thrum of the tractor's engine filled the air. And then Tony Holland put the car in gear and drove on.

For once, Holland paid no attention to the pitted, pot-holed driveway as he drove up to Inspector Jejeune's cottage. He gave the Audi full throttle until he pulled up at the front door, the tires skidding on the gravel.

He was out of the car and had knocked on the door by the time Maik made his way around to stand at his shoulder.

It took a long time for Lindy to open the door, longer than it should have taken. She leaned against the jamb, cradling a mug of tea against her chest. As a gesture it wasn't exactly defensive, but it occurred to Maik that a student of body language, some-body like Lauren Salter, say, might find something significant in the way it seemed to block the doorway.

"Danny, Constable Holland," said Lindy. It could have been surprise in her voice, or perhaps something else. "Domenic's not here, I'm afraid. Isn't he at the station?"

"Not at the moment," said Maik warily. "We were actually …"

"We're looking for a man by the name of John Damian," said Holland brusquely. "Ring any bells?"

Lindy shook her head uncertainly. "No, I don't think so." She looked past Holland to Maik. "What's this about, Danny?"

"Inquiries," he said simply. It occurred to him that in all the many times he had visited this cottage, he had never been on the doorstep this long without being invited in. But then, he had never timed his visit to coincide exactly with the DCI's absence before. Lindy seemed to register the awkwardness of their situation. "I was just about to have a cup of tea on the back porch. You can go on around if you like, and I'll bring you one out."

"No thanks, ma'am," said Holland. "Would you mind if we came in and had a look around?"

"Of course I would," said Lindy reasonably, albeit with a steeliness that Maik had long suspected existed. "What's this all about? Should I ring Domenic? Does he know you're here?" She turned to Maik. "Can you tell me what it is you're looking for, Danny? Perhaps I can help you find it?" She was still keeping things light, but there was an edge to her now, an uncertainty. Maik looked at her carefully, but he couldn't tell if she was hiding anything in the cottage ... or anyone.

"We were wondering if you knew anybody named John Damian," he said, watching her eyes for a reaction, as he knew Holland would be. But there was no flicker of recognition in them, and if they widened slightly, it could have been anything; puzzlement, surprise, even delayed outrage at this investigation so obviously being carried out behind the DCI's back. Lindy, though, wasn't about to give anything away. Maik would have expected no less.

"I have to say, I don't. Nice name though. Are you sure you don't want to come round the back?" The message was clear. *I've done nothing wrong; I have no idea what this is all about.* Danny had always known Lindy was a bright woman, but she was reaching new heights in his estimation today.

"Why are you looking for this man, can I ask?"

She was free to ask, but Tony Holland, for one, wouldn't be giving her any answers.

"And no one by that name has ever stayed here, as far as you're aware?"

"*As far as I'm aware,* Detective? It's Tony, isn't it? I live here, Tony, and as you can see it's not exactly a palace. I'm pretty sure I would be *aware* if anybody named John Damian had ever even crossed the threshold, let alone kipped down here."

"And you don't know anybody by that name?"

"You've already asked me that question, Constable."

"Do you think I'd ask the same question twice if I was happy with the first answer?" asked Holland, riled by Lindy's refusal to answer directly.

"That'll do, Detective."

"A North American, fairly tall, beard …"

"Asked and answered, Constable," said Maik. He had let this go on long enough. "Sorry to have bothered you, Ms. Hey. I'll make sure the DCI is aware that we came by, and why. We won't be troubling you any further."

Holland looked through the rear-view as the Audi made its way slowly down the driveway. "Not buying it, Sarge," he said. "She knows something."

In the passenger-side mirror, Maik looked at the door. Lindy was still leaning on the door jamb, tea mug cradled against her blue sweater. He had no doubt she would watch them every inch of the way until they disappeared from view.

56

Jejeune did not see the car he had hoped to in the university car park when he pulled the Range Rover to a stop. He was in the act of reaching for his phone to call Maik when he caught sight of a car he did recognize — the blue Kia he'd seen parked in Catherine Weil's bay at the Old Dairy. He knew there was no time. Not to call, not to wait. If she had reached Xandria Grey's office, it might already be too late. He sprinted across the car park and headed along the warren of bleak corridors, his steps echoing hollowly off the walls. The door to Grey's office was open. He entered cautiously, easing back the door fully and gazing around. No one. There was only one place she could have taken her. Jejeune pounded down the concrete stairs and ran along the hallways. He stopped short and crept the last few metres to the vault, pressing his ear to the door.

"Please don't," he heard a woman's voice say. It was weak with fear. "You don't have to do this. It's all over anyway."

Jejeune eased the door open. Inside the room it was dark, the air fetid and warm. A thin dagger of light from the corridor fell past him and lay on the dark floor like a shard of glass. He didn't turn on the light, but whoever was in here would have been able to see him coming in. He could hear whimpering coming from the far side of the room, in the file stacks. In the corner of the room, he could see a faint light moving. He felt for the wall behind him and slowly began to creep his way along it.

"You can't save her, Inspector Jejeune," said a voice from the darkness.

Jejeune continued easing himself along the wall. In the dark, he stubbed his toe on the base of the stack anchored against the wall. The penlight flashed at him, hitting him in the eyes, blinding him in the darkness. "My finger is on the remote switch, Inspector. If you move, I'll kill her now."

Jejeune looked away from the light and held up his hands to show that he would not move. "They say that killing for the second time is easier," he said cautiously. "But I suspect that's not true. The second time around, you know the feelings that are to come, the horror of what you've done, the knowledge that it's going to be on your conscience for the rest of your life. And having that insight, knowing before the act that you are going to have to face all those feelings again, all those emotions, I think that must make it so much harder to prepare to kill for a second time."

"Perhaps," said Xandria Grey coldly. "But she *is* going to die. She dares to come in here and accuse me, to confront me? After what she did. Scheming with him behind my back, to take away our research. I wanted it to look like an accident, like she had been going through the records when the stacks started up and crushed her. Now you'll know the truth. But that won't stop me."

From deep in the stacks, Weil whimpered again. With his eyes adjusting to the light, Jejeune could see her, a shadowy form only, pinned tightly between two stacks barely far enough apart to fit a human arm, let alone a body. "I didn't want the research," whispered Weil. "He never talked to me about turning it over. I had no idea he was planning to give it to me. Please, Xandria, I'm in so much pain." Jejeune heard the laboured panic of Weil's breathing, coming shorter and shallower with every breath. She was running out of time, he knew. They both were.

"It was the project. That was what Philip cared about." Weil's voice was weak, feathery. The pressure on her chest was squeezing the air from her lungs. Jejeune wanted to tell her to save her breath; the shallowness of her breathing wouldn't be able to replenish her supply. But he knew she was asking for her life, the only way she had left, with an explanation.

The penlight had disappeared, and he heard the faint sound of shoes shuffling. Grey had been in the corner somewhere, but she was on the move now. She could be anywhere. Could he risk going back to turn on the light? How long would it take to find her, snatch away the remote, stop the inexorable grinding of the stacks against Catherine Weil's frail body if Grey had already pressed the switch? Too long, he knew. She was pinned so tightly now he suspected she had already suffered internal injuries. Even the slightest extra pressure might be fatal. He had to keep Xandria Grey talking, keep her engaged, until ... what? Uniforms arrived, who might secure the area and wait in the car park for further instructions? Danny Maik and Tony Holland, once they had finished their mysterious duties elsewhere? No one was coming to help him, he realized. He was Catherine Weil's only hope. And he could not help her.

"I don't believe you intended to hurt Philip, Xandria," Jejeune called into the darkness.

"I was only trying to stop him," said Grey. He heard a single sob. "I was the one who believed in him, supported him. She showed him nothing but contempt. And he went to her."

"He loved you, Zan," called Weil softly. "I know he did."

"Not enough, though. Not enough to stop him coming to see you, to meet you, by that sign — PRIVATE PROPERTY. As if Philip ever respected property, let alone privacy." Grey's voice was flat, cold. The control she had fought so desperately for had turned in upon itself and become something terrible, something disconnected and inhuman. Jejeune needed words, any words to distract Grey, to buy Weil an extra few moments of life while he figured out where her assailant was. But he could find none. Instead, Grey supplied them.

"I knew you believed Philip intended to steal that data from the Old Dairy," she said, her voice devoid of any inflection, "but that would have made no sense. He would need their resources, all those piles and piles of money, if his project was ever going to be viable. It had to be the other way round. He had to take the work he had done here to them, instead. I kept waiting for someone to see that. But no one ever did."

Domenic Jejeune should have, he realized. And a Domenic Jejeune of the past might have done, he thought bitterly, one not so tied up in cases about Gyrfalcons, and his own problems. It had come to him too late, the idea that Swallows and Gyrfalcons, and just about every bird that flies around during the breeding season carries things only *to* a nest, never *away* from one. That it requires so much energy for a bird to carry food or nest-building material that it will only ever be one-way traffic. And so it was with Philip Wayland. Why would anyone need a heavy satchel, just to take away electronic data that could be stored on a flash drive? He wouldn't, of course. But to deliver a wad of folders somewhere? He would need a bag for that.

He should have realized all this sooner. He had failed to give Philip Wayland's murder the attention it deserved. And now, was his failure going to cost another person her life? Was Catherine Weil going to be another casualty of his personal distractions?

There was a shimmer of movement, and Jejeune could tell Grey was closer now. In the dark she had continued to move, and unknowingly, she had closed the gap between herself and him. He held his breath. He steadied himself, ready to make a move towards Grey, to make one last desperate gamble to overpower her and wrest away the remote. If she stepped close enough, if he sensed her presence before she could sense his, there was a chance he could subdue her. But what if she hit the button first? Would he know how to switch it off, stop the stacks from their awful, relentless progress? Or would he continue to fumble in the dark as Catherine Weil begged for her life, until her final silence told him he had failed? He needed to know exactly where Grey was.

"Your name," he called out. "Xandria. You said your mother was in Egypt before you were born. I think perhaps she intended your name to be a form of Alexandria. She wanted you to be special, unique, important. And you are."

Grey's voice came out of the darkness, nearby, startling him, and he froze once more. "You are a kind man, Inspector. I think you really cared about my loss. Your sergeant, too."

She was resolved now, final, so calm that, even across the darkness between them, Jejeune could sense the time had come. She was going to press the button, to set the motors running, to bring the stacks together so their crushing weight could extinguish the life of Catherine Weil.

"Let me help you, Xandria," he said desperately. "Let Ms. Weil go, and come in with me."

"No, I won't do that. But I will give you a choice. The same one Philip had to make. Her or me."

He heard the remote clatter to the floor somewhere in the distance and heard the churning of the motors as the stacks began to trundle on the guide tracks. He heard the door open and saw the same sliver of light as when he entered. Grey had gone. *Her or the remote.* Weil groaned and cried out. He went to her, reaching an arm in, grabbing her hand frantically, pulling, but he couldn't move her. The gears whined higher, protesting the resistance, grinding harder as they pressed in tighter. In the light from the doorway he could see Weil's pale face turned towards him, her head pressed tight between the racks. Tears ran down her cheeks and her lips opened in a soft, silent plea. She held his hand tightly. He felt the pressure on his own shoulder now, as the crushing force of the racks closed in on them. He tried to drag his hand away, but she held on. He could see her eyes burning into him, imploring him. "It's too late," she whimpered softly. "Stay with me. Please. Don't leave me."

The light from the hallway was blinding as the door swung wide open. There was a panicked shout and somebody picked up the remote from the floor and pressed a button. The stacks shuddered to a halt.

"What the bloody hell are you doing down here in the dark, Domenic?" asked the voice of Colleen Shepherd from the doorway. "Constable Salter, get those stacks reversed now."

57

Colleen Shepherd stood behind her desk looking at Domenic Jejeune. He had just come from the hospital. His right shoulder and his upper chest were severely bruised, but Catherine Weil had fared worse. She had been in surgery to remove a ruptured spleen, and a lung had been punctured by one of several broken ribs she had sustained. Other injuries, too — internal hemorrhaging and organ bruising — meant she was facing a long hospital stay. But the doctors felt she would likely make a full recovery. There was no smile to accompany this last piece of good news. Shepherd wondered if Jejeune had one left in him.

She regarded him carefully. A few shoulder bruises seemed a small price to pay for the predicament she had found him in. Perhaps there were other injuries he wasn't telling her about. Either way, she suspected getting any truth out of him about his condition would be more effort than it was worth.

"So, is there anything you don't know, Inspector Jejeune? Any blanks you haven't been able to fill in?"

It sounded peevish, petulant, and even Shepherd herself wasn't sure if she meant it that way. The words were a residue of other, unspoken feelings, the real reason Jejeune was standing there so silently before Shepherd now, and why she was having such a difficult time looking him in the eye.

"Wayland joined the university specifically so he could conduct his research into a biochemical solution," said Jejeune, "but I imagine he realized quite quickly that he was never going to have the resources to recreate all the work he had done when he was at the Old Dairy. Since he believed the answer lay in a combination of the two sets of research, he was faced with trying to get the initial data back, or giving his own findings to the one person who might have the resources, and the ability, to do something with it."

"And Wayland would really have been content to stay in the background? To let Weil and the Old Dairy project have the glory, and the money?"

"I imagine he saw himself in some sort of coaching role, guiding Weil as she pieced it all together. But yes, I do believe he would have given up the personal acclaim, to arrive at a solution to carbon storage that protected the coastline. It really was that important to him."

"I wonder if Catherine Weil understands how much respect he must have had for her, to believe she had the capacity to make the project work."

"I think she does now," said Jejeune. "Certainly Xandria Grey did."

"Grey hasn't been found," Shepherd told him hurriedly, as if having him ask would have made the news worse, somehow. "We've got all the usual travel alerts in place, though, and we're doing a thorough sweep of her known haunts. She'll show up soon enough," she added with a confidence that seemed to Jejeune to have no real conviction. They both knew Grey was intelligent and resourceful. If she had planned things in advance, and Jejeune believed she had, she would be difficult to find.

"And the murder weapon?" Shepherd looked at him over her glasses. "Do you think perhaps we might have done better on that? How many times did a member of the investigative team stare at that PRIVATE PROPERTY sign during the course of this investigation, would you say?"

Jejeune shrugged. "I don't think Grey ever intended to kill Wayland. I believe she grabbed the stake and swung the sign just to strike him with it, flat, as he walked away. The ME confirms the entry wound was at the back of the neck. But the metal skidded off the leather of his strap and there was enough force in the swing to slice right through the neck."

Shepherd nodded. "Danny Maik said the sign was barely staked in the ground at all when he went to retrieve it. Grey had simply propped it against the fence. It was ready to keel over at the slightest touch."

Had it fallen in among the bracken and leaf litter, it would have lain there undetected, covered year upon year by forest debris, until, finally, there would be no evidence left at all that this weapon of murder had ever existed. Swallowed up by the past, like the details of this case, which would one day be nothing but memories, a past history to be referred to, in admiration, perhaps, at the way Jejeune had solved it. Unless Grey remained at large. Then there would always be the tang of disappointment that no one had been brought to justice. No one had paid for leaving Philip Wayland, or Darla Doherty, to bleed out the last few moments of their lives in silent agony.

Other things, they both knew, would not be consigned to the past so easily. Shepherd had allowed her DCI to go into that place to pursue Xandria Grey unaccompanied, after all she'd said to Danny Maik about the value of having backup. She had erred on the side of her own suspicions, and even she wasn't really sure if it had been sound police judgment or something more personal, more vengeful. Either way, Xandria Grey had escaped because of her decision; a living reminder of her error, of their collective failures in this case. Shepherd picked up a sheet of paper and read from it. "The tragic loss of the project director has made it impossible for the Old Dairy Carbon Capture and Storage Scheme to pursue its goals at this time. While all avenues are being explored to allow the scheme to resume its valuable work, all operations have been temporarily suspended at this time."

She set down the paper and looked at him. "One assumes the university will be a bit less long-winded when it shuts down its own programme."

"Both projects have made important progress in the field," said Jejeune. "The data is too important to lose. Someone will come in and pick up the pieces. Philip Wayland's goal of uniting the research will happen. There will be a viable, environmentally sensitive solution for carbon capture and storage."

But it wouldn't be in the hands of the al-Haladins. Regardless of whether the project was ever resurrected, it was unlikely Ibrahim or Yousef would ever set foot in north Norfolk again. She could read Jejeune's thoughts and recalled Tony Holland's words — *too rich to face justice.*

"We don't know, Domenic, what el-Taleb would have said. He was facing an obstruction charge, at best, accessory after the fact, perhaps, if we got lucky. We didn't even have enough to charge him with conspiracy." She shrugged. "A man so dedicated to the al-Haladin family, years in their service. Would he have sacrificed all that, given us Prince Yousef, just to save his own skin? Or would he have stuck to his story, taken his pathetic punishment and emerged from his prison term to riches beyond his wildest dreams?"

She looked at him across the desk. She wished he would say something, tell her how disappointed he was to have watched that red ball of flame and those clouds of thick, black, acrid smoke consume his one hope of justice for Darla Doherty.

"The truth is, of course, without el-Taleb's testimony, we can't ever really be sure it was Yousef who killed the girl. Your theory ticks all the boxes. But it could have been someone else, using the falcon in the same way you describe, perhaps even escaping the same way, or by boat from the shoreline. As far as the CPS would be concerned, there can be no way to know with any certainty that Yousef al-Haladin murdered Darla Doherty."

But Jejeune knew, and, because of his conviction, she supposed she did too. Proof was for courts and lawyers, and the Crown Prosecution Service, but the truth, the absolute raw facts of what had happened, that was what Inspector Jejeune concerned himself with. The patterns, the answers, the knowledge he'd accumulated had removed all doubt for him. And what was certainty but the absence of doubt? Darla Doherty's death would remain an accident in the records. But buff folders or digitized files could never hold the truth of a case. That could only come from looking in the eyes of the people, listening to the messages behind their statements, tracing the tiny filaments that tied their lives together, that bound them to one another in so many tangled, complicated ways. He had done that, and he had his truth. Whether or not a court ever held anyone accountable, Jejeune knew. And she did, too.

Shepherd looked at him. He was so good at this, she thought, regretfully. He recognized the subtle shades that made up the human condition, and when you understood people that well, making sense of their actions was a lot easier. "Domenic. About this other business …"

"There is no other business." He turned an unblinking stare on her, and she met his eyes. For a long moment, they stood there, unmoving, locked in a wasteland between their shared past and their unknowable future.

A name, spoken alone, that was all it had taken. A single name in the hide that day, and Shepherd had seen the personnel file before her again, as vividly as if she might reach out and touch it. A new recruit, one she had studied, pored over at length, deciding, deciding: commendations galore, references glowing and stellar. A no-brainer, except for this one shadow, cast overseas somewhere, yet still extending its pall over the career of a young sergeant here in the U.K. A shadow involving a family member. An older brother, *Damian.*

"No," said Shepherd finally. "Perhaps there isn't. But if there ever was, if you did want to talk about anything, you know I would listen, don't you? You know I would be willing to hear all sides, before I ever came to a judgement."

She looked at him, knowing, as he did, that something had changed between them, something that perhaps could never be restored. *Was it me?* she wondered *Did I betray our trust, when I went behind your back to Quentin Senior? You did what you promised us you would, all you ever promise us. You found our killer, perhaps even two. And I stood by in silent amazement, as I always do, and watched as you unravelled it all and brought it to some sort of resolution.*

But she had waited for Jejeune's honesty, supported him and fought for him, and given him all the time he needed to come to her. And he had not repaid her with his own trust. And so, she found herself not quite able to believe in him as much as she once did. She wondered if she ever would again.

She felt an emptiness inside her, a disappointment that went beyond sadness, almost to despair. DCS Shepherd didn't quite trust herself to look up from her desk, and waved Jejeune away with a movement of her hand.

He seemed to understand, as always, and moved towards the door without a backwards glance.

Jejeune paused outside Shepherd's office for a moment, and then began to make his way down the corridor to the detectives' room.

Danny Maik was in his cubicle, hunched over some report, giving it the attention it deserved, but nothing more. Soft strains of Motown were coming from his laptop, voices entwined almost as one, until it was all but impossible to tell them apart. Jejeune had no idea who they were, but it was obvious they had spent some time working on their harmonies.

Maik looked up as his DCI approached, and reached out to turn down the volume. Jejeune held up a hand to let him know it was fine just as it was.

"The Supremes," said Maik, setting down his report. "You'd never know that Florence Ballard and Diana Ross had such a touchy relationship, would you, listening to them?"

Jejeune slid the phone over a touch and sat on the corner of Danny's desk.

"Nothing on Grey, yet?" asked Maik, looking at his DCI. "We could have looked a bit harder at Wayland's private life, I suppose. Maybe there would have been something."

Jejeune tilted his head. Perhaps. But perhaps Philip Wayland's life would have given them no clues, only more unanswered questions. Any life looked at as a single linear event, frozen at some premature end point, would seem the same curious tangle of unfinished narratives. Lives were organic, evolving things that grew and progressed and changed through caprice and circumstance. Threads were interwoven and overlaid, making sense of the unintentional, and leaving carefully designed plans in tatters. In the hindsight of death, Philip Wayland's life would have seemed a confusing miasma of unresolved conflicts, plans, intentions. But both men knew all lives, their own included, would look the same way if they were unravelled and rolled out for dispassionate analysis.

Jejeune looked down at the phone, absently running a finger over the buttons on the console. "Everything all right with the phones, Sergeant? No need to get tech in or anything?"

Maik looked up at him, his gaze unwavering. "You can ask them to come in if you like, but I'm sure they'll say everything's working fine."

Maik reached over and turned down the volume on his laptop just a touch. He leaned back in his chair and looked up at Jejeune. "In the army, your best gear has a tendency not to be around for very long, unless you're careful. It gets lifted, goes missing, gets ruined. You learn to value certain things, the ones you're better off having around. You do your best to look after them. You try to make sure nothing happens to them."

Like phones, thought Jejeune. Phones with speakerphone options that you could switch on and off without anybody noticing, so that if anyone was on the other end, and they kept quiet, they might hear conversations that perhaps they shouldn't. And no one else would ever know.

Jejeune laid a hand on Danny's shoulder and reached over him to turn up the volume on his laptop again. The searing harmonies were rising to a climax, the smooth, interlocking voices seeming to drive each other on to ever greater heights.

"I'll leave you to your Motown, Sergeant," said Jejeune. "Enjoy."

It wasn't just ex-army types who recognized the wisdom of keeping a close eye on the things you valued.

58

Domenic noticed the manila envelope on the table as soon as he entered. He heard the echo of Eric's booming baritone at the party that night, in this same room. *"Big envelope: good news, small envelope: disappointment."* No mention of the medium-sized envelope that sat there before Domenic now.

"Is this what I think it is?" he called, picking it up.

"Be out in a minute," shouted Lindy from the office.

"Don't be too long. I could use some good news."

"Or not."

It was only now that their world was beginning to settle back on its axis again, after the tumultuous events of the previous days. The helicopter crash had taken hold of Domenic's senses more than anyone had realized at the time, and more than once Lindy had come into a room and found him sitting, slightly hunched forward, staring into nothingness, starting wildly when she called his name. A doctor friend had told her not to discourage his flashbacks. As he revisited them, the shock would wear off; his visions would lose their intensity. Domenic would gradually become desensitized to the horror he had witnessed. The memories would begin to fade. In time.

But perhaps the other demons would not be so quick to disappear. Without Damian's presence, there was a palpable emptiness to the cottage, and in it rattled around Domenic's unspoken words to his brother, his intentions, his regrets. Lindy and Domenic had not talked about any of it yet. She knew he realized it could only have unfolded as it did, that it is never really in the power of one person to shape the destiny of another. But that did not make the ragged, untidy way the brothers had been forced to part any easier for him. The open wound of their unreconciled relationship would take a long time to heal.

Lindy and Dom would talk, she knew, as time passed, as the immediacy of Damian's presence, and the pain of his departure, receded. But it was still too soon, and she knew that for all the distress his brother had brought, all the turmoil and anger and hurt, Domenic missed him.

Part of it was that he knew, they both knew, Damian would never risk getting in contact with Domenic again. Damian was clever enough to realize how close they had come to being discovered, and how finely he had cut his escape. He had enough of a survivor's instinct to avoid that kind of risk again. But he was aware, too, that some people in Saltmarsh knew with certainty that he had been here, and others suspected it. For this reason, he wouldn't call, or email, or send any letters that prying eyes may be alert for. He cared too much for his brother, for the career he had carved out here in north Norfolk, for the life he had built for himself and Lindy.

Domenic knew all this, and understood it. But he recognized that it meant that life, or even Damian himself, would never give him another chance to help his older brother. More than once since Damian's departure, Domenic had told Lindy of his fear: that he would never hear from his brother again. She respected Dom too much, cared for him too much, to pretend that it might be otherwise.

Unless. She typed in one more URL with flying fingers,

tapping impatiently on the desk as she waited for the laborious, interminable load from the server.

"Are you coming to open this thing or not?" called Domenic impatiently from the other room. "I'd like to know, even if you don't want to."

"Soon," she called. "Pour us a drink. We can drown our sorrows. Or have a toast. I'll be there in a minute."

On the webmail site, she entered the username: *spoon_bellied_sandpiper*. She paused. This was the last one, the last of five universal email sites she had used to set up a free email account. The name, she was sure, Damian would try. They had even joked about it. Almost. But the password, that they had never discussed. The cursor blinked its interminable patience from the empty box below, impassive, indifferent. Feel lucky? Take your chances. I'll give you three tries. *Password:*

It could only be one thing. Surely? One shared, identifiable word that bound the brothers together. One word that would capture all that Damian was; his lovely sense of irony, his playful nature, his affection for his brother. She had chosen it so carefully, given it so much thought. But would Damian think to try it? Would he dare?

She hesitated a second before hitting the enter key after typing in the password: *Domino*.

The screen seemed to freeze for an instant, as if somehow aware she was holding her breath and wanting to draw out the moment. She closed her eyes for a second, not daring to look. And then the pixels melted and re-formed, and before her was her prize. There were no messages in the Inbox, read or unread; nothing in the Sent folder either. But she knew there would not be. The one item she had been hoping for, praying for, would not be in those folders. It would be in the Drafts. And it was. A single message, two days old, no recipient, no subject.

My guess? Big envelope.

It was all she needed. A single thread, a tenuous lifeline that could bind two brothers together across the world, across any divide. A way for Domenic to hold onto his brother. A way he did not even know existed. Yet.

"This is crazy," called Domenic. She could hear him tapping the envelope against his chest as he approached the office. She quickly shut down the computer and spun in the chair to face him, just as he entered the room.

"Trying to heighten the tension?" he asked. He was holding the envelope in one hand and cradling two glasses of wine in the other. He passed a glass to her, but whipped the envelope away from her as she reached for it.

"You look as if you already know what's in here," he said. He was smiling, just a little, as if the very possibility of good news was all he needed for now.

"I really don't," said Lindy. But whatever it was, she knew it could never be as important as the discovery she had just made. The discovery she would share with Domenic when the time was right.

She set her wine down on the desk beside the closed up laptop. Domenic held his own glass aloft, ready for a toast.

With a sigh for dramatic effect, Lindy took the envelope from Domenic's outstretched hand and, drawing a deep breath, she opened it.

THE GYRFALCON

The Gyrfalcon (pronounced jer-falcon), *Falco rusticolus,* is the largest falcon in the world, and arguably nature's most lethal hunter. In summer, the birds inhabit the circumpolar regions, breeding in Greenland, Iceland, Norway, Finland, Russia, and Canada. In some areas, Gyrfalcons share habitat with Golden Eagles, and despite being physically dwarfed by their formidable neighbours, Gyrfalcons will readily engage in spectacular aerial battles with eagles over territory. In winter, the search for food will often send Gyrfalcons south, and this time represents the best opportunity for most birdwatchers to catch a glimpse of these outstanding birds.

Despite the remoteness of its natural habitat, the Gyrfalcon has had a long association with humans, due to its hunting prowess. In twelfth-century China, Gyrfalcons were used for hunting swans, and the Liao emperor imposed an in-kind tax on some of his subjects, payable in Gyrfalcons. It is claimed that the Gyrfalcon tax was one cause of the Jurchen rebellion, which caused the fall of the Liao Dynasty. In Western medieval falconry, the Gyrfalcon was considered the preserve of kings, second only in the raptor hierarchy to the eagles of an emperor.

Gyrfalcon ecology has not been extensively studied, but research in Canada suggests climate change may be disrupting the predator/prey relationship between the Gyrfalcon and the Willow Ptarmigan. Population peaks for the prey species may be disappearing from the natural cycles. As a top predator in the food web, Gyrfalcons are also one of the species most at risk from the increasing accumulation of contaminants, such as chlorinated hydrocarbons, that are turning up in Arctic ecosystems.

Though many Gyrfalcons are responsibly and legally bred for the falconry industry, the mythical appeal of this magnificent predator means that there will always be a market for birds illegally taken from the wild, and this trade remains perhaps the greatest threat the wild Gyrfalcon population faces today.

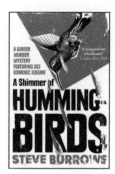